VOLATILE OBSESSIONS

The King
will reign.

DEE GARCIA

Photographer: Danny Woodstock
Cover Models: Jord Liddell and Lusy Logan
Cover Design: Dee Garcia w. Black Widow Designs

WARNING

Volatile Obsessions is a complete standalone.
It contains a variety of dark elements, some of which may cause triggers for those who have had such personal experiences. There's also a plethora of profanity thanks to Rome and Lux's give-no-fucks attitudes, scorchingly hot —detailed and explicit—sexual situations that will absolutely melt your kindle, detailed displays of graphic violence, and some drug use/references.
Proceed with caution.

DEDICATION

To Lusy and Jord.
Thank you for helping me bring this book to life.

PLAYLIST

Medieval Warefare - *Grimes*
Chandelier - *Sia*
Sucker for Pain - *Lil' Wayne, Wiz Khalifa, Imagine Dragons, X Ambassadors, Logic & Ty Dolla $ign*
you should see me in a crown -
Billie Eilish
Heathens - *Twenty One Pilots*
Everybody Wants To Rule The World - *Lorde*
I'll Sleep When I'm Dead - *Set It Off*
Wild for the Night - *A$AP Rocky, Skrillex, Birdy Nam Nam, and Lord Flacko*
Gasoline - *Halsey*
Mi Gente - *J Balvin & Willy Willam*
Wreak Havoc - *Skylar Grey*
Superman - *Eminem*
Kill Everyone - *Hollywood Undead*
Tag, you're it - *Melanie Martinez*
Courtesy Call - *Thousand Foot Krutch*
Every Breath You Take - *Chase Holfelder*
Bodies - *Drowning Pool*
Monster - *Skillet*
Dollhouse - *Melanie Martinez*

Playlist

Lucky You - *Eminem*

Gangsta - *Kehlani*

I Can't Stop - *Flux Pavilion*

Never Be the Same - *Camila Cabello*

Carousel - *Melanie Martinez*

Party Favors - *Tinashe*

Like Water - *Flume ft. MNDR*

Collide - *Justine Skye feat. Tyga*

My Demons - *Starset*

Pills & Automobiles - *Chris Brown and Yo Gotti*

Sex with Me - *Rihanna*

Spazzn - *Decap and Gyrefunk*

This is Halloween - *Marilyn Manson*

Be Together - *Major Lazer and Wild Belle*

Him & I - *G Eazy and Halsey*

Issues - *Julia Michaels*

Netflixxx - *Brytiago and Bad Bunny*

Bring Me To Life - *Evanescence*

Twisted - *MISSIO*

Acquainted - *The Weeknd*

All I Want for Christmas Is You - *Mariah Carey*

Partners in Crime - *Set It Off feat. Ash Costello*

Madness - *Ruelle*

Higher - *Rihanna*

Radioactive - *Imagine Dragons*

Mine - *Bazzi*

Circus For A Psycho - *Skillet*

Love The Way You Lie - *Eminem & Rihanna*

End Of Me - *Ashes Remain*

Elastic Heart - *Sia*

Venom - *Eminem*
Sarcasm - *Get Scared*
The Devil Within - *Digital Daggers*
In the Name of Love - *Martin Garrix and Bebe Rexha*
Secret - *The Pierces*
Die For You - *The Weeknd*
Nothing Without You - *The Weeknd*

Listen to it here: http://bit.ly/VOplaylist

PROLOGUE

♫ *Medieval Warefare - Grimes* ♫

I t all happened so fast, I didn't have time to process what was happening, much less react.

Roman's little hussies, however, were very much reacting behind us. They weren't happy, and he didn't seem to give a single fuck.

"But Rome, what about—"

Slam!

The harsh sound echoed through the office, rattling the walls and likely carrying through to the adjacent rooms. The lock seemed to echo, too, as he clicked it in place to keep them out.

A quick swivel and we were off despite their angered banging on the door.

Each step forward came with a grunt, his clasp on my arm a forceful vise. He didn't look back at me or speak a word either, just stalked further into the room with determination coloring his aura.

A baffled protest was building on my tongue when suddenly, my back hit the black felt of the custom pool table.

And I mean hit *the felt.*

Roman deposited me on it like he planned to eat me alive.

He wedged his way almost effortlessly between my legs, and in the time I merely gasped, he'd already thrown my arms above my head and locked my wrists in his grip.

I was trapped beneath this man once again with nowhere to go.

Still no words were exchanged. He looked me over once, just once, stare lingering on my eyes for a second longer, and then the domino effect went off like a bomb.

Lips collided.

Teeth crashed.

It was frantic, intense.

Unexpected.

Explosive.

I was scorching under his touch, reeling at the feel of his mouth on me again, and he was a ball of pent-up desperation, running a million miles per hour. He moved so fast, I literally couldn't keep up, panting wildly as he tore his lips away from my mouth and started down the column of my neck.

Kissing.

Licking.

Biting.

It was heaven and hell, so right and yet so fucking wrong. I knew I shouldn't be doing this with him, but I couldn't stop either. The taste of bourbon on his lips was addicting. He was addicting.

And I wanted more.

So much more.

Throwing all caution to the wind just to have it, even if for but a moment.

My body fell lax in desperation of finding a rhythm. Pliant beneath him, I let him explore, let him consume me, let him lead. Only idly—and momentarily—did I realize alarm bells would normally have been blaring by now.

But I wasn't remotely afraid.

If anything, the acute tempo of my breathing stemmed purely from carnal desire as he kissed me senseless.

He wasn't far behind either. His chest heaved with such ferocity, the air around us quivered. It reverberated through me, lanced right through my being until I was trembling.

Aching.

Zoning out from everything but right here, right now.

"Tell me why you ran," Roman hissed as he came up for air. He released me, only to grip me at the hips with both hands and push me further down on him.

My heat throbbed as his erection probed me, teasing me through all the layers separating us.

The veil of lust so was thick, whatever he'd asked had gone right over my head. "What?"

Draping himself over me, he met my stare. "Tell me. Why you ran from me. When I put my lips on you."

His breath was hot on my skin, drenched in bourbon, and his eyes, they swam in it, too—unfocused and reflective. He was so pissed I honestly wondered how he was still standing up right.

The thought instantly sobered me, reminding me he'd

3

been outside those doors just five minutes ago, balls deep in two women.

"It doesn't matter." I tried pushing him off me. "We have to stop, though."

"Why?"

"Why?" I croaked incredulously. "For starters, you're drunk—way past the limit. And did you happen to forget you were just out there in the hallway, getting your cock sucked by one female, while you played with an entirely different cunt?"

Silence.

He pulled back to full height and watched me beneath curious brows, taking me in spread out before him on the pool table. His gaze was so utterly penetrating, I could feel it searing through me like a laser.

Down my neck, over my breasts, along my stomach...

When he reached the barely contained space between my thighs, I swallowed down the whimper caught in my throat and snapped my legs closed, feeling unbearably vulnerable under his scrutiny.

The growl that thundered in his chest was feral. My reaction to his perusal obviously wasn't to his liking.

Fist clenching the very middle of my tank top, he yanked me up toward him in a flash, my legs naturally spreading to accommodate his hips.

"They're distractions," he grated into my ear, the tip of his nose buried in my hair.

"From what?"

"From you and everything you stand for."

4

"Which would be?" I asked on a shaky breath, my hands subconsciously gripping his tee, too.

"Everything I shouldn't want."

I squeezed my eyes shut. His words were agonizing. They're not at all what I wanted to hear, what I could bear to hear. I'd fallen weak enough to him already, had submitted in ways every man in my life only wished I'd given up so freely. I needed to be stronger. Self-preservation begged me so.

I couldn't do this with him.

"That's why we have to stop," I whispered, trying and failing to push him away once more. "We can't be doing this. You know we can't."

Solid as a rock, he gripped me tighter. "Then tell me. Tell me you don't feel this and I'll never put my hands on you again."

One second.

Two.

Three.

What was I supposed to say?

When I didn't respond, or rather, couldn't respond, he pushed me away and looked me dead in the eye, breaths ragged, unsteady.

"Exactly—let that sink in. I know you feel it too, Lux. That's why you ran, why you're trying to fight it," he snarled, waiting a beat or two before he continued. "So go on, run. *Run as fast as you can, but we both know the bomb will detonate sooner or later. And when it does, when you finally find yourself beneath me, begging me to*

wreck havoc on your body, I'm going to remind you of this moment right here. I'm going to remind you that you thought you could run from the King."

1. THE QUEEN OF MIAMI
Lux

♫ *Chandelier - Sia* ♫

June
Miami, FL

Ah, Jack, my old friend, I thought to myself with a blissfully inebriated smile as I pressed my lips to the bottle and took another long sip. I'd drunk so much already, the welcome burn didn't even burn anymore. Probably why Scotty-boy, the good 'ol bartender, passed me the bottle over half hour ago. He'd been pouring tumbler after tumbler while still serving the rest of the Blackbird Ordinary regulars.

But then the motherfucker started slacking, and I wasn't having it.

I was, however, absolutely okay with serving myself, hence why he found me halfway over the bar from the corner of his eyes when he'd turned his back to distribute a few beers. I would've knocked the unamused glare he shot me off his face had he not been such a good friend, *and a better client*. Scott wasn't stupid, though, and a quick reminder I had certain rights as the birthday girl, lead him to setting down the bottle in front of me without a glance back. I almost patted his graying head and praised him with a purred 'good boy' in tow, but figured a quick smack on the cheek and an additional black baggy would suffice.

"So, any calls from the folks?" Vic asked suddenly from his perch on the stool between my inked legs.

I stilled momentarily, eyeing him closely. "Nope," I answered, popping the P. "You should know this."

"I know, but it's your birthday. Don't you think they miss you?"

"Don't know, don't care. If they missed me, they'd have tracked me down a decade ago when I first left Leeds."

"True." He nodded awkwardly. "I just can't believe they haven't—"

"Can we not talk about this?" I growled, cutting him off. "They're dead to me, end of story."

"Okay, okay, my bad. I was just curious is all. So are you gonna share the rest or what?" he questioned, motioning the bottle lodged firmly in my grasp.

"By share, you mean a sip, right?"

"No, I mean like, let me kill it," he clarified.

I scoffed through my nose and raked a hand through my emerald green tresses. "Negative. That last lil' bit is mine."

"C'mon, L!" He protested, warm palms slithering up my thighs. "You've drank the entire bottle already. Let me have the rest."

His touch kinda made my skin crawl. I shooed him off

and narrowed my eyes. "It's my birthday, dickhead. I'll have however much I fucking want. You thirsty? Get your ass up and buy your own drink."

Vic scowled, dark brows furrowed and all, to which I rolled my eyes. God, he was a pain in my ass. But as my righthand man, he—unfortunately—went almost everywhere with me, mostly because he played multiple roles; business confidant, assistant, security.

He'd like a permanent role in my bed, too, after what spiraled out of control the other night, but that was never gonna happen. The mere thought could throw me into a manic fit of laughter.

Don't get me wrong, Vic somehow turned out to be a great lay, *I guess*, but that's as far as it would ever go for me. I didn't do relationships. Never had, never would. I'd learned at a very young age that the only person I could truly trust was me, myself, and I.

"You're a mean ass drunk, you know that," he added with a snarl.

"And you're wrong, on two different accounts," I countered, downing the last bit of whiskey he so desperately wanted.

"How I am wrong? You *are* mean as fuck."

"Exactly, but that's everyday common knowledge. No need to treat it as breaking news."

"Alright, fine, I'll give you that, but what else am I supposedly so wrong about?" he quizzed, inching closer as though it were confidential.

So I leaned in closely too, dragging one of my claws under his chin. "I'm not drunk," I whispered.

Vic threw his head back and howled a full-bellied laugh, prompting those in the near vicinity to look our way. "That's a load of bullshit. You're fucked the hell up, Lux."

"Fucked up, yeah, but not drunk. I'm not a light-weight, Vic. I can handle my liquor."

"You won't be saying that once I spark one in the car," he snickered, the confidence of his statement sending my eyes in another 360 spin.

"Just because you spark one doesn't mean I'm going to partake."

"*Please*, it's your birthday. You're gonna hit it at least once, and then I'm gonna take you home, and hit *that*."

Oh no he fucking didn't.

Whistling at Scott without so much as a cut of my eyes in his direction, I held up the now emptied bottle of Jack and arched an unamused brow at Vic, crossing one leg over the other. "Yeah? Well, it's unfortunate you don't call the shots then, huh? I know you like to think you do, since you do so much for me and all, but really, you don't. I do—a concept you should be quite familiar with by now. We slept together once, Vic. Stop assuming you now have access to my pussy whenever you please."

"Ouch. Jesus Christ, L, what gives? Who the fuck pissed on your birthday cake before we got here?"

"No one. Was part of your proposition not for me to come to you?" I questioned, examining my currently bright purple stiletto nails that were going to need a fill soon.

"For the first time, yeah." He sounded incredulous.

"*For the first time* was not specified when you stated your terms, Mr. Kane, therefore, your objection means fuck all to me."

Now he looked really offended, ivy green eyes blazing in the dim lighting of the obscure bar. The veins in his neck bulged as he grit his jaw together. "Are you serious," he spat. "So I can't come to you but you expect me to drop my pants and whip out my dick whenever you want? What makes you think I'll be so willing?"

"Simple," I stated, taking a swig from the new bottle Scott set beside me seconds prior. "Because you want me, Vic. As a matter of fact, those were your exact words when we discussed your offer in my office."

"Why do you sound so amused by this? Obviously I want you if I'm taking you to bed."

"No. No-no," I laughed out loud, "*No.* Taking me to bed and wanting me are two different things. You *want* me, Kane, for yourself, in and out of bed. Twenty-four hours a day, seven days a week, three-sixty-five a year. You have for a long time. But you wanna know a secret?"

Vic nodded, and while I knew the action was meant to be subtle, I could see the hopeful gleam sparking within his serious expression.

"That's not gonna happen," I murmured, smirking in satisfaction as his face fell before my very eyes. "You wanna roll around in the sack a few times a week and blow some steam? By all means, fuck me like a rag doll, but I'm not spreading my legs at your beck and call. It's either my way or you can toss your proposition in the trash and set in on fire, got it?"

Scoffing a laugh, he pushed his stool back in a hurry, one that clearly let on to how disappointed he was by the way it scraped against the floor. His stare remained downcast as he pulled out his wallet from the back pocket of his jeans and fished out a few bills, discarding them onto the polished bar top.

"It's all good, Lux, I got it. And since that's the case, I'm gonna go. I'll see you Monday."

"See 'ya Monday, baby cakes," I purred mockingly, flashing him a purposeful wink and all.

Again, he was not amused, but do you really think I gave a shit? Just because I let him fuck me once didn't mean he was suddenly entitled to screw me whenever he wanted. And this didn't just apply to Vic. I'd be damned if any man thought he owned me.

No one owned me.

NO. ONE.

Lux Mercier rode solo.

I always had and I always would because there was not one person on this planet who could handle me in all my depraved glory, let alone ride with me until the very end.

2. WELCOME TO THE 305

Roman

♫ *Sucker for Pain - Lil' Wayne, Wiz Khalifa, Imagine Dragons, X Ambassadors, Logic & Ty Dolla $ign* ♫

Two months later - Present day

The King has arrived.

Stepping out onto the pavement in the infernal Miami heat, I slammed shut the door of my rental Mercedes and quickly adjusted my off-centered obsidian tie. Through the Ray-bans aiding me from going blind under the oppressive rays, my gaze shot around the palm-riddled lot, then over the ordinary factory.

Dingy, white paint, and eroded vents, likely from the salt water nearby.

This is it?

I chuckled. Even the cloudless blue sky and lush view of the marina didn't help. Of all the places he could've chosen to start an empire, why here? This place was a shit hole. Literal hell.

Truth is, I didn't really want to be here. That alone was enough for me to nit-pick and dissect every aspect of my visit. But Vic needed my help, so despite my plethora of opinions, here I was—being a good-fucking-friend and all that shit.

With a resigned huff, I straightened my jacket, refastening the first of two buttons as I squared my shoulders and started for the only set of doors in plain sight. From what I could see, they were as dingy and eroded as the rest of the exterior. I shook my head in disdain. Clearly, Vic needed a proper lesson in business. Not that I was a businessman—*per se*—but even I knew the importance of aesthetics and appearance.

And this place screamed nothing short of filthy and unsanitary.

If he was hoping to get me on board of whatever *this* was, we were going to have to make some serious changes. No way in hell I was slapping my name on something so putrid.

Once at the mass double doors, I came to an abrupt halt, staring at the handles in revolt. My lip curled offensively. They looked like a tetanus breeding ground, layer upon layer of rust accumulated at the curves. I wouldn't even consider touching them, and I wondered how the hell Vic could possibly touch them on the daily, too, considering his obsessive habits.

What sounded like a zooming sound whirred somewhere on my left, shifting my attention away from my long time friend and the offending entry to his fairly new stab at success. I snapped my head in its direction, noting the security camera at the top of the doorway zeroing in on me, a small red light blinking every other second or so.

"It's about time you showed, King." Vic's voice

erupted from some hidden source. He sounded both amused and a little shocked.

"Blame it on your beloved city. How is there traffic at ten in the morning? Do people here not work?" I asked irately.

"Yes, they work"—he laughed—"but you're in Miami, Rome. Lots of retirees, college kids, tourists, and immigrants. Get used to it."

"Yeah, we'll see about that. Open up, will 'ya? It's hot as balls out here."

A low buzz met my ears, followed by what sounded like the lock mechanism coming undone. I laughed sarcastically, motioning toward the door. "You've gotta be kidding me, right? I'm not touching that shit."

Vic went on to laugh too, his more entertained than sarcastic. "Don't tell me you've turned into a prissy bitch since I last saw you, bro."

"Says the man who spends a fortune on hand sanitizer each month," I fired back.

"Touché, touché." He laughed again. "I was joking by the way. Wouldn't touch that door with a ten foot pole either. Roscoe's on his way. He should be there any sec—"

The door flew open, a hulking bastard of a man with leather-gloved hands stepping aside to allow me entry. I stared at him with much of the same disgust in which I'd stared at those detestable handles. I wasn't a small man by any means, but this dude made me look like a teacup puppy in comparison. A shoe-in for Jack the giant, he was more beefy than anything else, and not in the defined way women liked to see. He was balding, too, with a scraggly beard and an obvious beer gut, none of which helped deter from the slimy vibe oozing off his person. Other than the grunted directions muttered under his breath, Roscoe didn't move, standing stock-still with crossed-arms.

Taking care not to come within three centimeters of his body, I slipped in past him and followed the given route to the singular elevator bank, pulling off my sunglasses in the process. I tucked them into the breast pocket of my jacket and jammed my thumb into the call button promptly thereafter. The doors slid open almost immediately with a loud ding, leaving me absolutely no time to assess the conditions of the first floor. At a quick glance, it was nothing more than an emptied factory, but a full perusal would have to wait until later. That is, if I decided to actually lend my buddy a helping hand.

Otherwise, not my business. Not my fucking problem.

When I arrived on the second floor, the only route optional was that of a suspended, metal pathway that led to a large office situated dead-center of the vast space on the other side. Wrapped in entirety with floor to ceiling windows, it looked like something straight out of a mafia film, one where the mob boss could overlook his empire from any and every accessible point possible.

Typical Vic, I thought to myself as I trudged over the bridge, idly speculating whether this thing would collapse under my weight or not. Rickety shit looked about ready to do just that; all oxidized and unkempt like everything else around here. Regardless, I kept on, and from my vantage point up here, I could just barely make out a set of stairs the led up to the office from the first floor, along with several gargantuan machines and dusty conveyer belts. The rest was shrouded by darkness. Given the scarcity of people, I assumed what laid down there was of no working use or value.

Piqued my interest as to why he'd keep it in the first place.

Guess we're about to find out...

Just as I set out to rap my knuckles on the door, it swung open, revealing a grinning Vic. Clad in a black suit —strikingly similar to mine—with an olive green tie in place of my raven one, he was seemingly the picture of success.

"It's been a while, man," he said, offering me a welcoming hand.

It *had* been a while, for reasons I didn't care to relive in that moment, earning him a hiccup of reticence on my part. I eyed him steadily, mentally time traveling through years of unwanted memories, which in turn furrowed his brows in confusion. The simple action sprung me into action. I stuffed down those images and extended my hand in return.

"How's it going?" I offered, falling into that typical one-sided, slap on the back man-hug.

"Pretty damn good, not much to complain about," he replied, easing back and motioning for me to enter his office. "Come in, come in. Have a seat."

Vic's workspace was a stark contrast to majority of the building. Not one thing was out of place, much less dilapidated or run down. Everything appeared new and quite costly if I'm being completely honest. A massive inky desk with one hell of a throne sat at the very end of the room, all the other pieces of furniture, including the wrap-around bookcases and wingback chairs facing his desk the same dark shade, too. Decorative accent pieces and various abstract paintings in different shades of green were strewn about in strategic places, and yet somehow were still in perfect symmetry.

None of this was unusual really. In fact, it all but hollered Vic's style. But what I couldn't for the life of me figure out was what he could possibly need my help with.

I took the seat on the left as he shut the door behind us and ambled toward the liquor cabinet nearby, holding up a decanter of what I assumed was whiskey. It's all he drank.

"Care for a drink?" he questioned.

Despite knowing the time, I glanced at the steel face of my Movado. "A little early don't you think?"

"Perhaps, but it's five o'clock somewhere."

He has a point...

"Two fingers. I'm driving," I stated simply.

Vic poured our drinks without spilling a drop and shuffled toward me, holding out the amber liquid.

"What's with the inquisitive brow?"

"I'm confused," I said, taking the proffered glass from his hand.

He slipped around his desk and dropped into his chair, setting an ankle to his knee. "About?" he quizzed.

"I thought you needed my help," I clarified.

"I do."

"With?" My eyes danced around the pristinely

furnished room as I twirled a finger through the air. "You look pretty damn set to me, bro. Granted, the outside is an absolute dump, but I know you didn't call me all the way down here to restore a fucking building."

Chuckling, Vic took a generous sip of his whiskey and went on to arrange the glass on his desk, dead-center on the coaster. Not an inch to the right or on the left side of his desk; dead-center on the cork coaster, approximately five inches from the top right corner his laptop. Fucker had the worse case of OCD I know. Hell, if I hung out with him too long, shit started to affect me, too. I hated it. Made me feel crazier than I already was.

"I *do* need your help," he affirmed, steepling his fingers.

I waited for him to continue, even nodding to confirm I'd heard him, but, of course, Vic was always one who enjoyed dragging shit out.

"Again...with?" I waved impatiently, which in turn spread a Cheshire cat grin across his face.

"Rising to the top," he stated evenly.

My head reared back just slightly, unamused confusion cinching my expression. "To the top of what?"

"Of this city, Rome. The top of this city." He leaned back in his seat. "You see, I don't just want to be a member of society. I want power. Money. Respect. I want to run these streets."

I sighed with purpose at his concession, my line of sight trained on his form as I took a long and much needed sip from my glass.

A whole thing kind of sip.

Drained in entirety, the ice clinked against the tumbler, louder still when I set it on his desk.

"This again?" I questioned, leaning back into my seat to mirror his posture.

Vic assessed me, twitching at the sight of my disposed glass, and shrugged after a beat. "It's in my blood, King, and this right here is it. The opportunity is mine to seize."

"So seize it then," I deadpanned. "Why do you need me?"

He came forward, stabbing a finger on the polished, ebony wood before him. "Because this isn't a one-man job. It's a mass operation and I need your expertise, your diabolical mastermind."

Now it was me who had a good chuckle, offering him nothing more than a shake of my head as I rose onto my feet and perused the contents of his office. Vic remained silent throughout, probably because he knew better than to rush me.

"Let me ask you something," I started, leaning against the liquor cabinet, arms crossed over my chest. "What makes this different from all your other genius ideas? You seem to have a...*tendency* to drag me right to the forefront of your shit shows, and I'm not particularly too keen on finding myself in another. I've got my own circus to deal with."

"Because the idea is already in motion and it's full-proof," he replied simply, snatching my emptied tumbler off the desk.

"Full-proof, huh? What makes it so?"

Nothing with Vic was ever full-proof.

"I'll tell you, once you agree."

"The fuck? You expect me to agree to something I have zero knowledge of?" My retort came with an angered rear of my head and harsh bite in my tone.

"Yes, because as much as it benefits me, it'll benefit you as well," he countered.

"How so?"

"Again, I'll tell you, when you agree."

The fuck you will.

"Then I guess you're shit out of luck, Kane," I snapped, pushing off the cabinet. "If you need me as badly as you claim, then you'll call me with every last detail by tonight. Otherwise, I'll be on a plane to New York tomorrow morning, and I can assure you, I won't be coming back."

"Respect, Rome," Vic blurted out, just as I reached the door of his office. When I stilled and glanced over my shoulder, he went on. "That's whats in it for you. Power, money, and well-deserved respect. A new and better life."

None of that truly answered my questions, and yet, I found myself rooted in place, mulling over the possibilities. His promise held all the things I'd once had, luxuries I'd been robbed of by fear and jealousy. For a long time afterward, I'd been on a mission to reclaim what was mine, and in the end, all my depraved actions forced me to do was lay low. And when keeping to the shadows was no longer effective, I ran.

I ran from London to New York, and then I ran here.

Vic requesting my assistance was merely a perfectly

orchestrated coincidence and all the more reason to leave New York behind.

My life depended on it.

So, as much as I didn't want to dive in headfirst to what could possibly be another fail of epic proportions, could blindly aiding Vic with the vow of retribution really be so bad?

3. SAME SHIT, DIFFERENT DAY
Lux

♫ *you should see me in a crown -*
Billie Eilish ♫

"Your brand is exactly what I'm looking for, Miss Mercier. From what I've seen, I believe Black Widow can make it to the top with all the big-name competitors. You just need more exposure."

"And how would you provide that exposure?" I asked the woman, mostly because I had no choice.

She'd been trying to get a hold of me for months despite my PA having turned her away more times than I can count. Isabella was a semi well-known field marketing rep in the make-up industry and she was adamant on securing my line under her belt.

"We need to get you in all the major retailers like *Sephora* and *ULTA,* even department stores like *Macy's* would be great. The more women can see your products in the flesh and test them out, the more likely they'll be to abandon an old brand and try yours," she explained confidently, which in turn piqued my interest.

Clearly, Isabella was not a woman easily deterred. Problem with that was, I wasn't either. Sure, I could see how using her particular set of skills might play to my advantage in the long run, but I preferred to do shit my way, and there was just something about her that didn't sit well with me.

What the hell did she know about my brand anyway?

Black Widow Cosmetics was still fairly new. Did well for an online-only based company, but I knew she could be far bigger. When I started her up just over a year ago, I made sure my products had it all; high-quality ingredients that weren't tested on animals, fierce pigmentation and long-lasting wear, aesthetically pleasing and uniquely designed durable packaging. Prices were damn reasonable, too, when in reality they should've been a bit higher.

I was so sure of my brand, in fact, I dared to say I could compete against *Two-Faced or Anastasia Beverly Hills* with my eyes closed.

Reclining into my seat, I swiveled my chair around to the long rectangular windows at my back and gazed out at the prime view of the beach, wishing I had a margarita in my hand.

"How are you so sure you can get me into said retailers, though, Miss Cruz?"

"My connections are solid and reliable, Miss Mercier. *Sephora* and *ULTA* will be chomping at the bit to showcase your products once we present them with your bestsellers. It's really quite simple."

If it were so simple, I'd have done it myself...

"That all sounds fine and dandy, Isabella—really, it does, but unfortunately, I need proof. Mock-up a proper marketing scheme and get in contact with, at the very least, one of these companies. Once you've heard from them, and they give you the green light, then you and I can discuss a contract. Until then, I'm afraid I can't take a chance."

"I understand," she conceded, her tone only half-defeated. "I'll get a mock-up through to you this week for approval and then—"

"Absolutely not," I interjected, turning back to my desk. "You want this position as my head of marketing, correct?"

"Yes…"

"Then a mock-up shouldn't need my approval. It's your job to know my brand forwards and back, inside and out. Get it done, contact one of your supposed reliable sources, and we'll chat when agree. Clear?"

"Yes, Miss Mercier. Speak soo—"

Click.

Tossing the receiver onto the console without a single fuck to give, I buzzed my PA, Ellie, no less than five seconds later.

"What's up, L?" she responded immediately.

"I'm going to bloody kill you," I huffed, typing Isabel-la's website into my search bar with the tips of my nails.

"Why? What the hell did I do?" she laughed.

"You know damn well what you did. Why in the actual fuck would you put her through?"

"Because you were here? Every other time she's called, you've not been in the office."

"Still! I told you to turn her away until she gave up! Yes, her skill set could be useful and beneficial, but there's something about her I don't like…" I trailed off, scrolling through her dainty page in revolt.

Pastels? Really?

Literally *all* pastels and child-like flowers.

Pathetic.

"I'm sorry, L, seriously. I just thought—"

"I know what you thought, that you were like, *helping and shit*," I quipped, mimicking her typical Miami girl lingo. "And maybe you did, but we won't know until next week, possibly longer."

"You can thank me then," Ellie laughed again. "I know she seems like a prissy little bitch, but she's got some serious talent."

"Yeah, well, we'll see about that if she ever calls back."

"I'm sure she wi… About time, asshole," she growled, her voice further away from the receiver. "Vic's here." The annoyed announcement came just as the door to my office flew open.

Cutting my gaze in his direction—completely unamused, I might add—I noted he was donning that disgusting vomit green tie again.

The man had shit style sometimes.

Lack of courtesy and common sense, too, apparently.

I rolled my eyes and inched back into my seat as he approached. "So nice of you to make it in this afternoon, Mr. Kane. Is there anything I get for you?"

"Cut the Mr. Kane shit, L. I got stuck in traffic," he retorted, dropping into one of the chairs that sat before my desk.

"For the whole morning? I mean, I know these American twats can't drive, but you're telling me you've been stuck in traffic since 8 this morning? It's almost 1!"

Did he think I was stupid?

"No, not since this morning, Lux. I had a few errands to run before coming in and 95 had a four-car pile up blocking almost every lane."

Sure it did.

"Still doesn't explain *or excuse* your tardiness, Vic. You took the morning at your leisure without any notice at all, as you've been doing for several weeks now. Obviously, this job isn't very important to you anymore, so I'm only going to ask this once." I leaned forward, glaring him a down, a bitchy brow arching high. "Should I be setting up interviews with people who will be more reliable, respectful, and appreciative of their position? 'Cause I can do that if it works better for you. I don't need you if you don't want to be here."

Vic sighed frustratedly and scrubbed a hand down his face as he scooted to the edge of his seat.

I'd struck a nerve.

Good.

Served his ungrateful ass right.

"Lux, relax, please. It's not like that. You know I love working here," he all but gritted out, his green-eyed stare never wavering.

And yet, I could somehow see what I'd been sensing for weeks now. There was a difference in the way he looked at me. Not by a lot, but I *knew* Vic.

His ticks.

His tells.

I knew it all. At one point, he was with me more hours in the day than I was in my own solitary company. He did everything for me. Everything. From bringing me coffee to taking out the trash who abhorred my business. Hell, I'd even set aside the slimy part of him that put me off sometimes and had let the man fuck me a few times.

Yes, that means he finally agreed to my terms, by the way.

Aside from who called the shots, I had two rules; no kissing and no staying the night. The last one was more so for myself because I always went to him. Sure, Vic had been to my flat a few times, like all other friends, but I'd never allowed him anywhere near my room, much less my bed.

No man had.

I didn't allow dogs in my private space.

Anyway, things had been off between us as of late. Aside from the office hours he actually worked, we hadn't had much interaction. He was always busy, busy being a term I'd use loosely. Not that I cared—I could have any man I desired, but his newfound distance and sudden absence shed light on all the gray areas I'd ignored. I was starting to understand why they say not to mix business with pleasure.

Lines were blurring, and at this rate, they were going to get messy soon, too, if I didn't get a grip on it.

"Then act like it," I finally countered, relaxing my stance.

"I do act like it, L." He fell back in his seat with another sigh. "Shit's just…"

"Shit's just what? Spit it out."

"It's Ramos. He's making moves," he blurted out.

Really now?

"I see." I mirrored his posture, melting into my throne. "What kind of moves?"

"He's got eyes on the runners and Roscoe caught a few across the street scoping the lot."

My blood boiled. Apparently, Hector hadn't learned his lesson the last time he tried to move in on my territory. Unfortunately for him, there would be no lesson to learn this time.

"Kill him," I gritted out, my eyes tearing to the computer screen as a new email from Isabella pinged my inbox. "I don't care how you do it, just kill him. Chop him up into little pieces and feed him to the sharks if you have to. No one threatens me twice and gets away with it."

"THAT RAMOS BLOKE MUST BE ONE VAPID motherfucker," Suki laughed as I pulled the cork free from the wine bottle and refilled our glasses.

"Clearly. The last time he tried that shit, I carved a jagged line from his eyebrow to his jawline. You think he'd learn."

Suki hummed and swirled the merlot a few rounds, taking an ample sip that practically drained her glass. Again.

Figures it'd be a two-bottle kinda night.

"Rams, refill?" I asked Ramsey, who was curled on my couch with her nose glued to a book.

As per usual.

Without a word or a glance spared my way, she reached over her feet to grab the emptied glass on the coffee table and held it up for me to see. I rolled my eyes. Did I look like a fucking waitress?

"Rams...*refill*?" I queried again, with clear, irate emphasis coloring my words.

Big hazel eyes snapped up to where I stood behind the island. Jerking her shoulders up to her ears, she jiggled the glass in response and went right back to the words holding her hostage. As if I wasn't in enough of a ruffled stated already, her detached presence only served to piss me off all the more.

"Are you mute tonight?" I snapped.

"No." She shot me a testy glare. "I'm reading."

"Then why bother showing up?" Suki chimed in, swiveling her stool to face Ramsey directly. The wavy, bleach-blonde tresses of her hair swayed with the motion. "We're not here to watch you swoon over Mr. Darcy for the millionth time."

I smirked. Forever my main bitch, always down to back me up. They both were, truthfully, but Suki was my ride or die. Deranged as I was, if not more so, where as Ramsey was our voice of reason. Always the rational one; quiet. Tamed.

Ramsey puckered her crimson lips and slammed her

book shut, tossing it on the cushion beside her. "Don't start with me, Suk."

"Or what, Raggedy Ann?" Suki fired back, a devious grin darkening her expression.

Ramsey rolled her eyes in an unamused fashion and flipped her the bird as she trudged toward us, plopping down on the vacant stool to Suki's left. "Hit me," she grumbled, sliding her glass across the dark glittering granite.

"Anywaaay, you were saying," Suki drawled, circling her arms around Ramsey in a deadlock before licking her face.

I almost spilled what little remained of the wine, choking back a proper full-bellied laugh as Ramsey squealed in disgust and shoved Suki off, hastily wiping her cheek clean.

"You're disgusting," she hissed, swiping the remnants along Suki's inked arm.

Not that Suki cared, much to her dismay. She merely shrugged and reached across the counter for the bottle, swatting my protective hand out of the way.

"Once again, as you were saying, L. Hector—the imbecile—Ramos…"

"More like Hector—soon-to-be shark bait—Ramos," I snickered.

Suki and Ramsey both stared at me, chocolate brown and hazel eyes wide.

"You're feeding him to the fish?" Ramsey screeched.

"He deserves worse, trust me. Fool me once, shame on you. Fool me twice…"

"Except there is no twice with you," Suki jeered.

"Damn right. Told Vic to chop him up into pieces if he had to," I added.

"Speaking of Vic," she began, waggling her eyebrows. "How's that going?"

"Same place as it was before—no where. More so now."

"Why? He's hot as fuck."

"He's also stupid as fuck. Not to mention he's acting rather shady these days."

"Shady?" That was Ramsey whose curiosity was obviously roused.

"Very. Shows up late to work, does the bare minimum, takes all these mysterious phone calls. The list of shit I've noticed is endless."

"Have you guys, you know," she pressed.

"Not for a while, no. He doesn't even call me after-hours anymore." I tipped my head back, draining the contents of my glass. "Honestly, I don't give a fuck. He wasn't the greatest lay anyway. But like I said, shady."

"That bastard better not be fucking with you or I'll castrate him with my bare hands," Suki snarled, looking like she was ready to hunt him down, and Ramsey nodded in accordance right along with her.

"Agreed. I may be quiet most of the time but—"

"It's always the quiet ones," I joked, the sudden buzz of my phone dragging my attention away from the girls.

Plucking it off the counter, I glazed over the message displayed on my screen.

Stryker: *We still on for next week?*

A smile drifted across my face for two reasons.

"Ohhh, Sukiii," I sang, shoving my phone in her face. "It's your lover boy."

Suki's cheeks turned a bright shade of pink, little stars forming in her eyes at the mere sight of his name. "Now *he* is hot. Fine as hell to be exact," she stated, fanning herself with a quick hand. "One day he'll be mine."

Ramsey and I laughed at her not-so-secret fantasy as I typed out my response.

Me: *Without a doubt! See you then!*

4. CORRUPT

Roman

♫ *Heathens - Twenty One Pilots* ♫

T*his motherfucker.*

The answer to my last question—could blindly aiding Vic truly be so bad—was a definite yes.

Yes, it could.

I should have stuck to my gut and walked the hell away, spared myself the imminent grief. But no, he hit me with the right bait, and my stupid ass agreed.

Just like he knew I would.

What Vic wanted to do wasn't just insane. It was damn near suicide. Not only did it involve taking out Miami's biggest drug lord, it also involved wronging those who'd been bested by said drug lord, too. Those who dreamed of revenge and reclaiming what was once theirs.

Those like me.

The corrupt were far easier to prey on than one would think. Dangle their greatest weakness before them like a fresh slab of meat and we'd fight for it to the death like the rabid dogs we were.

"Yo, earth to Rome," Vic's voice boomed, reeling me back into the moment. "You good, bro?"

"Fuckin' peachy." I scrubbed a hand down my face, cradling my mouth behind it as I watched him steadily.

One of his perfectly polished brows shot up at the snip in my tone. "I hear sarcasm."

"No shit, Sherlock," I growled.

"Care to tell me why? You've been in a shit mood since you showed your ass at my office earlier this morning."

"C'mon, man. Do I really need to lay it out for you in black and white after what I told you?"

"I don't need a spiel, no. I just wanna know what happened to the Rome I knew," he clarified, which only served to boil my blood more than it already was.

"Dead and gone, Vic. The Rome you knew has been dead and gone for a long time."

"And yet, that's the Rome I need," he countered.

Scoffing through my nose, I shook my head, mentally chastising myself for feeding into his bullshit again. "Sounds like you're fucked then, huh?"

"Not particularly, no. Bringing him back from the dead shouldn't be too difficult with what's up for grabs and all."

"And yet, it will be, considering I'm not willing," I fired back.

"You already agreed," he asserted.

"Yeah, and now I'm withdrawing. You've lost your fucking mind, mate. What you're trying to do…" I trailed off, pinching the bridge of my nose momentarily before rising onto my feet. "It's suicide—seriously."

"Listen to me." He jumped up from the desk, nervously blocking my escape. "I'm not negating the fact that this is going to be difficult. It is, but that's why I need you, King. You're the key to this plan."

"As I said, sounds like you're fucked then. I've got enough of my own shit to deal with to worry about yours, too, and quite frankly, yours stinks a hell of a lot more than mine. I'm good on that."

"Hear me out, please. Wiping this leech out is the best thing we can do for Miami. We'd be doing them a goddamn service!"

"And why is that?"

"Because Lux is a backstabbing little thief and it's time someone finally taught her a lesson," he sneered.

Her?

Out of everything he'd just said, that one little word stood out most.

"Her? Right, funny." I chuckled, only to fall abruptly silent at his stoic expression.

"I'm serious," he deadpanned.

What the fuck?

"Your big, bad drug lord is a bird?" Amusement and partial intrigue practically dripped off my query.

Alright, fuck, full-on intrigue.

Vic hummed in satisfaction and dropped back on his desk, that eerie, despicable smirk curling his lips. He knew he had me, *again*. "Yep—Queen of Miami if you wanna get into specifics. Beautiful bitch...but lethal as hell. And before you ask," he cocked his head to one side, "no, you can't fuck her. You don't even stand a chance. Trust me when I say you don't want to either. She's psychotic; pure evil to the absolute core. Chew you up and spit you out kind of broad."

I huffed knowingly, moving toward the decanter of whiskey sitting on his bookshelf. Fucker hadn't even offered me a drink when I arrived. "Sure you're not embellishing to keep her for yourself, Kane?" I questioned, flipping over one of the sparkling glasses.

We'd been here before hence my asking.

"Hell no. Way too fucking crazy for my liking."

"That's what you said about Nadia," I reminded him.

A nonchalant hitch of his shoulders was my response, his eyes steady on the fact I was helping myself to his alcohol. He didn't seem pleased and I didn't give a fuck. "You don't have to take my word for it, Rome, I'm just trying to spare you from the chaos that is Lux Mercier. She'll rot what's left of your soul from the inside out, without an ounce of remorse."

I almost rolled my eyes. Was he for real? Did he not realize he sounded like a ginormous pussy?

"So, am I supposed to be afraid of her or some shit?" I laughed, swiveling toward him with glass in hand, my palm flush to the polished wood. "How bad can she be? She's a female for fucks sake."

"A female with a lot of man power. Really, just power in general. Lux is not an easy broad to subdue and she doesn't scare easily. She's smart, too, always five steps ahead. Bringing her to her knees is going to take an impenetrable plan and precise tactics."

Precise tactics my dick. He's scared of her.

Pathetic.

"Wanna know what I think?" I asked, pushing off toward him. "I think you have this girl on some non-existent, deranged pedestal. She's a *female,* Kane—a fe-male. Take what's yours and be done with it. What's the worst she could do?"

Vic chuckled, his shoulders bobbing around as if *I* were the one talking crazy.

"This bitch could start the motherfucking apocalypse. Trust me, Rome. She's not someone you wanna pick a fight with."

"Ohhhh, she sounds so scawyyy," I joked.

It really was a joke though. The relentless and ruthless Vic Kane was afraid of a chick. Quite priceless, if you asked me.

Maybe a little ironic, too.

"You see, *this,*" he motioned toward me, as appeased as ever. "*This,* is exactly why I need you. My warning means absolutely nothing to you. If anything, it's luring you right into my plan. Now that you know who she is, you're interested as hell to find out more about her, am I right?"

Yes...

But I wasn't going to admit that. I'd fallen deep enough into his clutches as it is. While he regarded me curiously, awaiting my answer, I dropped down into the nearest seat and took another sip of my drink, my mind racing in a dozen different directions.

Who was this infamous Lux Mercier and what kind of damage had she done on Vic? He could bullshit me all wanted but I knew his motives weren't just strictly business; they were personal above all else. I could feel it, smell it oozing off him.

But he didn't need to know of my sixth sense. I'd keep that little morsel of intel to myself. Could come in handy later on down the line should this entire scheme crumble to the ground.

"Exactly," he concluded, clapping his hands together. "So *now* my question is, are you in…or out?"

A smile slithered across his face as I contemplated my answer. Running the tips of my fingers along my stubble-dusted jaw, I watched him sharply, noting the nefarious glimmer in his eyes. What looked like hope with a hint of coercion, too. The man was hanging by a thread, pleading with satan himself that'd I'd firmly agree this time around so he could lock me in and throw away the key.

Did I really want to do this?

Was it really worth it?

For starters, I'd be putting myself in the shadowy spotlight of malfeasance yet again, and that presented a problem for me. Could attract a certain breed I had no intention of interacting with ever again.

"Does your previous offer still stand?" I blurted, 'cause if it didn't, I was out. I wouldn't be doing this shit for free, not when so much was at stake.

"Absolutely. I don't mind sharing with someone who's going to help make this possible," he affirmed.

And if he didn't, I'd kill him. Simple.

"Then you've got yourself a deal, Kane." Holding a hand out, I rose to full height. "But I want proof you'll hold true to your word. I need a *nice* place to stay and my own personal form of transportation by the end of the week. Otherwise, I'm afraid I can't help."

Didn't hurt to state my terms and remind him I wasn't his bitch. He wanted my help? Then we were doing this shit my way.

Vic nodded, grinning from ear to ear as we shook hands. "We can make that happen. C'mon, let's go meet the boys at Brickhouse and I'll brief you all on the Queen of Miami. We have moves to make soon."

"She won't be the Queen much longer"—I straightened my jacket—"We'll see what happens once Roman King turns her world upside down."

LATER ON THAT EVENING, AFTER A FEW CORONA'S AND A lucrative plan laid out for me in great detail, I finally made it back to my suite at *The Colony*. Weeknight or not, South Beach was thrumming with life, making it nearly impossible for me to drift off. The walls vibrated from the volume of the music and all the commotion outside as I laid there on the plush bed, staring at the tray ceiling above me in sick anticipation.

My entire body buzzed like a live wire at the many ideas racing to the forefront of my mind. The smell of a challenge hung thick in the air, exciting me more than it should've. Apparently, Miss Mercier was quite the busy woman; a true hustler focused on her money. Black Widow was her baby, a make-up company she'd launched on whim a little over a year ago. It did well enough that it served perfectly as a cover up operation for her drug ring, too, the drug ring that provided her the money to fund Black Widow.

Oh, but that's not all.

Oh no.

She was also co-owner of a highly popular dance studio in the city. The other half belonged to her best friend, who she bought the space and got everything started for.

The Queen seemed to be more of a jack of all trades, and I was thoroughly intrigued. Was beyond eager to meet this vindictive little pigeon…and turn her life into a living hell.

She deserved it, from what Vic shared with me.

Initially, I wasn't too fond of what all his strategy entailed, but the more he elaborated and the more I thought on it, the more I realized I'd do anything in my power to make it work.

Vic wanted *me* on the front lines, the leading pawn meant to hop across the chess board and dethrone the Queen.

And honestly, I was perfectly okay with that.

I'd done it once and I'd do it again.

Not just for Vic and all he'd promised me, but for those who'd been silenced and banished, too.

This woman had ruled over Miami for a minute too long, backstabbing and incinerating anyone who stood in her path along the way.

But not for much longer.

Lux Mercier was about to learn the value of loyalty and respect. And if she didn't, I wouldn't hesitate making a mockery of her for all the world to see before sucking the life from her veins.

5. SERPENTINE
Lux

♫ *Everybody Wants To Rule The World - Lorde* ♫

"That's gonna look sick as fuck," Stryker mused, a devious smirk flitting across his handsome face as he eyed my bare chest.

Well, almost bare chest. Aside from the black tape laid over my nipples in an X, everything else was on display. Not that there was much to see, really. I wasn't a part of the big ol' titty committee.

Swatting his arm with a playful hand, I rolled my eyes and sat up right in my seat. "Move out the way! Let me see, dammit!"

"Okay, okay, geez," he laughed, rolling away on his stool to allow me a look in the mirror.

Even from my vantage point, I found myself gasping, scrambling onto my feet to get a closer look. The design we'd discussed several weeks back literally had nothing on the masterpiece Stryker ended up recreating. The focal point was the raven laid out on my sternum, its beak parted as though it were croaking its call, wings splayed out amongst two roses on either side. Beneath it, a crown

43

sat surrounded by rose leaves that swept up the sides to tie the entire design together.

It was perfect, and gorgeous, and just—

"It's you," Stryker mused, reading my mind. "Flows well with the rest of your ink."

I might've been biased, but he was right. Everything just meshed well, and it wasn't even permanent yet.

With one last look in the mirror, I melted into the cool leather, regarding my friend with nothing but excitement. You'd think after all the tattoos already adorning my body that I'd be used to this, but each and every piece was a new adventure. A new rush.

It never got old.

"Ready?" he asked, slowly reclining my chair as far possible.

"As always. Let's do this."

That familiar, comforting buzz met my ears not ten seconds later. I took a deep breath and shut my eyes, allowing Stryker to work without the stress of my stare. Feeling the needles puncture my skin was instantly thera-peutic. The world around me, and all the problems within it gave away to the recesses of my mind, allowing me to fully relax under Stryker's hand.

"Sooo... How's Suki?" he quipped after a beat.

The grin in his voice was palpable, and for that, I smirked. He had absolutely no shame in his game, at least not when it came to her. The man had been pining after her probably as long as she'd been pining after him. Why they weren't together yet, I hadn't a clue.

"She's good—up to her neck in new students at the

studio," I replied, stifling down a laugh at the reaction I knew was coming.

Stryker groaned, louder than intended. "That girl has some serious moves. Doesn't surprise me Vybe is thriving."

Moves she wants to put on you.

"You should come one Friday night. It's kind of like a weekly showcase for all the advanced routines. By midnight, though, it's basically another club; drinks, black lights, good music. You get the picture, right?"

"Cover charge?"

"Newbs only," I conceded. "If you come with me, though, you're good. Plus, Suki would never charge you anyway, and I *know* she'd be happy to see you."

Like a broken record, the buzz of Stryker's machine stopped as he went completely rigid beside me, and once again, I had to reign myself in from bursting into a fit of laughter.

Intrigued blue eyes bore into me the moment I cracked open my eyelids. "Did she say that?" he questioned.

"No, but—"

Ping!

The abrupt chime of my phone halted the admission right on the tip of my tongue. Without prompting, Stryker reached over his station and passed it to me, studying me with a curious brow. I hoped it was Suki, just to see what his reaction would be, but it wasn't. It was Vic, and the text message illuminating my screen shot up all types of red flags I couldn't ignore.

Vic: *We've got a problem…*

Of course we do.
Everything with him was a damn problem these days.
I sighed in frustration and typed out a quick response.

Me: *Which would be???*
Vic: *Word on the street is there's a new guy sniffing around. He wants in apparently.*
Me: *And you heard this where?*
Vic: *Ramos.*
Me: *One minute. Answer.*

"I've gotta take this," I said to Stryker after sending my last reply. "Come with me outside."

"You smokin?" he asked as he set his machine down and ripped off his gloves.

"I'll pass this time. I just need someone to keep me from going nuclear on Vic."

Stryker laughed despite my unappeased expression, shaking his head sardonically. He knew about Vic all too well. Didn't care for him too much either. "C'mon, let's go out the side. Quieter than out front," he suggested, showing me out into the dimly lit narrow corridor.

We trailed its short length in silence, pushing out through the emergency exit to the humid alley way on the other side. Even tucked away back here, the vim and vigor from Ocean Drive carried over, a hint of *Bad Bunny's* latest track, too, and the pungent scent of ocean water.

Stryker immediately pulled out a pack and sparked up

a smoke as I tapped on Vic's name in my recents and laid my back to coral stucco of the building. Not a full ring later, our call was connected.

"Boss lady..." he answered candidly.

I rolled my eyes. Now was not the time for his games. "Cut the shit, Kane. Who is this asshole?"

"Ramos doesn't know all the details. He overheard his boys discussing it a few days ago. All they know is he's from New York and he wants a cut of the territory."

"Well, that's obviously not happening. You sure that's all Hector knows?" I pressed, tamping down the spike in my temper.

"Why don't you listen for yourself? One sec, lemme put you on speaker."

The softest shuffling scraped through the line, followed by what sounded like some electrical current and Hector's pained growls.

"Go on, tell her what you told me," Vic gritted out above the ruckus.

Hector's cries only grew louder, as did the voltage, prickling almost every hair on my body at attention. I ground my teeth together. The static was like nails on a chalkboard, licking up my body in burning waves.

I said kill him, not play with him.

"Enough!" I barked, snapping Stryker's head to where as I stood as he blew out a cloud of smoke.

Everything on the other side of the phone went silent, too.

"Tell her!" Vic demanded.

Thud.

47

Then a whimper.

That whimper said it all; he'd pistol whipped him, I could tell. Knew the sound. Would never forget that damn sound. I clenched my eyes together and tightened my grip on the phone as Vic bashed him a second time.

"*No se nada!*" Ramos screamed in distress. "I don't know anything!"

He wasn't lying. The agony in his voice was beyond genuine, an exhausted cry for help. Those who had something hide always put up a fight. Weakness shows your true colors.

"Take his word, Vic—he's not fibbing. Do what you need to do and be done with it. Enough with the theatrics," I hissed, my voice so deathly low, even Stryker shifted on his feet before me as he flicked his cigarette to the asphalt. "And when you're done, start asking questions. *Lots* of questions. I want to know who this phantom tosser is by Monday."

"I don't know if that's doable, Lux. I'm gonna need more than—"

"Make. It. Doable, Kane. Answers, Monday. Goodbye."

Click.

Shoving the phone into my pocket, I all but growled in exasperation, pushing off the brickwork behind me. My hands snaked into my hair, tugging at the roots. What the hell was happening to my city? First Ramos, now this newbie from Yonkers. Didn't anyone around here have fucking manners anymore?

"I'm not even gonna ask," Stryker began, holding his

hands up surrender. "Need me to have Deja book you in next week? I can move some shit around."

"Fuck that," I waved him off, "I came here to get tatted. I'm not walking out until it's done. Vic can handle this shit show. It's a joke anyway."

Little did I know that, not only was the joke on me, it was only just getting started...

6. LET THE GAMES BEGIN
Vic

♫ *I'll Sleep When I'm Dead - Set It Off* ♫

These poor, simple fools.

I smiled triumphantly, tucking my phone into the inner breast pocket of my suit jacket. This shit was turning out to be far more simple than I initially anticipated. It was laughable really; I had Roman eating out of the palm of my hand and Lux hanging on my every word. If things kept up at this speed, I'd be lounging in my throne with Lux on a leash between my legs in a just few months time.

"There, you called the little *puta*. Are we done now?" Ramos barked, his voice raspy and debilitated.

Dropping my gaze to where he kneeled before me, I could just make out his swollen, bloodied face in the dim lighting. My lips quirked ever so slightly.

He thought we were done.

Delusional imbecile.

The only thing to be done here was *him,* hence his immobility, arms suspended by shackles on the mildew-infested tiles behind him.

I bounced my gaze to Rome who was just about a foot

50

away from him, his knowing stare already waiting. Nothing but a mere look passed between us and Hector began wailing again, his face contorted in agony as he convulsed from the electrical currents zipping through his bindings.

Roman had the power source hidden away safely in his pocket. He was going rather easy on the drug runner now, the smallest of sparks bursting from the metal cuffs, but all it took was a simple turn of the dial and he'd be barbecued from the inside out.

As satisfying as it was to hear his stuttered pleas, though, they fell on deaf ears time and time again. I had somewhere to be, namely in Willow's bed. New little piece of ass I'd acquired as of late. She could suck the fucking life out of me and her cunt wasn't too bad either. A little used but, weren't most pussies these days?

Thirsty hoes.

Another quick exchange between Rome and I, and everything ceased.

Ramos fell dead silent. His upper-body sagged over, suspended in the air, breathing ragged and unsteady. The man couldn't pick his head up, bobbing around feebly as he swallowed mouthfuls of air into his weeping lungs.

Pity. His imminent death would've be so much more satisfying if he wasn't so exhausted.

Sinking onto the balls of my Oxford's, I waited in silence until his exhausted, weary gaze met mine.

"*Please, spare me,*" it begged. "*Not again.*"

Still, I didn't utter a word. I simply studied him; the lingering fear of death in his eyes, how his chest heaved faster upon each breath, the thick droplets of blood and sweat that dripped from his forehead onto the grimy shower floors beneath us.

"I would say you need a lesson in respect, Hector, but lessons are for those given another chance to live," I finally advised, relishing the moment realization flashed in his brown eyes.

"I did what you asked, man!" he spat. "I did *everything!*"

"You did, yes," I agreed. "But you also tried to move in on Lux last year. How am I to know you won't do the same to me a few months down the line? It would be grand mistake for you or anyone else who dares cross me, I can promise you that, but I prefer not to get my hands dirty unless it's on my own terms."

Ramos laughed, weakly, but I caught it, and it infuriated me. Mockery wasn't something I took lightly. And yet, I wanted to hear what he had to say, gritting down on my jaw to leave the ball bouncing in his court. Frail or not, he saw the challenge, accepted it like the idiot he was.

"Seems like you finally grew a pair of balls, huh?" he snickered, shaking his head to the best of his ability. "Last time I checked, you were Lux's little bitch. What happened? Got denied by the Queen one too many times?"

Zero.

One-hundred.

I was there in a millisecond, grabbing onto a fistful of his dark hair as I flipped my switchblade on him with an enraged growl. The very tip dug into his throat, bulging his eyes in shock.

In horror.

Clearly, he hadn't been expecting that.

Not so funny now, motherfucker, huh?

It would've been so easy to end him right there, *so* damn easy, and I almost did...but Rome's purposeful cough reminded me this wasn't part of the plan. That, in turn, did not help to placate me. In fact, it only made me far more incensed than I already was. Incensed with myself. Ramos provoked me and I struck, stupidly, revealing every last card in my hand. Cards I'd had no intention of sharing with Rome. He wasn't supposed to know the full extent of my vendetta, thought it was a business move, but my actions just proved otherwise.

Gave me away.

I was going to have to do some serious damage control tomorrow before he tried playing Sherlock Holmes. 'Cause he would, he definitely would. Roman was slicker than your average and in tune with every last detail, even the hidden ones.

"You can thank Mr. King this blade isn't jammed into your jugular right now," I gritted out, thrusting him backward as I rose to full height. "Though, you might actually prefer that if you knew what awaited you in about twenty seconds."

I'd had enough. It was time.

Flipping my blade back in place, I shoved it into my pocket and nodded at Rome in signal. Without a single word, he retreated several steps and made quick work of turning both eroded levers. A putrid colored water began pouring out from two holes where shower heads once sat, splashing onto Hector's hands beneath them.

"What the fuck?" he bellowed, undoubtedly confused at the sudden turn of events.

I didn't offer him an answer. Neither did Rome, who was lugging a bucket to my side.

He'd understand soon enough.

I took one last good look at the drug runner, grinning at his stupidity, and promptly tossed a tidal wave of water his way. Ramos sputtered under the assault as the bucket clattered to the ground, our cue to get the fuck out of there.

He protested at our silent retiring forms, yanking at his restraints, but we kept on for the exit, shutting out the clanking of metal from our minds.

And just as we made it to the threshold, Rome toyed with that handy dandy little device in his pocket…

A quick flick of the wrist, remember?

The sizzle of electricity meeting water was delightful, and the tortured scream that followed was music to my ears, but knowing that would be Roman one day soon was the icing on the motherfucking cake.

Soon.

One. Day. Soon.

7. WAGING WAR

Roman

♫ *Wild for the Night - A$AP Rocky, Skrillex, Birdy Nam Nam, and Lord Flacko* ♫

Burning Ramos to a crisp was oddly satisfying. It somehow seemed to melt away all the stress mounted on my shoulders, no pun intended. For the briefest moment, amongst the unrelenting sparks and voltage, bliss replaced grief. I felt weightless, yet brimming with such privilege and sovereignty.

His cries did nothing for me.

Nothing.

If anything, they prolonged that sense of peace within me.

Thinking about who expected him home, what his loss would do to his loved ones, what the consequences could be after the fact…nothing. Absolutely nothing.

Simply put, the man was a casualty of war. Nothing less, nothing more.

Cruel and heartless, perhaps, but I didn't have a heart. Sympathy wasn't a quality I possessed nor cared to possess. The world didn't give two fucks about me when everything I ever cared about was ripped away at the seams, so why the fuck should I give a shit about anyone but myself?

Why the fuck should I trust anyone else?

Instilling trust in people was pointless, and often times, entirely misplaced. Loyalty meant nothing to our species unless it suited them and their needs.

"We're ready, boss," grunted Roscoe as the last of my newly acquired army hopped out of the van and gathered in the alley way across the street from Black Widow.

The war on Lux was sheer minutes away from commencement. With Ramos out of the way and the Queen fully aware of the newcomer who was a clear threat to her business, Vic had finally given me the green light to get the ball rolling.

That newcomer was me by the way, in case you hadn't connected the dots already—if you hadn't…c'mon, mate, pay attention.

"It's showtime, fellas," I declared, glancing around my entourage as I took one last pull from my smoke. "Masks on. Let's rile up the Queen of Miami, shall we?"

They nodded, each of them knowing exactly what role they played in this preliminary and rather petty experiment. Tonight wasn't so much about hurting anyone or reducing numbers. It was more a test of Lux's strengths and capabilities.

A taste of what she was made of.

Judging by what I heard of her sultry voice, I imagined she tasted pretty damn sweet… Didn't share that shit with Vic, though. Not even a peep in regards to her accent, which for the record—yes, threw me off. I most definitely was not expecting the Queen of Miami to sound like that.

Slipping my mask in place, I blew out a cloud of smoke and flicked my cigarette into the street, cocking back the slide on my firearm with ease. "I truly loathe repeating myself, but for the sake of covering all my bases, I'm giving you lads the run-down one last time, so listen carefully. Move quietly, stay alert, and don't get too comfortable. No unnecessary noise once we get inside either. Keep your identity hidden at all times, and for the love of God, stay the bloody hell out of her office. Oh, and if any of you so much as tamper with one hinge on the outside of that building, we're going to have a massive fucking problem. Are we clear?"

Another round of silent nods ensued, their faces all hidden behind different masks; some creepy, some down-right terrorizing. It was like *The Purge,* except no one was dying tonight.

Not yet anyway.

Ten minutes later, the whole lot of us had broken into Lux's empire without incident. Bodies hard at work littered the first floor where all the make-up production clearly took place. Well, used to, because when she and her crew waltzed in later this morning, they wouldn't be getting much of anything done except clean up, and alerting customers their orders would be a tad delayed.

Happy Monday, Miss Mercier.

Materials used to create the make-up had been unpackaged and spilt around like confetti. Boxes ready for distribution had been ripped open and emptied onto the floor, colorful powders and shards of glass splattered around the now broken packaging. Several machines had been vandalized and broken, too, including conveyer belts and all their according electrical wiring. These guys were thorough, leaving not one thing unopened or standing.

As for me, I'd yet to touch a thing, and not because I didn't want to. I was just waiting, waiting and watching. Stalking along from space to space. My move would come last and I preferred it that way, gave me a moment to supervise these monkeys and enjoy the mayhem unfolding before me.

The brunt of it all was what would probably hurt Lux most.

Her weight.

Her supply.

The room used to separate and package all her, we'll call them pharmaceuticals, was the perfect cover-up. A well-thought out operation. One would think the scales and baggies were used to weigh and distribute make-up. Everything blended in seamlessly.

I was impressed to say the least, so impressed I found myself shaking my head in slight disappointment as I glanced around the space. It's a shame I had to ruin it for her. In another life, we might've been great partners. She was obviously an intelligent, resourceful woman, and those were two qualities I admired. Rare to come by these days when sharing a business with someone.

Alas, this wasn't that lifetime, nor would it ever be. Lux would loathe me through each and every one, in any way, shape, or form. Couldn't fault the woman, considering her life was about to go from lush to mediocre, but I didn't care either way.

She seemed to have what I wanted and I was damn sure going to have it.

The guys continued milling about, pulling me out from my daze as they ambled around me, transferring brick after brick of weed and cocaine out to the truck we'd arrived in. Some appeared as though they could be ecstasy or molly, too, but I wouldn't know until we made it back to Vic's factory, now better known as Noir Coast Distillery.

In any case, the sight of it all pleased me. There was plenty of money to be made here, and I mean *plenty.* An obscene amount, one Vic couldn't hide or deny, and I was already imagining all the ways I could blow my cut as I started up the stairs for Lux's office.

Unlike the distillery, Lux had taken care of furnishing every last nook and cranny of the building. The floors up here were a glittering white tile, a stark polar opposite from the ebony damask wallpaper on the walls that made up what appeared to be a small lobby overlooking the main floor. They curved inward slightly, leading you right to a dark Victorian desk that sat askew to a tall set of raven doors. Not one paper, folder, pen, or paper clip was out of place, everything neatly tucked in its place.

I assumed it was Vic's desk based on the anal vibe I got just looking at it, and I almost trashed it for shits and giggles—because why the hell not—but why waste my energy on something so trivial when the Queen's chamber was mere feet away?

After all, that's what I was here for, right? To help him purge Miami of the little bitch?

Actually, no, allow me to rephrase that—to help him purge *himself* of the little bitch.

He wasn't fooling anyone. Our evening with Ramos last week ensured it, and I didn't even have to coax it out of him. He did it all on his own. Tried to play it off afterward as though it were a simple lapse of judgement given the moment. As always, I kept my mouth shut, nodding in agreement at all the appropriate times. Better he think I didn't have a damn clue. Gave me the upper hand while I ran my own little experiment on his deceitful ass. I was interested to see how long he'd drag this facade out, how long he'd lie right to my face.

Each time I thought on it, it made me angrier, more skeptical of his word, too. And yet, I had no right to be. I'd brought this on myself when I jumped at the chance to leave New York. I hadn't much of a choice really. The past was creeping up on me quickly, leaving me little to no time to conjure a proper game plan, so I took off a second time.

Unfortunately for me, that's how it *would be* for the rest of my life.

Always running, watching my back.

The lone wolf.

Fucked up part is I'd do it all over again if I had to. I regretted very few things in my life, and what I left in London was most certainly not one of them. Helping Vic on the other hand...that might make the list if we continued on this route, and *should* that end up happening, there would be no 'apology accepted' this time.

He'd be dead to me. End of story.

Right now wasn't the time to dwell on Vic and his hidden motives, though.

I had a Queen to dishevel, and I planned to dishevel her well.

This is going to be fun.

Curling my hands around the finely curved steel knobs, I burst in through the double doors of Lux's dark office like a bull out the gate, only to stop short almost immediately thereafter. The distinct, sweet scent of sandalwood and roses rushed me in a flurry, firmly rooting my Converse-clad feet to tiled floor. I inhaled another deep breath, then another and another after that.

If this is what Lux smelled like, it's no wonder Vic had a perpetual hard-on for her. The scent was mouthwatering. No really, I was salivating at the mouth like a fucking dog. Somehow, it matched her alluring voice, too, leaving me to wonder if what she looked like would match as well.

Was she blonde?

Brunette?

Slim?

Curvy?

Tall?

Fun sized?

Vic wouldn't tell me.

"You'll just know," was all he'd offered when he'd briefed me on the woman.

I had an idea drawn up in my head based on his type and what I'd heard, but something about his resistance to talk about her led me to believe maybe she wasn't his type after all. Needless to say, I was thoroughly intrigued and equally anxious to finally catch a glimpse of her.

And if my plans worked out the way I hoped, she'd be banging down my door soon.

Very, *very,* soon.

My lips curled in an appeased smirk as I stalked over to her desk and dropped down in her plush leather throne. Everything was clean and pristine. Dragging a finger along the edge of her desk, I glazed over the minimal items on display. Judging by the decor out in the lobby and from what I could see here in the darkness, it was obvious Lux fancied a classic, gothic style. I'll admit, she had good taste, but perhaps that's because I gravitated towards gothic decor as well. Although mine was a bit more modern goth with hints of rustic thrown in the mix.

Who are you, Lux Mercier?

The question replayed in a loop as I spun around in her chair, glancing around the shrouded office. Ironically enough, she'd be asking the same question about me in just a few hours. The note I was leaving on her desk ensured it…

Your Highness,
I heard you were looking for me.
Let's chat soon, shall we?
Tag, you're it. – K

8. RED HOT RAGE

Lux

♫ *Gasoline - Halsey* ♫

I stared at the note on my desk for a good ten minutes, reading the finely scripted message over and over again.

Enraged.

Scandalized.

Befuddled.

I felt a little bit of everything as I sat back in my throne and clenched my hands around the arm rests to keep myself in place. I was ready to run a rampage through the streets until I found this wanker and dragged him to hell.

Let's chat, shall we?

Was he serious?

Did he think this little charade would grapple my attention in a good way? That I'd be impressed and oh so very pleased to meet with him for a fucking chat?

Piss off with that shit.

How the hell did he expect for us to chat when I didn't know a thing about him. Not one damn thing. I didn't even know *who* he was, for fucks sake.

Clearly, he knew all about me, though. Knew where to find me, *how to hurt me*. Something that never should've happened when I paid Roscoe good money to man the cams overnight.

Where the hell was he during this fiasco?

I didn't hear a single word from him until 7 this morning and he sounded utterly baffled as he delivered the news. Claimed the alarm system never triggered during the hours Phantom and his boys waltzed right in and destroyed everything.

Because that's what they'd done, destroyed everything I'd worked so hard to build in under ten minutes, and it all happened in perfect succession, too.

Phantom came into view first, alone. He glanced around, then inched up on his toes to stare into the lens, his masked face cocking around in a creepy fashion. On his signal, the rest of his calvary trickled into the frame, all masked as well. I swear I counted at least thirty bodies filtering in after Phantom somehow bypassed the lock code. Worst part was not seeing how he did it. Smart ass turned his back and blocked out the view. Once the last guy slipped inside, he offered a two-finger salute and slipped his way inside as well, like he owned the damn place.

Cunt.

By this point, I'd watched the footage over twenty times, speculating a little harder and focusing on something else each time around in hopes of finding a clue.

But there was nothing.

No clues.

No finger prints.

No trails.

Nothing.

The more I thought about it, the more my temper threatened to best me. I squeezed the phone in my grasp and counted to ten, silently cussing out Ellie for taking so long to pick up my call. What was she doing out there?

"What's up, L?" she answered after a beat, slightly out of breath.

"I need Vic and Roscoe in here, stat," I growled.

"Will d—"

Click.

I slammed the phone down so hard, I'm surprised I didn't crack the damn thing, my chest heaving like I'd just ran a mile. I hadn't been this infuriated in a long time. Wasn't my PA's fault, I knew that, but the girl was rather oblivious sometimes and I was on the verge of a break-down. I needed answers and I needed them now.

Time seemed to stand still as I waited for Vic and Roscoe to show their mugs. What part of ASAP didn't they understand? In reality, I didn't wait anymore than ten minutes, but that was ten minutes too long. Didn't take that long to walk their asses up the stairs, which led me to wonder where they were and what they were doing.

Two abrupt knocks at my doors cut my rumination short.

"Come in!" I bellowed, minimizing all the open search windows on my screen and pulling up the security footage.

Vic poked his head inside. "You wanted to see us?" he asked gingerly.

I assumed Roscoe was right behind him, probably cowering like a scolded dog with his tail between his legs. Took every ounce of restraint within me not to roll my eyes. He wouldn't be cowering if he'd done his blasted job right.

"Sit," I bit out, motioning toward the empty seats facing my desk.

Vic cleared his throat and gave a little nod, sauntering in first. Roscoe was promptly in tow as suspected. Neither one dared to make eye contact with me as they dropped into the wingback chairs, one fiddling with his silk tie while the other picked at his enormous finger nails.

They were so skittish, they would've bowed at my feet had I asked them to.

I almost laughed, but this wasn't amusing enough to lighten my mood. There was some serious shit to be discussed, and they better hoped they had the right answers…in the shortest amount of words possible. I wasn't about to sit here all day with them and waste more time.

"I've spent the entire morning watching the security footage over and over again," I started, turning the computer screen toward them. "And I keep coming back to the same questions. Who the bloody hell is he? How the fuck did he know where to find me? And lastly, what in the ever loving *motherfuck* does he want?"

"We don't know," Vic answered quietly. He had the nerve to look sheepish while he was at it.

"We don't know is not an option. I told you last week I wanted all the details by Monday, and well, today is Monday, Vic, so where are my details?"

"No one knows anything. I searched high and low all weekend, and there's nothing. Zilch. Nada. He's clean as fuck."

No one is perfect, idiot.

"Then how did Hector know he was from New York?" I quizzed, leaning onto my elbows.

"I told you, he overheard his boys talking about it. They have Poker night every week. Hector got there late and walked in on them discussing it."

"So where are his boys?"

"Gone," he deadpanned.

This time, I did laugh—softly, as I rose onto my feet and ambled around the desk. My patience had about reached its end.

"*Of course* they are. How convenient."

Green eyes narrowed defensively. "What are you trying to say, L?"

"I'm saying it's pretty damn convenient that his men just vanished into thin air, when they're the only ones who can help us at this point in time," I clarified.

"I swear to you, I've turned Miami upside down looking for them and any clues as to who this phantom is—"

"Any yet you've come up empty handed, so quite obviously you didn't look hard enough. Pro tip—look harder, Vic, look real fucking hard; between the lines, in every damn crevice, because the hit I'm taking no thanks to this asshole isn't a goddamn joke! Do you know how much product I have to replace out of pocket? How many orders for Black Widow need to be duplicated and sent out express? How much supplies needs to be ordered? How many machines need repairs? Again, *all* out of pocket. He. Fucked. Me. And now I want his balls on a silver platter," I bit out, literally tasting the venom dripping off my words.

This faceless, nefarious man was evoking the darkest of hate within me and I didn't even know who he was.

"I'll find him," Vic vowed, snapping my gaze back to where he sat.

The meager smirk he offered pissed me right the hell off. What could he possibly have to smile about? His ass was grass if he didn't get his shit together.

"Damn right you will or you can expect a severe decrease in your hours *and* your salary. I don't pay you to do mediocre work."

Vic nodded and nonchalantly turned towards Roscoe, reminding me of the giant's presence. Regret and guilt made up his massive aura. His posture, his demeanor, everything.

Good.

"What the hell were you doing while this shit show was going on?" I asked him, crossing my arms.

Roscoe eyed me cautiously, beads of sweat accumulating at his temples. His mouth popped open several times as he tried to work out a plausible explanation, but words seemed to elude him. You'd never think a man of his size was capable of such intimidation.

And I was going easy on him.

"I passed out, Lux," he finally answered. "I'm sorry—it wasn't intentional. The wife has been on my ass lately and I'm just... I'm exhausted."

"You're exhausted?" I puffed out incredulously.

Roscoe nodded, scrubbing a hand down the back of his buzzed head.

"Did it occur to you that sharing that information with me might've been beneficial to both you and I? Not only would it have ensured the security of my business, it would have given you the time you needed to rest. You know I'm pretty lenient when it comes to time off."

"I know, but I didn't want to waste time off because I'm tired. Yessika would kill me."

"Yeah? And now *I'm* about to kill you. You fucked up, Roscoe—you fucked up royally. I'm going to lose so much money, and possibly customers *on both ends* because you fell asleep. Give me one good reason why I shouldn't put your ass out on the street and bill you for my upcoming expenses?"

"It won't happen again, Lux, I swear," he blurted out, legs bouncing restlessly.

The sweat at his temples was a full sheen now. Nervous wasn't enough of a word to properly describe the state of this man.

"That's right," I leaned toward him, feeding off his vulnerability, "because there won't be a next time. Understood?"

He nodded briskly. "Yes, ma'am."

"Wonderful. Now both of you, go find...*something*." I

shooed them away. "And that still includes Hector's circle."

"What if we can't?" That was Vic as he rose to full height, straightening his ivy green suit jacket.

I stared at him for several moments, wondering how fucking stupid he could be. Apparently, more than I thought possible.

"You better," was all I offered, stalking back around desk. "Or we're going to have problems. Serious problems."

9. BOATS AND HOES
Roman

♫ *Mi Gente - J Balvin & Willy Willam* ♫

"Willow, be a doll and fetch Rome another beer, will you?" Vic said to the petite redhead perched contentedly on his lap.

With a swift slap to her ass, she was on her feet, scampering off inside the yacht's cabin to fulfill Vic's demand.

I shook my head as he glanced my way, his lips curving in an amused smirk.

"What?" he asked candidly, taking another sip from his Corona.

"She's not a dog," I answered.

"I'm fully aware."

"And yet you treat her like one."

"She likes it." He shrugged, relaxing further into the hazel wood leathered cushions lining the perimeter of the stern. "Well, she likes the money."

"So that warrants you to treat her like your personal slave?" I quizzed.

"When I take such good care of her? Yes, it's part of the trade-off."

"Trade-off?" A sarcastic laugh shot out from my nose.

"How about you just treat her with mutual respect instead? Would that be so difficult?"

"I do respect her, with my cock in her mouth," he snickered.

I couldn't help but look at him in complete and utter shock. His mum would knock him over the head with a frying pan if she heard him. Mine would've, too.

Don't get me wrong, I did my fair share of fucking around with different women on a pretty regular basis, but I respected them.

Unless they warranted a reason otherwise, that is.

Act like a slut, get treated like a slut.

Vic used to operate the same. As an army brat, it'd been engrained in his mind. Respecting women was a cardinal rule in their home, just as it was in mine. Our families were vastly different, but that was the same. Sure, my mum might've danced to make a living, but she never brought strange men home, except for the two who were serious. Not only did she want to set a good example for me, she wanted to set one for my little sister as well. As a single mother, she had to work twice as hard, had to play both roles in a child's life.

"I liked you better when you weren't so uptight and pissy," Vic said suddenly, pulling me out from a place I didn't like revisiting too often.

"What are you going on about now?" I sighed, scrubbing a hand down my face to rid my mind of that bloodied image.

"You and your perpetually ticked state. You seem as bitter toward me as you are about—"

I held a hand up to shut him down. We were *not* about to talk about my ex.

"What the hell is going on with you?" he bit out. "Are you still mad about—"

Again I held a hand up. Wasn't up for discussion. No matter how he worded it or tried to get around it, we were not talking about Liza.

Not now, not ever.

End of story.

Just the thought of her made me resentful.

"Nothing to do with you," I lied, catching wind of Willow emerging from the cabin with an enamored smile on her face.

Thank you, Willow.

The perfect distraction.

She bound right up to me, offered me the Corona, and legitimately slithered her way into Vic's grasp again.

Except her presence didn't distract him the way I was banking on.

"Then what's the problem?" he pressed, grazing his fingertips along her figure. "And don't tell me nothing, because I know you, Rome, and I know there's something going on that you haven't fessed up about."

Kinda like you, asshole?

I took a sip from the fresh, ice cold bottle to mask my irritation. "It's nothing, Vic. Just know that me helping you puts me at risk."

"Why?" Willow asked, totally rapt in our conversation.

I stared at her for a moment in confusion, then

watched Vic's face morph from curious to slightly irate. Very slowly, he turned his head toward her and waited for her attention. When she remained oblivious, he rushed a hand into her enflamed locks and reeled her back close enough for his lips to scrape against her ear.

"Don't speak unless you're spoken to, sweetheart," he growled viciously. "Understood?"

"Y-yes," she whimpered, squeezing her eyes shut as he tugged on her hair harder.

"Fantastic. Now run along and play with your little friends while you can. We'll be docking shortly."

He all but shoved her onto her feet and slapped her ass, not the least bit concerned she was gaping at him in both horror and betrayal. Idly, I wondered if this were the first time he lashed out at her like this.

Either way, he was one stupid motherfucker. Willow looked damn good.

"Why help me then?" he asked, as soon as she was out of earshot.

I shook my head and took another generous sip, pondering what had happened in the last few years for Vic to change so much. "Because you needed it," I answered.

"Anddd," he drawled, waving a hand for me to continue.

"And because Lux sounds a lot like…"

I stopped myself right there, quickly realizing I'd said too much. I wasn't ready to get into this with him, but of course, he already seemed to know. I hated how well he still knew me when I recognized so little about him.

"Oh, I know," he agreed, a little chuckle bouncing off

the end, completely unsurprised. "If I didn't know any better, I'd say they're related. Diabolical little bitches."

"Amen," I agreed, for the sake of letting it go, taking yet another sip as Cardi's "*I Like It*" began blaring through the speakers.

"She's losing her mind trying to figure out who you are, by the way." He laughed.

"So why not just tell her?" I asked, to which his head reared back in slight disgust.

"How is that even a question right now?"

"How do you expect her to retaliate if she doesn't know where to find me?" I countered.

"I plan to tell her, trust me. Just not yet. If I come back with answers too soon, she'll question it."

"Will she really, though?" My query sounded as skeptical as you're imagining. "If she's losing it like you claim, she'll be pleased you have, at the very least, one answer for her. One little clue will get this moving even quicker."

Vic shook his head definitively. "Not yet. I want to make her wait, want her to suffer, need her to beg on her fucking knees in desperation. *Then* I'll tell her."

On one hand, I understood where he was coming from. Revenge made people do the most daft shit sometimes. Wearing her down to the last thread was part of the appeal, something I'd once been hellbent on doing to Liza.

Correction, something I did do to Liza.

But on the other hand, I didn't understand why he'd want to drag this out.

Okay, wait—I'm lying out of my ass. Vic loved himself a lengthy drama, loved the spotlight on him.

My point is, though, for someone who was so anxious to reclaim what was supposedly his, why wait any longer than necessary to do so? Why waste time on petty moves?

I was tempted to ask, so tempted the question burned hot on my tongue, but I knew the chances of getting an honest answer were slim to none, not when he was still withholding so much from me.

"If you say so," I conceded, cutting my eyes toward all the commotion on the upper level.

Willow's friends were having the time of their lives with no Willow in sight. I'd bet money not one of them knew what their dearest friend had to endure in order to make this possible.

"So what's the next step in your plan?" He questioned, slicing through my silent observation.

I shrugged and turned my attention back on him, draining what remained of my beer. "Tip off the cops, lead them right to her distributors. At least the top three anyway. She'll find herself quite lost without them considering they purchase the most weight and have the most clientele, right?"

One of Vic's brows shot up in a perfect arch. "Absolutely. I like that," he cooed, nodding in approval. "She's going to go nuclear."

"Good. That's the goal, is it not?"

"Yep."

"Next move is on you, though, mate," I clarified, pointing the emptied bottle at him. "You *have* to give her one teensy sliver, make her think you're doing your job and all that."

"I will, I will. She'll be begging for sure by then. Perfect timing if you ask me," he chortled, the devious glimmer in his eyes practically shining through his Aviators. "Told you I needed your mastermind."

Sureee.

I could have rolled my damn eyes. Bloody miracle I didn't, really.

"Oh, and I keep forgetting to mention…" I added, scooting to the edge of my seat. "I'm taking the office."

Vic looked at me like I'd sprouted five heads. "The hell you are," he spat, enjoying a good laugh.

By himself.

My lips didn't even quirk.

"I am. I have to," I asserted.

"Yeah? And why is that?"

"Because if I don't, it'll blow our cover. What is Lux going to think when she finally pieces everything together, storms into Noir Coast, only to find an office that screams Vic Kane?"

Silence.

I could see the cogs working in his head, see it painted all over his face. He knew I had a point.

"Fuck, you're right," he sighed, dropping his head back against the cushion.

I smiled in satisfaction and lifted onto my feet as the yacht began approaching the bay. "I know."

"Whatever, do it." He waved me off, not noticing I'd already taken off. "I'll clean it out Monday and you can move your shit in. But as soon as Lux submits, I'm taking it back."

"You can have it," I called out over my shoulder, heading right for a frightened Willow at the other end of the boat with a smirk.

The girl was going to have a good time, even if it was just for a few minutes, and she was going to realize she didn't need Vic to do that.

She just needed the King.

10. ENEMY LINES
Lux

♫ *Wreak Havoc - Skylar Grey* ♫

Phantom returned before I could retaliate.

After a week and a half or so of losing my goddamn mind, he struck again, randomly and unannounced. And let me tell you, this *K* fellow was ballsy. Ballsy as fuck to be exact. Smart, too.

Crafty.

Resourceful.

I hated him. No, more like loathed him with a fierce passion. Loathed him more than I did my piece of shit father. His masked face haunted me day in and day out, haunted my dreams, too. I was exhausted, constantly on edge. But mostly, I was livid.

All I wanted was to rid myself of him, but if he'd proven anything in the last few weeks, it's that he wasn't going anywhere.

The million dollar question was—*what exactly did he want from me?*

There were obvious factors of course; the money, the power. But why target me specifically? Phantom could've chosen anyone in the world to pick a fight with. So why me?

And why hide while he was at it?

He had balls of steel when it came to intimidation tactics, so why not just be a man, period?

Why not face me directly and tell me he wanted a cut?

I'd have said no—obviously—because there's not a chance in hell I was going to share something I shed blood, sweat, and tears for, but he didn't know that...

Or did he?

I'd run across the thought several times, and no matter how much I tried to convince myself it just couldn't be, I couldn't seem to dismiss it completely either.

Was Phantom someone I knew?

Someone I may have burned a bridge with on the way up?

Sadly, no, he wasn't, because it couldn't be that easy.

I still had no idea who he was, even after Vic finally did his job. All we had to go by was a location. Oh, and the infamous *K* signature from his note, of course. Despite the lack of an ID, though, his supposed coordinates led us to some newly restored factory along the marina.

Noir Coast Distillery.

Was this really his place?

We're about to find out...

"Ready?" I asked Roscoe and Vic, as we stood head-on before the enemy, ready to tear the place upside down until we found him.

Oh rather, *until I found him.* If anyone was going to

DEE GARCIA

rip him to shreds, it was me. I smirked. He wanted to chat, right?

Well, let's chat then, motherfucker.

Roscoe and Vic yanked open the doors for me, allowing me to run in with a handgun lodged in each hand. Machines and conversations immediately came to a screeching halt as everyone—men and women alike—stopped what they were doing, their wide, fearful eyes trained on me in all my furious glory.

It was dead silent as I peered around the room, both Vic and Roscoe right on my tail again, rifles extended.

"Who the fuck runs this shit hole?" I gritted out.

At least ten people pointed up to an office over-looking the main floor. The blinds were drawn but I could just make out a shadowed figure standing beside the window.

My pulse quickened all the more.

Was that him?

"On your right. The stairs," Vic commented softly in my ear. "Go, I'll watch these guys down here."

My gaze followed his directions, then up the zigzag trail of the rusty stairs.

Perfect.

"You guys remember the plan?" I asked them both, taking one last look around the first floor.

"Yup," they answered.

"On my mark only… Cover me," I ordered Roscoe, holstering one firearm at the small of my back as I sprung into action and hustled up the steps. The iron floor clanked beneath my heeled boots, growing louder and louder as I zeroed in on the door. Each step pumped in time with my heart.

"As you were!" Vic barked powerfully. "C'mon, nothing to see here!"

I heard, rather than saw them all scramble back to work just as I curled my hand around the cool knob.

This was it.

The moment I'd been waiting for.

And it turned out to be nothing like I expected…

Bursting into the office fit my vision perfectly. Falling dead in my tracks, however, did not.

My breath caught as my feet rooted themselves to the ground. This man, Phantom or not, he was…*me*. Only in male form.

A handsomely grim mug.

Intense eyes.

Hard lines to his jaw.

Almost every plane of skin tattooed in entirety, or at least it appeared that way beneath the all-black suit that fit him like a second skin. Even his face was tattooed. Two stood out most; a spider crawling down one side and the word *compel* scripted over his eyebrow, almost in the same spot I carried one of my own. I felt like I was looking into some weird mirror from an alternate universe and was completely taken aback at how strikingly good-looking he was.

"Take a picture, Pigeon, it'll last longer," he mused, a deviously cocky smirk playing on one corner of his mouth.

That word, *pigeon,* and the amused fashion in which

he'd spoken to me—with an accent like mine nonetheless
—both shook me to my core, and yet rekindled my initial
purpose for being here.

Fire rushed through my veins as I narrowed my eyes
and started for his desk with determined strides. "First
and last time you call me Pigeon. I'm not a fucking
bird."

The handsome man chuckled, a dark, sexy rumble in
his chest, and lazily reclined into his seat, crossing his
arms behind his head. "On the contrary, Miss Mercier, you
are quite the little bird. Not at all what I was expecting the
Queen of Miami to look like."

It *is* him.

"And what were you expecting?" I asked sarcastically,
trying my hardest to seem as unaffected as possible.

"I don't know…maybe some class?" he bit out, his
smirk spreading further at the offended expression that fell
across my face.

Oh hell no.

I could've killed him, right then and there, simply for
being such a fool. But because I was so intent on finding
out who he was, what he wanted, and how the hell he
knew who I was, I swallowed his words down, the gun in
my grasp burning my palm.

Wasn't lost on me he had me bouncing from one
emotion to the next in nanoseconds..

"I'm going to let that slide this time seeing as we have
more important things to discuss than your low blow
tactics. How's that for some class?" I tossed back.

My answer was a sinister grin. Nothing less, nothing

more. And it only served to irk me further. He wasn't fazed. Not remotely.

"Who the hell are you?" I blurted out angrily, stopping at the foot of his space, my fingers twitching on the trigger.

Icy blue eyes dropped to my 9mm for a split-second before slithering up to my face. He just stared at me, studying me closely. That was hard enough in itself, but I wasn't at all prepared to catch his tongue peek out and swipe along his bottom lip. And I sure as hell wasn't prepared to feel it everywhere either.

"Roman. Roman King," he purred, breaking through the overwhelming haze. "It's a pleasure to finally meet you."

K for King... Roman King...

Something about his name made my stomach flip wildly.

What the fuck is happening to me right now?

"Can't say I feel the same," I barely gritted out, shocked at my body's reaction to toward this man.

"Let's see if we can change your mind then, yeah? I did agree to a chat after all. What is it you'd like to discuss, Miss Mercier? Tell me everything."

"Or we can just cut to the chase," I countered, leaning onto his desk. "I believe your time in Miami has come to an end, Mr. King."

"Has it now?" He questioned on a chuckle, yet again way too amused for my liking.

"Indeed it has." I swallowed as his scent hit me. Mahogany...and teakwood, with the subtle hint of some mouthwatering cologne. "I might've considered letting you accumulate the odd client here and there, because everyone has to make a living, but you decided to fuck with me—not once, but twice. I'm not very pleased about that."

Roman shrugged, one-hundred percent unaffected by the bite in my tone. "You have what I want," he explained, inching forward closer to me.

I had to force myself in place. "And that would be?"

"Everything." He grinned, cocking his head to one side, wayward strands of his dark coiffed hair falling in his face.

Another swallow. "Define everything," I demanded.

"Money, power, respect. You seem to have it all, *and I want it.*"

"But why me?" Why choose to screw with me?"

"Because you're an easy target, love. Women are too emotional, and emotions elicit vulnerability. See where I'm going with this?"

He was absolutely right, and that right there was the tipping point for me. I hated that he was right. Women *were* vulnerable creatures, especially women who'd survived the deepest, darkest parts of hell.

Women like me.

"So why not just come forward and state your terms? Why was any of this necessary?" I asked, wanting to focus on anything but how right he was.

"Because I knew you'd never agree to anything my assistant offered you," he conceded.

"Yeah, you know why? Because I don't negotiate with

messengers. You want to tread my streets, *you* come to *me*, not send your minions to sway me to your liking. And you most certainly don't take out my people either. What you did was wage a war, Mr. King, and let me tell you, you picked a fight with the wrong woman."

"Ooohhh," he cooed in mock horror. "Am I supposed to be afraid?"

"You should be," I warned.

Roman laughed softly. "I'll make a mental note for next time."

"There won't be a next time. You need to get the fuck out of here if you know what's good for you."

"Not going anywhere, Pigeon. Get used to seeing this mug a lot, since you don't want to play nice and share. All that can change, though. Just say the words and I'll be out of your hair," he said, bringing a hand of ringed fingers up to twirl an emerald strand around a digit.

I stilled at his unexpected touch, all but holding my breath as I eyed the ink adorning his skin. The words etched on that curve between his thumb and forefinger called out to me most.

Your throat here.

I almost whimpered aloud at the visual his tattoo offered. *Heaven help me.* "Nothing personal, King, but I don't share with anyone," I murmured, inhaling a shaky breath.

The air, thick and heavy around us, drowned out the conversation in entirety. He was just watching me again and I couldn't stop myself from staring back either, completely hypnotized by the glow of those glacial blues.

"And that right there will be what ends your reign," he whispered, dropping his gaze to my lips. "Just remember we had this conversation when your throne goes up in flames. Remember you could have spared yourself imminent doom, Lux."

The way he purred my name, how his tongue caressed it, dotted my skin with dozens of goose pimples, those small, thin baby hairs at the nape of my neck rising at attention. Still, I held my head high, reminding myself to breathe. "If anyone should be worried about imminent doom, it's you. I wasn't kidding, Roman. I'm not the woman to mess with."

"Do your worst," he challenged, like he *still* didn't understand—*or believe*—the gravity of my words.

Suddenly, I was all for feeding into his childish little game. He truly wanted to war with me, then a war we would have. It was on without question.

"You can count on it," I promised him, pushing off his desk and sauntering toward Roscoe by the doors. "Oh, and Roman?" The question came from over my shoulder.

"Hmmm?"

"*Tag, you're it,*" I purred, snapping my fingers at Roscoe as I slipped past him and started down the way I came.

And just as I was pushing out of the distillery into another humid Miami night, Vic and Roscoe lit the place up without mercy, the rapid firing of their rifles sounding like fireworks on the fourth of July.

11. CELEBRATING THE WORLD'S IDIOTS

Vic

♫ *Superman - Eminen* ♫

I fucking loved when Willow sucked my cock.

She did it with such gusto, always so eager to please me. And lately, that's all I'd allowed myself to do with her. She'd gotten too whiny. Too clingy.

The girl clearly wanted more, and unfortunately for her, I didn't do more.

More was fucking bullshit.

But apparently, debasing her three times a week automatically called for such ridiculousness, thus rendering her an instantaneous downgrade. I refused to put my dick inside her used cunt anymore.

Hell no. Wasn't doing it.

Still needed something to take the edge off, and her mouth did the job well.

Without complaint I should add.

Willow wanted me too much to protest about what she could or couldn't have. In her mind, sucking me off was better than nothing at all. I could call her at three in the morning and she'd answer. Didn't matter if she was dead asleep. The girl would drive across town, attend to my needs, and take her ass back home with her pretty little clit throbbing in need if it meant having me to herself for half an hour.

So, after a shit week that consisted of Lux barking down my neck about Phantom at every turn, I went out for a few hard drinks with the boys, then came straight home and gave my little pet a ring. As expected, she answered promptly, and within thirty minutes, she was knocking at my door.

In nothing but a robe.

Had her on her knees in my office—completely naked —shortly after that.

Sprawled out in my chair, I let Willow work her magic between my spread legs. Stress was melting away in waves and I was about three pumps away from nutting down her throat. Eyes downcast, she worked the base of my cock with her hand while her tongue swirled around the head over and over again. Every few seconds or so, a content little moan would escape her lips.

Loved that, too.

That sexy little sound would vibrate from tip to base, enhancing her ministrations in tenfold. It felt so damn good.

Another moan rattled down my length then. Teeth grit, I glanced down at her, and it was then I realized she was playing with herself, too, rubbing her clit with soft strokes.

"God-fucking-damn," I gritted out, thrusting a hand into her hair for leverage. Scooting closer to the edge of my seat, I forced my cock further down her throat and held her there, suffocating her, gagging her.

It was glorious.

I could feel her throat stretching and shrinking around me.

She was wailing about for air by the time I let up. But I allowed her only a few mere breaths before I started face-fucking her without mercy. Stares entwined, I didn't hold back, pummeling harder and harder the more her eyes watered around each gag.

"Such a good little whore," I cooed, gripping her hair tighter. "You love this fucking cock, don't you?"

Willow couldn't nod from the strength of my hold, but I heard the hum of approval loud and clear, saw the answer flickering in her flooded green eyes.

Yes, sir, they said. *Use me. Own me.*

That sense of prolific power tipped me over the edge. Growling, I struck my palm across her cheek and held her down on my dick as I came violently, hot and thick. Her moans prolonged my climax, milking my balls for every last drop. Even when the spurts ceased, she kept at it, licking me clean with a devious smile on her face. Willow was a greedy little thing and I'd have relished it longer if my damn phone hadn't started vibrating somewhere on my desk.

"Fuck!" I hissed, pulling myself free from her mouth.

Rolling back a few feet, I glazed over the illuminated screen as I tucked my cock into my pants. The name displayed clear as day tripped me up for a second.

What the hell does she want now?

"Finish yourself," I ordered Willow, snatching my phone off the desk. "Then show yourself out. I've gotta take this."

I didn't have to look back to see the disappointment now etched on her face. I could feel it as I stalked to the door and rushed out into the hallway.

Not that I cared. She had no respect for herself, so why should I or anyone else?

"Moxie," I answered, as I ambled down the dim corridor en route to the back terrace.

"Must you call me that every time, Victor?" she growled, her Brit accent thicker than I remembered.

A plethora of music and laughter blared behind her as though she were in a club.

"It's a term of endearment and you know it."

"Mhmm," she hummed skeptically.

"It is," I chuckled.

"I'm sure. In any case, I have to make this short. Just checking in to see how things are going…"

Of course.

I should've known. She couldn't've just waited until *I* called *her,* right? Always so impatient.

"They're…going," I said, stepping out into the muggy night through the large sliding glass door.

"What is that supposed to mean?"

"It means they're just getting started."

The little bitch sighed deeply, the sound equally aggravated as it was displeased. "And why is that?" she questioned.

"Because it just is. These things take time."

"I've wasted enough time," she gritted out, just as I dropped into one of the loungers near the infinity pool.

I could imagine her pretty face as she said that. Could see it so clearly it's like she was sitting right in front of me.

"Well, I hate to break it to you, but you're going to have to wait a little longer. Relax, love, I got this. You'll get what you want at the end of it all," I assured her, relaxing in my seat.

"Get it done, Vic, soon—or I'm coming for you, too," she threatened, and while I knew she was entirely serious, I wasn't the least bit concerned.

Everything was going according to plan thus far, and unless Rome somehow managed to fuck it up, I didn't foresee there being issues in the future.

Lux would go down, and Rome would follow.

My lips quirked at the visual that all presented. "That won't be necessary. You have my word."

"I'm counting on it," she concluded, mumbling something I couldn't make out to whoever she was with. "Listen, I've gotta go, the pub's closing up. Expect a call from me in a few weeks time."

Wonderful, I thought to myself. Another follow up from her evil ass.

"Noted," I conceded.

"Good night, Victor."

"Good night, *Liza.*"

12. FATAL ATTRACTION
Roman

♫ *Kill Everyone - Hollywood Undead* ♫

I finally understood why Vic hadn't given me anything other than the bare minimum on Lux. I understood it loud and fucking clear.

The motherfucker was sneaky. He knew damn well if I'd gotten even the slightest hint she looked like *that,* I would've washed my hands of it all from the get-go and left him to handle this vendetta on his own.

In retrospect, I probably should've put two and two together based on what little I did know, but it hadn't crossed my mind this could even be a possibility.

I mean, what were the chances?

One in a million, that's what and, apparently, the world had tipped on its axis or some shit because this was that one.

It'd been a few short days since Lux stormed into my office and I was still in utter shock. Shocked to my goddamn core is more like it.

She looked so much like Liza.

So. Bloody. Much.

Not quite identical, but if someone told me they were

related, I'd have believed them without question. From the blue eyes to those plush lips, to the defined lines of her gorgeous face and all the tats. Down to the slim physique and style, too.

It was simply uncanny.

I might've appeared calm and collected as I caught my first glimpse of her, but on the inside, I was completely taken aback. A bit creeped out, too, if I'm being honest.

I was so drawn to it, though.

So drawn to her and the challenge she presented.

And it had nothing to do with her appearance.

She was just this...force. This unstoppable, alluring, intriguing force, and *I wanted to see more*, so much more. Wanted to see how hot I could make her, just how far I could push her before she snapped like a twig.

The possibilities were endless, and what got me most was knowing she felt the same, too.

I could laugh remembering how she tried to hide it.

To deny it.

Her entire performance was quite possibly the most—I can't believe I'm about to say this—*adorable* thing I'd ever seen in my life.

So adorable I gave her an A plus for effort.

But I could see right through her wicked little armor, clocked onto everything she didn't want me to see; the unintentional seductive lilt of her body language, the lustful fire in her eyes, the throaty rasp to her voice.

Even those dick-twitching little gasps.

I caught them all.

The attraction was instantaneous—on both our parts—

and while I knew this frame of mind could lead to dangerous destinations, I was going to use it to my advantage. I'd build her up, play on her crazy with our twisted little game of cat and mouse until she broke…and then I'd build her up again, feed her desires, and slither my way into every last part of her being before shattering her from the inside out.

A smile touched my lips at the vicious thought, my grip tightening around the steering wheel in anticipation as I eased onto I-95 from the Palmetto. I'd been driving around for the last hour, aggressively weaving in and out of traffic in hopes to calm the erratic thrumming in my veins.

But nothing helped.

The next move was mine to make, it had been for a while, and I couldn't seem to settle on a new attack, especially now.

I *needed* something that would demand her handling it herself. Something that would lead her right back to me.

And this time, I wouldn't be confined to my desk.

Lux was about to find herself toe to toe with the King, and I could hardly wait to sink my claws deep into her pale, ink-adorned skin. Could hardly wait to inhale her scent, run my hands over her body, feel her pulse flutter wildly as I held the gun to her temple…

It was right about then, as I pulled up to my new chill spot, that I realized this was going to be more fun than I ever thought possible.

Fuck Vic and his bullshit power play. This wasn't about him anymore. This was for *me*.

I'd have the money.

The Power.

Respect.

Soon I'd have Miami under my rule, and I'd have little Miss Lux Mercier, too.

Let the gruesome, nefarious games—*officially*—begin.

13. TIL THE LAST DROP
Lux

♫ *Tag, you're it - Melanie Martinez* ♫

"I just don't understand why he's suddenly stagnant," I snapped at Suki, as I stomped around my bedroom in an anxiety-induced cleaning spree.

It'd been almost two weeks since I barreled into Noir Coast, and I'd not heard a single peep from Roman.

Let's just say, my nerves were officially at an all-time high.

"I mean, you did threaten him to get the hell out of Miami, did you not?" she pointed out from her place on my bed, as she went about perfectly polishing her toes in a villainous purple.

"Yes, but after all I've told you about him, do you really think he'd just heed my warning and bolt?"

"If he's intelligent, yes."

I stilled in my half bent over state and glared at her. "You're not helping, Suk."

"What do you want me to say then?" She sighed, meeting my stare with dubious eyes. "That he's coming for you?"

"No," I grumbled, snatching my pajamas off the floor.

"Then what?"

"I don't know!" I blurted out, fidgeting under her scrutiny. "I don't fucking know, okay?! It's like, I want him to disappear, but at the same time—"

The smirk that curled Suki's lips shut me up real quick. And I mean, *real quick.* I couldn't believe I was about to admit that I *wanted* to play his stupid little game.

How insane would that have sounded?

Evidently, not *that* much considering my best friend was looking at me like she already knew what I wanted to say.

Was I insane, though, for even entertaining it? Hell, I felt like I was, and I loathed Roman that much more for making me feel this way.

"But at the same time you what?" she pressed, leaning toward me expectantly.

I shook my head and held my hands up in surrender. There was no way in hell I could tell her. I loved Suki with my whole life, but she'd never let me live this down. "Nothing, forget it. Let's just hope his silence does, in fact, mean he's gone and done one."

Suki hesitated only a couple of seconds before piping up again. "I see what's going on here," she chuckled, screwing the polish bottle shut.

"Yeah? And what is that?" I crossed my arms.

"You want him, Lux."

My eyes nearly popped out of their sockets. "What?!" I screeched incredulously, heart suddenly racing into overdrive. "Are you daft?"

Suki choked out a laugh, thinning her lips and all. "No, I'm not, thank you, but you are, apparently. "

Is she serious right now?

"I do *not* want him," I muttered indignantly, storming into the safety of my closet.

With shaky hands, I slammed my clothes into the hamper and huffed out a breath, trying to block out her cackling in the background. She was way beyond daft. Totally fucking delusional. How could she even think that—

"Don't hide from me, Lux," she called out, shooting my shoulders up to my ears. "You're only making it more obvious."

Rolling my eyes, I walked back out in the bedroom with my head held high, trying to appear as blasé about the entire situation as possible.

But she wasn't buying it one bit, sitting at the edge of the bed with her head tilted aside. "You know I'm right."

"You're not," I retorted.

"I am, and you wanna know how I can tell? Those killer cheeks of yours ran bright red when I mentioned it. Tell tale sign right there. Plus, you were on the defense before I could blink."

I went completely rigid as a tense silence engulfed the room. The only thing I could hear was my pulse thundering in my ears.

"I know you too well for you to play dumb," she continued, snapping my attention her way once more. "Is he hot?" she queried, waggling her eyebrows.

"Why does it matter?" My head reared, which earned me another satisfied smirk.

"Because you never told me what he looks like."

"Because it's irrelevant!" I bellowed, arms shooting out to my sides.

Suki chuckled and shook her head. "Judging by your reaction, I'd say it's pretty relevant. Spill, L," she ordered, motioning to empty space on the bed beside her.

But I didn't move.

If I took the bait, I'd only be encouraging her assumptions, and I was blatantly refusing to believe she could even be partially right. Something was wrong with me, that's a definite given, and it was one-hundred percent Roman's fault. But no, I did *not* want him in any other way than gone, dead or alive.

I couldn't.

I don't.

And yet you do, whispered that bastard little voice in my head.

Shooing her away with a shake of my head, I forced myself to focus on all Roman had done up to this point. So what if he was good looking? I could acknowledge his beauty and still hate him.

Right?

Nothing but laughter greeted me, both in and out of my mind. Suki and my subconscious were enjoying quite a good chuckle at my expense.

"I'll take that as a yes," she snickered, and I groaned, because I was contradicting myself left and right, at every fucking turn.

My body was not at all in sync with my mind.

"Yes, he's striking, okay," I admitted, shuffling toward the bed and dropping down beside her in a heap. "But like I said, irrelevant. His looks don't change what he's done or how I feel about it all."

"Sureee," she drawled.

"I just want him to make a move already."

"On you or—"

I shot her another glare. "Drop it, Suk."

"Okay, okay, fine." She giggled, holding her hands up. "Provoke him then."

"What?"

"Provoke him. You want him to react, right? Fuck with him like he fucked with you. Nothing too extravagant, but enough to make it clear you're waiting on him."

"What do you mean clear? I *was* clear that night in his office. Vic and Roscoe wiped out every body on the first floor, for crying out loud."

"Obviously wasn't clear enough, or perhaps he just didn't believe you. *Make him believe.*"

"How?" I questioned, genuinely intrigued by her suggestion.

Suki bounced onto her feet excitedly and held a hand out to me. "Wanna take a little trip?"

"Where?" I asked warily, slipping my palm in hers.

"Noir Coast, of course.*"

"The distillery? Why?"

That evil Suki smile split across her lips. "Because we're going to let it pour til the very last drop."

LESS THAN AN HOUR LATER, SUKI AND I WERE HIDDEN IN the shadows on Noir Coast's grounds waiting for Stryker. The original plan didn't call for his assistance, but after further consideration, it was clear we were going to need another set of eyes on the lot. He wasn't sold at first, but once he realized Suki was tagging along, too, he agreed to help us keep watch while we did the dirty work. For the most part, Stryker did a good job at staying out of trouble for the sake of his custody battle, but the man just couldn't resist my girl.

Suki asked.

He delivered.

Always. No matter what. Again, why they weren't together yet was beyond me.

"Will you stop fidgeting?" Suki hissed from our place beneath a large tree.

"I can't help it, bitch. I'm dying under all these layers!" I hissed back, pushing up the sleeves of my black hoodie. "Remind me why it's necessary for us to wear all this shit?"

"Do you want to get caught on camera?"

"I don't really give three flying fucks, Suk. The man is going to know it was me the second he opens those doors tomorrow morning. Who fucking cares if he catches us on tape?"

She glared at me like I'd lost my damn mind. "I don't know about you, but I'm not too keen on ending up at the county jail for breaking and entering. Oh, and vandalizing, too."

"I'd say you have a point, but you seem to forget we're dealing with Roman. All this is going to do is fire him up and, hopefully, get him moving. I can guarantee you there won't be any cops involved."

"I didn't forget, I'm just not willing to take the chance. From what you've told me, King is a wild card. Locking you up would make things a lot easier for him."

She has a point...

"True," I agreed. "But no, I'm telling you. He wouldn't do that, not when bringing the cops into this could end badly for him as well. He'll handle it himself, trust me."

"Yeah, while he handles your pussy," she quipped, voice hushed.

My mouth popped open, an only half-amused scoff bursting its way out.

This bitch.

"What the hell did you just say?"

Suki flashed me that wannabe angelic smile, batting her long lashes and all. "Oh, nothinggg."

I was just about to backhand her arm when a formidable voice boomed suddenly mere feet away.

"Hey! You two! Don't move!"

Gasping, Suki and I withdrew our weapons at the same, pointing them toward the source, our chests heaving.

"Don't shoot, don't shoot! It's me!"

I deflated like a balloon. So did Suki.

Stryker.

Sure enough, emerging from the shadows with his hands thrown up in the air was the bastard himself.

"Jesus Christ, Stryker! What in the actual fuck?" I gritted out, re-holstering my gun at the small of my back.

"I'm sorry!" He laughed. "It was too good to pass up."

"Wouldn't have been so funny if one of us had shot your dumb ass," Suki grumbled, her cheeks reddening as he pinned her with his gaze and closed the distance between us.

The closer he got, the more stiff she became at my side, sucking in a heap of air as he slid up beside her and curled an arm around her shoulders.

"How's it going, baby doll?" he asked smoothly, cocking his head to one side.

I had to stifle a laugh as I watched my best friend succumb to his charm. She tried hardening her expression to the best of her ability, but anyone in their right mind could see the desire in her eyes from a mile away.

"You're a dick, you know that?" The rhetorical question came with a shove to his chest.

Not that he cared.

Stryker simply chuckled and squeezed Suki closer to his side. "Not always, but I will admit, it is fun sometimes."

"Oh, she knows. She can be a dick too," I chimed in, grinning when she hit me with another glare.

"Fuck you, L."

"I'll pass, but Stryker may want a go at it."

Both their faces paled—and flushed—right before my

very eyes. I couldn't contain my amusement, throwing my head back in a proper laugh that brought tears to my eyes.

"I'm going to bloody kill you," Suki snarled, which in turn only made me laugh harder.

"On the contrary," I wiped the droplets running down my cheeks, "you'll thank me one day. But that day is not today and we have shit to do. Think you two can focus around each other for fifteen minutes or…"

"If by focus you mean on her ass, yeah, I can do that." Stryker grinned devilishly.

Suki gasped in surprise. Her blue eyes bulged and her cheeks heated all the more than they already were, but she didn't utter a single word.

Surprisingly.

"Are you done?" I glanced at Stryker, deciding not to ask for further elaboration.

Yet.

I'd cross that bridge once we were out of Noir Coast.

Stryker nodded and zipped his lips, motioning for me to continue.

"We need to make this quick, in and out. Stryk, you pick the locks and stay by the door. Suki and I will find the barrels."

A firm shake of his head was my response. "Hell no. I'm not leaving you two alone in there. I'll keep an eye on things, but I'm going inside, too."

"If that makes you feel better," I sighed, "then fine. Once we've gotten all the barrels, we're out of here. No horsing around or fucking with anything else. Got it?"

After rounding the entire perimeter of the building,

Stryker deemed the back entrance our easiest option. Considering it was likely that the barrels would be back here anyway, Suki and I let him do his thing. Took the man no more than five minutes to toy with the locks and pull the doors open.

Flashlights and hammers in hand, Suki and I made our way through the darkened factory in search of the whiskey barrels with Stryker looming not too far behind.

The search didn't last long.

They were right where I thought they would be, all of them neatly and chronologically organized in floor to ceiling wooden shelves.

"Do you wanna do the honors?" I asked Suki. It was her idea after all.

"Na, you do it, babe. Leave the motherfucker high and dry."

A delighted smile curled my lips as I tightened my grip on the hammer.

Oh to be a fly on the wall...

14. WHISKEY AND RED FLAGS

Roman

♫ *Courtesy Call - Thousand Foot Krutch* ♫

Monday morning rolled around and I was no more certain of what my next move would be than I was last week. If anything, I was all the more unsure. I'd gotten ahead of myself by taking out Lux's biggest clients so early in the game.

Then again, I had no idea we'd be in for such an interesting turn events just days later. And unbeknownst to me, things were about to get all the more interesting.

7am.

The sun was just beginning to rise through the clouds. Punching in the passcode, I let myself into the quiet factory and took a deep breath as I surveyed the room. Usually, I'd relished the silence and enjoy a piping hot mug of coffee in the comfort of my office, before the day got started, but today… Today was definitely not one of those days.

The entire place smelled like a giant bottle of whiskey. I don't mean the usual smells that infiltrated the factory on a day to day basis.

No.

I mean it *reeked* of whiskey.

Burn your nose hairs, eyes watering blindly type of reek.

With an arm to my nose, I took two steps inside to assess the problem and quickly deduced what happened. Anger consumed me in seconds. The floor was flooded in at least two inches of the amber liquid. Not a couple of random puddles here and there.

Oh ho.

The entire fucking floor.

And I'd just stepped my brand new Derby's in the mess.

Smoke all but billowed from my ears, my hands curling into fists at my sides as I trudged through the factory to the back where Vic housed all the barrels.

Barrels that would now have to be replaced, seeing as every last one had a lovely hole smashed right through the bottom.

I knew who it was before the thought even crossed my mind.

Lux.

It had to be. I mean, *who else* could be responsible for this?

Ramos was dead.

His boys had long since fled. Either that, or they were doing a fine job at laying low.

In any case, this was hands down Lux's doing.

"What in the actual fuck is all this?" Vic's voice boomed from the front of the factory.

Wonderful.

Just what I needed.

On an exasperated sigh, I stalked out from the back, silently cursing Lux the entire way for ruining, not only my brand new shoes, but my slacks and my morning as well.

"What do you think?" I tossed back once he came into view, grappling his attention from the mess at his feet. "Or rather, *who* do you think?"

Vic's already irate expression darkened all the more, his upper lip curling in a silent snarl. "Lux," he gritted out.

"Ding, ding, ding—we have a a winner!"

"Son of a bitch!" he hissed.

Humming, I stepped around him and clapped him on the shoulder en route to the parking lot. "She's a cunt alright."

"Where the hell are you going? We need to clean this shit up."

"Which is exactly why I need to change out of this." I pointed to my suit.

"Right." He glancing down at his own suit. "I suppose I should too. When you get back, though, we need to talk."

My head jerked back. "About?"

"Liza," he deadpanned.

Her name immobilized me.

I stood there like a mindless idiot, staring at the man that, at one point in time was like a brother to me, like he'd just uttered something in a foreign language or grown five heads.

Holding his stare, I clenched and unclenched my fists. "What about her?"

"She called me."

"She what?!"

Vic nodded and ambled over to his charcoal gray Rover parked in the first spot, leaning up against the grill. "You heard me, brother. She. Called. Me."

Fuck.

"What did she want?" I asked, trying to keep my voice steady.

"She's looking for you," he explained, confirming my suspicions.

"And what did you tell her?" I hedged.

"That I haven't spoken to you since...well, you know."

Of course I knew.

How could I forget *that?*

Flashes of that day, the day I lost my fucking shit and sent my life in a downward spiral, flickered viciously in my mind. I wouldn't be standing here today if that shit show hadn't gone down.

But it did.

It was very real, and despite the fact it'd been years since then, it still hurt like hell. It hurt because every painful thing that followed, every person I loved and lost, happened because of me.

"Wanna tell me what's going on, Rome, 'cause, I haven't heard from Liza since before my parents and I left London, so why the fuck is she calling me all these years later, looking for you no less? How does she even have my number?"

"I don't know," I gritted out, willing any and every thought having to do with Liza and her vindictive ass out of my mind.

"Bull-fucking-shit, bro. That's bullshit and you know it! Liza doesn't just do things without a reason. There's always a reason, a method to her madness, so what the hell did you do now?"

He was right, unfortunately. One-hundred percent right. If my ex did something, there was a story behind it, whether it was true or not. And now, I was going to have to tell him about what drove me out London, because if I didn't, there's a chance she might call him again…and she'd tell him without hesitation if he asked.

Better he hear it from my mouth than her false, twisted version.

"I killed Leo," I said softly, like it were the most natural thing in the world, trudging the short distance between us to post up beside him.

"You what?!" he hollered.

"I. Killed. Leo." I enunciated, meeting his incredulous stare. "Returned him the fucking favor for what he did to my mum. What he did to Sio."

Just mentioning my family constricted my chest as though someone were wringing me like a sodden towel.

"Are you out of your goddamn mind? Why the fuck would you do that, Rome? Why? When?"

"Almost two years ago," I started, gazing off toward the marina as the harrowing memory of that blood bath began flooding me. "Do you really need to ask why, though? You know what went down, mate. Bottom line is, he deserved it. Why do you think he stopped fucking with me after forcing me to bury my blood? It wasn't because he wanted to. He wasn't doing it out of the kindness of his heart. He *had* to leave me alone, Vic. After what he did, he knew I'd come for him. So I laid low, kept my head down. I made myself out to be a man destroyed, someone he'd no longer consider a threat. And he bought it. *I* made him believe that. I made him believe he was in the clear."

"And then you hit him when he least expected it. Unprotected. Completely blindsided," Vic said quietly, pulling me back into the present.

I nodded. "Exactly. He never saw me coming."

A thoughtful silence fell between us then. Nothing strained or excruciatingly long, but long enough for both of us to process what I'd just come clean about.

"How'd you do it?" he asked after a while, reaching inside the inner pocket of his jacket to retrieve a perfectly rolled blunt and his lighter.

I scoffed as he sparked it up. "What didn't I do is more like it."

Vic took a few hits, sucking it in deeper and deeper before letting out a mass cloud. "So now Liza's out for revenge..." he stated, passing me the cigarillo.

"Yep."

"How long have you been running from her?"

"A little over a year," I admitted, taking a long pull.

"Has she had any luck finding you?"

Nodding, I tipped my head back and exhaled. "Why

do you think I was so willing to leave New York? I was already looking for someplace new to go when you rang."

"So you've seen her?" he questioned.

"No, she's not shown her face, but she leaves me clues at the most random times."

Vic's head cocked to one side, curiosity painted clearly on his face. "Clues? Like?"

"White lilies, Minstrels, those pink notebooks she used to carry everywhere, packs of Benson and Hedges. The list goes on. Anything and everything that could possibly make me think of her, she leaves it," I explained, passing back the blunt.

"And where does she leave it?"

"Anywhere she knows I'll see it. It's like she has someone following me, memorizing my daily schedule. There were a few times I found some items in my flat, too."

"She's going all out then."

"Seems that way," I agreed. "I figured she'd have given up by now, what with how long it's been, but the more time passes, the angrier I feel she becomes. She won't stop until I'm dead. Won't be too long until she shows up here if she's already called you."

Vic scoffed through his nose as he took another hit. "I'd like to say I sounded very convincing," he said, holding in his puff. "I don't think you have anything to worry about, but we'll add her to the list of shit to handle."

"Adding her on the list next to Lux?" I couldn't help

but laugh, scrubbing a hand down my face. "Fuck me, that damned letter is cursed or some shit."

"Lux and Liza, two peas in a demonic pod." He laughed, too, and clapped me on the shoulder, offering me the cigarillo again. "They're one in the same, brother, one in the fucking same."

Were they ever.

This whole whiskey charade proved it.

Revenge was clearly their forte and something they weren't afraid to dish out.

"How did you even meet Lux?" I couldn't help but ask, because once again, what were the chances he'd find someone in Miami who could pass for Liza's long lost sister?

Vic sucked in a heap of air through his teeth as I pulled a few hits. "It's a long story, something we'll leave for another day. Just know that, when I first saw her from afar, I thought she was Liza. That's the only reason why I approached her."

"And when you realized she wasn't? What happened then?"

"I helped her anyway." He hitched a shoulder. "She damn well needed it, the poor street rat."

15. LATE NIGHT MONSTERS
Lux

♫ *Every Breath You Take - Chase Holfelder* ♫

"I didn't think I'd hear from you again," I said to Isabella, thoroughly intrigued to hear what she had to say after a month of silence. "I'm assuming you have good news for me?"

"Took me longer than usual to get in contact with everyone, but yes, I do!" she exclaimed proudly.

"Fantastic. Let's hear it then," I conceded, leaning back in my seat.

"Oh." She sounded confused. "Right now?"

I glanced at the time displayed on my computer, noting it was well past business hours. Still, she was calling, right?

"Is now not a good time?"

"No, no, it's fine. I just wasn't expecting to catch you at this time."

"And is that a problem, Miss. Mendoza?"

"No, no, of course not!" she blurted out. "What I'm trying to say is, I was prepared to leave a voicemail thinking you wouldn't be in the office at this time, that's all."

"Well, I'm here," I stated the obvious, "so go on, tell me what was going in your voicemail."

"O-okay, well, ummm... I spoke to *Sephora* and *ULTA*. They'd love to showcase Black Widow in select stores for a 90-day trial period to see how it does. If it's a hit, they'll expand you to every location without question."

"Oh wow." I couldn't hide the surprise in my voice. "That's actually wonderful news."

"It is," Isabella squealed. "I'll admit, *Macy's* still hasn't gotten back to me yet, but I've heard their process is a bit more trying. I'm sure I'll hear from them soon."

"Even if you don't, you got two mass companies to agree. I commend you, Isabella. I truly didn't think you had it in you."

"Thank you, Miss Mercier. I appreciate it."

Her smile was palpable, and while I'd been skeptical of the girl at first, I found myself smiling as well. She proved me wrong, pleasantly so, and because of it, Black Widow was finally getting the attention it deserved.

"So, where do we go from here? What's next?" I questioned, pulling out a notepad and a pen from my drawer.

"We'll need to start with that contract, then from there we can set up meetings with both corporations to review and finalize their propositions," she explained surely.

"Ah yes, the contract." I laughed. The girl was adamant as ever. "I'll tell you what, since it's getting late... My PA usually handles any and all paperwork for me, and she's already gone for the evening, so I'm going to leave a note on her desk to ensure she gives you a ring first thing tomorrow morning. Then we'll go from there. How does that sound?"

"That sounds perfect! So does this mean you're hiring me?"

"If we mutually agree to the terms, yes it does."

"Holy fuck," she said, but the gasp that followed led me to believe she hadn't meant to say that out loud. "Oh my God, I apologize, Miss Mercier. I cuss and gush when I get ner—"

"Isabella," I interjected, chuckling under my breath. "You're fine. If we move forward, you'll find out rather quickly I cuss like a fucking sailor. A crass mouth doesn't offend to me."

"Oh, thank God," she sighed in relief. "I legit thought I just blew that for myself. World record job offer."

We both shared a laugh then.

"No, alls good. It'll take more than a few 'holy fucks' to piss me off. So I'll hear from you tomorrow, yes?" I hedged.

"Absolutely! I have you as number one on my to-do list for tomorrow."

"Organized, I like it. We'll speak soon then. Have a wonderful evening, Miss Mendoza."

"You too!"

Click.

I hadn't even moved my hand off the receiver when two quick knocks and a voice I knew too well sounded off by my door.

"What are you still doing here?" his voice boomed.

I'd have startled if I hadn't caught a flash of white from the corner of my eyes.

What the hell is he *doing here?*

Dragging my gaze to where he stood at the threshold, I shrugged and returned my attention to the catalogues on my desk. "Mehhh, got consumed in the new product catalogues. I could ask you the same question, though."

"I left my charger," Vic explained meekly, holding the cord up for me to see.

Okaaay.

"Interesting." I nodded.

"What?"

"Nothing. I just don't see how that matters when you've not been in the office much. Surely you have another trusty cord somewhere else, right?" I countered, setting a sticky note on the glossy page to avoid losing my place.

"I do, yeah, at home, but I'm heading out for a bit and the office was closer."

"I see," was all I answered, when really I wanted to ask where he'd been.

And it wasn't in a possessive manner.

I truly wanted to know where the hell he was all the time. Roman was an issue, we all know that, but he wasn't something that required 24-hour surveillance. I guess the more important question is, why was I allowing it?

I paid him *damn good* money, and yes, he was doing his job, but at the same time, he wasn't. I should've fired him, but a part of me felt like I couldn't. Indebted would describe it best, and I think he knew that. Hence his *'I do what I want'* attitude as of late.

"Well, looks like you're all set then." I flashed him a forced smile. "Have fun, don't drink and drive."

"Yes, mom," he laughed, striding toward my desk.

I froze for the briefest second, not expecting him to have stepped foot in here. When he was just a few feet away, I pushed my seat back and hustled onto my feet, meeting him head-on.

"Will you be gracing us with your presence tomorrow or..."

"Yep, I'll be here." He smirked.

"I assume that means you haven't heard anything on the Roman front?"

His brow arched. "Not a word. Why? Should I be expecting something?"

"Maaaybe," I drawled.

"Maybe clearly means yes. What did you do?"

"Oh, nothing too fancy. Suki and I just broke into the distillery last night and wrecked every last whiskey barrel."

The expression that washed over his face was as shocked as it was amused *and* impressed.

"No, you didn't."

"We did indeed." I smirked proudly. "Tit for tat. Bet his Monday morning was rather...soggy."

Vic shook his head and smiled that bright mega-watt smile of his. "You're evil."

I hitched a shoulder. "We established this a long time ago."

"I know, it just...never ceases to amaze me, that's all."

Humming, I waved my fingers at him and turned slightly to fetch my purse. "Well, good night, Vic."

"Night, L," he chuckled.

I swear to you I thought he walked away. It sounded as such anyway, but when I swiveled back around with bag in hand, he was standing right there, donning that sinister smirk of his.

"Christ, Vic, what the hell?" I hissed in alarm, digging my heels into the floor beneath me to avoid slamming into his chest.

"I'm sorry, I just couldn't help myself," he murmured, stepping impossibly closer. "Seeing you reminds me how much I've missed you..."

I smiled tightly. "I'm sure you're just fine."

"I am, but that doesn't change the fact I miss you. You literally cut me off from one day to the next." His large hand swooped up and cupped my face.

"I didn't cut you off." I gritted out, cringing under his touch. "Phantom happened. Shit's been busy."

Vic nodded as his thumb skated along my jaw. "Very true. You're right."

No shit.

"Well, we're alone now," he pointed out, gliding his other palm up my side. "How about we pick up where we left off?"

"I think it's better we don't."

"C'mon, Lux, you're gonna stand there and tell me you don't miss my cock demolishing your pussy?" His question came hot and heavy on my neck.

"My toys do the job just fine," I answered, squeezing my eyes shut as he engulfed me in his arms. Alarm bells blared but I tamped them down, breathed through each wave in attempt to calm myself.

Vic would never...

Would he?

"Toys aren't real, baby, and you know it," he tossed back, teeth grazing the shell of my ear.

"They aren't, no, but they sate my needs perfectly."

An amused chuckle erupted from his chest. Shaking his head, he pressed himself against me with purpose, *all of him.* "I'm calling bull on that. I doubt any dildo of yours feels better than my dick stretching you out."

God, no, please.

My heart started racing, breathing ran ragged. Dread creeped its way up my spine in sickening anticipation of what his next move would be. I hated this feeling, this all too familiar feeling, and though I hadn't felt it in a long time, now that it was working its way through every part of me in rapid succession, it felt like just yesterday since the last time it burned me alive.

"Vic, stop," I grated out, sliding my arms between us to fend him off.

"Relax, L," he cooed, pulling me closer. "Let me make you feel good."

No.

"I said I'm fine. Please stop," I huffed again, struggling a bit harder.

But his hold on me was much too strong, and before I knew it, he had me pinned to the top of my desk, his erection probing me through all the layers of clothing separating us.

"What you need is some stress relief. Lift this little skirt up and spread those legs for me."

"No." I tensed.

"Shhh, just relax," he tried cajoling me, holding me steady with a firm arm around my waist as his hand effortlessly yanked up my fitted pencil skirt. "You know you miss me. I'm sure your cunt misses me, too."

"I said no, Vic. Stop."

The more I resisted, the more he held me down.

The more a smile tore across his face.

I could barely look at him, barely recognized him. The fire in his green eyes was truly alarming. I couldn't believe the direction this was going in, especially when he knew *everything* about me.

Why was he doing this?

Full-blown panic seized me. My pulse was sky high as every hair on my body stood at attention. "Don't do this, please," I begged him shamelessly, which only seemed to please him more.

He smiled brighter, clamping a hand down on my mouth while the other slipped beneath my panty line and found my sex. I mewled when his middle finger slid between my lips, but it was far from pleasured.

"Goddamn, look how wet you are," he growled, working his finger inside me. "You *did* miss me."

I shook my head and tried feebly to shove him off, but once again, I was no match for his muscle or his dexterity. In seconds, he had my arms behind my back, my weight keeping them secured beneath me, before he was pinning me down with that palm on my mouth again. I was completely immobilized and at his mercy, laid out on my desk for him to do as he pleased.

And that included ripping my panties off my body.

"Such a pretty pussy," he said, pulling his cock free from his pants. Fisting it tightly, he pumped it a few times and promptly slapped my clit before rubbing it along my slicked opening. "Feels good, baby?"

"No," I mumbled against his palm, but he didn't care. He kept on, sliding against me over and over again, his length rigid, scorching to the touch, veiny, *angry*.

Why the hell is he doing this to me?

That's all I could think as he continued on in his feat.

Until he impaled me. From one moment to the next, he was filling me to capacity, jolting the air out of my lungs. Vic wasn't the biggest I'd been with, but he was still large, and he had girth. I squeezed my eyes shut as my body struggled to accept him despite how wet I was.

"Fuuuck, so tight, so warm. Just like I remembered," he mused, working in and out of me with ease.

I hated that it was so easy for him.

I wanted it to hurt, wanted it to hurt so badly, so badly that I'd scream, but it didn't. It never hurt. After the first few occurrences, I learned to shut it off. Shutting down and giving in were part of my body's natural reaction, a coping mechanism if you will.

By some miracle, I didn't have to cope for much longer. Someone must have been watching over me; God, a guardian angel, some special force—I don't know, but as quickly as this all began was as quickly as it ended.

The end a result of Vic's phone buzzing in his pocket.

"Fuck!" he hissed, stilling inside me as he fished it out and glanced over the screen. Clearly, it wasn't someone to be ignored. A litany of expletives slipped past his lips as he pulled out with a quickness and shoved his rigid length back into his pants, his stare trained on my shivering form.

He must've like what he saw because that amused, evil grin slid across his face once more. My stomach turned painfully. And then he was on me again, dragging the tip of his nose up my cheek, fingers toying with my sex.

"We'll finish this soon, L," he promised me, his voice deathly low. "Money calls. Think of me when you come later, okay?"

And with that, he was gone, leaving me exposed in the cool confines of my office with nothing but the demons of my past.

16. HARLEY VS THE JOKER
Roman

♫ *Bodies - Drowning Pool* ♫

Took me two days after the Great Whiskey Flood of 2017 to quell my anger enough to finally react. Had I taken action on Monday morning after walking into the distillery, things would've ended badly for anyone who stood in my path.

Lux especially.

It had nothing to do with the whiskey, by the way. That I couldn't care less about. The whiskey business was all Vic, though he didn't seem too bothered by the loss, if I'm being completely honest. He was more concerned about Liza resurfacing, and while I was, too, I was far more preoccupied by the fact Lux seemed to have pinned me for a fool.

My thoughtful silence obviously gave her the wrong impression. While I was contemplating the next best attack, something that would top my last charade, here she was, laughing at me, pissing all over me, asserting her dominance.

Trying and failing to prove her goddamn point.

And she was about to find out just how wrong she was.

"Can I help you, sir?" asked this elfin blonde at the tidy Victorian desk I'd seen all those nights ago.

"I'm here to see, Miss Mercier," I answered, in the smoothest voice I could manage.

"And your name is?"

Grinning, I shoved my hands into my slack pockets. "Just tell her it's an old friend."

"Okay..." She eyed me keenly, but went on to dial Lux's extension without further questioning. "L, you have a visitor... Mhmm... An old friend? Are you sure? O-okay..."

Setting her phone back in place, the small woman rose onto her feet and waved a polished hand toward the doors. "She was just leaving, so you'll have to make it quick, but go right through those doors."

"Thank you, love." I tipped my head at her graciously and strolled to the doors with leisure strides as directed.

Curling my hands around the cool handles brought back the same rush it did the first time around, only this time it was amplified in tenfold. I could already smell her, could just imagine her pretty face as I stormed in on her much in the same way she'd barreled in on me.

My grin widened.

Showtime.

"Knock, knock," I sang cheerfully as I threw open the doors without care.

They slammed against the walls with a loud bang,

snapping Lux's head up toward me immediately, baby blues widening in genuine surprise.

Clearly, she hadn't thought *an old friend* could be me.

Score one for the King.

"What the fuck are you doing here?" she barked, shooting onto her feet.

Almost instantly, I felt the shift in the air around us.

Intoxicating us.

Suffocating us.

My entire body buzzed like a live wire. I couldn't help myself from devouring her whole with a singular sweep of my eyes. They slid over her subtly curved form, mentally removing the strapless mauve dress clinging to her figure along the way.

She was fucking stunning, and I was itching to get closer, *for multiple reasons.*

"Oh, nothing… Just paying you a little visit." I smirked, shutting the doors behind myself.

One of her perfectly arched brows shot up curiously. "Is that so?"

"Indeed," I conceded, starting toward her with purpose. "You see, it appears my business was vandalized a couple of days back, now I'm simply doing my due diligence."

"And that would be?"

"Crossing you off my list as a possible suspect."

"A whole list, huh?" she asked on a chuckle, crossing her arms.

"It's not very long, but nonetheless, it *is* a list that needs to be addressed, and you're at the very top,

Pigeon. Not that I'm implying it was you or anything, but you—"

"Cut the shit, Roman. You know damn well it was me." The snarl in her tone left me hanging onto my words.

Well, shit.

Had she really just admitted that?

Cocking my head to one side, I stilled mere feet away from her.

"So you're saying it *was* you?" I questioned, the black hole in my chest kick-starting into overdrive when she started toward me.

"That's what I just said, is it not?" she purred, dragging an ebony claw along my chest as she sauntered around me. "How's the distillery doing by the way? Still flooded? Bet it reeks to high Heaven in there."

Burning.

I was burning with anger, frustration—*lust.*

Denial, too.

This woman made me crazy in a ways that made no sense whatsoever. The hold she had over me made no sense whatsoever. I *hated* her, or at least, I did. Tormenting her, bringing her pain and hardship, brought me great pleasure. But in the same hand, that hate somehow bled into something else, something I didn't want to feel for her.

I didn't want to want Lux, yet here we are, the force between us unstoppable.

Relentless.

Inevitable.

Consuming.

"You're much too close for your own good, love. I suggest you back up," I warned her, breathing through each wave of temptation that rattled through me.

"All bark, no bite, Mr. King," she cooed in my ear, her body pressed flush to my back. *"You don't scare me."*

I was about to respond, to follow that up with a '*you should be,*' until I heard the safety click of a pistol on my right. Then she pressed the cool tip to my temple, chucking quietly as I righted myself all the more.

"Weren't expecting that, huh?"

"Drop it," I gritted out, pulse roaring in my ears.

"Or what?" she challenged.

"Or this won't fare well for you."

Lux choked out a laugh, adding more pressure to her weapon. "Somehow, I doubt that."

"Last chance, Lux. Drop it," I warned again, breaths ragged and unsteady.

"Go on, Roman. *Do your worst,*" she hedged, mimicking my exact words from that night in my office.

One...

Two...

Three...

I tried taking deep breaths, eyes squeezed shut in attempt to block her out, but the heat radiating off her body was impossible to ignore. That primal need within me, the one that drew me to her despite every red flag set raised before me, was raging like a storm.

I wanted her.

Wanted to wreck her.

Possess her.

Fuck her.

Own her.

Christ, I was so screwed if these were the directions my mind was going to so early on. They were dangerous, dangerous thoughts, thoughts that had the ability to wreck us in one simple implosion.

How was it even possible this woman could make me feel so insane?

More over, the better question was, did she feel this way, too?

I was so sure of it the other night, so damn sure, but here in this moment, she didn't seem as fazed by my presence anymore.

And I didn't like that.

Needed to change that.

With lithe speed, I ducked and swiveled around, body slamming her into the nearest wall. The force of my strike dislodged the weapon from her hand, dropping it right in my grasp.

I grinned, and struck again.

Digging the tip of her pistol deep under her chin, I pressed myself impossibly closer, watching in complete fascination as she gasped for air like a fish out of water.

That stare of hers, though…it didn't waver, lethal blues biting into me as she tried clawing herself free.

My grin widened.

There it is.

"What's wrong, Pigeon? Did you really think the big, bad wolf doesn't bite?" I hissed, relishing the feel of being this close to her.

She fit perfectly against me.

"Stop calling me that," she choked out, and then with a growl I wasn't expecting, she kneed me almost right in the nuts, whacking her palm straight across my cheek.

She struck me so hard, the bloody gun went flying out from my grasp, clattering to the floor several feet away as I folded over just slightly. The entire left side of my face burned from her assault.

Little bitch had good aim.

Chuckling, I snapped my jaw back in place and swiftly trapped her throat in my hand, touching my forehead to hers as I forced her further into the wall. "That's fine, Pigeon," I snarled again, placing emphasis on her favorite word. "Hate me all you want. I can assure you the feeling is fucking mutual."

"Fantastic, so get the fuck out of here already," she tossed back, chest heaving.

"Not a chance in hell, especially now. You wanna play? *Let's play*, *love*. I guarantee you'll lose," I murmured, dropping my stare to her lips.

They looked so soft, so damned plump and delicious. I wanted to suck them between my teeth and lick into her mouth…

"I'm fast, King," she growled, distracting me from my wayward thoughts.

"*And I'm faster,*" I countered.

"I'd never guess considering I had to provoke you a second time to get you moving."

"Because you have no patience. Trust me, I was coming for you, sweetheart," I advised softly, bringing my lips impossibly closer. They were so close, I could almost taste her. "You just never gave me the chance."

Lux swallowed, the action defined by the prominent bobbing of her throat, and yet still, she held her head high, as if she weren't at all affected by our proximity.

"Don't think, Roman. Just do," she grated softly. "Like I said, do your worst. Ball's in your court. That, or you can leave, and you'll never have to worry about me again."

"I told you, I'm not going anywhere," I reminded her.

"Then make a move and don't keep me waiting. The faster I can wear you down and knock you out, the better."

"You have no idea what you're asking for," I growled in warning, because it was the absolute truth.

She wanted me to do my worst?

Then the worst she shall have.

17. GROVELING

Vic

♫ *Monster - Skillet* ♫

I don't know what the hell happened to me in Lux's office that night, but I never intended for it to go that far. Hell, I hadn't even expected to run into her when I went back for my charger, which for the record, was the absolute truth.

Not the point, though.

Seeing her there, all alone, briefly reminded me of old times. But then she questioned my presence and hit me with that fake smile, and I remembered exactly why she needed to go. The woman had used me and abused me for too long.

Regardless of how I felt about her, I know I fucked up. I let my emotions get the best of me, and as a result, could end up catching a case for my stupidity. A major case, and orange was most definitely not my fucking color.

That left me one choice and one choice only, whether I was fond of the idea or not; groveling.

I needed to grovel like the lovesick bastard she once knew, work my way back onto her good side and apologize profusely until she forgave me. Otherwise, the entire operation could be ruined.

I'd come too far and had way too much on the line to let that happen. Not to mention, Liza would behead me without hesitation.

So I was starting with a simple clue. Something that would make her think she was one step ahead of Roman, which in actuality, she would be. Rome had no idea I knew about his little spot. He hadn't shared it with me and I assumed it was for the same reason as always; that was *his* spot, somewhere he could go and think, unwind, enjoy the solitude of his own company...

Not anymore, brother.

I chuckled at his expense as I signed my name on the sticky note and stuck it to Lux's computer monitor, hoping like hell this was a move in the right direction.

And considering what his next move was, it should be...

18. SPECIAL DELIVERY
Lux

♫ *Dollhouse - Melanie Martinez* ♫

H*e's down there.*
He's still *down there, drinking in excess, playing Rummy with his friends.*

I groan in frustration.

Can't he just go to bed already?

I've been waiting to go downstairs for what's felt like hours, hiding out in the safety of my room. I can't keep myself locked up much longer, though.

I'm parched, so parched my tongue sticks to the roof of my mouth. I'm starved, too—especially after skipping supper—but I don't want to face him.

I don't want to face them.

My stomach grumbles in protest, reminding me the last time I ate was a small lunch at school. Wasn't too hungry at the time, but I'm sure regretting it now. I rub at sore spot in attempt to quell that gnawing sense of hunger, but it rumbles again, louder this time.

It hurts, too; twisting, turning, and contorting.

I will myself to calm down, to breathe through it like all the other times, but it doesn't work. All I can think about is how hungry I am, how wonderful a warm, cheesy sandwich would taste right now. I'm salivating just imagining it, and I know without a doubt, I'm going to have to brave the storm and make it down to that kitchen before I make myself sick.

Sucking in a heap of air, I turn the doorknob as quietly as possible and poke my head out into the darkened corridor. The door to their room is shut. No light shines beneath it either. I know mum is in there, though, probably preparing herself for what awaits when my father finally calls it a night. Just the thought of what she endures brings tears to my eyes. She hasn't a clue I know, that I can hear them through the wall of my bedroom every time it happens.

But even if she did, I know she wouldn't speak of it.

Just like I don't either…

I've contemplated telling her, have come so close to spitting it all out when she's just laying there in one of her dazed states, but I don't, and I won't. She'd deny it if anything, tell me I'm making it up and to stop accusing my father of such atrocities…

Laughter and a loud bang reel me back into the moment. I startle at the sound and reconsider my decision to tread downstairs, but my stomach rumbles yet again.

I don't need a full plate. I'll be in and out, *I war with myself, shutting my door with the softest click.*

On another deep breath, I pad carefully down the stairs in the darkness. My heart thumps with each step as though it might burst from my chest at any moment. I'm barely breathing, yet it thunders in my ears, spiking my pulse into a wild gallop. I have three steps to go when I hear voices from the telly drift into the foyer. It's nothing but background noise, a concept I find rather pointless when it's not like they can hear it. They're louder with every beer consumed.

As I round the corner into the living area, my father's icy stare collides with mine, penetrating me to my core. I fall rigid in place. The corner of his mouth quirks in the most subtle, satisfied smirk, but he says nothing, returning his attention to the men surrounding him as he takes another swig from his bottle.

You can do this, *I remind myself.* Grab what you need and get out.

Despite how small and afraid I feel, I hold my head high and amble into the kitchen with soft steps, hoping none of them will pay me any mind. I know it's impolite not to acknowledge them and I may get in trouble for it, but I don't even glance their way. I simply gather all I need from the refrigerator and take a place at the counter where I can see them, fixing myself a quick sandwich as quietly as possible; turkey, cheese, a leaf of lettuce, and some mayonnaise.

When I finish, I stow everything back in its rightful spot, pull out a fizzy drink, and grab a bag of crisps from the basket on top of the fridge, thinking all is well.

The moment I spin around, though, all eyes are on me. It's only then I realize the conversation had run quiet while I was storing my ingredients.

Crap.

I swallow deeply and remain in place, holding their stares. Stares that are hungered.

Familiar.

Every last one.

Get out, *that little voice in my head advises.*

My body instantly reconnects with my brain. I offer them a small smile and scamper out of the kitchen, making it just into the foyer when my father's voice booms behind me.

"Lux, get back in here."

I skid to a stop and eye the stairs. They're so close. I could just run and lock myself away.

But deep down, I know that wouldn't end well for me.

The sick realization clogs my throat. I whimper and set both my plate and my drink at the foot of the stairs, then retrace my steps, stopping at the arched threshold between the living area and the kitchen.

"Where are your manners?" he asks, him tone seemingly friendly as he gestures to his guests.

My arms come around my middle as all four men, my father included, stare me down. "I apologize," I say to them. "I'm just so hungry."

"Not an excuse," my father growls, racking another shiver down my spine.

"I'm sorry," I say again.

A mere second ticks by before Fredrick chimes in.

"I'm hurt, little L."

I snap my gaze to where he sits in time to catch him holding a hand to his chest. "Had me waiting all night. I wanted to see you before I left and you don't even say hello?"

Of all the men, Fredrick likes me best, and my father lets him have sex with me the most, doesn't even make him pay like the rest. They have the kind of relationship I once used to wish my father had with me. He loves him—genuinely loves him—like a son.

Technically, he could be his son. He's only twenty-one.

And I'm fifteen, just to put things into perspective for you.

My father loves him so much, he let Fredrick take my virginity two years ago. It was nothing like they say it should be. Wasn't sweet or slow. There were no kisses or soothing touches either.

I did bleed quite a bit, though, but perhaps that's because I fought him the whole way through, begging him not to strip me of my innocence as tears rolled down my cheeks. I hadn't made any sort of vows to keep it intact, but I'd hoped someone special would claim that card, someone who took my breath away, someone who loved me.

It was brutal, and a part of me died that day.

The next time, I fought him harder, tried screaming louder. I even bit him when he sealed a hand over my mouth to keep me quiet. But the third time, the third time I learned it was best to just keep my mouth shut. No one was coming to rescue me, especially not my father, not even when Fredrick pulled out his uncle's pistol and whipped me across the face.

I wore that gruesome marking for weeks, and my mum truly believed I'd fallen down the stairs.

With time, the rest of the men followed suit, some more aggressive than others. Either way, I simply took it, no protest.

Because what was the point?

My cries would only fall of deaf ears.

"*Well, you saw me,*" *I snap at him.*

My father's eyes bulge at my disrespectful tone. "*Watch that tone, young lady.*"

"*I'm sorry,*" *I apologize for the third time.* "*I'm just hungry. I've said hello...can I please go now?*"

"*I'll walk her back up to her room, Pops,*" *Fredrick offers immediately, and of course, my father nods without a word, clapping him on the shoulder with pride in his blue eyes.*

That twisted, blood-chilling sound of approval is what dissolved the memory into nothing. When my stare refocused in the moment, I found myself standing before the bathroom mirror, eyeliner wand in hand.

I sighed at myself in frustration.

I'm doing it again.

Staring off mindlessly as flashes of my past played at the forefront of my mind. I'd do it at the most inopportune times, too. Can't say I missed this one bit, not when the last few years of my life I'd finally been able to keep them at bay, tucked far, far away in the very depths of my mind.

But after what happened with Vic, they flooded me with a vengeance.

They'd evolved, too, which was the worst part of it all.

Now, they all ended with Vic. I could start off seeing Fredrick, or James, or Ronald, or any man who'd used my body, but eventually, they all morphed into Vic.

And what they did to me was mind-numbing.

As a result, I'd been keeping my time in the office to a bare minimum. I couldn't look at it the same, not without breaking into a sweat or goose pimples dotting my skin as my stomach churned in revolt. I kept telling myself I simply needed to work through my demons, and that time would, once again, heal these vicious wounds.

But after Roman's surprise visit, I'd just been avoiding it at all costs.

Told Ellie—in my best congested voice—that I was feeling under the weather. We were going on four days now of my so-called super flu, but could you blame me? Black Widow used to be my safe haven, my command center, a sanctuary I'd worked so hard to build, and within days of each other, I was attacked there, twice.

Granted, Roman's encounter had a vastly different effect on me than what Vic's dished out, but nonetheless, it contributed to running myself mad. The sheer amount of emotions both of these men had me fluctuating through was enough to drive anyone to the point of insanity.

Regardless of my instability, though, four days was still four days of missed work, and while I knew Ellie was doing all she could to keep me up to speed, there was still a lot I was missing out on, including that meeting with Isabella.

Well, both of them.

I'd cancelled the re-schedule the day of and Miss

Mendoza was obviously not pleased. If I missed this third one, I knew she'd walk, no matter how badly she wanted to work with me.

Which brings us to now.

Clicking the home button on my iPhone, I took note of the time. I'd promised Ellie I'd be there before noon.

Didn't look like that was going to be possible after wasting so much time spiraling into the past.

I'd dragged my ass out of bed and showered, put my face on, threw on something work-appropriate, and hustled out the door less than twenty minutes later. I'd go in for this meeting and come right back home after everything was finalized—no big deal. The chances of running into either of them, Vic especially, were slim.

Or so I hoped.

When I arrived at Black Widow, Isabella was already waiting near Ellie's desk, looking a million times more confident and prepared. She seemed a bit uptight, too, her lips a firm line when I smiled, but I suppose that was my fault with the double reschedule. The girl probably thought I was trying to play her.

I wasn't, in case you were wondering.

"Good morning, Miss Mendoza, I'll be ready for you in ten minutes," I said to her as I sauntered past quickly to my office, the clip-clop of my heels echoing off the glittering floors.

Stealing a peek at an expectant—and relieved—Ellie, I motioned to my office with a tip of my head and burst through the doors. The initial sight of my desk made me shiver, but I blocked the memory out of my mind, focusing on the fact that if this meeting didn't go off without a hitch, Black Widow wouldn't be getting the attention it deserved.

Ellie was skittering in behind me just seconds later, a notepad in hand. "Do you need anything?" she asked sweetly, gauging my reaction.

"Tea, please, and bring one for Isabella, too. Milk and sugar on the side."

"On it."

She was out the door not ten seconds later, leaving me to scramble about and attempt to prepare myself for this meeting. Attempt being the operative word. Dropping into my chair, I booted up my computer and began frantically pulling things from my drawers; her file folder, a notebook, sticky notes, my favorite pen with the gold dipped Maleficent head.

I was going to need her contract as well, which I'm sure Ellie printed out at some point. I just didn't know where it was and I was not about to go on a wild goose chase to find it.

Just print another one.

That's when I saw the note, right as I turned to my computer to pull up my email.

Stuck on the monitor was a sticky note with Vic's signature. The mere sight of it made my heart palpitate in all the wrong ways. That overwhelming feeling of dread dispersed through my body with such speed, I almost folded in on myself in agony.

Breathe. Just breathe, I reminded myself, inhaling deeply through my nose and out through my mouth.

He's not here, you're safe.

At least for now. If I kept wasting time letting him get to me, though...

Dragging my gaze back up to the note, I peeled it off the monitor in determination and quickly read the short message scribbled perfectly in the center.

KING HAS A SPOT YOU MAY WANT TO CHECK OUT.
MIGHT GIVE YOU THE UPPER HAND
IF YOU CATCH HIM OFF-GUARD.
ROOFTOP OF THE PANORAMA.

X - Vic
P.S. I'M SORRY.

He's sorry? HE'S SORRY?

Chuckling in disbelief, I crumpled the note in my shaky hand and promptly tossed it into the rubbish bin regardless of the information supplied. He was sorry? He was fucking sorry? Did he truly think a meager apology would amend what he'd done to me? Just like that?

The man had to be delusional. Insane. Or maybe he was using? He had to be, had unparalleled access to anything he wanted.

Or maybe he's just that evil...

"L!" Ellie reappeared at my door then, face pale, breathing ragged, her blonde hair mussed up as if she'd running through the factory.

Every red flag known to man kind shot up at the sight

of her distress. The already frantic beating of my heart raged, threatening to break free from my chest.

"What's wrong?" I asked, shooting onto my feet.

"You're gonna wanna see this," she said simply, motioning for me to follow her.

Stat.

Abandoning my desk, I scampered out of my office behind my PA, promising a befuddled Isabella I'd be right back along the way. She didn't seemed too pleased, but nodded anyway, pulling her phone out from her purse to busy herself in the meantime.

Thank fuck.

The last thing I needed was for her to storm out after I'd come in just for her sake.

With brisk footing, Ellie and I hightailed it down the stairs to the back room where at least a dozen people were hard at work, packaging new palettes for online orders. Their greetings went unanswered, aside from a simple wave, as we barreled through each station and out the back door onto the delivery deck.

The scorching afternoon sun blinded me as I rushed out behind Ellie. Hand raised to shield myself, I skidded to a stop when I saw Vic standing next to Roscoe, their backs turned as they assessed whatever was in the lone delivery truck.

Thump, thump, thump.

Every instinct within me told me to run. I wanted to, wanted to turn back while there was still time and he hadn't seen me, but Ellie outed me before I could so much as take one step.

"She's here!"

Both men spun around in a flash, their eyes pinning me in place. Vic's were glacial, almost emotionless to an extent, while Roscoe's were more concerned, dark brows bunched together tensely.

"He's not playing around anymore," Roscoe said, and at first I didn't clock on to who he was talking about.

I couldn't focus with Vic standing not ten feet away from me, staring at me in the most unnerving fashion.

"W-who?" I asked nervously.

"King."

My stomach flipped at the mention of his name.

"What did he do?" I hedged, taking cautious steps forward.

Roscoe glanced at Vic, then turned back to me and hitched a thumb over his shoulder. "Inside the truck, but brace yourself... It's not pretty."

I don't know what I was expecting to see as I slid between the two and padded down the docks edge, but awaited me surely wasn't it, even after reading the note taped onto the door.

Inside the crisp white delivery truck was a mangled Javi, our delivery driver, and a large shipping box. He knew everything that went down behind these ebony doors, and now, *he was dead.*

Gasping, I tried processing the harrowing image before me. From the looks of it, he suffered a great deal of pain before Roman finally let him die. His body remained upright solely by the thick, course rope binding him to the chair, uniform shirt drenched in his blood.

This is where it got really ugly.

His eyes—gouged.

His ears—sliced off clean.

And his lips—sewn shut.

I didn't have to open the box to know what was in there, but a part of me wanted to believe Roman wasn't sick enough to do such a thing…

In the end, I was wrong.

Very, very wrong.

Inside the box were two eyes, two ears, and one bloodied tongue.

Hear no evil.
See no evil.
Speak no evil.

This bad enough, Pigeon? Or do you want some more?

Anxiously awaiting your reply. Tag, you're it.

—K

19. I DARE YOU
Roman

♫ *Lucky You - Eminem ft. Joyner Lucas* ♫

The delivery guy never stood a chance. Poor bloke never saw it coming. Not to worry, I didn't drag it out *too* long, just enough to expel the demons.

For the time being anyway.

They'd return soon enough and demand another taste of death to quench the thirst.

To answer your obvious question—no, I didn't *have* to kill him.

But did it send a message?

Yes, it sure as fuck did.

You see, I'd not been left much of a choice really. I had to do it. Lux underestimated me. Hell, I think everyone underestimated me, Vic included. Lux I could somewhat understand, given the woman didn't know very much about me.

But Vic?

How could he truly be surprised when he knew first-hand what I was capable of?

I suppose it didn't matter either way.

What I did moving forward wasn't for his benefit anyway.

Not that he'd figured that out yet since I was still playing along without missing a beat.

All part of the plan.

Dismembering the delivery bloke, though, was *not* part of Vic's plan, and he wasn't pleased about it in the slightest.

As you're about to find out…

Parked outside of Noir Coast after hours, I was rolling up a little stress reliever to enjoy up on my spot when all of a sudden, someone banged their fist on the driver's window.

Startling just slightly, I snapped my head toward the sound to find Vic on the other side, green eyes blazing.

"Open up," he demanded, starting around the front end of the Benz.

Sighing, I clicked the magical button and waited for him to slip in the passenger side as I went about resealing the cigarillo between my lips.

"You butchered the delivery dude?" he questioned furiously, sliding inside the peaceful confines of my car and slamming shut the door.

There goes my peace and quiet.

I stared at him for a moment, sealing the final end of the blunt with a vacant expression on my face. "That's a rhetorical question, right? Clearly you already know since you're asking me."

The look he flashed me practically screamed he was about to blow a gasket. I almost laughed.

"Why the hell would you do that?!" he barked.

"Another rhetorical question?"

"Cut the fucking shit, King! Do you have any idea how much this little charade of yours has complicated everything?"

"How so?" I questioned, stuffing the blunt into the inside pocket of my jacket and returning my supplies to their rightful spot within the center console. "Do tell."

"Lux is going ballistic," he spat, cinching my entire face in confusion.

"Um...was that not the point?"

"Yes!" he bellowed. "But not this way!"

"Then how? What else did you expect after she had you and Roscoe wipe out more than half of *our* guys that one night. Did you not think I'd retaliate on the same level?"

Vic opened his mouth to counter, but not a single word slipped free.

Not one.

He just sat there, eyeing me indignantly, until finally he laid an elbow on the window sill and turned to observe our shrouded surroundings.

"They were casualties, Rome, casualties we've replaced," he explained quietly.

"As is the delivery driver. He's replaceable," I retorted.

Chuckling, he shook his head and sighed deeply as if I were clueless. "She doesn't just trust people like that. Finding someone who's going to keep quiet isn't as easy as you think."

"You do realize that makes no sense, right? There's an excess of people willing to keep their mouth shut for the right price. As you so kindly pointed out, you just replaced over thirty-five people in a span of mere days," I stated, jamming the key in the ignition.

The engine roared to life with a simple flick of my wrist.

"That's different!" he snapped, turning back toward me.

"How is that different, Vic? It's the same damn concept. They *know* they can't talk."

"It's different, trust me. Lux and I are two different people. How we operate business is different, too."

They weren't really, but I didn't feel the need to exhort my opinion. In fact, I had no inclination to keep this conversation going much longer. If Vic wanted to believe he and Lux were so different, then by all means, the man could live in denial for all I cared. What bothered me most was the fact he was questioning me about something that shouldn't've been an issue to begin with. He knew damn well many a pawn wouldn't make it out alive.

"So let me get this straight… Eliminating people off the board is okay, but only if it's on your terms?"

"That's not what I said," he muttered.

"But it's what you implied. You had absolutely no problem with us taking out Ramos, or letting Lux wipe out our people, which for the record was a grand betrayal on your part. I'm surprised anyone was willing to fill in their shoes after the fact."

Silence, once again, fell upon us. He could try to spout

it however he wanted, turn it inside out and all around, but the bottom line is, he knew I was right.

"You could have at least warned me, allowed me to prepare myself," he said after a beat, his tone resigned. "The day I had... Trying as fuck."

Interesting...

"Explain," I demanded, falling lax in my seat. *This* I could tolerate another five minutes for.

Vic shrugged. "Having to go through Roscoe for everything just made the process more tedious than necessary, that's all."

"Why did you have to go through Roscoe?" I pressed, and although he tried brushing it off with a wave of his hand, I didn't miss the way he initially tensed up.

"Lux and I are not exactly on speaking terms right now."

Very *interesting...*

"Why?" I pressed harder, and again, he tried playing the nonchalant card.

"We had a disagreement."

"About?"

"Not important. She'll get over it. Like I said, we're very different people. Don't always see eye to eye on certain things."

She's not the only one.

"You mean, kind of like us?" I pointed out, earning me a dubious smirk, one I didn't return.

"I think we're more alike than you think."

"We used to be," I stressed. "I'm not sure the sentiment still applies."

"Please," he huffed. "Here we are again, working to together, trying to take over the world."

"For your benefit."

"And yours. I promised you half." He sounded offended, but I pulled a page from his book and shrugged it off as well.

"Wasn't sure that still stood when I was just repri-manded for getting us ahead."

Vic sighed and ran a hand over his faded head, shaking his head in what I sensed was defeat. "Apologies, okay? Just truly took me off-guard. But yes, it still stands."

"Then stop bitching and let me do my job like you asked," I advised.

Hands in the air, he smiled. "Warn a bloke is all I'm saying."

"Will do, now get the fuck out."

ALL WAS WELL ABOUT AN HOUR LATER.

That ridiculous conversation with Vic was a thing of the past and I was feeling fantastic, higher than a damn kite. The weed had done its job and there was not one thing in this world that could've bothered me in that moment.

Breathing in the fresh air, I stood huddled over the thick glass ledge, enjoying the view from the very top of the Panorama, one of the highest sky rises in Miami. Down below, the typical sounds of the city erupted in waves, briefly transporting me back to my time in New York. I'd chosen this building as my spot for that exact reason. The city just called to me, soothed me. It was home in its own insane, chaotic way.

"Roman-fucking-King!" a woman's voice shrilled, jolting me in place.

That voice. It can't be.

In a brisk swivel, I was met with her approaching form as she sashayed toward me with purpose, hips swinging side to side in these tight leather pants that clung to her legs.

My jaw almost hit the floor.

"How in the…" I couldn't even finish my sentence as I stared at her in confusion.

"How in the hell did I find you?" she finished amusedly, an irate little laugh bubbling in tow. "An anonymous tip off."

Anonymous my dick.

It had to be Vic.

He's the only one who knew I always had an escape spot.

"You need to go," I warned her.

"I think not. I have a huge bone to pick with you."

"I'm sure you do, but you're not doing it here."

"Like hell I'm not," she spat, stopping toe to toe with me. Blue eyes lifted to my icy stare. "You must really have a death wish after that special delivery. Is it not more simple for you to just leave?"

A small gust of wind rolled by then, slamming me with her scent every which way possible. It seeped into my pores, knocked me off my game for a split-second. Breathing in only made it worse.

"It is, but I told you, Lux. You have what I want and I'm not leaving until I get it," I grated out, trying my damnedest not to focus on the fact she was right *there*. "Besides, you know deep down you don't want me to leave."

Her face contorted in disgust. "Oh, please. Don't think so highly of yourself."

"I'm not. Simply calling it like it is. You wouldn't have acted out in my silence if you didn't."

"L-O-L. Right." She laughed. "Guess you got me all figured out then, huh?"

Shaking my head, I moved impossibly closer, dropping my lips to her ear. "Not yet, but I will eventually. I know enough, though."

Lux scoffed and pushed me away, but not before I felt her shiver in delight. "Get over yourself, Roman, seriously. You don't know shit about me! I hit you a second time to send the message loud and clear."

"And that would be?" I questioned, stepping closer once more.

"Don't. Fuck with me," she threatened, shoving me backwards so hard my back hit the glass ledge.

All the noises down below—car horns, music, laughter—suddenly seemed louder than before, rattling up my spine, and despite being cornered, a smirk played on my lips. "As I demonstrated today, I could do a lot more than just fuck *with* you, Pigeon."

Those bright blue eyes bulged. "Piss off, got it? Just

quit while you're ahead. The distillery was nothing in comparison to the hell I could bring you, to the hell I *will* bring you after your little stunt today."

"So bring it then. Let's see what you can do, love," I cooed, waving my palms challengingly.

Smoke seemed to billow from her nose as she bound up to me and prodded my chest with one of her perfectly polished claws.

"You really wanna go there?"

"I wanna go *everywhere;* all over it, in it, behind it," I admitted, my gaze skating over her petit figure.

"You're delusional," she barked, and all I could do was shrug.

I'd been called a hell of a lot worse.

"Maybe, but I like to think of it as more of a wild imagination with a penchant for danger."

"You're digging yourself a grave, King," she gritted out.

"As are you, love. The more you push, the more I pull. I could make it so easy for you, you know? Just give me what I want and I'll be out of your hair. No one else has to get hurt," I explained, bringing a hand up to finger those curled emerald locks.

Lux eyed me fiendishly, her chest heaving wildly beneath the lace cage of her halter top. The small swells of her tits, adorned with roses and a striking raven, all but called to me, begging me to set them free and worship them with my mouth. I was so far gone within my own imagination, I didn't notice her whipping out a weapon until the tip of the blade pressed against my skin.

"Or I could just shove this right into your jugular and *make you* go away," she sneered.

"Do it." I grinned devilishly, heart racing with adrenaline. "*I dare you.*"

A growl tore free from her chest as she moved closer, eyebrows bunched together. She held my stare as firmly as ever, but made no move to see her threat through.

I held steady, waiting, and waiting, and waiting, counting down the seconds…

But it never came.

That's when I struck.

Snatching the blade from her hand, I flung her into the ledge I'd been trapped against, and pressed my body against her soft planes, caging her beneath me.

"See what happens when you hesitate?" I growled, bringing the blade to her erratic pulse. "You get yourself into trouble."

"I'll scream," she announced, holding her chin high.

"Oh, I know. They all scream. *Yes, Rome, harder, please!*"

A quiet gasp met my ears, but she recovered quickly, narrowing her eyes. "You know that's not what I'm talking about…"

"Well aware, Pigeon." I chuckled. "What can I say? I just like pressing your buttons."

"Is there a button I can press that'll make you fuck off?"

Ever so lightly, I dragged the blade across her throat to the other side. "Now why would I ever do that when we're just really getting started?"

"Because I'm ready to finish it!" she barked, swatting my hand away deftly. With it went her weapon tumbling to the floor. "Clearly, you must seem to think I'm joking. I don't know why, honestly. I will make your life a living hell."

"My life's already hell, love. I can handle the heat."

Lux groaned, the sound loud and adorably frustrated. Once again, she tried shoving me away, but I was strong as iron, an impenetrable force with the grin of a Cheshire Cat.

"You're fucking impossible, you know that?!" she seethed. "You talk all this crap out of your ass about negotiations and what not, but all you've done is harass me."

"Because you don't listen."

"Because I don't listen? Jesus-fucking-Christ—who the hell do you think you are?!"

"Roman-fucking-King, sweetheart," I reminded her, which only riled her up all the more.

"I hate you!" She shoved at me again.

"Scream it louder for me, Lux. You what?"

"I hate you—*shove*—I fucking hate you!"

"*Excellent*," I whispered, slithering a hand around her throat. My grip was so tight, I felt the bob of her swallow. "Hold on to that feeling tight, Pigeon. Hold onto it real fucking tight, 'cause if you let it go, I swear I'll wear you down to the bone, and I promise you that you'll regret it."

20. INTERVENTION
Lux

♫ *Gangsta - Kehlani* ♫

I was shaking in my seat the entire drive home, my hands white-knuckling the steering wheel from the strain of my hold. I wasn't just angry—I was beside myself.

With myself.

With him.

Once again, this man proved he had the ability to diverge a dozen different emotions through my body in one go, and I couldn't wrap my head around it in the slightest.

How?

How was this bloody possible?

I kept telling myself I hated him, kept telling *him* I hated him, but the second he was anywhere near me, I lit up from the inside out, forgot all about what a trying pest he'd been since stepping foot in Miami. And the more it happened, the harder it was to continue denying there was an obvious attraction burning between us.

An attraction I wished didn't exist.

Running him out of my city would be a million times easier if I didn't feel so...

I shook my head.

No, I'm not going there...

Go on, say it, pressed that little voice in my head. *If you didn't feel so...*

"Intimidated," I whispered, slamming my foot on the brake at a red light.

That singular yet loaded word shot a horrified gasp out of my mouth. My head started spinning. Panic clawed its way deep into my being, wiping out every last bit of denial clouding my judgment.

No. NO. This can't be happening.

Hands shaking, I reached for my iPhone lodged in the cupholder and quickly opened up my group thread with Suki and Ramsey.

Me: *911*

Their replies were nearly instantaneous and came in within seconds of each other.

Suki: *I'm here! What happened?*
Ramsey: *What the hell happened? Are you okay?!*

I was about to punch in my response when several cars behind me honked angrily, snapping my gaze up to see, not only the now green light, but other drivers zooming past me on my left.

"Shit!" I hissed, dropping my phone into my lap as I

stepped on the gas, gunning it through the intersection. Palm tress, street lights, and buildings alike were nothing but one big blur.

This can't be happening. This can't be fucking happening.

Oh, but it is, went that little voice again. *And no, you're not over-thinking it.*

More pings sounded off between my legs, reminding me I hadn't replied to my girls after calling for help, something I hadn't dared to do after what happened with Vic. If I told them, Suki would've snapped like a damn twig and gone on a rampage with Ramsey closely on her tail. They would've ripped him apart piece by piece, fed him to the wolves.

Yes, he deserved it, worse than that if I'm being honest with myself, but I wouldn't fare well without them if they ended up in prison on my behalf.

Some things were just better left unsaid.

Approaching another red light, I slowed to a stop and scooped my phone up with a quickness, their frantic messages clogging the notifications on my screen.

Ramsey: *Lux, what the hell is going on?*
Ramsey: *Helllloooo?*
Suki: *I'm gonna kill you myself if you don't answer! You can't text us with an emergency and then disappear!*
Suki: *LUX!!! GET YOUR ASS BACK IN THIS CHAT!!!*
Ramsey: *Jesus fucking Christ! What the hell, Lux!*
Ramsey: *Suk, I'm starting to worry for real…*
Suki: *I know…*

As worried as they were, my little black heart swelled as I read their messages. They loved me, and I them, hence why dragging them into dark places with me was a strict no go. I couldn't lose them.

They were all I had.

Me: *I'm here! I was driving dammit!*

I giggled almost right after I sent it, imagining the both of them sagging in relief. Suki was probably cussing me out, too.

Suki: *What in the hell happened?*
Me: *Him.*
Ramsey: *Who?*
Suki: *R-O-M-A-N.*
Ramsey: *Ooooh! Spill! What did he do now?*
Me: *Both of you free?*
Ramsey: *Sure am.*
Suki: *Just closing up!*
Me: *My place, half hour! Green light—gotta go!*

∾

"My question to you is, do you still want to put a bullet through his head or not?" That was Suki, curled in the corner of my couch with wine glass in hand.

We were twenty minutes into the Roman conversation and I was about done. Not because of opposing views or anything like that, I just didn't want to talk about him anymore. They were having too much fun with this, and well, I wasn't.

"I should, especially after today," I admitted, taking a sip from my own glass. "But I don't."

"Why?" she hedged, and all I could offer was a feeble shrug.

"I don't know." When he was just Phantom, the thought was a no brainer..."

"But the second you met him..." Ramsey chimed in from her place on the tiled floor. "It disappeared?"

I nodded.

It was the complete and awful truth.

When Roman was just Phantom, hating him was simple, a given based on how he'd attacked me and what he'd done to my business. But then I stormed into his office, and everything changed in a nanosecond.

I'd been trying to keep myself in check, had been relentlessly reminding myself of all he'd done no matter how petty, but in the end, it only proved one thing.

Denial was real, and I was drowning in it.

"So are you finally admitting that you want him?" asked an amused Suki.

I wasn't even looking at her and I knew there was a smirk sitting her face.

More like painted. Permanently.

"I don't want him," I said surely, or at least what I thought was surely. "But I will admit to his looks affecting me more than they should."

"Better known as, you want him," Suki snickered,

prompting Ramsey to choke back a laugh as she took a sip from her glass.

"I don't wa—" I started to protest, but Suki was quick to cut me off.

"L, want him or not, you admit he's attractive, yes?"

Nod.

"You also admit that attraction not only complicates things, but isn't a one-sided affair, right?"

Another nod. "Feeds off of it any and every chance he gets."

"And you don't want to kill him?" she clarified.

"Or rather, she *can't* kill him," Ramsey corrected.

"Right, what she said," Suki agreed.

Once again, I nodded, stare trained on the tinted wine in my glass.

"I can't," I said quietly, swirling the liquid round and around and around. "He dared me to hurt him tonight, literally dared me as I held the blade to his neck... But I hesitated and he turned it on me, trapped me beneath his hard body. It's like, all he has to do is come within one foot of me and my body locks up, my brain shuts down. He intimidates me in that respect, and I keep telling myself I don't like it but—"

"For the record, you *do* want him," she cut me off, holding a hand up when I attempted to protest again, "but I'm not pushing the topic. We'll talk about that when you're ready. My question now is, do you love your job enough to continue fighting him for it? He's obviously not going to disappear any time soon, so why not just give him what he wants and send him on his way?"

My entire body jerked backwards, eyes bulging in outrage at her suggestion. "Are you insane? There's no way in hell I'm handing over Miami just because he won't piss off. If he wants to continue this incessant game of tag, then so be it, I'm not giving him shit other than hell. All I want is for him to go away."

"But why, L? He's already making it impossible for you to do your job. Why not just let him have what he wants and focus on Black Widow instead? Hell, I know you prefer not to, but I could really use your help over at Vybe, too," she explained. "Ram, what do you think?"

Ramsey sat up straighter and crossed her pale legs, criss cross applesauce style. "I don't think she should just hand Miami over on a silver platter. It's hers, rightfully so, but do I think she should give him a cut? Yes."

My already bulging eyes nearly popped out of their sockets as I stared at my best friends in disbelief. "You're both off your rockers," I muttered, scrubbing a hand down my face.

"I'm just saying, L. Clearly, he's feeling exactly what you're feeling. You said it yourself, he feeds off it. Says and does things based off that feeling. Sounds to me like fighting it is useless, so why not team up with him?"

"Team up with him?" I laughed cynically. "Who do you think we are? Bonnie and Clyde?"

"Bonnie and Clyde, Harley and Joker, Thanos and Lady Death," she clarified, waving a hand. "I'm just saying, he's into you, and whether you agree or not, you're into him. Why not take advantage of that?"

They've lost their bloody minds.

"No. Just no," I asserted.

"Then you're going to have to work him out of your system and get him out of here before things escalate more than they already have," Suki piped up again.

"How am I supposed to do that? It's hard enough as it is."

"Which is why we're both telling you to give him *something*, but you don't want to," Ramsey countered.

"You're damn right I don't," I huffed, crossing my arms. "I worked too hard for him to—"

"Then shut him out, L. Shut him out of your mind and keep it moving. You're going to have to think smarter when it comes to scaring him off," Suki advised, rising off the couch.

"That's not how this works," Ramsey laughed.

"Of course you'd see it that way," Suki called out over her shoulder as she reached over the island to grab the wine bottle.

"The hopeless romantic in me *is* squealing," Ramsey sighed, holding a hand to her chest, "but that's not what this is about. She can't just shut him out, Suk. The more they see each other, the more it's going to fester and spread, the more it'll evolve. They're not going to be able to fight it forever."

I scoffed indignantly. "I will fight it forever, forever and a day if I have to. I'm not letting my body call the shots."

"Who said it's only your body?" Ramsey grinned, a knowing look glazing over her features as my face paled.

Hearing her those words—words that were more probable than I cared to entertain—ran my blood ice old. I couldn't even respond, gaping at her in horror. I almost spilled my wine in the process.

Was she right?

Were they both right?

Was this more than just a physical attraction?

21. DOWN THE RABBIT HOLE
Roman

♫ *I Can't Stop - Flux Pavilion* ♫

"**I**'m gonna come!" Lux screams, her back arching off the bed as my lips clamp down on her clit.

I pump my fingers in and out of her cunt only twice more before her thighs lock my head between their grasp, her hands roughly fisting my hair. The moans that erupt from deep in her throat completely undo me, unleashing the beast within.

On a growl, I tear myself away from her and plant my feet on the floor, breaths ragged, cock aching.

I need her so badly it hurts.

My hands clasp her ankles and yank her shivering form to the edge of the bed. She gazes up at me as the last of her climax rolls through her, and the look I see in her eyes says it all...

Fuck me.

Own me.

Possess me.

I'm over her before either of us can say another word, sliding into her effortlessly with an urgency I've not ever felt before.

"Fuuuck," I hiss, losing all sense of sobriety as her heat envelopes me, sucking me in deeper.

I'm in so deep, I can feel the very end of her entrance straining to keep me from pushing in any further.

"So greedy," I coo in her ear, hitching one of her legs around my waist.

Lux nods shamelessly. "So good, it's so good," she breathes, clawing at my back, her nails breaking skin as I increase the pace.

She's not wrong. Good is only putting it lightly. This right here is sublime, the only damned sliver of Heaven I'll ever get to experience.

And I don't want it to stop…

"Right, Rome?" Vic's voice suddenly cut through another explicit daze.

Another vividly real, cock-jolting daze I couldn't seem to escape these days. The semi barely contained by my tuxedo pants was proof. Thankfully, neither one of the men standing before me—or anyone else for that matter—seemed to notice.

Vic placed a firm hand on my shoulder. "Roman…you good?"

I nodded and tamped down the ridiculous amount of desire swimming through my veins. "Yeah, apologies, man. Just remembering a few things that need to get done before the weekend is over. What were you saying?"

He eyed me keenly but didn't seem inclined to press me on the matter.

Yet.

I'm sure he'd be up my ass about it later.

"I was telling Ryzhkov here that Lux hasn't been very easy to wear down."

Of course he had to bring her up.

I glanced over at the older Russian man who was watching me like a hawk. According to Vic, he was Pahkan of the Ryzhkov Brotherhood from Chicago, which left me wondering what the hell he was doing here in Miami. Couldn't be solely for this so-called charity gala, that's for sure…

"She hasn't been, no," I agreed, snatching another champagne glass from one of the waiters passing through with a giant sterling silver tray. "But we're getting there."

"It's about time," Vic grumbled, taking a sip from his flute.

Ryzhkov chuckled darkly and shook his head. "You can't rush such things, Victor. Not if you want them done right. Give the man some credit and have a little patience," he advised, his Russian accent thick as molasses.

"*Thank you.*" I smiled.

The satisfied gesture seemed to deepen Vic's scowl, and on the inside I was damn satisfied about that, too.

"I realize that, but we're falling behind. She's a stubborn broad with tactics of her own. Not to mention Roman's last travesty set her off like a bomb," Vic explained.

Ryzhkov seemed very intrigued, his blue eyed gaze bouncing between us both. "I see. Well, there's always a way, and if she becomes too difficult, then simply eliminate her completely. Problem solved," he countered, offering a shrug when Vic's expression paled.

"I don't want to kill her. I just want what's mine."

"Then you don't want it bad enough. If she's such threat, you'd be willing to do anything to rid yourself of her presence. And since that's obviously not the case, I suggest you start *taking* rather than *asking*."

"How?" Vic asked, glancing at me from the corner of his eyes.

Ryzhkov laughed and clapped him on the shoulder. "Women are easy to subdue, Victor, far easier than you think. You just have to figure out how they like it. Now, if you'll excuse me, there's someone here I must introduce myself to."

And just like that, the man was gone without a glance back, leaving Vic and I alone amongst the masses.

"That's not part of your plan, correct?" he questioned after a beat, staring out at the sea of elegantly dressed people.

I mulled it over for a moment.

If Ryzhkov's suggestion took him aback so blatantly, I was curious to see what his reaction would be if I agreed.

"If it comes down to that, yes," I lied, sipping my champagne.

He tensed beside me, but continued watching the crowd as if I hadn't struck a nerve. "We're not going that route, so go ahead and cross that off the list."

Interesting.

"I thought you agreed to stop bitching and let me—"

"The answer is no, Rome," he growled. "End of discussion."

"So touchy," I chuckled, mentally shaking my head at his stupidity. "My bad, mate."

"I just don't see it being necessary, that's all." His tone was clipped, like he was just realizing he'd given himself away, *yet again*. "Oh, I forgot to mention earlier. Your house is finally ready."

I almost laughed and pointed out the abrupt subject change to further my point, but considering the news he'd just thrown my way, I decided to humor him. After all, I'd been at the *Colony* for weeks while the house was being remodeled, and it was bloody-fucking-torture at this point.

"Fucks sake, about time," I replied.

"Just in time, actually. You heard about the hurricane right?"

What?

"No, what hurricane?"

"Hurricane Glenn. He's a Cat 5, supposed to hit us as a Cat 4 on Wednesday."

Again, what? I was genuinely confused.

"Okay, you lost me," I admitted. "What does that have to do with my house?"

Vic plucked the drained glass from my hand and set it on a tray of empties as another waitress strolled by. "Hurricane party, brother, that's what."

"Still lost. What the hell is a hurricane party?"

"A party during a hurricane?" he said, though it sounded more like a question.

"Seriously? That's a thing?"

"It's almost a tradition, really."

"And you just volunteered my new home for the occasion?" I snapped, turning my head toward him.

"Well," he grinned, "I would hope you don't mind. You've got the most space, after all. Just consider it a house warming party."

He couldn't be serious.

"What's in it for me?" I asked as steady as possible, tipping my head graciously at an older couple scouting around us.

"Pussy, lots of it, and good company. You don't want to ride out a storm this large alone. Truuust me," he drawled.

Was that supposed to make it better?

I enjoyed my space, enjoyed it quite a bit, and I wasn't afraid to pass some storm in my own company.

"C'mon, Rome," he cajoled knowingly. "You got the guest house and all. You have my word we won't overdo it on the body count. Don't forget, the power *will* go out eventually. With a storm this big, that's a given. It'll get quiet and you'll have your space."

He had a point. Unfortunately.

Despite not ever having a experienced a hurricane, I knew power loss was a probability. Sometimes it lasted hours, other times days. Depended on how bad the storm was and how quickly the power company could stitch things up. Having people around *would* make the blackout period less excruciating, I suppose.

"I guess we're having a party then," I sighed, resigned.

There was no use arguing him, honestly. He'd gone and organized it without my knowledge. What's done is done.

A pleased grin spread across his face at my concession. "There's my boy," he said excitedly, squeezing me to his side. "I asked the reno guys to go ahead and put your shutters up, so that's done too. We just need to prep."

See?

Presumptuous dick.

"What all do we need?" I was already regretting my decision to let this slide.

Vic smirked gestured for me to follow him. "Some weed, food, and of course, drinks."

This shit wreaked terribly, and unfortunately for me, no amount of weed or alcohol could have prepared me for the storm headed my way.

22. TWENTY-ONE QUESTIONS
Lux

♫ *Never Be the Same - Camila Cabello* ♫

After my little chat with Suki and Ramsey regarding The Phantom Menace, I actually found myself ready to go to work on Monday morning.

I wanted to go to work.

It appeared that, my situation with Roman somehow trumped what Vic had done to me, and while I still wasn't one-hundred percent—had no intention of seeing or speaking to him—that perpetual state of paranoia had vanished once more. The flashbacks had subsided to mild night terrors, too, ones I could handle and, overall, I hadn't been dwelling on the sordid affair anymore, period.

That was new for me.

Really new for me.

I suffered years of trauma and PTSD after such harrowing occurrences, with no simple or instant fix along the way. Took several therapists, lots of medications, and overall time to even find a way to cope with it.

But this thing with Roman made it go away like nothing ever happened, which kept bringing me back to, *were my girls right?*

That's exactly what I was dissecting to the final translucent thread when I pulled up to Black Widow and saw all my employees gathered outside.

It looked like damn riot.

What in the fuck?

All thoughts of Roman briskly fizzled away to the back of my mind as I eased into my usual spot and killed the engine, hopping out of the G Class at lightning speed.

"What the hell is going on?" I asked, throwing my door shut.

Dozens of heads snapped my way, a lot of them which proceeded to cower just from my tone alone.

"Power's out," said one of the packagers.

My brow quirked high in a perfect arch as I dragged my gaze his way. "The entire building?"

He nodded. "Every last room."

"Did we check the breakers?" I hedged, turning my attention to the factory's exterior for any clues.

"We flipped them three times," he explained. "Nothing."

Of course there was nothing.

Nothing, as usual, which meant one thing and one thing only.

Roman.

"I see. Thank you." That was all I offered the man before stalking off to the front doors with anger swiftly bubbling in my gut.

I had it in my right mind to haul my ass over to Noir Coast and wring the bastard's neck, give him a piece of my damn mind, but I'm sure that's what he was he was expecting.

What he wanted.

And I wasn't going to give him the satisfaction this time.

Swiveling around on my toes, I cleared my throat and waited until I had the crowd's undivided attention.

"Good morning."

"Good morning," they hummed.

"As you're all fully aware already, the power is out, and it looks like this is something that's going to take some time to resolve. Quite obviously that means some of you won't be able to operate your usual stations, so I'm doubling you up to work on packaging. Once everything is packaged, you can go home—if the power hasn't been restored by then, that is. Easy enough, yeah?"

A loud round of "Yes, ma'am" erupted around me, most of them nodding in agreement.

"Wonderful, then let's get to work." I smiled as genuinely as possible and tipped my head every so often as they all began filing in past me.

When the last few trickled in, I whipped out my phone and scrolled through my contacts for Roscoe's number. The man was likely dead asleep but…he was basically all the help I had at the moment, aside from Ellie.

Me: *Good morning. I hate to possibly wake you, but we have a problem. Roman was here at some point between last night and this morning. We have absolutely no power and, apparently, some of these guys already tried flipping the breakers before I arrived. It's not a* *simple fix. I need someone out here to come take a look at it ASAP. Thank you in advance.*

With the text delivered, I slipped my phone back into my purse and headed upstairs to my office, head held high —all seemingly calm, cool, and collected.

I was fuming, though, positively livid.

Burning.

Loathing every facet of what made up my acquaintance with Roman, and that visceral, overwhelming connection.

This mindset was good, how I needed to think at all times.

I welcomed it, embraced it with open arms.

Yes.

This is how things between Roman and I should be.

How they needed to stay.

Enemies.

Forever.

Anything else was unacceptable, a danger to well-being, to my sanity.

The past—though not vast—proved confronting him was pointless and, all the while, *lethal*, a deadly concoction of rage and unadulterated lust.

I had to stay away from him.

Wouldn't be remotely easy, but I had to try.

My heart would never survive Roman King otherwise.

I FAILED, ROYALLY.

Despite being dead-set on not giving Roman the satisfaction of eliciting a reaction from me, I ended up doing just that anyway.

As the morning went on, the temperatures in the factory continued to rise, my office included. I was sweating bullets, could feel my hair protesting against the humidity, sticking to every inch of my damp skin. No doubt my make-up was smearing off, too.

By the time the electrician finally arrived, I was a hot mess.

Literally.

An irritable hot mess who went nuclear when said electrician explained all the wires had been snipped, thus confirming this would be a lengthy—and quite costly —process.

Right then, in that moment, denying Roman of what he so justly deserved suddenly seemed stupid.

What he needed was a taste of his own damn medicine. He wanted to get this petty?

No problem, I could do petty with damn eyes closed.

So I returned him the favor, sent hell right to his doors, and when the sun finally set just beyond the horizon, I raced like a bat out of hell to the Panorama.

I was already waiting on the rooftop beneath the full moon when Roman finally showed his face. I hadn't been certain he'd actually show at all, but if his day was as trying as mine, he'd need an escape like he needed his next breath.

Leaned up against the glass ledge, I smiled inwardly

when the metal door slammed shut on the other side of the roof.

If he hadn't realized he wasn't alone yet, he would be in three...

Two...

One...

"Well, well, well, look what we have here." His voice boomed perfectly on cue, footsteps growing louder and louder as he approached.

"An indignant female," I retorted, cutting my eyes to his approaching form.

Jesus Christ...

My jaw almost fell slack as he came closer into view. Thankfully, I was able to keep myself together and swallowed deeply instead, hoping like hell he hadn't caught onto the blatant action. Tried as I might not to stare, though, my gaze moved of its own accord, following the defined lines of his tailored clothing.

He was all broad shoulders, built arms, and slim waist beneath them, and he looked...

Ugh, do I even have to say it?

You're going to make me, aren't you?

He looked... Well, he looked... Delicious.

There's no other way to word it. He looked absolutely delicious, and more so than ever because he was actually wearing some color.

I'd never seen him in anything other than black.

The rusted ruby of his dress shirt brought out his eyes impossibly more, especially with the top two buttons undone.

No tie.

Just a peek of the colorful ink on his chest on display.

I was straight up gaping by the time he came to a full stop beside me, not a trace of anger or hostility anywhere to found.

The spell was thicker than ever this time, and we were caught tightly in its web.

"Indignant female, huh? Well, we seem to have a pissed off bloke, too," he tossed back, leaning one arm on the ledge. "My day was rather…heated."

"Funny, so was mine. Turns out some asshole snipped my electrical. Had to have it all rewired."

"Wow, what a maggot," he said sarcastically, shaking his head.

"Oh, he is—a total pest." I bit back the smile that was trying to break free. "Alls good, though, I returned him the favor."

Roman nodded and scoffed a laugh through his nose. "That you did."

"If only he'd listen to me. He'd have spared himself a sample of hell."

"I've told you this before… I'm not afraid to burn, Pigeon. Been through hell and back more times than I can count."

"As have I, but seriously, the power? You had to cut the power?" I asked, more inquisitively than anything else.

Shrugging, he turned into the ledge and leaned over, watching the cars below. "Set you back a day, right?"

"Unfortunately."

"And there you go. So, yes, the power." A genuine grin split across his face, and it wasn't one of the evil ones he'd flashed me a time or two.

No.

This was a full-on, genuine, mega-watt smile, with a little sinister playing on the corners.

I had to look away, because if I didn't...

"Why are you still here, Roman?" I inhaled a deep breath as I glazed over the booming city below us.

"Why do you keep asking me this question when you know what the answer will be?"

"Because I keep hoping you'll take the hint and move on to the next place. Miami isn't for you. Go pester some wanker in Chicago, or in Detroit, Boston, *anywhere*. Anywhere but here."

"I told you that's not happening, I'm not a man easily deterred."

"I can see that," I agreed, walking off a short distance.

I needed the space.

Needed to be out of his bubble. He was too close, and that was my weakness.

When he intimidated me most.

With how loud the city was, it wasn't exactly quiet per se, but an awkward lull fell upon us. Neither one of us spoke for several minutes, allowing all different types of ideas and scenarios to play out in my mind.

"Why don't you just get to know me?" Roman asked suddenly, rooting me to the ground beneath my feet.

Was he serious right now?

"Get to know you?" I spun in place, looking at him like he'd gone completely insane. "You're joking, right?"

Roman shook his head. The expression on his face was entirely serious. "Not remotely. Get to know me, Lux. You'll see I'm not a terror unless I have to be. Just a man trying to get ahead is all."

"Yeah, off something I built. That's not someone I want to know."

"You might, if you knew the story behind it."

"And that would be?" I hedged, clearly intrigued by his response.

But he shot me down, just like I should've expected.

"I can't tell you. That's part of getting to know me."

"Well, that's not what I came up here for, so I'm going to go ahead and pass," I exhorted.

"What *did* you come up here for? And don't state the obvious, because we both know damn well I'm not giving up that feat any time soon. I'll play this game with you as long as you want, Pigeon."

My blood burned.

Him and that damned nickname.

It made me cringe every time. I hated it.

Shuffling over to him, I groaned profoundly to get my point across once and for all. "Can you *please,* for the love of all things fucking holy, stop calling me that?"

Rome chuckled. "You really hate it, don't you?"

Blue eyes clung to me as I leaned over the ledge once more.

"Yes, please stop. Lux will suffice."

"Tell me something about you and I will."

And there went my body locking up again.

I couldn't even look at him, completely thrown off by his asinine request. He really *was* insane. He had to be. After everything we'd been through and all we'd done to each other, how the hell could he stand there and ask me to share myself with him, like everything was all good and gravy?

Why?

Why would he want to know me anyway?

Didn't he realize getting to know each other would only make our predicament more difficult? It was difficult enough as it is, for fucks sake.

"Lux," Roman's voice boomed through my internal struggle.

He didn't call you Pigeon...

Dragging my gaze to where he stood, I found that lopsided smirk awaiting me. The simple gesture was becoming too familiar, something I both expected—*and wanted*—to see.

"Stop scheming over there for five seconds and tell me. I'll even make it easy for you. Just give me one thing. If there's one thing the world should know about Lux Mercier, what should it be?"

"That she's a tough bitch," I said proudly.

"True, but that doesn't count."

"Why not?"

"Because the world already knows that. Gotta give me something better. *More.*"

This man...

"Flattery thing isn't a good look on you, Roman. Stick

to the plan."

"That is part of the plan." He waggled his eyebrows, the tip of his tongue caught between his teeth through a wicked grin.

Fuck, I liked that.

I'm not even going to try to deny it. I liked it, maybe a little too much, and he must've known it, too, because his grin slithered into that devious smile I knew all too well.

My insides twisted like a wrung tee.

"And no, I'm not telling you the plan," he added, sliding closer to me.

He was so close, our arms brushed.

"Figures," I scoffed.

"Stop averting—I'm still waiting on that one thing."

"I wasn't averting, you're the one who—"

"Eh, eh, eh," he chided, tapping the tip of my nose. "See? Averting."

Ughhh.

He was maddening and I was cheesing. Me, cheesing, no holds barred! What in the actual fuck was he doing to me?

"You're a pain in the ass, you know that?"

"Guilty, but you like it. Now, back to the question," he pressed, shooting another groan out of me.

He really was relentless.

"You're going to be the death of me."

"Probably, but you're averting again. The question, Lux, let's go—tell me one thing the world should know about you."

"That I don't back down. Ever," I blurted out,

desperate to be freed from his ludicrous game of twenty-one questions.

My heart was suddenly hammering, spiking higher and higher as he leaned in toward me. Alarm bells sounded off, but fuck me if I could move.

I could barely breathe.

Too close. He was too close, like all up in my bubble close. I could feel him, all of him; his vibe, his warmth, his fucking everything in my bubble and I couldn't fucking breathe.

"I knew that already, too, but I'm gonna let it slide this time. Next time, though, don't give me some obvious bullshit answer, or I'll pester you until I get the one I want."

Something about his threat snapped my eyes up to his, and unbeknownst to me, it was a wrong move on my part.

A trap.

The second they fused together he was quick to hold on and not let go. That *compel* tattoo scripted over his eyebrow had never been more apt, because that's exactly what he was doing to me.

I couldn't look away, watching his every move. When his gazed dropped to my mouth, I was there, struggling not to squirm as his tongue lashed out across his bottom lip.

I felt it everywhere and no where all at once.

He inched a spec closer and I sucked in a heap of air, squeezing my eyes shut to save myself from falling deeper under his spell.

"Don't do it, please" I whispered, because I knew what was coming.

I knew it with every fiber of my being.

"Hell yes I'm doing it," he whispered back, lips hovering so tangibly against mine I could already feel their softness. "I have to. Been dying to. Let me."

"Don't."

"Yes. Just relax. Those street rats can't see us—it's all good."

"I know, but still, don't…" I beseeched him.

If he did this—if I *let* him do this—nothing would ever be the same again.

"If I put my lips on yours right now, are you going to move?" he questioned, ever so softly clasping my chin between his fingers.

"N-no," I admitted, breathing hitching.

"Then yes, I'm fucking do it. One taste, Lux. Quick and painless…"

"But deadly—"

And then he was kissing me, dragging me down further into his depraved rabbit hole of sin and temptation.

My brain screamed for me to get the hell out of there, and yet once again, I was helpless against him. This man had me stuck, melting into him as he kissed me with purpose, like his life depended on it. What was supposed to be one kiss, went on and on, building rapidly from gentle to urgent. His fingers speared into my hair, pulling me closer until I was trapped beneath him with no escape route in sight. The way his lips moved over mine was unlike anything I'd ever had the pleasure of experiencing before. He knew when to kiss, when to nibble, *when to lick,* intoxicating me beyond repair. I couldn't control myself, opening wider as he sought out proper entrance into my mouth, his hands trailing along my body like we'd done this a million times before.

I was lost, so damn lost in this moment... Until a breathy moan bubbled in my throat and reality threw a bucket of ice water over my head.

Gasping, I pulled away from him, shaky hands flat on his hard chest to put some much needed space between us.

"I've gotta go," I said in a rush, scrambling to get around him on jelly-like legs.

"Lux." He tried reaching out for me, but I was too quick. "Lux, don't go."

"I have to," I called out over my shoulder, nervously booking it to the door.

What have I done? What the hell have I done?

23. IT'S ALL FUN AND GAMES UNTIL...

Lux

♫ *Carousel - Melanie Martinez* ♫

That kiss. *That electrifying, inebriating kiss. His lips devouring mine. So warm and demanding.*

It was on replay.

Wet mouths.

Haunting me…

Frantic hands.

Enticing me…

Dueling tongues.

I couldn't stop thinking about it.

Even now, as the scalding shower pelted my face, all I could focus on was the way Roman's mouth nearly devoured me. He would have for sure had I not left when I did.

Truthfully speaking, I think he did regardless because I could still feel every bit of it diverging through my body.

Just one taste, Lux—quick and painless.

That moment right there, the one where he first put his lips on me with abandon…

That's what I felt most.

Electrifying my fingertips, burning up my neck.

Searing my lips.

My nipples puckered at the reminder, the warm rivulets of water running down my breasts clinging to each rigid peak. I squeezed a small globe in each hand to wane off the sharp bite and threw my head back.

Eyes shut.

Heart palpitating.

If this is what he could do to me with a kiss alone, imagine what he could do...

Fuck.

That image was hazardous. I shouldn't be thinking such thoughts, shouldn't be thinking about *him*, period, but I couldn't stop.

Didn't know how.

He'd left a whole new mark on me, and I didn't know what the hell to do about it.

Was there even anything I *could* do?

No, probably not. I mean, I hadn't done a very good job at running him out of Miami thus far, so how in the ever-loving fuck was I supposed to stop this?

Whatever this was...

The remainder of my shower continued on in the same torturous fashion. By the time I stepped out and reached for my towel, the space between my thighs was throbbing.

Aching.

Begging for relief.

I considered it for all of two-point-five seconds, eyeing my nightstand where B.O.B laid to rest, but all too quickly I realized indulging in this manic, lust-driven episode would only reiterate the fact Roman had managed to settle himself deep under my skin.

Nope.

No way.

Not happening.

There's no way I could touch myself with his blasted face entrained in my mind and not be a ruined mess after the fact.

Nope.

Hell the fuck no.

It was bad enough as it is.

Cursing him to hell and back, I finished drying myself off and padded into my closet with the damp towel now wrapped around my body. Every single article of clothing was whipped from one side of the rack to the other as I searched for something to wear, the angry scrape of metal on metal a tell-tale sign of my frustration.

I couldn't decide whether I was more angry with him or myself.

How daft could I be to let him put his lips on me? I should've run when he got too close. Hell, I should've run the second I deduced what his intentions were. Could've spared myself from all this nonsense. But no, of course not, because I was an idiot.

A masochist, too, evidently.

As the last blouse joined the rest of my wardrobe, I groaned aloud in defeat and stomped to my bed, falling onto my back in a disheveled heap.

What the hell is wrong with me?

No, seriously, what the hell was wrong with me? Why

was I letting a man, a man whom I loathed no less, have this inexplicable effect over me?

Because you don't really hate him...

Right as the ridiculous thought crossed my mind, my phone began blaring on the nightstand. I shot up with a gasp and snatched it with a quick hand, thankful for the perfectly timed distraction like never before.

"Hey Rams," I answered, keeping my voice as even and unsuspecting as possible.

The last thing I needed was for her to pick up on my crazy and start another round of twenty-one questions.

"What are your plans for the hurricane?"

The blurted query caught me off guard, contorting my face in confusion. "What do you mean what are my plans?"

"Like, where are you staying?" she clarified.

"Um, in my flat?" I answered, though it sounded more like a question.

Ramsey gasped just slightly, a loud clatter arising in the background behind her.

Sounded like dishes clashing in the sink.

"Are you insane? You're in a high-rise!" she squeaked, and I rolled my eyes, clutching my towel as I rose onto my feet.

"And? Your point?"

"It's not safe, L. Those buildings sway with high winds. Not to mention you're surrounded by windows, windows that won't be protected."

"I understand that but, I don't really have much of a choice," I chuckled, wandering back into my closet. "It's not like I have family I can hunker down with. I'll be fine."

"No, you won't," she deadpanned. "It's a big storm, Lux—you're coming with me."

"Where?" I was intrigued to say the least, rummaging through my wardrobe once more.

"To this hurricane party Marco invited me to."

"Marco, as in Stryker's mate?"

"Yup." She popped the P, whipping my head back in disbelief.

"Since when do you talk to Marco?"

"Since the other night when I showed up at Vybe and he was there."

And where was I?

If it was within the last week, probably obsessing over Roman...

"Does this mean Stryker and Suki will be there, too?" I hedged, swallowing down the abrasive lump in my throat as those vicious thoughts of our kiss plagued me yet again.

"No actually," Ramsey snickered. "Suki's staying at Stryker's."

I heard the words, both my mouth and eyes popping in surprise, but it took several moments for what the full extent of that statement meant.

She was staying with Stryker and she hadn't told me?

"What?! When did this happen?"

"I don't know. She literally just told me about ten minutes ago when I called her to ask if she wanted to come with."

My hand clenched around one of my little black dresses. "You called her before me?" I couldn't hide the disappointment in my voice.

"L, c'mon—don't take it personal. Shit, I don't and you two leave me out of a lot," she countered, ripping what sounded like a paper towel free from the kitchen roll.

"We do not," I blurted out, yanking my dress off the hanger.

"Yes, you do, but that's okay. You've known her forever. I wouldn't expect anything less." I could almost see her shrugging. "Not the point, though...are you coming or do I have to drag you?"

Sighing, I set the phone on speaker and tossed it on my bed.

"Where is this supposed party?" I questioned, dropping my towel as I pulled out a pair of panties from my nightstand and shimmied into them.

"I don't know, somewhere near *Star Island* which means plenty of space, lots of booze, and a good time."

"You really want to stay at some random house for God knows how many hours?"

"It's better than your flat or my shit hole in Carol City. Besides, if Marco is going, I'm sure that means whoever's throwing this shit must be cool people."

Somehow, I doubted that. Cool people didn't exist nowadays. Our world was beyond fucked up, humanity included. Most people—myself included—had cruel intentions.

Sad, but true.

"We'll check it out," I conceded doubtingly, "but I'm

not making any promises. One measly bad vibe and I'm out of there, you hear me? I don't care if it's raining a tsunami outside, I'm leaving."

Now had I only stood my ground and held onto the already festering bad vibe roiling my gut, I could have avoided what I would later deem the night the devil finally possessed me.

24. HURRICANE FORCE WINDS

Roman

♫ *Party Favors - Tinashe & Young Thug* ♫

I knew I was fucked when it came to Lux from the moment I first laid eyes on her, but that kiss just about signed my name on the dotted line.

In my blood.

I couldn't get it, *or her,* out of my mind.

Couldn't get the horrified look on her face or the way she ran from me out of my mind.

She was shook—rightfully so—bolted before I could grab her, and I wouldn't be surprised if she went into hiding regardless of me hand-delivering another threat. Might've been a good thing honestly, because I would-n't've have been much help. Other than pinning her to the wall and kissing her senseless a second time.

And a third.

And a fourth.

I knew I was in the wrong, knew I should *not* have gone anywhere near there, but I couldn't reign myself in.

I had to do it.

She was *right there, her lips were right there*, and after

showing me a side of her I never expected to see—no matter how brief—I reacted accordingly.

She wanted to me to do it, too.

Lux could deny it all she wanted. She could overthink it until she made herself sick, but I knew she wanted me to do it.

The way she melted against me proved it.

Ding, dong!

The abrupt chime of my doorbell sucked me back into the present. I nearly groaned in exasperation.

I was no more thrilled about Vic's audacious and covertly planned hurricane soiree than I was when he first informed me several days back. It was cracked, and considering he'd arranged the entire thing behind my back, dodgy as fuck.

"It's party time, bro. You ready?" the bastard himself asked as he sauntered through the kitchen to the front doors to welcome our first guests.

He was almost dressed to the nines in a crisp ebony dress shirt and slacks, which made absolutely no sense to me. Was he expecting the red carpet or the paparazzi?

I nodded wordlessly and flashed him the horns as I went about stocking the last few beers in the fridge. The thing looked like it belonged at a frat house.

Thank fuck for having all the strong shit locked up in my office. I was damn sure going to need something a hell of a lot stronger than just beer to get me through the rest of the night.

A little over an hour later, the festivities were officially in full swing, and the hurricane was moving in quickly. Most of our attendees were present and accounted for, and the majority of them had congregated in the main living area off the kitchen.

Music blared from space to space, as did random bouts of laughter and mixed conversation. I did my best to greet everyone, offering drinks when necessary, but the sheer amount of bodies packed in here was already overwhelming.

Again, thank fuck for bourbon.

By my third, there wasn't a thing in the world that could ruffle my feathers. A king in my castle, I was actually starting to have a good time—chatting, networking, even a little dancing. I'd even forgotten about Vic and his overly cheery self.

Until I caught a flash of emerald from the corner of my eyes.

I almost spit my drink out, had to do a double-take.

At first, I thought I'd already drank too much, but reality is, I'd know that bright emerald mane anywhere. Had it engrained in my mind, along with the sharp edges of her profile, and the supple pout of her lips.

And those eyes, fuck me—don't get me started on those feral, sexy eyes; the perfect, blue cat eyes, slanted with malice and all.

They locked right on me and held me captive to her allure.

Black tank top.

Minuscule denim shorts.

Inked legs for days.

I couldn't look away, and neither could she, apparently. We just stood there, gaping at one another with the very same question sounding off between us.

What the fuck are you doing here?

I almost couldn't believe it.

She was here, *in my home*, mere feet separating her and my chamber. The images of her beneath me— writhing, begging, *screaming*—were more prominent than ever before. Could hear it all with such clarity, my cock was one moan away from rising to the challenge.

I could smell her.

Taste her.

The urge to scoop her up and press her into the nearest wall was nearly impossible to subdue but, somehow, I held onto my restraint and forced myself in check *real quick*.

Lux had this uncanny, maddening ability to get deep under my skin and cloud my judgement like no other.

And she wasn't even trying.

She just did, effortlessly so.

The woman completely blindsided me and this sudden fixation I'd developed for her was wearing me thin.

I'd gone from a sure, solid fixture determined to take her out, to an entranced, royally fucked up bloke hanging by a deranged thread.

A deranged thread that wouldn't hold much longer.

My own fault.

I had no one to blame but myself, not when I'd single-handedly paved the way for such self-destruction when I decided to play on her weakness.

But still, I blamed her.

I blamed her for making me so damn crazed, and after the blow I'd felt when she fled, I knew I had to distance myself before I did something else we'd both regret later.

Flashing her the most schooled smirk I could manage, I took another sip of my drink and disappeared through the crowd with determined strides as *Tinashe's* "Party Favors" blasted behind me, propelling me faster.

I didn't need to imagine a blasted party favor from Lux.

One drunken, sultry look or a mere gander at her body swaying to this music, and there's no telling what I might do.

Once on the other side of my office door, I deflated like a balloon, my hand firmly gripping the knobs at my back as the black hole in my chest thrashed about frantically.

What the fuck was she doing here?

What in the *actual fuck* was she doing here?

Was this her next move?

No, it couldn't be, wasn't her style. She liked taking me by surprise. Showing herself this early on would defeat the purpose.

Or would it?

Perhaps the element of surprise *was* revealing herself, throwing me for a loop from the usual.

What I really wanted to know was *who* invited her? Everyone present was very well aware of Vic and his anarchy movement. The role I myself played, too. Quite a few had helped me vandalize Black Widow several weeks back as well.

That said, this could, of course, be Vic's doing. Another one of his tests. It *would* explain his suspicious behavior.

I downed another sip of my bourbon, lip curling in a snarl around the rim.

On second thought... Na. He wasn't that idiotic. Revealing our friendship to her—if you could even call it that—would only hurt his efforts.

He'd never risk that.

If this wasn't another one of his games, though, did that mean he was clueless to her presence?

Shit.

This could get nasty real quick.

One look at Vic and I together, and Lux was bound to connect the dots sooner or later. She was far too intelligent not to. Same went for him catching me with Lux. If he so much as felt a sliver of the force between us, he'd know something had shifted.

Fucking hell. I need another drink.

Or five.

This party was turning into everything I'd been dreading.

Stalking over to the antique liquor cabinet between the bookcases, I refilled my tumbler and nearly drained it in entirety before even sinking into one of the high-backed parlor chairs.

At this rate, alcohol wouldn't be a distraction for much longer.

I needed something warmer, something with a nice set of tits and a pert little ass. Something to get lost in a few hours and make myself scarce altogether.

Something to make myself briefly forget Lux, and Vic, and all the ever-present bullshit in my life...

Slam!

The doors to my office burst wide open, banging rudely against the walls.

I snapped my head over to see a small group of drunken lads stalk through—clearly with no regard for other people's property, *or privacy*—and head straight to the pool table before my desk.

Their noise-level was instantly obnoxious, like that of a toddler running on an unnecessary burst of caffeine, and just as I was about to make my presence known and kick them the fuck out, a curvaceous redhead came barreling in with Lux on her tail.

I froze stock-still and watched quietly, melting back into my seat to avoid being seen.

The redhead whipped her inside and signaled back out into the hallway with an impatient hand. The content of their conversation was drowned out by the music, but it didn't look like a friendly discussion if you asked me, which left me more curious than anything else.

Especially when Lux went rigid and all the color stripped from her face.

From here, it looked like she mouthed *I'll tell you later* as she shook her head, but I wasn't certain, not when my head was swimming in a hazy bourbon pool.

A hazy bourbon pool that flooded over as our eyes collided.

She gasped.

My cock jolted.

We held it for several moments, long enough for me to see the image of that damned kiss reflecting off them, to feel the electricity surge between us, supercharging the air to a stifling degree.

And then she was gone, leaving me with the intoxicating taste of her mouth burning my lips.

Damn her.

My already buggered mood plummeted to downright sour.

Tightening my grip on the tumbler, I drained the remaining contents and inhaled a deep breath in attempt to calm myself.

But it didn't do shit if I'm being honest.

There was just way too much going on.

Way. Too. Much.

I was going to explode if I didn't find a proper distraction soon.

Seconds later, said proper distraction trailed right into my line of sight like an encouraging gift from satan himself. She looked good; teeny tiny with long lilac waves that hung to the small of her back. Sashaying past me to the bookcase, she bent over at the waist and scanned the titles on the bottom shelf.

All ass.

She was all ass in this skin-tight mini skirt. If she bent over any more, said ass would be on full display.

"Psssttt," I hissed at her, and immediately her head

whipped around to where I sat—as if she'd been hoping I'd do that all along.

Apparently, she was, because when I crooked a finger at her, she abandoned her search and came hustling toward me without any hesitations at all.

Standing before me now, I could feel her expectant gaze as she awaited my next move. I lifted my eyes to meet her stare and offered her a lopsided smirk. She really was very pretty; regal gray eyes and full pouty lips.

I can work with this.

Disposing my emptied tumbler on the small table beside us, I leaned back further into my seat and patted my lap. She crawled right in and crossed her legs, flashing me a salacious smile as she gave me an appreciative sweep of her own.

"I'm gonna need your name," I said to her, running a finger along her chin.

"Azalea," she murmured coyly. "But my friends call me Zay."

"Well, *Zay*, care to take a walk with me?"

"Where?"

"Oh, I don't know…" I grinned, twirling a finger through the air. "Around."

Azalea eyed me curiously for a beat or two, probably debating whether or not she could trust me. "I suppose we can. It's not like we can go very far. Just let me tell my best friend I'm disappearing for a few so she doesn't freak. She's out in the kitchen."

You'll be disappearing for more than few but okay…

Tipping my head, the grin on my lips morphed into a

sinister smirk. "I'll get us drinks then. What's your poison of choice?"

"Got any tequila?"

I gave a subtle nod. "I do, yes."

"Tequila it is then—what did you say your name was?" she asked, prompting me lean into her personal bubble.

"I didn't."

Azalea seemed completely unfazed, leaning in closer, too. "Well you know mine, so..."

I could smell the tequila on her breath.

Chuckling, I raked a finger along her collar bone. "Roman King."

"Mmm, the king huh?" Her voice was a purr, goose-bumps dotting her skin.

"I like to think so, yes."

"Well, treat me right and I'll make sure to treat you like a king. I'll be back, handsome." She pecked my cheek, then slid off my lap in one fluid movement, taking care to give me another full, unprecedented view of her ass as she did so.

A glint of a smirk settled on her lips when she caught me enjoying it.

"You're cheeky."

"And you like it," she countered.

"Guilty. That said, run along now. Go find your friend and say what you need to say. I'm not fond of waiting very long."

25. BLACKOUT
Lux

♫ *Like Water - Flume ft. MNDR* ♫

I think I forgot how to breathe.

Seeing a casually-dressed Roman—beanie, gray sweatpants, and all—no more than five minutes after arriving knocked me sick. Literally sucked the wind right out of me and turned my stomach upside down.

And he wasn't just here as guest.

No.

After further explanation, I was told *this was his home* —all gray walls, white clean-lined furniture, and modern goth decor.

Shock gave into silent rage within sheer milliseconds.

I wanted to kill Ramsey.

Had Marco not taken the brunt of my wrath when he saw me going off on her like a psychopath, I might have snapped her neck and left her for dead on the lush patio.

Okay, so I'm exaggerating; I could never actually kill my girl, but holy hell was I livid.

Ramsey swore she didn't know and Marco claimed he'd not had a clue either. That, apparently, he was invited by someone else and took it upon himself to extend the invitation a few times over. I don't know how much of that I truly believed, solely because I didn't know Marco as well as I knew Stryker, but I decided to let it go.

Ramsey would never purposely do this to me.

Suki, yes.

But Ramsey, never.

So I drowned myself deep in the whiskey hole instead, a naive attempt to abolish Roman's presence from my mind.

Within thirty minutes, I'd downed about six fingers worth and was working on another few when Marco and his buddies led Ramsey and I through the dimmed house.

Flume resounded off the walls.

Bodies writhed and swayed around to the beat.

I was having a good time, and with Roman no where in sight, I actually let myself believe all would be okay. That he had enough sense to lock himself away and leave me alone. There wasn't any need for us to interact, hostile *or otherwise.*

But that's when I saw Vic...green eyes trailing me like a hawk.

My stomach skyrocketed to my throat.

On a small gasp, I gripped Ramsey out of reflex, expecting him to roll up on us, but he simply raised his glass by way of greeting, then disappeared down the hallway with a small push off the wall.

If I didn't know the man as well as I did, I would've wondered what the hell he was doing here.

This was prime Vic behavior, though—a serpent always slithering around undetected, always watching.

Waiting.

He'd stepped it up after Javi's murder, too, which would explain why he was here.

And yet, my heart still seemed to race.

My focus kind of tunneled. Everything was out of sorts. Ramsey was talking as we moved along but I didn't hear a single word of it. I hated being near Vic and it showed. Was the first thing she questioned me about when we followed Marco and his mates into what appeared to be Roman's home office. I brushed it off, promised I'd tell her later. This wasn't the time or place for me to come clean about *that*. Not when Roman's stare was striking me from across the room.

I felt it long before I even saw him. Tried to avoid it, to avoid him, but the pull was too strong, like a beacon in the night. My eyes moved of their own free will, tangling with those piercing blue orbs. They were an intimidatingly icy shade beneath his cinched brows.

Another breath escaped me.

I held in what little air remained within my lungs and forced myself to hold his stare, too, adamant on squaring him off. On seeming unaffected. But the flashback hit me in double time, more vivid and louder than ever before.

Wet mouths.

Frantic hands.

Dueling tongues.

I nearly went weak at the knees as my core clenched, betraying me in the worst way possible. All I could think was I had to get out of there. I knew Ramsey was going to unload a whole new set of questions on me, but so be it.

Anything was better than this inferno of crazy.

Everything following me dragging Ramsey out of the office was one gigantic, tipsy rollercoaster of emotions I'd barely remember later.

I *did,* however, remember chugging two beers in succession.

I remembered Ramsey yanking me into the powder room after the fact.

I remembered her texting Suki and filling her in on what was happening in her absence.

I remembered her bitching like the mama bear she often could be.

And I, unfortunately, remembered stumbling back out into the hallway, right as Roman was trailing down its length with a woman on his arm.

Which brings us to now...

2am.

The storm was going at full force and the power had officially gone out. All you could hear was the rain pattering against the window and the palm fronds slapping about with the terrifying howl of the wind. It was much worse than I'd been anticipating despite the warning over the last week, and as a result, I couldn't sleep. Ramsey, on the other hand, laid passed out beside me on the couch. I kept going back to Roman sauntering down the hall with that girl's hand in his grasp. The sight of them together filled me with instant jealousy, jealousy he caught onto clear as day. The way he looked at me when he passed by confirmed it.

Satisfaction.

Triumph.

Just the thought resurfaced the green-eyed monster with a vengeance. Throwing the pillow over my face, I groaned aloud in irritation. What the hell was wrong with me?

Why was I acting so ridiculous?

Why was I letting him affect me like this?

'Cause you don't have a choice.

No. I dismissed the thought faster than it'd hit me. This wasn't me. I didn't fuss over men like this, ever.

But he's not just any man…

No, he wasn't.

I groaned again and shot upright from my place on the couch. Ramsey stirred slightly, mumbling something about ten points to Ravenclaw, before rolling over on her side and falling silent once more.

How could she sleep so soundly when I was wired?

Probably because she wasn't busy obsessing over a man she had absolutely no business obsessing about.

I felt myself pale.

My God…

I really *was* obsessing, wound tighter than a fucking spring. If I didn't zen myself soon, I'd likely combust before morning.

Alcohol hadn't done a thing except magnify my vulnerability. Marco had the weed, and we'd lost him hours ago. But Suki had cigarettes in her purse.

I eyed it on the floor with the rest of our belongings.

Very rarely did I smoke, more socially than anything

else, but a smoke had honestly never sounded so good. A little burst of nicotine was sure to chill me out...

Snatching it off the light travertine, I rifled through her mass of shit. The pack was near the bottom. I pulled a cigarette free and the lighter, too. Both went into my bra before I enabled the flashlight on my phone, and then I was out the door.

Sans boots for the sake of being quiet.

There wasn't a soul in sight as I trailed through the house. Most of the doors were shut for privacy, though you could still hear the sounds of sex, or laughter, or various handheld radios every few feet or so.

I couldn't help but wonder what room he was in.

If he was fucking her.

If he was enjoying it.

If she was still in his bed, caught in a naked tangle with him, her lilac hair splayed out all over his inked chest.

Indignation bloomed deep in the pit of my stomach. Teeth baring slightly, I clenched my fists at my sides and kept on down the hallway, beseeching the voice in my head to spare me of those images.

But as I slipped around the corner, maybe a hundred feet from the front door, the images in my mind were laid out before me in the flesh.

Only worse.

26. INEVITABLE
Lux

♫ *Collide - Justine Skye feat. Tyga* ♫

It was so much worse.

I think it's safe to say I was not expecting to see *that*.

Nearly swallowing my tongue whole, I slung back behind the wall and turned off the flashlight on my phone with shaky hands.

I didn't need it anyway.

The erotic sounds bouncing off the walls was enough of a given.

But if one really wanted to see, the candlelight showering out from the office was enough to illuminate them.

Them.

Stealing myself, I peeked over my shoulder, keeping my body flush to the wall at my back.

Right beside the office doors was Roman, *and two women*; Lilac and a blonde.

Lilac was on her knees, head bobbing up and down on his impressive length. Her breasts spilled out over the brim of her tank top, probably for Roman to unload all over like the nasty little porn star she clearly thought she was. Meanwhile, Roman had the blonde pressed into the wall beside her, grip on her throat tight as he worked her sex.

Her pajama pants were halfway down her legs, as were his, showing off the curve off his ass.

Damn.

As livid and scandalized as I was, I found myself biting down my lip.

His body was just…

Everything you were expecting it to be.

The apex of my thighs clenched as if agreeing with the little voice in my head.

It's true.

I couldn't see all of him yet I could just imagine the way his muscles were probably flexing and rippling.

Flexing and rippling as he pleased *them.*

UGH.

I was pea-green with envy.

I shouldn't be, but I was.

And I wanted to ruin him.

A part of me knew I shouldn't react, that I should just turn around and head back until the hurricane subsided, but raining on his parade was just too good to pass up.

Sucking in a deep breath, I settled my expression and held my head high as I started down the hallway with confident steps. Not one of them seemed to notice me until I loomed within their line of sight.

Surprised and suddenly bashful, both women froze,

and at their wide eyes, Roman snapped his gaze on me, too.

Bewildered and glassy.

"Don't mind me," I cooed, running a claw along his back as I slipped behind him. "Just passing through for a smoke."

I didn't get very far, though.

Roman's signature displeased growl filled the air, followed by the pop of his cock slipping free from Lilac's mouth. Seconds later, a strong hand wrapped itself around my arm and I was dragged back a short ways, then whipped into the office.

It all happened so fast, I didn't have time to process what was happening, much less react.

Roman's little hussies, however, were very much reacting behind us. They weren't happy, and he didn't seem to give a single fuck.

"But Rome, what about—"

Slam!

The harsh sound echoed through the office, rattling the walls and likely carrying through to the adjacent rooms. The lock seemed to echo, too, as he clicked it in place to keep them out.

A quick swivel and we were off despite their angered banging on the door.

Each step forward came with a grunt, his clasp on my arm a forceful vise. He didn't look back at me or speak a word either, just stalked further into the room with determination coloring his aura.

A baffled protest was building on my tongue when suddenly, my back hit the black felt of the custom pool table.

And I mean *hit* the felt.

Roman deposited me on it like he planned to eat me alive.

He wedged his way almost effortlessly between my legs, and in the time I merely gasped, he'd already thrown my arms above my head and locked my wrists in his grip.

I was trapped beneath this man once again with nowhere to go.

Still no words were exchanged. He looked me over once, just once, stare lingering on my eyes for a second longer, and then the domino effect went off like a bomb.

Lips collided.

Teeth crashed.

It was frantic, intense.

Unexpected.

Explosive.

I was scorching under his touch, reeling at the feel of his mouth on me again, and he was a ball of pent-up desperation, running a million miles per hour. He moved so fast, I literally couldn't keep up, panting wildly as he tore his lips away from my mouth and started down the column of my neck.

Kissing.

Licking.

Biting.

It was heaven and hell, so right and yet so fucking

wrong. I knew I shouldn't be doing this with him, but I couldn't stop either. The taste of bourbon on his lips was addicting. He was addicting.

And I wanted more.

So much more.

Throwing all caution to the wind just to have it, even if for but a moment.

My body fell lax in desperation of finding a rhythm. Pliant beneath him, I let him explore, let him consume me, let him lead. Only idly—and momentarily—did I realize alarm bells would normally have been blaring by now.

But I wasn't remotely afraid.

If anything, the acute tempo of my breathing stemmed purely from carnal desire as he kissed me senseless.

He wasn't far behind either. His chest heaved with such ferocity, the air around us quivered. It reverberated through me, lanced right through my being until I was trembling.

Aching.

Zoning out from everything but right here, right now.

"Tell me why you ran," Roman hissed as he came up for air. He released me, only to grip me at the hips with both hands and push me further down on him.

My heat throbbed as his erection probed me, teasing me through all the layers separating us.

The veil of lust so was thick, whatever he'd asked had gone right over my head. "What?"

Draping himself over me, he met my stare. "Tell me. Why you ran from me. When I put my lips on you."

His breath was hot on my skin, drenched in bourbon, and his eyes, they swam in it, too—unfocused and reflective. He was so pissed I honestly wondered how he was still standing up right.

The thought instantly sobered me, reminding me he'd been outside those doors just five minutes ago, balls deep in two women.

"It doesn't matter." I tried pushing him off me. "We have to stop, though."

"Why?"

"Why?" I croaked incredulously. "For starters, you're drunk—way past the limit. And did you happen to forget you were just out there in the hallway, getting your cock sucked by one female, while you played with an entirely different cunt?"

Silence.

He pulled back to full height and watched me beneath curious brows, taking me in spread out before him on the pool table. His gaze was so utterly penetrating, I could feel it searing through me like a laser.

Down my neck, over my breasts, along my stomach...

When he reached the barely contained space between my thighs, I swallowed down the whimper caught in my throat and snapped my legs closed, feeling unbearably vulnerable under his scrutiny.

The growl that thundered in his chest was feral. My reaction to his perusal obviously wasn't to his liking.

Fist clenching the very middle of my tank top, he yanked me up toward him in a flash, my legs naturally spreading to accommodate his hips.

"They're distractions," he grated into my ear, the tip of his nose buried in my hair.

"From what?"

"From you and everything you stand for."

"Which would be?" I asked on a shaky breath, my hands subconsciously gripping his tee, too.

"Everything I shouldn't want."

I squeezed my eyes shut. His words were agonizing. They're not at all what I wanted to hear, what I could bear to hear. I'd fallen weak enough to him already, had submitted in ways every man in my life only wished I'd given up so freely. I needed to be stronger. Self-preservation begged me so.

I couldn't do this with him.

"That's why we have to stop," I whispered, trying and failing to push him away once more. "We can't be doing this. You know we can't."

Solid as a rock, he gripped me tighter. "Then tell me. Tell me you don't feel this and I'll never put my hands on you again."

One second.

Two.

Three.

What was I supposed to say?

When I didn't respond, or rather, couldn't respond, he pushed me away and looked me dead in the eye, breaths ragged, unsteady.

"Exactly—let that sink in. I know you feel it too, Lux. That's why you ran, why you're trying to fight it," he snarled, waiting a beat or two before he continued. "So go on, run. Run as fast as you can, but we both know the bomb will detonate sooner or later. And when it does, when you finally find yourself beneath me, begging me to wreck havoc on your body, I'm going to remind you of this moment right here. I'm going to remind you that you thought you could run from the King."

27. SILENT OBSERVATIONS

Vic

♫ *My Demons - Starset* ♫

I had a bad feeling.

A really fucking bad feeling.

Irrational or not, I couldn't say for sure yet, but something was off. It had been for a while now, and after the hurricane passed, I couldn't ignore it any longer.

There'd been a shift in my world, with both Rome *and* Lux. I hadn't seen much of them during the storm, locked myself up with Willow and two of her friends, but even then I felt it. The bastard was up to something. I could smell it brewing on the back burner, saw it smoking in his eyes whenever I brought up Lux. The mere mention of her name coiled him up like a serpent ready to strike.

And Lux, well, she'd completely nixed me from her life without fully cutting the cord. She didn't seem inclined to forgive me any time soon, if ever at all, and had gone as far as issuing Roscoe tasks she'd have normally appointed me.

Yet she hadn't fired me.

What stood out most, though, was how everything was at a standstill on both ends. Neither one had made a single advance on each other since Javi's murder, and I couldn't for the life of me understand why, much less what had changed.

Yes, what Roman did was gruesome, but Lux was a tough little bitch. There's no chance in hell something like that would make her retract.

"You think he's fucking her?" Liza asked, her silken voice erupting through the speaker in my office.

She'd called, as promised the last time we spoke, leaving me no other choice but to fill her in on all recent developments.

Taking another sip from my drink, I reclined into my throne and crossed my legs on the desk. "Highly doubt that."

"But you said she's a touchy subject for him. You know how Rome is when he's hiding something."

"I know, but there's no way in hell he's fucking her after all that's gone down. She wouldn't allow it either."

"I'm just saying, sounds an awful lot like the Roman who beat one of Leo's mates to a pulp when he overheard him mentioning I looked good."

"I remember that." I chuckled. "Came over to mum's afterward with the poor bloke's blood splattered on his shirt. Seriously, though, Moxie, I doubt it."

"Just…watch him is all I'm saying. I wouldn't wanna have to drop in unannounced and babysit you," she threatened, voice dripping with vindictive delight.

A delight I knew too well.

I sighed. "I've got it under control, no need for all

that. I'll let you know when it's time, then you can swoop in for the grand finale."

Liza hummed appreciatively. "Always such a good friend, Vic."

Goosebumps broke out along my skin. The way she purred my name jerked my cock beneath my slacks. I nearly cringed, hating myself for still reacting to her like this.

Righting myself in my throne, I swallowed down the images of me balls deep in her cunt all those years ago....

"I'm sure there's a few who would beg to differ," I countered.

"Of course there is. Not everyone understands what it takes to make it to the top."

Ain't that the truth.

"Can't say I don't agree."

Again she hummed, but the sound far more sensuous this time around. "You know, as the years go by, I regret not keeping you instead. Would've spared me a hell of a lot of pain, that's for sure."

"Don't," I gritted out, squeezing my eyes shut. "That ship has sailed, Moxie."

"Says who?" she asked dubiously.

"No one has to say it. Just the way it is."

That quintessential Liza snicker erupted through the line. I could all but see her tsking through her teeth. "We'll see about that."

"What is that supposed to mean?"

"Whatever you think it means, Vicsy Bear," she quipped, sounding way too much like *Harley Quinn.*

I winced at the decade-old nickname. "Please don't."

"Tit for tat, love. You still call me Moxie, remember?"

Silence.

She was right.

Knowing how much she hated when I called her that —despite how true it was—I still did it anyway.

"Exactlyyy," she drawled, throwing in a very *Harley* giggle before she went on to sing, "*Vicsy Bear and Moxie sitting in a tree, upcoming King and bad ass Queen.*"

"Queen, huh?" I couldn't help but be intrigued. "You plan to stay in Miami when it's all said and done?"

"Given a reason to stay, yes."

"And what would you consider a reason?"

"Curious, are you? Well, I'll let you ponder that over the next few weeks. Perhaps you'll have it figured out before our next chat. In the mean time—Roman, keep an eye on him, and make sure you watch the little bitch, too."

Click.

28. VYBE

Roman

♫ *Sex with Me - Rihanna* ♫

Restless. Bitter. Deranged.

Those words best described the volatile mess I'd become in the week following Hurricane Glenn. I was living off bourbon and one heaping, unrelenting dose of self-loathing.

I couldn't sleep.

My appetite was shot to shit.

Pinning Lux to the pool table really was the worst thing I could've done for myself. I'd been obsessing about her enough after that first kiss, but now I was completely unhinged.

Enraged at my inability to control myself when it came to her.

Suffering greatly from the worst case of blue balls known to man kind because of it.

I could wank off for hours, spurt jet after jet of my release all over the place, and it did fuck all to sate this deep-rooted, savage need I felt for her.

Because it wasn't even a want, it was a need.

I needed to have Lux.

I didn't give a fuck that my own plan was blowing up in my face.

I needed her, and I was going to have her.

One way or another.

She could make it easy and drop the 'I loathe you' charade, or brace herself for impact—because I was coming for her.

Which is why when Vic told me we were going to be keeping an eye on her for the evening, I didn't object.

It wouldn't be easy to get my hands on her with him present, but I'd figure something out after scoping out the area.

"So how are we doing this?" I asked him as I stepped out of his Rover on Vybe's lot.

"You're going in first. Get her attention, keep her engaged, then I'll check her out." He said it completely straight-faced, too, slamming shut the driver's door and coming around to meet me at the front end.

I couldn't help but laugh, leaning back against the warm grill. "Seriously? We're at a club, Vic. Do you realize how hard it's going to be to get her attention, let alone keep it?"

"It's not a regular club, Rome," he chuckled, posting up beside me. "During the day, it's a dance studio, but Friday nights are Play Nights."

I had to motion for him to continue because I wasn't familiar with this so-called Play Night.

Vic shrugged, flashing a grin as he locked his vehicle and shoved the fob into the pocket of his jeans. "Good music, drinks, and every so often, the girls show off some of their routines. Lux is quite good."

His grin widened, but I didn't miss the side-eye gauging my reaction.

I gave him shit, though.

Outside, I appeared aloof. Uncaring. Unfazed by the knowledge that Lux knew how to work her body.

But inside, I was gaping, twitching at the images flashing through my mind.

"She dances?" I hedged evenly.

"On occasion. One of her best friends owns it. Lux actually bought the place for her when the space went up on the market," he explained, throwing me for a loop.

"That was generous of her." I couldn't hide my surprise.

Vic nodded, but his expression was nothing short of bitter. "With her girls? Always. The rest of the world, however, we don't matter. Hence why we're here."

Glancing over at the two-story shopping strip, I noted Vybe dominated the entire second floor. Must've cost Lux a pretty penny. Seeing the establishment teeming with life shed a whole new light on her I never expected to see.

Perhaps she wasn't as villainous as she wanted the world to believe…

"Right, well, where do you want her then?" I questioned, anxious to get inside the building.

"As long as she's away from her friends and I can watch from the shadows, it doesn't matter."

"You say it like I know who these friends are. Quick

profiles would be helpful, mate," I snapped, luring another chuckle out of him.

"Suki's a shorty, on the curvy side with bleach blonde locks. She's loud, wild, covered in ink. Fat ass, too."

"Noted. She the only one?"

"Usually yes, but sometimes their third wheel makes an appearance. Ramsey's a redhead, thick girl, heavy goth style. She's more reserved than the other two."

The redhead from the party...

The one berating Lux in the middle of my office.

I remembered her clear as day.

"Anyone else I need to look out for?" I pressed.

Vic shook his head. "That I know of, no."

"I'm going in then." Pushing off the Rover, I fished out my beanie from my back pocket and pulled it over my head. "Make it quick, though. She goes off in seconds."

"Don't worry, I won't be far."

The inside of this place was nothing like I'd imagined. I was expecting a true dance studio, but there was seating, and a bar fully stocked in the far corner.

Classy yet industrial, the east and west walls were a glittering gold, a stark contrast to the exposed steel pipework above. The other two were nothing but mirrors. Everything popped against the ebony settee's and it was all tied together by the bare factory-style floors.

The eye-catcher was on the far wall, though—a mass neon sign that read Play. It flickered every few seconds, adding to the edginess of the overall aesthetic. The space before it was littered with bodies, but the lack of furniture made it clear that was the main performance area.

I became more impressed with every detail noticed, in awe of what Lux had so generously done for her friend… and then I saw her.

Tiny black caged halter top, loose army fatigues that still managed to hug her bubbly little ass, and black ankle boots. Those emerald locks were far more sleek tonight, too, cascading down her sparsely inked back.

But the genuine smile on her face as she chatted with the blonde Vic told me about was the cherry on top.

My mouth watered.

Every time I saw her, she looked better than the last.

More sexy.

More alluring.

More fucking beautiful.

I wanted to rush her, invade her personal space, drown her in my insanity as punishment for beguiling me without consent.

But I hung back, digging my feet into the concrete beneath me to keep myself in place.

After all, Vic was here. I had to play my cards right. One wrong move and he'd understand the sudden silence he kept pestering me about.

Chris Brown and *Yo Gotti* erupted through the speakers then, prompting Suki to squeal and drag Lux out onto the dance floor. Bodies that had been dancing just seconds prior made some room for the two, cheering and clapping as the blonde immediately broke out into a dance. It was clearly a practiced set, one Lux must've known, too, given how Suki cajoled her to join.

Lux laughed coyly, intent on not making herself the

center of attention, but Suki backed her ass up all over her and sucked her right into the rhythm.

The second her body started following the notes, I was rapt, on high alert. My dick pulsed to life, hands clenched at my sides. I had to grit my teeth, loathing the way every male eye in the room was suddenly on her.

And it only got worse as the seconds went on.

Vic was right, she was quite good, fluidly instep with Suki at every turn.

Rolling.

Grinding.

Spinning.

The routine was skilled yet highly seductive. Some women in the crowd danced along, others watched. The male population was completely fixated, and I was growing more agitated.

This madness went on for a full minute, a full torturous minute I didn't want to relive ever again. If Lux was going to shake her ass for anyone, it'd be for me.

And me only.

Not that she knew that yet.

"Told you she was good," Vic's voice slithered in my ear.

I swerved aside, not having expected him right in that moment. The smug look on his face raised my hackles all the more.

Chuckling, he slapped me on the back and stalked right past me towards the crowd.

As the song came to an end, the music faded out in entirety before the DJ switched on a microphone, tapping it several times. I snapped my head over in that direction just as he passed it to a panting Suki.

She smiled and thanked him with a tip of her head, turning toward the masses with an inked arm in the air.

"How's everyone doing tonight?" she bellowed, the heavy Brit of her accent taking me aback yet again.

How long had Lux know this bird?

Clamors arose around me, tearing me away from my silent observation.

"Sounds like you're all having a good time then, yeah?"

They cheered again.

"Well let's make it a better one, shall we? A sexier one."

More cheers and rowdy concurring whistles.

"I figured you'd agree," she chuckled. "Over the last two weeks, my advanced girls learned a little routine from Miss Lux here that'll knock your socks off. To show you, though, we need a volunteer, preferably male."

Lux.

Routine.

Male.

Volunteer.

I was there, at the front of the crowd before I could process what the hell I was doing. Literally front and center, chest heaving, eyes blazing, willing Suki to catch me.

Every second she spent looking elsewhere, I grew more anxious, barely containing myself from keeping silent.

When our eyes finally met, hers widened in shock. Clearly, she knew who I was.

A devious smile stretched her lips as she turned to Lux.

A clueless Lux, I should add, brow arched and all.

Suki tipped her head in my direction, prompting Lux to cut her eyes my way, and almost instantly, the color drained from her face.

I could practically hear her heart slamming in her chest from here.

"You," Suki spoke through the mic, pointing at me. "You. Right. There. Come take a seat in the hot seat, old chap."

A younger girl, possibly a student, deposited said seat beside Suki right as I stalked up to her with determined strides.

"Go on, sit," she ordered, motioning to the chair, devious smile still in place.

I sank as instructed, legs spread, draping my arms over the narrow back. My heart was lodged in my fucking throat.

What the hell was she planning?

"Helix, music please." She pointed at the DJ, gaze trained on Lux. "That's allllllll you, baby girl."

I heard the gasp loud and clear.

Watched those blue pools widen impossibly more from the corner of my eyes.

Lux shook her head and retreated several steps, holding her hands up. "Hell. No. Hell to the fuck no, Suk! Not happening!"

"Give it up for Lux, everyone!" Suki yelled into the mic.

Another round of cheering ensued, leaving Lux no room to rebut, especially when the music started up too—slow, sensual.

She looked mortified, begging her friend with a tortured stare not to do this to her. But Suki simply shrugged and retreated to the shadows.

Alone.

There were eyes *everywhere,* and yet it felt like we were alone. In a tunnel-like vision, all I could see was her, standing so close, yet so fucking far away. She must've felt it too, because those blue orbs fell on me, piercing me.

They were raging.

Intense.

She was on one fucked up rollercoaster of emotions right now, and I was to blame for most of it.

I both loved and hated it.

I *wanted* her to feel everything with me—every single solitary emotion—because ultimately, owned would be her favorite.

Lux was going to love being mine.

I just had to lay that claim first...

Sitting perfectly still, I allowed her to take me in. I didn't move. Didn't taunt her. I just sat there...until renewed purpose burned bright in her eyes.

A small curl played on my lips.

Snapping my head over to the DJ, I whistled for his attention. His dark stare lifted toward me almost instantly, headphones around his neck.

"Start it over," I ordered, circling a finger through the air.

Our audience seemed to agree.

Amongst their whistles, he nodded and got right to work, first slowing down the track, then scratching it out deftly to the beginning.

The sensual beat started building again.

Lux closed her eyes and brought her arms up above her head, rocking slowly side to side. I should've known right then this would be the best dance of my lips, but I was far too hypnotized to acknowledge my fate.

As soon as *Rihanna's* voice started crooning those provocative lyrics, Lux's hips started rolling.

Swaying.

The enticing motion traveling through her stomach to her arms.

Up to her head.

A quick roll fanned her hair around as she bent forward toward one leg and snapped back, stare on me as those green tresses fell over her face in a mess.

Fuck me, this was torture. The lines of her body were just... They were goddamn perfect—delicate curves adorned in a plethora of ink.

Curves I wanted beneath me again.

On top of me.

Trapped in my hands.

And the erotic words splashing through the speakers didn't help.

They only amplified her movements, doubling—no, tripling—their effect on me.

It took everything in me to stay fused to that damn chair, and once again, she picked up on it before I could slide the mask in place.

Sinking to her knees, she rolled her head around once more and stretched out onto her hands, a wicked smirk puckering her already pouty lips.

Goading me, she was purposely goading me.

Look at her—rolling around on the floor, eyes pinning me to the seat as she arched her ass in the air, shaking it around for everyone to see.

And then that crawl, that dick-twitching little kitty cat crawl with claws and all before she slithered into my lap, pressing her back flush to my front. An inked arm wrapped around my neck from behind as she ground all over me in time to the music, that sweet scent of hers slamming into my senses faster than three lines of blow.

I was fucking salivating like a dog.

All I wanted to do was snake a hand around her throat and take a bite into her neck, sink my teeth as far in as her adorned skin would allow.

Suck the bitch right out her until she couldn't refuse me anymore.

But I didn't do a damn thing, mostly because I was so focused on not going rock hard beneath my jeans, which wasn't the easiest feat when driving me mad was quite obviously her ultimate goal.

Felt like some unspoken revenge.

Maybe it was.

"Such a tease," I growled in her ear, trying my damnedest not to put my hands on her.

Vic was watching—hard. I could feel his stare.

Fuck, I needed to get her alone.

"You literally volunteered for this, remember? Deal with it," she snapped, pushing off me with another roll of her ass.

But I slipped a finger through one of the loopholes at the back of her fatigues and pulled her back on my lap.

She squeaked softly, but quickly adjusted the flow of her routine as hoots and hollers went off around us.

"I need you to listen to me. Don't look around or make it obvious—but you're being watched," I lied.

Well, only half-lied.

"By who?" she quizzed.

"I don't know. Never seen him before in my life. I followed him here after overhearing your name come out of his mouth."

"What does he look like?" Another fucking torturous roll of her ass right on my dick.

"It doesn't matter right now," I gritted out. "We need to get outside."

"How?"

"Slap me."

"What?!" she hissed, pushing off me long enough to spin around gracefully and climb back into my lap, emerald green tresses falling over us like a veil.

"I'm gonna get handsy, love. Slap me and run out back. I'll come after you."

"Are you serious right now?"

"Yes, do it," I cooed, trailing my hands up along her thighs to her ass.

The second I gripped it with force, Lux gasped and reared back, whacking her palm straight across my cheek.

My head snapped sideways from the blow, face burning from her strike. Our audience was gaping, sucking in heaps of air as Lux flew off my lap and ran through the crowd.

The DJ cut off the song, drowning the room in a heavy silence.

Everyone was watching me.

I sat there for a moment or so, cupping my cheek to make it appear as realistic as possible, especially with Vic's gaze being all the more palpable than it was before.

I'd handle it, but first I needed to handle the reason why he was even here.

29. I CAN'T STOP
Roman

♫ *Spazzn - Decap and Gyrefunk* ♫

I sat there for a good three minutes before finally racing out behind Lux. On the way, I shot Vic a quick text letting him know I was taking care of it and to disappear before someone caught wind of his presence.

That *should* take care of him, but I wasn't holding my breath. He was more curious these days, more vigilant. Always asking fucking questions and showing up anywhere at the drop of a hat. But anonymity was still that of importance to him, so although there was a slight chance Lux or Suki might have already seen him, there's no way he'd risk it further by following me out the door.

Barreling down the steps, I jumped off the final three and bolted to the back of the building as soon as my feet hit the pavement. I couldn't seem to move fast enough, my limbs still somewhat weak after the strain I'd put my body through to keep my dick in check.

Took every fucking ounce of self-control within me, and let me tell you, it wasn't easy.

A smaller, mostly emptied car park was all that

awaited me when I made it around back. Surrounded by tall palms, there wasn't a soul in sight.

At least none that I could see within the lighting from the streetlamps.

"Lux?" I hissed, stepping around three large dumpsters, the gravel crunching beneath my boots.

No answer.

But then suddenly, I was pulled into the shadows between two of the receptacles.

"Woah!"

Lux had me cornered, small hand clenching the front of my tee, eyes paralyzing me in entirety.

"Were you lying to me?" she growled.

"About?"

"About the stalker! What else?!"

"No," I shook my head, "why would I lie about that?"

"Because you're you, you idiot, that's why!" She pushed me further into the steel at my back with a grunt. "Who is he?"

"I told you, I've never seen him before."

Why did you follow him here?" she pressed.

"Because…"

"Because what?!"

"Because it's clear he wants to hurt you, and that's not gonna fly with me," I grit out.

Those baby blues jutted out, but she didn't speak a single word. I couldn't decipher the expression on her face.

From the erratic tempo of my breaths, you'd have thought I ran a mile. My heart was jackhammering and I couldn't understand why after what happened inside that building not ten minutes ago.

But then I saw it.

That fire.

It didn't just spark in her eyes—*it burned every-where.* Hotter than any hell. From the inside out, I could feel it.

Scorching me.

Calling to me.

And just like the last time we were alone, we collided, more intensely if that were even possible.

Lips scraping.

Hands seeking purchase.

Her stalker was a thing of the past. I gripped her at the waist and tossed her in my spot, frantically reaching for her thighs thereafter to lift her off her feet.

She complied without protest, throwing her head back as she wrapped her legs around my waist.

Can't run now.

"We have to stop doing this," she panted, mewling softly as I nipped a trail up her neck.

"I can't," I bit down, my grip on her thighs forceful and possessive, "it feels too good. I fucking need you."

Lux's laugh was breathy, bordering on manical. "Why me? Why are you doing this to me?"

"What part?"

"All of it—from beginning to end. Why me?"

Did it matter?

It's not like I could tell her the truth anyway.

"Just shut up, Lux. It's not important." I slammed my

mouth against hers once more and kissed her with purpose.

Or at least I *tried* to.

"Like hell it's not!" She pushed me off, arm bent like a shield. "You've spent months harassing me, making my life a living hell, then you stupidly kiss me and suddenly you need me? Are you insane?"

There wasn't a lick of humor in her voice. She was completely serious.

This I could be honest about.

"Yes," I answered.

Evidently, that's not the answer she wanted to hear.

"Oh my God, you're fucking maddening!" She groaned, wiggling herself onto her feet.

Whether she was trying to run or not, I threw my hands down on either side of her, caging her in, the receptacle booming from my force.

"So are you—that's what you don't seem to understand."

"How am *I* maddening?" she spat incredulously. "I've done fuck all to you!"

"Fuck all? Really?" Now I was laughing. "And you think I'm insane? You've fucking possessed me—worse than any demon ever could."

"Oh, please. You kissed me once, Roman. Stop acting like—"

"Stop fucking calling me that!" I exploded.

I don't know why, but I was so fucking tired of hearing it come out of her mouth.

"It's your name, psycho!" she squeaked. "The fuck

would you like me to call you? Asshole? Douchebag? Motherfu—"

"Rome, Lux." My hands were on her again, nose in her hair. "Just Rome."

I'd been dying to hear her say it, especially in that little breathy tone of hers when I was touching her.

Just as I inhaled deeply, coiling around her like a snake, she pushed me off a second time, holding up a warning finger in my face.

"Stay away from me."

"I can't do that." I shook my head.

"I'm serious," she growled. "Stay. Away. from me, Rome. We aren't good for each other."

"I've already told you that you can't run from the King, kitty kat, but if you wanna continue living in the land of denial, then be my guest. I'll catch up to you eventually."

I would, too.

Eventually, Lux would give into me.

Into this.

The force was too strong for either one of us to escape.

"Kitty kat?" One of her sleek brows shot up as a scoff broke free. "What is it with you and animal names? Do I look like a damned cat to you?"

"No, but those eyes of yours are quite feline." A single step forward. "And those claws, those claws are quite sharp."

"I'm not afraid to use them." She firmed her finger, pointing one of said claws in question right at my throat.

"I believe it." I pushed her arm aside with ease, inching toward her again. "Can't wait to feel them running down my back when I finally—"

"When you finally nothing. Nothing is going to happen, Rome. Seriously, stay away from me. This," she motioned between us, "is a volatile mess, a disaster waiting happen."

"So you're going to keep denying you don't feel it?" I asked, insulted enough that she was able to slip past me and put at least five feet between us.

"I never said I didn't, but I'm not willing to risk anymore of my sanity to explore it. Promise me you'll stay away from me…"

Fuck no.

"Lux…" I tried, but she shook her head.

"Promise me, goddammit! In return, I'll leave you alone, too. I'll even give you a cut of my territories, whatever you want. Just stay away from me, please. I'm fucking begging you, and I never beg anyone for shit."

I heard the plea in her voice, but it was the ache in her eyes that hit me hardest.

I hated her all over again for doing this.

For torturing us both when she knew running away from this wasn't that easy.

A pointless feat.

I wanted to wring her neck, shake the common sense into her. But in a split-second decision, I decided to go along with it.

For now.

I'd bend her soon enough.

"Fine," I conceded, balling my hands into fists. "But who do I call for—"

"I'll have my PA get in touch with you. Goodnight, *Roman,* and goodbye."

And as quickly as she'd pulled me behind the dumpster was as quickly as she was gone.

30. TRICK OR TREAT

Lux

♫ *This is Halloween - Marilyn Manson* ♫

Two weeks had rolled by since the night Rome showed up at Vybe and, thankfully, he'd kept true to his word.

I hadn't seen him.

Hadn't heard from him.

Nothing.

On the one hand, I was grateful. Everything had spiraled *way* out of control, and we were falling captive to desires at an alarming pace. The only way to keep it at bay was to stay away from each other altogether.

A task easier said than done.

I was constantly astir. On edge. Wanting to seek him out. My body craved his touch, his kisses, the low timber of his voice in my ear when he growled in satisfaction. I wanted him so badly it—

"Earth to Lux."

That was Suki as she snapped her fingers in my face.

Refocusing on her dolled up features, I found Ramsey looming behind her, too, both of them staring at me with curious eyes.

"Are you okay?" she asked, arching a tattooed brow. "That's the third time you've zoned out in the last half hour."

The sad part was, she was absolutely right.

Drowning in a Roman King-induced Lala Land was all my brain seemed to be able to do these days. The flashbacks were so lucid, I actually felt the loss of his touch whenever I came to.

But since I was still somewhat ticked at Suki for forcing him on me that night, I hadn't bothered telling them yet. It would only confirm Suki's point, which would lead to a speech.

One I didn't care to hear.

Rolling my eyes, I shooed them away instead and rose onto my feet from Suki's cloud of a bed with a sigh. "I'm fine."

"You sure about that?" she called out right as I sauntered into her bathroom to get myself ready for our evening.

Black Widow make up covered the entire countertop, along with a straightener, a curling iron, and a large jug of fake blood.

Can't have Halloween without some gore.

"Yes," I lied, reaching for the eye primer.

"Positive?" she pressed.

"Mhmm."

"Hundred bucks says she was day dreaming about King again," I heard her murmur to Ramsey.

Wand in hand, I jerked still. "I heard that!"

"You were supposed to!" she yelled back.

I loathed when they did this shit.

Slamming the small bottle back onto the counter, I poked my head around the threshold and glared at my two so-called best friends. "Fuck you, okay? I was *not* day dreaming about him."

"No?" Suki crossed her arms, distributing all her weight on one stocking-clad leg. "Then what were you dwelling on so hard? And don't say nothing because you know I'm not that vapid."

Ramsey followed suit, daring me with the quirk in her expression to lie, and still all I could do was shrug.

"It's nothing. Just some work shit."

Suki and Ramsey exchanged a knowing look before they pinned it on me.

"I'm calling bull, L," Ramsey piped up first.

"Oh, it's bull, alright," Suki agreed, bounding up to me with an accusing finger pointed at my chest. "Do I need to remind you I was there? I *saw* you, L, and I don't mean *just* your performance. I *saw* you and King outside after the fact. All of it."

Ramsey gasped and shuffled forward, too, as my entire body broke out in goose pimples. "What happened?"

"You wanna tell her or should I?" Suki snapped.

I bounced my gaze between the two.

Should I tell them?

Had Suki really seen or was she spouting shit out of her ass to get me to talk? Wouldn't be the first time.

"Well, I'd like to know what you supposedly saw before I tell Rams how insane you are."

Suki looked at me like I'd lost my mind, her mouthing popping open and all. "Are you kidding me right now? Is he frying your brain cells that much?"

"Just tell me what you saw Suk!" I barked.

My patience had about reached its end.

"They were arguing." She turned to Ramsey. "I couldn't hear about what exactly with the music blaring, but they were arguing, Lux had him cornered. And from one second to the next, they were on each other like rabid animals. Like they needed each other to breathe."

Ramsey's eyes blew up. I could almost see a million little hearts swimming to the surface within them.

"Is this true?" she asked.

I didn't move a single muscle. Didn't speak. I just stared at them with the most blank expression possible.

Wasn't blank enough, though.

The answer must have been written all over my face given the way realization dawned over hers. "You're sleeping with the enemy?!"

Fucks sake.

Attempting to remain as calm as possible, I offered them a simple shake of my head. "We haven't slept together."

"Yet," Suki chimed in.

"No, not yet, for your information," I retorted. "We came to an agreement actually."

An anxious silence briefly filled the room as they stood before me, waiting for me to elaborate.

The sigh that left me could not have sounded more exasperated. "We agreed to stay away from each other."

Suki scoffed and rolled her eyes while Ramsey busted out laughing, shaking her flaming red head.

"I'd like to point out that I—"

"If you say called it so help me God, Rams," I growled, beyond irate at their reactions.

"She did, though," Suki countered in her defense. "We both did, but that's beside the point. I could give three fucks if you're turning him inside out or not. What I want to know is why the bloody hell you've been hiding this from us? I mean, I suspected, hence why I did what I did, but really? Really, L?"

The was a tinge of an ache in her voice. An ache I'd put there by being unnecessarily secretive, an ache that lanced right through me and wound itself around my heart.

I couldn't have felt more like scum than I did in that moment, swallowing down the lump of guilt that had briskly accumulated in my throat.

"I'm sorry, okay? It wasn't intentional. I barely knew how to handle it myself so I kept my mouth shut."

"Yeah? And now I'm going to keep my mouth shut before *I* say something that's going to ruin our evening to shit," Suki grated.

"Both of you stop." Ramsey stepped between us, holding a palm out to our chests. "Now is not the time to hash this out, but we will discuss this later, got it?"

The question was clearly directed at me, and while I really didn't want to go into depth on this topic just yet, I knew I didn't have much a choice anymore. They knew and there was no way to backtrack from here.

"Fine," I conceded, my voice even and surprisingly steady. "I'm going to finish getting ready then. If you need me, I'll be doing my makeup."

"Don't put on too much," Ramsey called out behind me. "Our masks will cover it."

Yeah, yeah, yeah, whatever.

She had a point, but only to an extent. *Purge Crew* or not, I didn't intend to wear the damn thing all night. Ladies drank for free until ten, and I planned to be blasted by then.

Twenty minutes later, I'd made myself up to near perfection and was mid-way through applying falsies when my phone vibrated on the counter. I stole a quick glance at the screen as I set the lash in place, only to do a double-take and nearly drop the damn thing in the sink.

Unknown: *I can't stop thinking about you…*

My heart immediately started banging in my chest. I stared at the message for several long moments before dropping the tweezers and snatching up the phone.

Me: *Who is this?*

Deep down, I knew damn well who it was, but I tried convincing myself otherwise. I mean, it couldn't be, right?

When the reply came through almost instantaneously, I peeked out into Suki's room to ensure they weren't going to barge in at any given moment, and shut the door, pressing my back flush against its cool surface.

Unknown: *Take a guess…or do you really have that many poor blokes caught under your spell?*

It *was* him.
Thump, thump, thump.
My fingers moved at lightning speed.

Me: *JFC. How the hell did you get my number?*
Unknown: *I have my ways.*
Me: *What do you want, Roman?*
Unknown: *Let me see you.*
Me: *NO.*
Unknown: *Five minutes, Lux. Give me five minutes. I'm going mad.*

So was I, but no. I couldn't allow it. We all know what happened the second I let that man anywhere near me…

Me: *Not my problem.*
Unknown: *It is very much your problem considering it's your fault. Five minutes won't kill you.*
Me: *And yet that's five minutes I don't have, especially for you. Goodbye, Roman. Lose my number.*

Setting the phone back onto the counter, I dragged my gaze up to my flustered reflection. Getting rid of Roman of was going to be harder than I thought.

My phone buzzed yet again.

Unknown: *What could you possibly be doing that you don't have a spare five minutes?*
Me: *Not that it's any of your business, but I'm going out.*
Unknown: *Where?*

If I told him, he'd show. There wasn't a single doubt about it in my mind.

So I opted for vague.

Me: *Halloween party.*
Unknown: *Where is it?*
Me: *Noneya.*

And that's how I left it, hoping like hell he'd take the hint and leave it at that, too.

Spoiler alert…he didn't.

CREEPY GLOWING MASKS WITH THE X'D OUT EYES.

Blood-stained white tees.

Black thigh-high nylons.

By nine o'clock—and without further inquisition on the Roman front—the girls and I made it to *Club Space* in our full-on *Purge* gear.

By nine-thirty, Stryker and his boys joined us at the bar, also in *Purge* ensembles.

And by ten, I'd effectively accomplished my goal for the evening.

I was feeling good.

Really good.

The kind of good where everything is wonderful and comical, where everyday problems and stressors don't exist—leaving you weightless.

Dazed.

In a state of bliss.

Smile on my face, I swayed around on the crowded dance floor with my girls, jamming out to *Major Lazer.* We were packed together like lab rats, but I didn't care.

I couldn't be bothered to give a single fuck.

The vibe in here was insane.

Freeing.

Strobe lights above flickered and flashed in different colors, heightening the energy rippling through the club with every minute that passed. Bodies writhed to the beat, drinks were passed along, substances of all kinds were consumed at every turn.

It's like *Ultra* and Halloween fucked on ecstacy and had a baby.

Taking another sip from my drink, I dragged my gaze over to Suki. She was shamelessly all over Stryker, staking her claim for every woman in the near vicinity to see. Ramsey wasn't too far behind with Marco either, though hers wasn't as possessive as it was drunk and horny.

I shook my head amusedly.

Fucking slags, the both of them.

When *G-Eazy and Halsey* faded in with "Him and I," hoots and hollers of approval erupted all around us. Even I belted out an appraising scream, lifting my arms in the air.

I threw my head back.

Shut my eyes.

I loved this song despite what it stood for and *who* it made me think of.

No, we're not going there…

Pushing him back to the recess' of my mind, I continued swaying my hips, rocking side to side sensually, completely lost in the music.

But that's when I felt it…

Searing body warmth.

A strong arm around my waist.

A possessive hand at my hip and warm lips ghosting along the column of my neck.

No.

I stilled in place, melting inadvertently into this familiar touch regardless of my girls standing not five feet away.

Regardless of my brain screaming, "*Abort, abort!*"

"Didn't I tell you that you couldn't run from the King?" His voice somehow boomed in my ear above everything else, reeling me further into him.

Not a single word came out of my mouth.

And believe me, I tried. *My* mouth popped open, ready to outcry my demurral.

But words failed me.

Suddenly, I was ten times more buzzed; light-headed, weak in the knees, my stomach one giant knot.

He was here.

How?

Why?

"Tongue tied, are we?" Roman chuckled, rolling his hips against me.

Again, I couldn't answer. It felt like every set of eyes in the room was on me.

On us.

The girls' were for sure. Stryker and Marco, too. I didn't have to look their way for confirmation; their stares were more than palpable.

Fixated.

Downright shocked.

I had to get Roman out of here before the drunken inquisition started.

Reaching back, I gripped his wrist and yanked him off the dance floor without any explanations. In my half sensible state, I trudged through the masses in an emotional fog, the palm of my hand aflame at the feel of Roman's skin beneath my own.

Why the fuck was he here?

How did he find me?

Is this what it had come to? Him stalking me because I wouldn't give him what he wanted?

Correction, what you both want, commented that little voice in my head.

I almost groaned aloud, frustrated at everything, especially myself. I never should have let him kiss me. Never should have let him put his hands on me. Never should've given him that fucking dance either.

I should've stood my ground and told Suki to handle it.

But no, the masochist in me wanted another taste, and I gave in.

Twice over.

The span of the club seemed to go on forever until finally the front doors came into view. I picked up the pace, desperate to fill my lungs with fresh air, to put an infinite amount of space between us and end this once and for all. I was literally dragging him, weaving in and out of every person standing between me and some sort of freedom.

The second we made it out into the muggy October night, I yanked Roman across the street without regard for oncoming traffic and whipped him onto the sidewalk with a growl. Chest heaving, I released him with purpose and took several steps back, inhaling heaps of air.

"What? What the fuck do you want?" I questioned, arms flying out in frustration, my gaze colliding with every set of eyes on us.

It seemed we'd enraptured an audience in our hasty exit.

Roman laughed softly, clenching and unclenching his fists as he began advancing on me. "You know what I want."

Each step forward felt like the ground shook along with it, propelling me backwards on shaky legs until my back hit the stucco exterior of another club.

"I want *you*," he gritted out.

"And I've already told you no."

He was on me in seconds flat, looming over me, his face illuminated by the streetlamps around us. Hands falling to my hips, he pressed himself against me as the tip of his nose skated along my jaw.

Fend him off, fend him off, fend him off!

Ridiculously dazed after two point five seconds of contact, I somehow managed to shove his chest and jerk him off me just slightly.

But he was back in double the speed.

The look that awaited me—while satisfied to have me where he wanted me—was also completely serious. "No isn't really an option."

I saw red, pure flaming indignant red.

Who the hell did he think he was? How many times did we need to go through this for him to understand?

"You agreed! What part of stay away—"

"EHHH," he cut me off with this obnoxious buzzer sound, cocking his head to one side. "Don't come at me with that bullshit again because right now, at this point time, it's the wrong fucking answer, *and you know it damn well.*"

He growled that last bit.

So deep and so deliciously malevolent, I actually found myself shivering, drawing that sinister grin across his face.

Feeling victorious, he assessed me closely from head to toe, blue eyes blazing, his breath hot against my cheek. "You know you're mine, Lux—have been for a while now. Since before that kiss if you want to get technical."

I rolled my eyes, hoping the darkness would hide the heat building in my cheeks. "I'm *not* yours, and you seriously need to get over that."

"Don't tell me what to do, kitty kat. I'll obsess about whatever and whoever I want," he purred, dragging the pad of his thumb along my bottom lip.

I laughed sardonically to keep up the appearance, but he was already wearing me down. I'd been alone with him less than five minutes and he was already wearing me the fuck down.

My heart galloped.

My stomach flip-flopped a million times.

How did this man always manage to do this to me, and more importantly, why did my body always betray me?

"You laugh, but I don't hear a no. You know I'm right," he added.

"No, you're not."

"I am, trust me. I can see right through that shiny metal shield you hold in front of me. You want me as badly as I want you. Two fiends in one fucked up pod."

"You're delusional," I stated and he chuckled.

"Sometimes, I suppose, but I'm not when it pertains to this. Have you taken a moment to really think about what this could mean? Do you know how powerful we could be together, Lux?"

"I'm already powerful," I barely grated.

"Yes, you are. Now imagine that doubled. Double the power, double the rewards. The benefits," he growled, rolling his hips against me. "You know I'd never let anyone hurt you, right?"

A blatant scoff left me. "Yeah, cause you'd rather hurt me yourself."

"Only in all the delicious, torturous ways you like, love."

I swallowed deeply, trying my damndest not to envision the filth his words brought to mind.

"We had an agreement," I reminded him. "Why do you insist on making this harder than it needs to be?"

Breaths shallow, his nostrils flared. "Because I can't stay away from you. I only agreed for your sake—that doesn't mean it's what I want."

"You want Miami? Take it! Take it all! If it means you'll leave me be then just fucking take it all!" I bellowed, trying and miserably failing to push him away.

He was far too lithe, though.

Catching my wrists in his grip, he shoved me back into the stucco as a growl unfurled from deep within his chest.

"I don't want it if I can't have you. What part of that don't you understand?"

"All of it. I was serious then, and I'm still serious now. Stay away from me, Rome. Go find someone else to aim your crazy at!"

Not really what I wanted, but I hadn't accepted that yet.

Hadn't even realized it yet.

Until I stormed back into *Space* and he didn't come after me...

31. WARMER

Roman

♫ *Monsters - Ruelle* ♫

"**M**um, I'm home," I call out, as I shut the front door behind myself.

I expect to hear her reply from the kitchen—as she usually does around this hour—but nothing follows.

I drag my eyes to the clock on the wall; 6:30 p.m.

She should be definitely home, so should my sister, Siobhan.

The lights are on both upstairs and downstairs, but not a sound resonates. The hairs at the nape of my neck prickle as silence lingers around me.

Something isn't right.

Dropping my bag in the foyer, I trail through the house quietly, keeping my eyes peeled. For what, I don't know, but I can't shake the bad feeling suddenly looming over my shoulders.

In the living room, the telly sits on one of mum's favorite crime programs. There's a glass of wine on the coffee table and one of her romance novels laid out with a bookmark lodged in the spine. Clearly, she's home, and at a glance, nothing seems out of place.

Except for the silence.

It's so silent I can hear my pulse thundering in my ears as I continue on to the kitchen.

"Mum?" I call out a second time, skidding to a stop upon crossing the threshold.

She's not here either, but it's the sight that greets me that runs my blood ice cold.

A puddle of wine and shards of glass cover a portion of the floor.

I try to not panic, try to convince myself it was a simple accident and perhaps she's upstairs cleaning herself up, but the remainder of the backdrop all but screams there's been a struggle of sorts.

The oven door is wide open.

The roast she'd clearly been preparing is still inside.

The stove top is on, too, two pots boiling away on the highest setting.

Forget thundering—my heart now slams violently in my chest.

"Mum?!" I bellow a third time, racing through the kitchen to the threshold on the other side.

That's when I see red.

Blood.

Dark.

Fresh.

I freeze.

They're the smallest of droplets, but as I step into the dining room, the droplets grow larger, forming puddles of all sizes.

Then I realize they're no longer contained to the floor.

A long smeared hand print paints the wall beside the china cabinet. My eyes follow it a short ways, noting how it ends abruptly.

My stomach churns.

That bad feeling is now full-on ominous. I feel a cold sweat coming on. I'm trying not to think the worst, but how can I not?

In my search of another clue, I find two hand prints on the floor, prints that were clearly dragged out of the dining room to the...

Stairs.

I stare up it's height.

Sporadic droplets stain the worn carpet all the way up.

Bracing myself, I follow them to the very top, stopping at the landing to examine both sides of the corridor. There's nothing on my right, where mine and Sio's rooms are.

But on the left...all the lights are on.

Swallowing deeply, I inch down it's length, only then realizing should there be someone in my home who's not meant to be here, I have nothing to defend myself with other than my fists.

I look around.

All that's readily available are the family photos on the walls.

Plucking one down, I figure this is better than nothing. I can bash an intruder over the head, then use the glass that breaks free as a shank.

And it's as that gruesome image plays in mind that I walk in on the most gruesome image of them all.

The image that would strip me of the last bit of my humanity and officially sell my soul to the devil...

The white Lillies sitting on my bed mocked me, as all her little gifts usually did.

It's because of *her* any of that even happened in the first place..

That selfish, vindictive little bitch.

My ex was a million times worse than Lux, despite what Vic would say, and she'd fucking found me.

Again.

Swiping the bunch with an aggravated hand, I bent them in half until they snapped and tossed them onto the floor, destroying the petals bit by bit with the soles of my Oxford's.

If Liza was here, that meant I was going to have to get the fuck out of here soon.

And at that moment, it meant without Lux...

I was not about to let that happen.

If she were mine, I'd say we could leave together, get to know each other better, travel the world...

But she wasn't, and I was on the verge of a nuclear explosion.

I couldn't take it anymore.

I only let her go last night simply because she'd been drinking. I could smell the fruity concoction on her breath. A lot of her bravado was all liquid courage. There were cops, too, and way too many people stopping to watch, as though we were some street-side act hoping to go viral on Instagram.

But this front of hers wouldn't last forever.

Hell, she was already showing signs of throwing in the towel and giving in.

I just had to push a little harder... Before it was too late.

♫ *Issues - Julia Michaels* ♫

Roman: *I can't do this. I'm going fucking crazy, Lux. I need to see you.*

Glued to my couch with wine goblet in hand, I'd been reading and re-reading that damned text for over ten minutes.

Not forty-eight hours had passed since I last saw him, and here he was, seeking me out yet again.

Worst part? I wanted to respond, too.

Sighing, I took another long sip from my glass, draining it in entirety. There wasn't enough wine in the world to deal with this dilemma. Hell, even the stronger shit wouldn't help at this point.

I didn't know what else to do.

The man was immune to rejection and I was driving myself mad trying to keep him away.

Because you're not really rejecting him...

It's true, I wasn't. I knew it, he knew, even you know it. As convincing as I tried to make myself out to be, we all knew I was only playing myself...

Which led me to wonder what would happen if I let myself indulge once?

Just once.

Nothing I'd done up this moment had worked, so perhaps giving in to this obsession would aid us in working each other out of our systems.

Yeah, okay.

I groaned at the sheer ridiculousness of my thoughts. Who was I kidding? Indulging would only worsen the problem.

My phone pinged again.

And again.

And again.

Dropping my gaze to my lap, I read the new messages now displayed on my screen.

Roman: *I'll beg if I have to.*
Roman: *I just want to see you.*
Roman: *We can chill, smoke, whatever you want.*

Every text hurdled me back and forth between livid and frenzied. The man was not easily deterred and it was becoming more and more impossible to say no. I had so many other pressing matters to be worrying about, like Phantom 2.0, that I wasn't sure how much more energy I could put into holding the door closed on Rome's face.

Ugh.

My eyes drifted back to the screen, re-reading the last text.

Roman: *We can chill, smoke, whatever you want.*

I *could* do with a smoke...

Call it a crazy spur of the moment decision, or maybe I was willing to take advantage of the man for my own selfish reasons, but with a muttered "fuck it," I typed out a quick, one-line message and sent it before I could give myself the chance to overthink it.

Me: *We need to talk.*

His reply came within minutes.

Roman: *I'll meet you anywhere.*
Me: *Your spot. Half hour.*
Roman: *I'll be there.*

Shit.

What the hell had I just gotten myself into?

Flying off the couch, I raced down the hallway to my room and scrambled into the closet like a lunatic. I'd gone from zero to one-hundred in seconds flat. Completely frazzled, I couldn't find anything to wear, mostly because everything I had was either too provocative or what I wore to work.

Storming back into my room, I ripped through my dresser and decided to go with black sweatpants. A simple white t-shirt. I threw my hair up in a messy bun, too, and kept my face as make-up free as possible.

Small wing, a bit of mascara, and a nude lippie.

I was out the door shortly after that, nervously sliding into the G-class.

If Suki and Ramsey found out I was doing this, they'd hold it against me forever. I still hadn't heard the end of the Vybe ordeal or Halloween.

Twenty minutes later, I made it to the top of the Panorama, my steps much quieter in my Converse joggers than in my usual heels. I was so quiet Rome didn't notice me until I was mere feet away from him.

That sly grin tilted up one corner of his mouth as he pivoted toward me. "Hi there."

"Hi." I smiled weakly in return, trying not focus on the fact he was wearing those gray sweatpants again.

"You alright?" he asked.

The question caught me off guard, cocking my head backwards just slightly. "Yeah, why?"

Rome chuckled and motioned to where I stood. "You said we needed to talk."

"Oh, yeah." *Fucking relax, Lux.* "It won't take long."

"I'm not worried about that. I've got time."

I felt my cheeks heat in slight embarrassment. "Shall we sit then?"

Nodding, Rome sunk down against the ledge and patted the spot beside him. "Shall we smoke?"

"*Please,*" I stressed, dropping down beside him, leaving a somewhat safe distance between us. "It's been a hell of a long few weeks."

"I'm going to take a guess I have something to do with it?" he asked, pulling out a small pipe and a ziplock bag with at least three grams of bud from his pocket.

"Yes and no."

"How does that work? It's either yes or no."

I didn't know how to answer.

He'd already sworn to me the stalker was very much real and not just a ploy to get me alone, but Phantom 2.0 was nowhere to be found...

"Were you truly honest about the stalker?" I blurted out, keeping my eyes on what he was doing rather than him.

"I told you that night at Vybe—yes. Why?"

"My boys can't seem to find him or any information about him."

"Your boys?" The slight hint of jealousy in his voice prompted me to snap my gaze up to his face.

"Roscoe and Vic," I explained hurriedly. "Roscoe is head of security. Vic acts as a personal assistant of sorts, or well, he used to be."

"Used to?"

I nodded. "We're not really on speaking terms these days. He's been rather MIA, too."

"I see," he said simply, passing me the pipe and a lighter. "You get greens, love."

Taking the proffered paraphernalia, I held the pipe up to my lips and flicked the lighter, bringing the flame up to the end and sucking in a drag.

All the while, those blue eyes, curious as ever, regarded me throughout.

I instantly regretted inhaling so deeply. Whatever the strain was, it was strong as hell, the mass cloud of smoke catching roughly in my throat. I let it go with a quickness but still found myself nearly coughing up a lung, to which Rome grinned and shook his head. His expression was both delighted and a little surprised.

"Rookie cough," he joked, tucking everything back into his pockets.

I took another quick hit and passed it off, blowing this one out—thankfully—without incident. "I don't smoke often. Plus, it's strong as fuck."

"Sure, blame it on the bud."

"I'm serious," I squeaked, shoving his arm playfully.

Me, squeaking, being playful.

What the hell was wrong with me?

Rome must've clocked on to my unease because he doubled back on the conversation. That, or our little moment made him anxious as well. "So back you were saying... Stalker. Your men can't find him?"

"No." I shook my head. "He's another you—a ghost. Phantom 2.0."

"Phantom, huh?" He smirked.

Cocky ass.

"The Phantom Menace," I corrected him.

Chuckling, he shook his head. He didn't seem at all fazed by my jab, his smirk darkening all the more as he lifted the pipe to his lips and took another hit.

I watched him, completely entranced—the way he took a pull, how he tipped his head back before letting it go. It was all just so fluid...so sexy.

"I can assure you he's not a ghost," he exhorted through his puff, blowing out a few perfectly shaped O's.

"He's very much real, and he sounded highly determined to get to you."

"Again, kind of like you."

Rome grinned slyly. "Pretty much."

My stomach whirled.

This was all so chill it bordered on bizarre.

I actually *wanted* to be here with him.

Swallowing down such realizations, I laid my head back against the ledge and curled up my knees, hugging them to keep myself grounded. "What exactly did you overhear him saying again?"

"I didn't catch all of it. Really only paid attention once I heard your name. Said something about paying you the visit you deserved."

"What did he look like?"

"About my height, maybe a tad shorter. Fade. Tanned skin."

I scoffed a laugh, eyes glued to the dark sky above us. "I'll never find him—there's a million of those in Miami. "

Typical fuck boys.

"We'll find him," Rome assured me, that one little word snapping my head toward him with such speed, I nearly gave myself whiplash.

"*We?*" I hedged.

"I can help." He shrugged casually. "That is, if you want me to."

"Enemies don't usually help one another," I pointed out.

"They also don't do this, but fuck it. Come here…"

"Where is here?"

Rome crooked a finger, pointing it almost on himself. "Right here. Come closer."

And I did, without my usual hesitations.

He said fuck it, right?

Leaning in closer, I broke through his personal space like he wanted, bursting my own now barely withstanding bubble in the process. The heat radiating off him wrapped around me as he lit the pipe and went in for the kill.

I should've been expecting it, but God, when his lips pressed flush against mine, they seared me.

His fingers clasped around my chin as he blew the cloud of smoke in my mouth, slowly, teasing my lips in between.

It was some hellish type of heaven.

My eyes fell shut through his gentle assault and I found myself having to stifle down the moan that threatened to break free, my entire body buzzing to life at the simple feel of his skin on mine.

Light-headed, heart thundering, I pulled back, breezily blowing out what remained of his puff, and tried to collect myself.

To move away from him.

But all too quickly, I found him even closer, shattering what little remained of my resolve. His minty breath was hot against my skin as his lips ghosted along my cheek. And then he was kissing me again, hand cupping the back of neck to keep me in place. I couldn't stop him if I wanted to, opening for him as he deepened the kiss.

"I want you, Lux," he mumbled against my lips,

attempting to pull me into his lap. "I want a truce."

"What?" I eased back on a single breath.

"I want a truce," he repeated, holding my stare. "I meant it when I said it; I don't want Miami if you're not part of the package."

"Rome, I..." I didn't know what to say.

A truce changed everything.

If he wasn't against me then that meant...

"Please. Give me a chance to prove myself to you. Give me a chance to prove to you how badly I need you. How badly I fucking crave you."

My subconscious was screaming 'yes,' all but belting it from the rooftop for him to hear, but the words wouldn't come out of my mouth.

"You're killing me," I somehow managed, barely containing the smile quirking my lips.

"I'm dead already, trust me. If I can have you, though, a motherfucker might just rise from hell," he quipped.

And there went my smile. My cheeks flushed along with it.

That pesky question I'd been dwelling on came racing back to the forefront of my mind.

What would happen if I let myself indulge once? Just once.

"You get one chance," I blurted, "and it stays between us."

"Sooo truce?" He grinned, holding a hand out to me.

I observed it before a split-second before leisurely slipping my palm in his.

"Truce."

33. AFTER HOURS
Roman

♫ *Netflixxx - Brytiago and Bad Bunny* ♫

That night on the Panorama was the turning point in our relationship.

I had her.

Maybe not in a sole proprietary sense, but after all we'd been through, including trying to outsmart destiny, I finally fucking had her on the same wave-length as me.

No more running.

No more denying.

No more pretending this shit between us wasn't real as fuck.

I had her, and soon, she'd officially be mine. I knew it was going to take a lot more than a little weed and calling a truce to get there, but this was a start.

Now more than ever, I was going to have to lay the charm on real thick, though. With Liza only two steps behind, time was undoubtedly limited.

Of the essence.

And when the time came to pack my bags and leave, Lux would be coming with me. I refused to leave her behind.

Unless she wanted to stand beside me and go to war.

But that would mean having to regale her with the painful pieces of my past…

No, too soon. It was too bloody soon for all that. With my luck, she'd revert to old ways and push me away again.

I'd fought too hard to lose her because of my demons and what they'd forced me to do.

Who they'd forced me to become.

I'd cross the bridge when we got there. For now, I was going to relish every goddamn moment she allowed me to spend with her.

In the flesh.

On the phone.

Every single one.

"What are you doing for Thanksgiving?" I asked her, falling flat on my bed after a shower. Throwing the phone on speaker, I laid it on my chest as she replied, her sultry voice filling my room.

"Nothing—I don't celebrate it. It's an American holiday."

"Newsflash, kitty kat, you live in America."

"I know, but I'm not American." I could practically see her shrugging. "What about you? Any plans?"

"Naaa," I drawled. "I don't celebrate it either."

"So then why ask me if—"

"I was fucking with you."

"As always," she laughed.

I couldn't help myself from laughing, too. She was right.

But I was about to change that...

"Serious question this time, I swear."

"Go on."

"What are you doing tonight?"

"Well," she sighed, "as soon as I get the fuck out of this office, I'm going straight home and plopping my ass on the couch to watch some Netflix."

"You're still there?" I checked the clock on my nightstand. "At this hour?"

It was almost 9.

"Yup—I've been deep in the legal jargon hole that is *Sephora's* contract for hours now. My eyes can't take much more, though, neither can my brain. I may tap out within the next five minutes or so."

Lux and tap out in the same sentence brought one thing to mind. "Would you object to me inviting myself over for your Netflix night?"

"Are you trying to Netflix and Chill?" Humor dripped off her tone, but there was a provocative edge to it, too.

One I hadn't expected.

If my dick could grin, it would've.

"I mean…" I trailed off, unsure of how to answer. "If the opportunity were to—"

"It won't," she snickered, dissolving any and all of the crude visions swimming through my mind.

It was worth a shot…

"Is that a yes, though?" I hedged.

Lux hummed exaggeratedly. "Only if you promise to be a good boy."

Boy?

"I'm not no boy, Lux," I reminded her, my voice deathly low. "I'm a grown ass man, but yes, I'll behave."

"Fine. Meet me at my place in an hour. I'll text you the address."

I grinned victoriously. "See you soon, kitty kat."

Click.

~

EXACTLY ONE HOUR LATER, THE SHINY METAL LIFT DOORS slid open on Lux's floor; the penthouse.

I was in awe almost immediately at the elegantly dark foyer that greeted me.

Round in shape, the walls were adorned with an ebony damask-print wallpaper, the wainscoting wrapped around the bottom half an equally dark shade. The tiled floors were a glittering black as well, and in the very center of the room was a small Victorian-style rounded table with an obsidian gothic-inspired chandelier hung above. On the table itself sat a dozen white roses in a crystal vase, contrasting nicely against the ominous tinge around them.

And then there were the front doors—tall and dark, like the entrance to an enchanted castle with large rounded gold knockers.

Curling my hand around one, I dropped it against the hard surface beneath it twice, the sound echoing through the room around me.

"Coming!" her muffled voice called out from inside.

Twenty seconds later, the locks were coming undone, and one of the doors flew open.

Lux smiled, almost shyly, and raked a hand through her hair. "Hi."

"Hi, yourself." I smiled back, shoving my already restless hands into my pockets.

This was going to be fucking torture.

Stepping aside, she opened the door wider and motioned for me to enter. "Come in."

I tipped my head graciously and followed her lead.

Crossing the threshold somehow felt like yet another milestone in our relationship. Sure, the woman had already been to my home, but it wasn't under the same circumstances.

Not even close.

"Make yourself comfortable. I'm just gonna pull the pizza out of the oven," she said, slipping past me in a hurry.

But that's when I noted what she was wearing; a white thinly-strapped crop top and teeny tiny pajama shorts covered in little bats. They hugged her ass, and the white fabric was nearly translucent, leaving almost nothing to the imagination.

She'd done this on purpose, the little minx.

She *wanted* me to react.

"Where do you think you're going?" I lunged for her, twirling her back toward me with a quick hand at her wrist. "I told you I'd behave—that doesn't mean I'm not kissing you."

"I never said you couldn't kiss me." She fell lax in my grasp as I wound an arm around her waist.

"The question is, do you want me to?" I asked, taking her chin between my fingers.

Nodding, she shut her eyes. Shifted closer and clenched my tee in her fists.

It was the tiniest sliver of submission, but fuck, I loved it, tightening my hold around her.

Pressed so closely together, her scent suddenly invaded me. I inhaled deeply, relishing it, savoring it.

It awakened the beast, waiting to be unleashed at any moment. My dick twitched beneath my sweats, luring my hands to the swell of her ass.

If I wasn't careful, I'd end up eating her alive.

And that would definitely violate the terms of my promise.

Flashing my tongue out, I licked at the seam of her lips first, coaxing her open for me. She complied without reservation and slid her small hands around my neck, willing me to go in for the kill.

I did, only softly, sensually, like our first kiss up on the Panorama. I wanted her to feel every last bit of it, feel it slither its way through her body like a venom.

"You're trying to kill me," she mumbled against my lips.

"Says the woman who wants me to behave but greeted me in scraps of clothing." Pulling away, I bore my stare on her until those blue pools fluttered open.

Her cheeks heated, a devilish yet subtle smirk curling her lips.

Yeah, she'd definitely done it on purpose, and she

cemented the notion when she decided not to comment on it, leading me further into her home.

"I'd give you a tour but, it's nothing like your place."

"Yeah, it's better," I countered, taking in its beauty. It matched the foyer perfectly, but the wall of floor to ceiling windows was my favorite part. "This view is stunning."

From this high up, you could see the entire city, including the Panorama standing tall in the distance.

"Agreed, main reason why I snatched this place up."

"So, what are we watching?" I questioned as I spun around toward the sound of her voice.

The sight that awaited me was just…

Fuck.

She was in the kitchen, bent over at the waist as she pulled out that pizza she'd been talking about from the oven. The swells of her ass were on display, and maybe it was the macho man in me talking, but something about seeing her so confidently in the kitchen was arousing.

Or perhaps I'm full of shit and it was just her, period.

Setting the pie on a wooden chopping block, she dragged her gaze to where I stood, yanking the oven mitts off her hands. "You don't happen to be into docuseries types of things, are you?"

"I don't mind them." I shoved my hands back into my pockets, shrugging. "Why? What did you have in mind?"

"I've been meaning to watch *Drugs Inc.* for a while now. Interested to see what all they've got in there."

"I'm down for it."

"Do you want anything to drink?" she asked, twirling

around to shut off the oven as I ambled toward the breakfast counter separating us.

"Whatcha got?"

"Whiskey, Bourbon, Vodka, Tequila," she named a few from the built-in liquor cabinet beside the pantry.

"Bourbon, please." I winked.

"Good choice. Two or three fingers?"

I could ask you the same question...

"Uh, two for now," I said, tamping down the wayward thoughts trickling through my mind.

"Two it is. If you wanna get the telly turned on, it's right over there. Remotes are on top of the coffee table. The biggest one is for the T.V. Do you want a slice of pizza, too?"

"I'm good for now. Just get your ass over here already," I demanded.

An hour later, we were about half way through the second episode, and I was getting fucking antsy. The first one wasn't so bad—it was actually damn good—but after a quick intermission and another refill to our tumbler's, I'd about had enough of sitting this far away from her.

It was only a mere sixteen inches that separated us, if that, but it was still too much in my opinion.

Unnecessary and quite useless, really.

The pull was distinctly there, urging us toward one another. I kept it together purely because I swore to her I would, but I could see the way it was starting to wear her down, too.

Every couple of minutes, she'd peer over at me from the corner of her eyes, shifting slightly in her seat.

Usually, I'd take that as a green light, an invitation, but this was Lux—Queen of hot and cold—and I wasn't trying to fuck it up for myself so early in the game.

"Shit," she hissed suddenly, leaning forward to deposit her tumbler on the table.

My brow lifted curiously. "You okay, there?"

"Fucking dribbled like an invalid," she muttered, staring down her shirt. "My tits are probably intoxicated."

And there was the green light.

The blatant green light.

I was on my knees in between her legs in nothing flat. "Allow me to clean that up for you."

Lux fell back against the couch, eyes wide, breathing unsteady. "You promised you'd—"

"I know, but that was before you deliberately drenched yourself in bourbon."

"It wasn't deliberate!" she retorted, painting the most dubious expression on my features.

My lips pursed. "Sure it wasn't. I wasn't born yesterday, kitty kat. Shirt off, now."

This time, no smart ass response followed. Coy eyes observed me in her hesitation but, eventually—probably after realizing I wasn't going to give it up—she sat up in my grasp and yanked the shirt over her head.

It fell somewhere beside me, I think, but I wasn't focused on that. I was focused on her, on the glisten of alcohol trailing down her chest between her small tits.

"The bra, too," I pressed, taking a moment to sweep my eyes over the rest of her.

Flat stomach adorned in ink.

Legs spread around my torso.

My mouth watered at the sight of her shorts cinched so high up. If she spread herself any wider, her cunt would be out there for me to see, too.

"Rome…" she whimpered in protest, but it was more meek than anything else.

"Take it off, Lux," I demanded, running my hands up her thighs.

That sense of reservation was still there, lingering for several beats.

But it dissipated from one moment to the next.

Reaching around herself, she unhooked the single clasp keeping her decent and tossed the bra aside.

The second it hit the ground, I flicked my tongue out around her navel and started upward, following the trail laid out before me.

"*Oh, fuck,*" she breathed, falling back against the couch.

"Mmm, tastes better off you," I cooed, licking and sucking my way up to her neck. "But I bet *you* taste even better."

Lux moaned softly, threading her fingers into the longer strands of my hair, arching herself into me. "Don't stop, please."

Her plea came with a sharp tug on my head. She wanted me closer, *on her*, forcing me onto the couch as well.

Trapping her between me and the back of the couch, I draped her legs over my own, and slid my hands up the line of her figure, actually taking her in for the first time.

Her tits were perfectly rounded globes, small nipples a pale pink.

I could just imagine them bouncing softly as I gave her every inch, robbing her of all the air in her lungs…

Goddamn…

My dick couldn't withstand much more, throbbing almost violently beneath my sweats.

A sheer battle of wills was all that kept me—barely—from devouring her right then. Every part of me shook with the need to take those globes within my grip and suck them into my mouth.

"I thought you wanted me to behave," I gritted out.

Lux nodded, her eyes clamped shut. "I did, but then you did *that,* and now I'm just… Touch me."

Leaning forward, I settled my lips beside her ear, her waist caught in my death grip. "Are you wet beneath those tiny shorts right now?"

"Probably," she breathed.

"You're making it hard as fuck to keep my word."

"Fuck it all to hell right now. I don't care about that," she asserted, picking her head up to look me in the eye.

The fire within them raged, calling to the beast once more.

"A promise is a promise." I breathed through the rush, my cock fucking aching in agony. "So now I'm promising you this….I'm taking this pussy soon, Lux—really fucking soon. Do you hear me?"

"Mhmmm."

Really, really soon.

34. TALES OF THE PAST: PART ONE

Lux

♫ *Bring Me To Life - Evanescence* ♫

Thanksgiving came and went. November then swiftly rolled into December.

With the holidays now looming around the corner, my tolerance for anything and everything was declining at an alarming rate.

As it did every year.

I was an acrimonious jumble of silent and distant chaos.

Naturally, Rome clocked on to said change without missing a beat, and after a couple weeks of sparse and limited interaction, he insisted I spend the weekend at his place.

In fact, he wouldn't take no for an answer, going as far as threatening to storm into my flat, pack my bag, and throw me over his shoulder if I didn't come on my own terms.

So I went, because if the last five months we'd known one another taught me anything, it's that the man didn't fuck around.

He'd keep true to his promise, no holds barred.

"So are you finally gonna tell me what's wrong, or am I gonna have to force it out of you?" Flicking the lighter, Rome lit the blunt he'd rolled not five minutes prior, taking a few deep puffs.

We were laying on his bed, his massive circular bed, surrounded by the dark of night. Only a sliver a light poured in from the windows thanks to the full moon.

"Nothing's wrong," I lied for the fifty-millionth time.

Rome sighed, releasing a thick cloud as he fell onto his back. "I know you're lying. Do you not trust me or something?"

"I do trust you, it's just—"

"See?" he interjected, passing me the cigarillo. "Lying."

Shit.

I'd literally walked right into that one without even realizing it.

"I'm sorry." I scooted closer to him, taking in my own hit. "I'm just not used to anyone caring."

"Well, I'm not just anyone, Lux." His voice held a dash of exasperation.

It stung a little, regardless of the fact I knew it wasn't intentional.

I couldn't blame him, really. I'd been aloof, had isolated myself to avoid marring those around me with my Grinch-like attitude, him included. And yet, here he was, making an effort to get to the root of the problem, and I was lying right through my teeth.

"I know you're not." I exhaled, hating myself a little more than I already did.

"So tell me then. You know I'm not going to judge you."

"It's such a long story, though…"

"And we have nothing but time, baby. A whole weekend to be exact. Tell me," he demanded, shifting back onto his side.

Baby.

That name.

That damned name.

It'd slipped a few times over the last several weeks, and each time we played it off, simply continued with our conversation like it didn't happen.

But this time…this time I couldn't pretend it didn't happen, much less that it didn't affect me. Might seem juvenile to some, but I'd never been anyone's "baby."

This was new for me in a way I fancied a little too much.

"I was never that girl," I somehow started suddenly, grappling Rome's attention in a nanosecond. "You know, the one who lived a perfect life, with her perfect loving family, in their perfect little white picket fence home. Perhaps in another time and place, we could have been…" I took another quick puff, shaking my head. "But we weren't. We were far from it. Anyway, I don't know the whole story because it wasn't shared with me, but I do know that my parents married young, like fresh out of secondary school young. They traveled around a bit, had plans for a whole lot of kids, but those plans quickly went spiraling down the drain when mum was unable to sustain a pregnancy. After five miscarriages, I finally managed to stick. Not wanting to get their hopes up, they refused to find out the gender—though my father was positive I was a boy."

Rome rested his head on his hand as I passed him the blunt. He took a few puffs, and as always, I found myself enraptured at the sight of him letting it all go. The smirk he flashed me when he caught me staring prompted me to continue.

"So yeah, after all that, June rolled around and mum finally went into labor. She ended up having me via c-section after I'd, apparently, flipped breech at the last minute. I'm sure you can imagine my father's surprise when the good Doctor told him I was a girl and not the strapping son he wanted. Any and every photo I've seen showed his disappointment, from the fake smile on his face to the awkward way in which he held me. Never mind the fact he was finally holding his own flesh and blood. I wasn't a boy and it was clearly unacceptable," I scoffed the last bit and fell onto my back, combing a hand through my hair, my gaze stuck on the circular tray ceiling above Rome's bed.

Dread spilled itself into every nook and cranny of my being, undesirably so. We hadn't even gotten to the worst part of it all yet and I was ready to call it quits. I didn't want to share this shit with Roman.

Didn't want him to know how ugly my life had been.

Certainly, I didn't want him to feel sorry for me either. Because he would, I knew he would.

Once he learned the extent of it all, he'd understand why I was the way I was, and he'd feel nothing but pity.

I didn't want his pity, or anyone else's for that matter.

All I wanted was respect.

A thoughtful silence fell between us while the wheels of the past turned in my head. Rome didn't say a word as he put out the cigarillo in the ashtray we had on the floor and wrapped an arm around my middle, pulling me closer to his side. It was a simple gesture of comfort, yet it felt so much more intimate than anything we'd shared thus far.

Following the colorful designs adorning his arm, I was met by his awaiting stare, a mindful expression furrowing his brows. He reached out and tucked a wayward strand of hair behind my ear.

"I'm listening, continue," he urged softly.

Ugh.

"Everything went downhill from there. When he found out it'd be very unlikely my mum could carry another child, he completely pulled away from her. Maybe he thought it was her fault? That there was something she did or didn't do to not bear him a boy, to not have the ability to reproduce like a normal woman? I don't know. The point is, he pushed her away, started working more. When he came home, he'd toss back a few beers and plant his ass in front of the telly until he passed out. He rarely ever made it to bed, and when he did, it was just to fuck my mum. I heard his drunken profanities and her forced moans through the walls more times than I can count."

An ill shiver racked through my body at the memories.

"What about you? Did he at the very least try having a relationship with you?" Rome asked.

"Never." I shook my head. "I grew up virtually alone,

always fending for myself. Yeah, I had mum for a while, but in the later years, she wasn't present, too caught up in her own depression to give me the love and attention any kid needs. She loved me, but parenting, unfortunately, took a backseat to her own sufferings. I made my own meals, washed my own clothes. I walked to and from the bus stop alone. Homework and projects were done alone, too. Forget about holidays and birthdays; those didn't exist in my home."

"Holidays?" Rome picked up on it immediately, as expected.

And I nodded, because what else was I suppose to do?

"In my entire life, I think I had maybe three Christmases, and I was too young to even remember them." A bitter laugh shot from my mouth. "Birthdays went on a little longer, but not by much. Once I was six or so, mum died altogether. Not physically, but she might as well have been."

Rome was staring at me in complete shock, but the pity I expected to see wasn't there.

No.

In its place, was ire.

A hint of sympathy billowed around the edges as well, but it was mostly contained fury.

It was terrifying because if he was this upset now, only knowing so little, I couldn't imagine his state when I dished out the rest.

"Lux…I-I don't even know what to say," he rasped.

I was so used to shrugging it all off, that's exactly

what I did. "No one ever really does, especially when they realize it only gets worse."

Blue eyes flashed in disbelief. "Go on…" he gritted out, swallowing deeply as if steeling himself.

Good, he should.

None of this was pretty.

"I'm just gonna say it, mainly because it makes it easier for me to get out, but also because it's better to just get it over with," I explained awkwardly.

Rome nodded, his jaw grit.

Inhaling a deep breath, I went for it. "I was ten the first time he hit me. Before that, he mostly just ignored me. Guess ten makes you of age for beatings when your father hates you," I scoffed, feeling him tense beside me. "They weren't really a regular occurrence, but I guess that's because mum got the worst of it. They did get worse with time, though, and when I turned thirteen, he violated me during one of his manic episodes. He didn't actually penetrate me, but every act was unwanted, against my will. I guess my cries finally sobered him and, following that night, he never tried it again."

The bed was shaking.

Literally shaking.

I couldn't even bring myself to look at Rome from the sheer amount of heat radiating off his body.

It was suffocating.

Debilitating.

More than I could bear.

And story time wasn't even over yet.

"By this point, I'd met Suki at school. She was a

problem child transfer from the Liverpool orphanage. We hit it off her first day in class and the rest is history. It's like she was sent to me to keep me from checking out so young. To help me through the next shit card and every one thereafter."

My heart was thrashing. I could hardly breathe, so much so that I had to sit up.

Risking a peek at Rome only made it worse.

He looked positively murderous and I wanted to die. Watching him suffer on my behalf, having to burden him with this because of who he'd become in my life, was forcing me to relive these memories through a whole new painful perspective.

"My father may not have tried to touch me again," my voice cracked a little, "but he had no problem selling my body to his friends when I turned fifteen. Fredrick was the first of the bunch. He took my virginity, shed me of my dignity. I endured it for a year—one long excruciating year of being used as a receptacle. That's when Suki and I left. Neither one of us had anything to lose by doing so, so why not, right? Little did we know how hard it was going to be. As two sixteen-year-olds who ran away and fled their country, we found ourselves permanently living on the streets. No one wanted to help us. We slept under plenty of park benches and bridges, starved for weeks at a time. Eventually, we had to sell ourselves on street corners to make a buck for sheer survival. But then two years later, Vic found us on a corner in Brickell, begging for petty change. He took us in, got us jobs at *Tootsies* now that we were legal—"

"I can't listen to any more," Rome growled suddenly, jolting me back into the here and now. "I can't fucking listen to anymore... Let's go."

My stomach almost purged itself from my body. "Where?"

"For a drive."

I didn't protest, offering him a silent nod that prompted him onto his feet in a flash. He was equally as silent as he extended a hand and helped me onto my feet as well.

Five minutes later, we were in the car.

He was speeding, weaving in and out around vehicles like a lunatic. I wanted to say something, but I couldn't seem to form words. My mind was racing. I was relieved the conversation was over and done with, and yet petrified at the same time at the abrupt way in which it ended.

What was he thinking?

Gripping the door handle, I could do nothing but sit and watch him maneuver us up I-95, then onto the MacArthur Causeway.

We were headed toward the beach, apparently.

"I get it now," he finally said, his grip on the steering wheel white. "I get it and I'm so fucking sorry for you, baby."

"Rome, don't..." Tears sprung to my eyes. The pity party was coming, the one where he left me because he'd realized how fucked up I was.

"But mostly, I'm so disgusted, I don't know what the fuck to do with myself. What's festering inside me right now..."

Here it comes.

"I'm going to kill your father," he seethed. "Maybe not today, or next month, even next year, but one day, he'll pay his fucking dues. That disgrace of a man will pay for every single thing he did to you—emotionally, physically, psychologically. *All of it.*"

"You can't—" I started, but he held a firm hand up, popping my mouth closed.

"I can, *and I will.* Unless you express a desire to keep him alive—for whatever the reason may be—I'm dragging that motherfucker to hell with my bare hands."

All the air just about left my lungs.

That malevolence, the possessively-fueled growl of his voice...

My God, I was suddenly so turned on.

I can't explain it and I probably sound crazy for admitting such a thing, but I'd gone from downright depleted, to the most aroused I'd ever felt in my entire life, at the flip of a switch.

Whether he sensed it or not, we fell silent yet again. I think we were both processing, yet they were two completely different things.

He understood me.

And I finally understood him.

I truly did.

Whatever this thing between us was, it was as real as he'd sworn, and it was all the more real now, after I'd laid my soul bare to him.

～

WE PARKED UP AT THE BEACH AS EXPECTED, CLOSER TO the pier. It was darker here, more secluded at this hour.

Away from all the boisterous night life.

The minutes continued to tick by in silence and I wasn't sure how much more I could tolerate. It was stifling, brimming with fierce sexual tension pent up from weeks upon weeks of repression.

I felt every bit of it pulsating between my thighs, through my veins, in my head.

My fucking heart.

"Wanna go for a walk?" I suggested, hoping to get us out of the damned car for a little while.

But Rome shook his head and turned toward me, eyes ablaze. "No," he rasped. "I need those lips on mine."

He didn't have to tell me twice.

I was unbuckling my seatbelt and climbing into his lap faster than either one of us could blink. The second my mouth crashed into his, that was it.

It was pure chaos.

That primal sense of need was so intensely magnified, there wasn't anything that could rip us apart.

We were drowning in a rabid clusterfuck of emotions, drowning so damn deep the windows began fogging out around us. Each kiss was more feverish than the last; desperate, impatient, hungered.

And none were enough.

I both needed and wanted more, needed and wanted *all of him,* my hands shaking as I fumbled to loosen the waistband of his basketball shorts.

I was so far gone, I didn't even register him

restraining me until my arms were clasped behind my back and his hand snaked into my hair, pulling me flush against him.

"We need to stop," he growled against my neck, teeth lightly grazing my skin, "or I'm going to eat you alive."

Yes. God, yes.

"Do it," I coaxed purposefully, whimpering when he tugged my head back with force.

"Don't test me, Lux. I *will* hold true to my word, and you don't want that right now."

"Yes I do, I want it all," I gritted out, hissing in bliss as he tugged harder. "You know you want to."

"There's not a single doubt about that, but not here. Not now, we can't."

What?

I went completely rigid.

My entire body stung, immobilized by the unexpected pride-jostling slap of rejection.

"Why?" I hated how pained I sounded.

"Lux, you just finished telling me all of *that*..." he trailed off, releasing me.

"I know, and your reaction to it all is what has me riding this high. You're not sitting there pitying me. You're not disgusted or put off. Somehow, you understand it all in a way no one has before."

"It wouldn't be ri—"

"I need you, Rome," I cut him off. "More than I've ever needed anyone or anything in my life."

His lips thinned, the cogs visibly rolling in his head.

"Do you really want me to fuck you out here like a twenty pound slag?" he asked suddenly.

I shook mine, leaning in closer. "No, I want you to fuck me *as me*, as the woman you so clearly desire. Take it all away, mark me with your stamp. Show me how it's supposed to be..."

"You understand what you're asking me for, right? What this means?" The man was entirely serious, not a hint of amusement anywhere to be found.

"I think so, but tell me anyway."

"You give me *you, all of you—and you're mine.* Got that?"

"I do." I nodded.

"Do you really though? I'm not fucking around, Lux. I don't share," he growled.

"I don't want you to share."

Everything stopped. The entire fucking world came to a screeching halt as we bore into one another with his decree hanging thick in the air.

Fifteen seconds.

Thirty.

Forty-five.

No words were exchanged.

After an excruciating minute, his palms, warm and reverent started up my thighs. "This right here is an exception, kitty kat, a one-time free pass. The next time I take you, it'll be in *my* bed with you spread out for me, naked, writhing, nails clawing down my back. Understand?"

That image...

God help me the day it came to be.

He was going to ruin me.

"Yes…" I was practically shivering in anticipation.

Rome dropped his gaze to the apex of my thighs, his tongue flashing out along his bottom lip. "Slide those little shorts to the side for me."

Suddenly, I couldn't breathe.

This was it.

We'd shared a couple of moments that led us to the point of no return.

But this time, *this,* right here, was the real deal.

There was no coming back from this.

Bracing myself for what would be my ultimate demise, I obliged to his request, pulling the soft fabrics of my shorts and panties aside.

The rest of me remained hidden beneath my clothing, but holy fuck, I had never felt more exposed.

So bare.

And yet, the possessive, adoring look in his eyes set me on fire.

It was everything I'd never had, and everything I'd always wanted.

Lips parted, his nostrils flared as he dipped his thumb between my lips and dragged it up to my clit. "Fuuuck… It's prettier than I imagined."

"Rome, please," I whimpered impatiently.

He could look later, up close and in detail if he wanted to. But right then, I needed him inside me. Needed him filling me until I didn't know where I started and he ended.

"Spread it for me, baby," he rasped crudely, pulling himself free from his shorts, stroking it slowly.

Long, thick, hard—my pussy clenched at the mere sight of it.

I was salivating like a bitch in heat, spreading myself wantonly between two fingers.

I'd never felt like this before…

Rome hissed, his eyes darkening. "Goddamn, you're perfect." He slid his length along my heat, flooding me, drawing my essence all over him.

It. Was. Torture.

Exquisite-fucking-torture.

"Come here," he gritted out, yanking me flush against him. "I wanna see you. Look at me while I take you."

Stares entwined, he pushed into me without warning, filling me inch, by inch, by delicious inch—until I was gasping for air, fully seated on his length.

Throwing my head back, I clamped my eyes shut. "Ohhh my God…"

Rome hummed, as if agreeing to my plea. Gripping my hips, his fingers dug into my skin as he rolled into me skillfully. "So. Fucking. Tight."—*thrust*—"So warm."—*thrust*—"So wet."—*thrust*—"You're perfect, fucking perfect, Lux."

His words…

The way he fucked me…

I was high on it all, creeping up on the precipice of ecstasy, ready to fall over the edge into sweet oblivion at any moment.

"Oh, God, please… More…" I begged, riding him with equal fervor.

"It's Rome, baby—get it right. Remember it. Engrain it in your mind. It's the only name you'll be moaning from now on."

"Rome, *please.*" I begged again, chasing that decadent feeling building deep within my core.

Pushing me back the tiniest bit, he shifted the angle just slightly, enough to thumb my clit, sending lightning bolts of pleasure coursing through me.

"Fuuuck, right there." My eyes rolled, legs quivering. "Don't stop."

"You gonna come for me?" he questioned roughly.

I nodded, panting, rolling against him frantically. "So close."

"I know, you're fucking milking me already."

I was, too, pulsing and throbbing, pulling him in deeper. My body had never been so greedy.

"So. Damn. Close," I warned him, moaning excitedly when his hand slipped around my throat.

Squeezing.

Robbing me of my air supply.

As those tingly little stars began flooding the corners of my eyes, he yanked me toward him once more. "Eyes on me when you come, Lux. Give me that orgasm, all of it."

I lasted all of a minute more, erupting from the air of determination playing on his features as he fucked me rabid.

My body locked up tight, pussy clenching and gushing all over him. "I'm coming, I'm fucking coming!"

He groaned appreciatively, slamming me in place as he chased his own release. "So. Fucking. Beautiful," the words came grunted through thrusts that left me breathless, limp, reeling.

Owned.

35. TALES OF THE PAST: PART TWO

Roman

♫ *Twisted - MISSIO* ♫

Mine.

She was mine.

The circumstances in which we arrived here were less than ideal, an unexpected bomb, really, but in the end, I got what I wanted.

I was on cloud-fucking-nine, feeling so damned victorious I didn't know what the hell to do with myself. I wanted to bury myself inside Lux over and over again, to erase the memories of her past, of any man who'd used her and abused her before me.

Her story was heart-wrenching. Gutting. It lacerated the blackened stone in my chest and set it ablaze with wild rage. I was entirely serious when I told her I'd end her father one day, too. He deserved every bit of it and then some. An eternity in hell wouldn't be enough in my eyes.

No.

He deserved much worse; a slow and painful death.

What he'd done to his daughter was... I couldn't even think about it.

Couldn't think about how his years of relentless abuse literally led her right into Vic's arms.

It took everything in me not to react when she'd said his name. I laid there quietly, fuming after what she'd shared with me, willing myself to sit through what remained.

But I had to cut her off there.

I couldn't bear to hear if he'd hurt her as well.

Couldn't bear to think that, eventually, I'd have to tell her the truth.

I say eventually because there wasn't a chance in hell I was going to come clean then. I'd just gotten her, had just won her over.

It had to wait, even if it weighed me down in the process.

"I'm getting in," Lux announced the following evening.

Poolside with drinks in hand, the night was crystal clear, a little cool, too, which was odd for Miami.

I set my tumbler on the small patio table between our loungers and steepled my fingers. "I'll join you, on one condition."

"And what's that?" She seemed genuinely intrigued, sliding her legs off the side of her seat.

"We go in naked." I waggled my eyebrows.

Lux smirked knowingly.

We'd been at it three different times today already.

I couldn't get enough of her.

"I'll agree if…" she held a finger up.

"If what?"

"If you tell me about you."

Her proposition threw me for a loop, rising faint alarm bells in the back my mind. "What all does that entail?"

"It's your turn," she clarified, confirming my worst suspicions.

What she wanted me to tell her wasn't just painful, it involved Vic, too….

I sighed, resigned almost, and shook my head. "It's a pathetic story. I could really do without retelling it."

"I don't think you've got much of a choice. You made me dish out my past even though you knew I didn't want to."

"I didn't *make* you. I asked you to."

"And I complied, despite cringing the entire way through. C'mon, Rome—you know I'm not going to judge you. It's only fair," she pointed out, using the exact words I'd thrown at her just last night.

Was fair point if I'm being honest. I'd seen the way it physically hurt her to rehash the shit she went through, yet she found the strength to tell me, all because I'd asked.

Would it be so bloody difficult for me to do the same?

"Please?" The softness of her voice pulled me away from my anxiety-driven thoughts.

On another amenable sigh, I leaned onto my knees and raked a hand through my hair. "I have a love-hate relationship with the letter L."

One of her sleek brows arched curiously. "What?"

"I sound crazy, I know—but the people who made Roman King the man he is today, the man you see in front of you, their names all started with the letter L. They were either taken from me, or fucked me over."

"Who are they?"

"Leigh-ann, Leo, and Liza," I counted each on a finger. "Leigh-ann was my mum. Leo was my best friend. And Liza," I paused, gauging her reaction, "Liza was my ex."

At the mention of a past lover, Lux sat up a little straighter, crossing one leg over the other. "I'm listening."

"My mum was a single mum. Young, boyfriend left her and the kids type of story. She turned to the pole, and while she *did* make money, we still struggled. Her addiction basically ate a lot of her paychecks, leaving just the bare minimum to scrape by."

"What was her vice?" she asked.

"Coke," I answered in disgust. "I won't touch that shit because of her."

"It's bad news," Lux agreed, prompting me to nod thoughtfully.

"Well, between *that* and the long hours she worked at the club, I was left responsible for my little sister at least ninety percent of the time."

"Did she have an L—"

"No," I chuckled. "Her name was Sio. Siobhan."

Lux smiled as she mulled it over for a moment. "Roman and Siobhan. I think they mesh well."

"I like to think so, too." A small smile tore across my face as well. "Anyway, Sio and I obviously spent a lot of time together. Mum helped when she could, but for the most part, it was just her and I. I was a good kid back then."

"What happened?" Lux hedged, leaning all her weight onto one hand.

"Mum started getting beat on at the club. Every week she had new bruises, and for the more prominent they were, the less her boss let her work. Said it was bad for business. By this point, I was about fifteen or so, and I wanted to help—that's how poorly we were doing. So I started looking for jobs after school, all quick cash, and eventually, I found Leo and his family."

I'd met Vic around that time as well... But I couldn't do it.

I couldn't bring myself to admit it then.

To come clean and confess.

It was too. Fucking. Soon.

Swallowing down that monster sense of guilt gnawing at my conscience, I continued. "The Milani's were mafia, drug-trafficking was their trade. They gave me work, I started selling, running the streets to protect their territories—"

Lux lifted a hand, bidding me to pause. "Where did this all happen?"

"What do you mean?"

"What city?" she clarified.

"Oh, right. London."

Reaching for her drink on the table, she took a generous sip, her lips quirking around the rim. "So close yet so far away that whole time..."

"Liverpool, right?" I hedged.

"No, that was Suki. Leeds, here."

"And we all ended up Miami." I smirked. The world was so damn small. "Anyway, while I was wreaking havoc on the streets with Leo, Sio was staying at the Milani's main warehouse. Some days, she'd go home after school with a friend, but usually, she wanted to tag along with me. Leo had twin sisters who were only a year younger than Sio, so she had fun with them. They did homework, played out on the dock, and I got to make money. It was a win/win for me."

"Did your mum know about all of it?"

"No, and I never gave her the money personally in fear she'd spend it. She had an envelope in one of the kitchen drawers—I used to slip some in there every few days."

Lux's features cinched dubiously. "She never noticed the money?"

I hitched a shoulder. "That she brought to my attention, no, but again, coke destroyed her. She was oblivious. Bills were paid, though, there was food on the table. Things were pretty damn decent for a while there... And then I met Liza." A regretful scoff shout out of my mouth of its own accord. "Originally from Wales, she ended up in London after becoming an orphan overnight. She ran circles around her foster family, which I never understood, considering they gave her the world. The girl literally had everything handed to her, but she had a wicked penchant for trouble. We met at school, starting hanging out together. She got to know Leo, too. Few months in, we started dating, and within a couple weeks, she started coming out with me, feeding her desires. I fell for her, hard. I thought she had, too. We were making moves, handling bigger projects for the Milani's, making more money. I gave her—and them—five years of my life. Until that one day…"

Lux shifted slightly in her seat, car-piling the words on my tongue.

I tried analyzing her expression, but the mask was firmly in place. "You sure you wanna hear the rest of this?"

"From start to finish," she assured me, reaching behind herself to untie her bikini top. The black triangles keeping her decent gave away, falling to the brickwork beneath our feet.

Lips parted, I took her in ever so slowly, dragging my gaze from her perfect little tits up to her hooded eyes.

"Some motivation." She shrugged coyly.

"I need you closer than that to get the full effect." I grinned, holding out a hand to her.

She came more than willingly, straddling me, her inked arms falling gently around my neck. "There, I'm closer. Go on. Until that one day what…"

My stomach sank just thinking about it. "I walked in on her and Leo"—*and Vic*—"in the office."

Her stare widened. "Were they…?"

"Yup. I went fucking ballistic; destroyed the entire office, beat Leo an inch from his life. But my biggest mistake was threatening to expose his family."

And that was the gods-honest truth.

It was both my biggest mistake, and my biggest regret.

Had I controlled my temper, *my rage*, I could have spared myself a lifetime of excruciating and irreversible pain.

But twenty-year-old Rome didn't know how to reign himself in.

"The worst is coming, isn't it?" Lux's voice was incredibly soft, her grip tightening around my neck. "I can feel it."

"Yeah." I nodded, burying my face in the slope of her neck. "Short version of the story? I came home one night to both mum and Sio, dead."

Gasping, she stilled in my arms. "Leo?"

I nodded again. "He raped Sio, slit her throat, tossed her in the bathtub like a rag doll when he was done with her. She bled out in the water. And mum...he tied her to her bed, spread eagle. Abused her and slit her throat, too. I'd never seen so much blood in my life, not even on the streets."

Lux took a hold of my face then, gripping it with urgency as she pierced me with her stare. "Tell me you fucking slaughtered him?" She was entirely serious.

"Years later," I proclaimed. "Almost five."

"Why'd you wait so long?"

"I wanted him to think he'd gotten me. That he was safe... Then when he least expected it..."

That sinister smile of hers, the one I hadn't seen in a while, stretched her lips before she leaned in the tiniest bit and hit me with a chaste kiss. "You're an evil genius."

Scoffing in amusement, I pecked her back. "You say that like it's a good thing."

But I should've known she, of all people, *would* think it was.

"There's honor in revenge sometimes, baby," she murmured, rising onto her feet.

Then she hooked two fingers at the sides of her bikini bottom and leisurely slid them down her legs, until they fell the rest of the way.

"Take your clothes off, Rome." It wasn't a request. "That's enough for tonight."

"For the rest of the weekend," I corrected, regardless of the fact we hadn't even touched on Liza's revenge. "And next weekend, I'm taking you out, so don't think we're continuing story time then either."

Case closed.

36. MAGIC
Lux

♫ *Acquainted - The Weeknd* ♫

When Saturday finally rolled around, Suki, Ramsey, and I spent the entire day prepping. Unfortunately.

They'd dragged me along against my will.

I'd planned on wearing one of my little black dresses and calling it a day, but Ramsey and her hopeless romantic self wouldn't hear anything of it. She was insistent on manicure's and pedicure's, on getting my hair done, a new outfit, new shoes.

Everything.

I wanted to kill her, and I'd expected Suki to side with me on the matter, but she didn't.

The little bitch betrayed me.

She wasn't fully on Ramsey's side of the fence either, but kept reiterating that Ramsey had a point and that it "would be fun."

Her words, not mine.

Not even half hour into the shopping trip, I was seriously regretting my decision to allow them turning me into their personal life-size barbie for the day. I tried explaining, almost relentlessly, that tonight wasn't a big deal, but of course, neither one agreed.

"He's putting time in, Lux." Suki claimed at one point. "This isn't a joke to him. That man is playing for keeps—permanent keeps—and you're the million dollar prize. He's falling in love with you."

I'd rolled my eyes so damn hard I'm surprised they didn't explode from their sockets. But that was all a defense mechanism, because deep down, I knew she was right.

So much had changed between Roman and I in the last several weeks, especially that getting to know you thing I'd been terrified of. At this point, we were way past that.

He knew me, and I knew him.

I'd given myself to him.

He'd staked his claim.

Marked me with his stamp.

There was no turning back now.

I couldn't lie and say I wasn't scared out of my mind, though.

I know, I should've been honest. Should've told my girls how I felt and turned to them like the sounding board they'd always been. But this was different in a way I knew neither one could offer a sliver of advice on. They simply had zero experience in this deep of a realm.

Ramsey, maybe, what with her high school sweetheart and all, but not even their tumultuous love affair compared to this.

So why bother trying to explain it when they wouldn't

understand? They'd do nothing but worry, and I hated being fussed over.

Not to mention, it would also give them something to giggle about; how I'd fallen hopelessly in love with the enemy.

How I gave into his charms and dropped to my knees in submission.

No thank you, I'll pass.

The day went on in much of the same fashion. Either Suki or Ramsey would gush randomly about how exciting this was for me, and I played it off like they were missing one too many screws.

But come 7p.m, I couldn't hide it anymore.

As I stood there before the large mirror in my bedroom, gazing over my new and polished reflection, the blanched expression on my face gave me away.

They'd asked, obviously.

I, however, never got the chance to tell them.

Rome was right on time and he didn't seem too inclined to wait outside after taking a good look at me, regardless of what the reason may be.

Not gonna lie... I was kinda happy right then my girls had dolled me up.

Seeing the fire ignite in his eyes was exhilarating.

Worth every damn cringing moment.

I held my head higher as all my reservations melted away, remaining perfectly in place under his scrutiny.

"Your hair." He seemed to be in awe. "You changed it."

I shrugged nonchalantly. "It was time. Suki and Ramsey's idea really."

"It suits you," he cooed, fingering a lock. "I love the silver hue, somehow brings to your eyes more."

A fresh wave of heat crept up my cheeks. "Thank you."

Rome tipped his head by way of reply, only for his eyes to roam up my body in another appreciative sweep.

I thought I'd imagined the deep rumble that seemed to reverberate from his chest, but not ten seconds later he was caging me into the door of my flat.

"You look incredible, seriously," he rasped, the tip of his nose skated along the curve of my neck: "Are you trying to kill me in that little thing?"

He was referencing the black lace romper clinging to my body; extremely short and backless, with a plunging sweetheart neckline held up by thin spaghetti straps. Almost every inch of my inked skin was exposed and it was blatantly obvious I was bare beneath.

"You can thank Suki for that. She picked it out," I chuckled, angling toward him as his warm lips sought me out.

"Thank her for what? Subjecting me to torture for the rest of the night?"

"I'd hardly call it torture when you've got your hands all over me right now."

Said hands trailed over the curve of my ass and up my back in a feather-light yet purposeful caress. "It's torture because I know what's under this scrap of a garment, and

I'm lusting after it so hard, I don't know how I'll be able to contain myself."

"Behave, and you can have it," I whispered, locking my arms around his neck to lure him closer.

Our lips brushed.

"Is that a promise?"

Another brush.

"Cross my heart."

And another.

"I'm holding you to it."

Face cupped in his grasp, he left no room for me to counter, pressing our lips together with such ferocity, I couldn't breathe under their assault.

Slick, enticing sounds instantly filled the foyer as he invaded my mouth, hips shifting closer to the heat between my legs.

We'd never leave at this rate, but I couldn't for the life of me stop him if I wanted to. Opening wider, I allowed his impatient tongue to wickedly duel with my own, drawing out a feverish, wanton moan from deep within me.

"Fuck," he hissed, as carnal and consumed as I felt.

Then he pulled away, leaving me so bereft I almost whimpered at the loss.

"Let's go, before I give your friends a reason to come to the door." His chest heaved.

As did my own, pulse rampaging beneath my skin. "I'm sure they're already there."

We never found out if they were or not, and quite frankly, I didn't care either way.

I just wanted to get Rome alone.

Once we made it outside and strolled up to the Benz, Rome—ever the gentleman—opened the door for me and ushered me inside, even pulling the seatbelt out a ways for me to grab. As I went about buckling myself in with still shaky hands, he slid around the front end and effortlessly slipped inside beside me.

"So, where are we going?" I asked to distract myself from the ache between my thighs.

It'd been a week since our last romp in the sheets.

A simple flick of his wrist, and the engine roared to life, rolling a sensuous vibration through my seat. "A light dinner, but after that, well, I can't tell you."

"Why not?"

"Because it's a surprise." He grinned and reached over the center console for my hand, lacing our fingers together. "You'll see."

I groaned inwardly.

I absolutely detested surprises, could've sworn he knew that already…but his excitement was palpable, and I didn't want to ruin it.

So I kept that little morsel of information to my myself, offering him a small smile and a nod instead.

"Don't worry, you're going to love it," he added, reversing out of his spot. "Or at least I hope you will."

"Well, give me a hint," I cajoled.

"I can't."

"C'mon, Rome, just a small hint."

He shook his head with finality. "Not happening, baby."

"Please?" My query came with a squeeze to his hand, and then, instant silence.

His eyes came off the road for a split-second. When we stopped at a red light near the on-ramp for I-95, he turned toward me in entirety and simply observed me.

I could practically see the wheels turning in his head. What he was contemplating so firmly, I'm not sure, but I didn't ask. I just sat there and watched him, too. Studied the hard lines of his face, the perfect arch of his brows, the fierce blue of his eyes...

It's times like these I wondered how I ever thought I could kill him. How I ever thought I could stay away.

"Magic," he said suddenly, refocusing my attention in the moment.

Our eyes met as my brow quirked. "What?"

"You wanted a hint. The hint is magic."

The light flipped from red to green, like the magic he'd just spoken of. Rome tapped on the gas and we were off, zooming through the intersection onto the South-bound ramp.

Glued to my seat, I found myself mentally repeating the word over and over again.

Magic?

Such a loaded yet vague hint.

Magic could be anything if one so believes.

"Got you thinking now, huh?" he questioned, voice dripping with amusement.

"Obviously. That was the most vague hint of all time," I muttered.

Rome gave a little shrug and flipped his blinker on

before switching lanes onto the interstate. "A hint is a hint, baby, and that's all you're getting. Stop over-thinking it. Just sit back and enjoy the ride, we'll be there soon."

So I did.

For the sake of not unnecessarily dragging our evening through the mud, I bit my tongue and shut my trap.

It wasn't an easy feat by any means.

The need to retort and sass him was there, *right there*, but I managed to quell it.

I mean, he'd obviously spent a lot of time planning this out, right? What type of—dare I say it—*girlfriend* would I be if I threw it all to hell because the thought of surprises gave me anxiety?

Sensing my unease, Roman reached out and turned up the volume on the radio, effectively killing the dreadful silence and the tension in my shoulders.

I melted into the seat and took a deep, calming breath, listening to *The Weeknd's* voice croon about putting time in for a chick.

The more I listened, the harder the lyrics hit me.

They were Suki's words from earlier in the day...

He's putting time in, Lux. This isn't a joke to him. That man is playing for keeps—permanent keeps—and you're the million dollar prize He's falling in love with you.

Thankfully, the volume was loud enough to mask the gasp that shot out of my mouth.

Was this a sign or the stars aligning to prove a point?

The point being we had one-hundred percent crossed over into uncharted territory.

"Still over-thinking I see." His voice boomed.

"I'm not," I lied.

"You are, I know you. Talk to me, tell me what's running through your mind."

Sinking my teeth into my lower lip, I shook my head and busied myself with tracing the rose vibrantly inked on his hand.

"Lux…" his voice boomed, darting my eyes back on his form. "Tell me."

"I don't wanna talk about it tonight."

"Should I be concerned?" he pressed.

"No."

"That doesn't sound very reassuring."

"I promise, it's nothing. I'm just…"

"Over-thinking." He chuckled, and I smiled.

"Pretty much."

A LITTLE OVER AN HOUR LATER, ROME AND I SLIPPED OUT of the Japanese restaurant hand in hand, and set off for the second half of our date.

The surprise half he still hadn't budged and told me anything about.

Yet again, the thought of what exactly this surprise was made me anxious, but I stuffed down that vicious sense of unease and told myself all would be well.

How could it not after we'd had such a nice dinner?

Headed South on the Palmetto, I tried piecing together where we could be headed based on the landmarks we passed, but I came up empty-handed on more than one occasion.

Rome stifled a laugh beside me. "Tell me you're not still trying to figure it out?"

"I can't help it." I shrugged, biting back a smile at the amusement etched on his handsome face. "I'm anxious."

"Hate to break it to you, kitty kat, but you're about to be even more anxious here in a second or so."

"Why…?"

"Because I need you to close your eyes," he explained.

I froze solid in my seat. "What? No."

"Yes." He nodded, grinning devilishly.

"I'm not closing my eyes, Rome," I gritted out, gripping the door handle for dear life.

"You are, or I'll pull over and blindfold you instead."

Thump, thump, thump.

"Rome…"

"I know, baby, I fucking know, which is why I'm asking you to please, for the love of God, close your eyes."

"I don't believe in God," I muttered.

"Do it for me then. Close your eyes for me," he countered.

Ugh.

That face.

His excitement.

"I hate you." My eyes narrowed.

Unfazed by my glare, he waved me off. "That's fine, we've been here before. I promise you it'll be worth it."

"Fine. Fineee," I yielded, slipping shaky hands over my eyes.

"Keep them closed. No peeking, okay?"

"Okay."

Pulse erratic.

Stomach in my throat.

I began counting in my head as a distraction.

It literally felt like I'd counted to a million by the time Roman finally piped up again.

"Now, look now, baby!"

A deep breath, then I snapped my head up. The sight that awaited me was the last thing I'd expected to see.

Christmas lights—hundreds and hundreds of Christmas lights put on by *Santa's Enchanted Forest.*

I sucked in a heap of air, my hands shooting up to my mouth.

"Surprise." He sounded pleased.

Had he not been driving, I would have climbed into his lap and mauled him by now.

He remembered.

"Tell me we're going there," I squealed, my eyes glued out the window.

In all my years living here, I'd never been. Could never bring myself to come alone.

"We are indeed," he agreed.

This man…

"Pull over," I demanded.

"What? Here?"

"Yes! Pull the damn car over!"

"Okay, okay." Roman flipped on his blinker and

slipped into the emergency lane. "Fuck, did I do something wrong?"

I didn't answer.

The second he put the car in park, I was yanking off my seatbelt and rushing into his lap.

"What are you—"

I cut him off with a harsh, desperate kiss, my fingers raking into the longer strands of his hair, tugging with force to emphasize my point.

"Thank you," I mumbled against his lips. "Thank you, thank you, thank you."

Rome chuckled in relief beneath my sudden assault. "Had I known Christmas lights would work you up this much, I'd have done this ages ago."

"You didn't know about this ages ago," I pointed out, kissing him senseless, the Benz rocking sideways every few seconds with each car that whirred past us. "Now take me to see my lights, King, before a cop pulls behind us and gives you a ticket for public indecency."

37. ALL I WANT FOR CHRISTMAS
Roman

♫ *All I Want for Christmas Is You - Mariah Carey* ♫

I hadn't felt the holiday cheer in years.

But as Lux and I walked around this Christmas-themed wonderland, the young lad in me was seeping outward through my fucking pores in innocent delight.

The lights, the music, the constant laughter and sheer sense of excitement filling the air…

Mum would have loved this place, Siobhan too.

It was everything Christmas magic was made of.

A smile tore across my face as one of my favorite childhood memories flashed through my mind.

"What are you thinking about?" Lux asked around a mouthful of what these American's call an elephant ear; deep-fried dough covered in cinnamon sugar and confectioners.

"The year mum bought us tickets to Disneyland. Sio screamed for half hour straight, completely lost her shit," I laughed.

"How old were you two?"

"I was thirteen, Sio was eight."

"Was it fun?" She munched on another piece. "I've never been."

"We never got to go. Mum ended up having to pick up more shifts at the club just to scrape by after buying the tickets. Passports, plane tickets, hotel stay—it was just too expensive, unfortunately," I answered, far more forlornly than intended.

Lux's face fell, brows cinching together. "Was Sio crushed?"

"Shattered is more like it. She cried about it for months."

"That's so sad."

"Anddd this is where we end this conversation." I slipped my arm around her shoulders, burrowing her in my side. "What do you wanna do now?"

Blue eyes peered up at me from the very corner, gauging my reaction. "Take me on the Ferris wheel? I'm dying to see what this place looks like all the way up there."

"Well, then, m'lady—shall we?" I grinned, releasing her only to offer up my arm in a gentlemanly fashion.

Lux grinned in return, the smallest giggle escaping along with it. Tossing what little remained of her sugar rush in the rubbish bin, she took a hold of me, tightly.

"We shall."

The damned Ferris wheel was packed. Took us over twenty-five minutes just to get to the front of the line, and another fifteen after that to be seated in one of the pods.

It was so fucking worth it, though.

The look of enchantment on Lux's face as we rose higher and higher to the top was all worth it.

"It's breathtaking…" she gasped, taking in every bit of the scenery splayed out before her in awe.

"It is," I agreed, but we weren't talking about the same thing.

Lux turned to me then, as inquisitive as ever. "Why are you looking at me like that?" she questioned.

I tried playing it off, hitching a shoulder nonchalantly, but the tone of my voice gave me away. "Because you're breathtaking."

"Shut up." She shoved at my arm, cheeks heating beneath her blasé facade.

"Give me those lips and I will," I murmured, reaching out to cup her face in my palm.

She came willingly, leaning in closer with heavy-lidded eyes. The briefest of smiles danced on our lips before they fused together softly. Whipping my phone out of my pocket, I accessed the camera with a swipe of my thumb and captured the moment in a single swift tap.

The shutter went off, snapping Lux's eyes open. "Did you just take a selfie of us." She was cheesing, prompting me to hum as I nodded.

"I did, yes."

"So basic," she quipped.

"Cheesy too, I know. But I want you to remember this." I pulled up the image and turned the phone for her to see it.

It looked like it belonged in one of those multi-million

dollar romance movies—the glimmer in her eyes corroborated it.

"I won't forget it," she decreed, leaning in to kiss me once more. "Never."

After the Ferris wheel, we wandered around the rest of the fair grounds, and rode a few more rides. I suggested we play a few games, too, for the sole purpose of keeping her out longer, but Lux declined graciously, suggesting we go home instead.

I knew exactly what she was getting at, the sly little thing.

Could practically feel the heat emanating off her, slowly but surely unfurling the beast with in me.

"One last picture before we go?" she questioned with a squeeze to my hand as we passed an illuminated gazebo. "You can add it to tonight's cheesy collection."

"Do you wanna do the honors this time?" I waggled my eyebrows, leading her up the pathway.

"Your arm is longer," she pointed out.

"*Or,* we can have someone else take it."

Lux seemed to like my suggestion, glancing around us in search of a possible photographer.

"Excuse me?" She released me and approached a young woman with a small lot of children off to the side."Would you mind taking a quick photo of us in the gazebo?"

The woman nodded pleasantly and took Lux's phone, instructing her children to stay put as she got into position. On her cue, Lux slipped her arms around my neck and I snaked my own around her waist, dropping my lips to her cheek.

"Got it!" The woman called out, rushing back over to us. "So cute!"

"Thank you!" Lux waved her off, giddily showing me the newest image.

Another silver-screen worthy image.

"That *is* a good photo," I agreed, once again living for that genuine megawatt smile of hers. "Send it to me."

"Then send me the Ferris wheel one," she concurred, swiping through several screens on her phone as I did the same on mine.

But then suddenly she froze, jutting her neck out on high alert. "Do you hear that?"

"Hear what?" I didn't hear anything.

"Shhh, listen."

Still I didn't hear anything, straining my ears. Until I did. Faint at first, it sounded like…

"Is that a cat?"

"It sounds like a kitten," Lux squealed, dropping down on her haunches near a cluster of bushes. "Rome, *ohmigod*, look!"

Curled up beneath the closest bushel was the teeniest kitten I'd ever seen in my life; midnight black coat with bright green irises.

"Are there anymore?" I queried, squinting to see further into the bushes.

"I don't know—I can't see. Flash your light."

Enabling the light on my phone, I shined it over the

area in question. "Looks like she's the only one. Grab her, baby."

"I'm trying! C'mere, girl," Lux cooed, reaching out with a cajoling hand while making adorable and unbelievably realistic little mewling sounds.

And then she wondered why I called her kitty kat...

Took several minutes and a whole lot of patience, but the kitten finally approached her, climbing right into her grasp. Rising to full height beside me, Lux lifted the little feline and nuzzled the top of her head.

"No collar—she's probably wild," I pointed out.

Lux nodded, completely taken with the teeny animal.

"I'd ask if you're superstitious but..."

"Yeah, I'm not," she laughed. "And even if I was... look at her little face. She's co cute!"

"We should keep her," I suggested.

My proposition snapped her gaze on me in record timing.

"*We?*" she stressed.

Nodding, I reached out to pet the little thing. "I quite like felines, and she *is* rather cute."

"Cuter than me?" Lux quipped.

"Just about," I joked. "What should we name her?"

Lux lifted her in the air and observed her closely, tilting her head from side to side. "She looks like a Wednesday."

Christina Ricci was the first thing that came to mind. "As in Addams?"

"Don't you think so?" she asked, turning back toward me.

The more I examined the feline, the more I could see it, but even if I hadn't, it was Lux's choice. She was elated to have come across this little creature, and all I cared about was her happiness. She could have wanted to name her Beans and I'd have agreed.

Chuckling, I pet her again. "You're right, she does."

"Wednesday it is then," she conceded. "*Wednesday Mercier-King.*"

I kinda liked that sound of that…

38. ALIGNED FORCES
Roman

♫ *Partners in Crime - Set It Off feat. Ash Costello* ♫

In the weeks leading up to the new year, Lux and I spent a lot of time talking about what the future could look like for us; business goals, wanderlust, moving in together. It might've seemed like a quick affair to some—some being Lux's friends—but everything with us had been a whirlwind from the start.

Could they really expect anything else moving forward?

Personally, I didn't give a flying fuck what anyone thought, especially those bitter, close-minded folk who weren't thrilled with the announcement that a new silent partner—aka yours truly—would be taking over reign of territories and all things related to distribution. We used a factious name for the sole purpose of keeping my identity, and our budding relationship, hidden.

Lux wasn't pleased with their resistance, but I urged her to brush it off. The way I saw it was, she didn't owe them an explanation. If they valued their jobs, they'd shut their mouth and get to work. Otherwise, the door was there and they were free to walk.

Besides, my Queen had bigger fish to fry, namely focusing on her cosmetic line.

With Black Widow doing so well on *Sephora's* shelves, it was paramount now more than ever that she expand into other retailers. That was the main goal here, where her focus needed to be, and where it needed to stay.

But during the transition from drug lord to solely entrepreneur, there was an important meeting she couldn't sit out due to what all it entailed. It'd been planned for quite some time now, regarding large quantities of high quality bud from Cali. The shipment couldn't be shipped, and with Lux not an easily trusting individual, she was not okay with just anyone driving across the country to secure it and deliver it.

Roscoe, evidently, knew someone willing to drive to and from for the right price, though, which is who she was interviewing when I stealthily arrived at Black Widow late one evening.

Slipping inside her office, I shut the door behind myself quietly and took a seat off to side to avoid a disruption. The man took notice of my presence immediately, blanching when I tipped my head in silent greeting.

"My driving record, seriously?" he turned back to ask Lux, determined to sound confident.

She was not amused by him. At all.

Holding his stare, she leaned back into her seat and crossed one leg over the other, the tip of her pen bouncing impatiently on the glass surface of her desk.

"Yes, Mr. Fernandez, I'm serious, and if you need the cash as badly as you claim, you'll shut your trap and provide the paperwork needed without further exclamation. This isn't some easy as shit free-ride job. You've gotta drive the best you've ever driven in your entire life or highway patrol will be all over your ass. I don't particularly think you're wanting prison time, am I correct?"

Fuck me.

Instant hard-on.

I loved watching my Queen lay down the law on these fools. It was sexy as fuck.

The bloke had nothing to say except shake his head by way of response. Glancing nervously between her and I, he swallowed deeply. "Okay, fine, I'll have it to you by tomorrow afternoon. I have one more question, though."

Lux sighed frustratedly and motioned for him to continue.

"Why do I have to drive both ways?"

Could he be more stupid?

Apparently, I wasn't the only one who thought so. The unimpressed look on Lux's face said it all. I had to stifle a laugh as she glared a hole through his head, probably cursing Roscoe to hell and back for his so-called recommendation.

"You see that man over there?" she went on to question him, a black polished finger pointing to where I sat.

At his nod, she went on.

"*Our* product is what you're picking up. It's a mass amount that cannot be shipped. *That* is why you have to drive both ways."

You'd think the motherfucker would've take the hint and quit while he was ahead.

But he didn't.

Wait for it…

"Is this a joke?" He laughed nervously. "Everyone on the streets knows you two are sworn enemies."

"Not that it's any of your business, street rat, and it's something that stays between us, but Mr. King and I recently decided to align forces. Is that going to be a problem for you?"

"I don't know, Miss Mercier, should it be?" he snapped.

I wasn't laughing anymore.

The fact he had the balls to even dare speaking to her in such a manner, when she providing him with quite the opportunity, was where I drew the line.

"You're out," I chimed in, rubbing my jaw between two fingers as I observed him.

His head snapped back over to where I sat, expression perplexed. "What?"

"You're. Out," I enunciated slowly.

"Why? I need this cash, man!"

"Should've thought about that before you decided to disrespect the Queen, mate. Don't bite the hand that feeds you."

"I'm sorry! I'm sorry, okay?" he bellowed, shifting anxiously in his seat. "I'm just nervous! I've never done anything like this be—"

"Yet another reason why you're out. This isn't a rookie position. We need someone skilled and reserved by nature," I explained evenly.

"I can do that, I sw—"

I held a hand up to spare him. "Have a nice evening."

Fernandez tried piping up again, pivoting back towards Lux in hopes she'd hear him out, but she shook her head and held a hand up as well, ending his feat before a single word could make it out of his mouth.

After he stormed out, I rose from my seat and made my way over to Lux, who had quite the satisfied look on her face.

"That was hot," she said, swiveling her throne around to meet me.

Grinning, I flashed her a wink and dipped my head to her level. "We'll find someone else."

"I'm not even worried about it. I know we will"—*kiss*—"How was your day?"

"Long, tiring." I set my hands on the armrest, wedging my way between her legs. "I'm ready to go home, take a long shower, and lose myself in you for a couple hours."

Coy, blue eyes regarded me beneath playful lashes. "That can be arranged. You should spend the night."

"Oh, I was planning on it. I loathe the solitude of my bed these days."

"Right there with you, baby." She kissed me again. "Wednesday misses you, too."

"And I her. When do you wanna head out?" I was eager to get out of there, and it showed in zealous waves.

Lux smirked knowingly, checking the time on her computer screen. "Twenty minutes, maybe? I just need to add a few things to Ellie's calendar and respond to some emails."

"Or you can leave all that for tomorrow morning and I

can get our evening started early," I suggested, peppering featherlight kisses along her neck.

"Oooh, I'm intrigued. Do tell." She hitched her legs around me.

"In detail or no detail?"

A tug to my tie put her lips at my ear. "I want every, single filthy detail running through your mind."

She asked for it...

"You, on that desk. Pencil skirt bunched high above your hips. These silky, creamy legs of yours spread wide open for me while I eat this pussy from your throne."

"And then what?" she breathed, nipping the lobe.

"You tell me. Tell me what you want, baby. You want the King to fuck you right here, to own that tight little cunt all over your workspace? Make it drip down on the glass?" Snaking a hand between her legs, I caressed her softly over the lace of her panties with the pad of my thumb, eliciting a little mewl with every rotation.

"Did you lock the door?" Her query came panted.

"No, why?"

"Hit extension two."

I did as instructed, reaching over her desk for the phone. A simple tap of the button and it beeped only twice before her PA's voice filled the space.

"What's up, L?"

"I'm wrapping up here in a few. You can go early," Lux said to her, voice schooled to perfection.

"You sure? I don't mind staying until 6."

The hell you will.

"Not necessary," Lux blurted, obviously thinking the same. "Have a good night, babe."

"If you say so—I'll see you tomorrow. Have a good night!"

The line clicked, and Ellie was gone, leaving us alone once more.

Lux promptly returned her full attention my way, seemingly more appeased at the fact no one would be strolling in unannounced.

"Where were we?" she questioned.

"I was about to turn you out on your desk," I reminded her.

"Oh, yeah—*that's right.*" She grinned salaciously.

As she threw her arms around my neck, I gripped her at the backs of her thighs and lifted her off her seat, all but throwing her into the desk.

She squealed excitedly.

I pinned her down.

Lips crashed instantly, tearing into each other with rabid nips of our teeth.

Hot.

Needy.

Roused by our setting.

My hands trailed down her body, reverently, bunching the hem of her skirt. Yanking it upwards and over her hips, she was left on display for me.

Sheathed only by black lace.

Calling for my tongue.

I could practically taste her, slipping my middle finger around the thin fabric between her lips.

"So wet," I cooed, increasing the pace.

But the reaction I received was far from what I was expecting.

"Stop. Stop! Rome, stop!" Lux pushed me off, eyes wild.

She even clamped her legs shut, throwing up all kinds of red flags.

"What's wrong?" I asked tensely, holding my hands up.

"I-I can't do this here..." she stammered, and for the briefest moment I thought she was referring to the door again...

"Ellie left, baby. No one is going to—"

But she wasn't.

It was so much worse.

What came out of her mouth so much worse than I ever could've imagine...

"Vic raped me..."

39. FIGHT OR FLIGHT
Lux

♫ *Madness - Ruelle* ♫

"What. The. Fuck. Did you just say?" Rome gritted out, his eyes darkening in that demonic way that could clear out a room.

"He violated me," my voice cracked, tears welling unbidden in my eyes as the nauseating memory rushed me. "He fucking violated me right here." I motioned to my desk.

"When did this happen?" he pressed sharply.

"Months ago, when you and I first met."

"What happened *exactly*? Tell me everything so I know how to gauge where he sits on the scale."

I wiped the wetness clinging to my cheeks. "What scale?"

"The scale of death, 'cause I'm going to fucking rip him apart," he growled vehemently.

"Rome, please, just—"

"Just tell me what happened, Lux!" The boom of his voice bounced off the walls, shooting my shoulders up to my ears.

Thank God I'd sent Ellie home early.

"I was here late one night. Got wrapped up in a phone call with Isabella, my now head of marketing, and when we hung up, Vic was standing at the doorway. Said he'd forgotten his charger," I explained hastily, hoping that if I started talking, he'd calm down a bit.

An abrupt flash of skepticism rained over his enraged features. "His charger?"

I nodded, wringing my hands together.

"And you believed that?" he spat.

"He'd never given me a reason *not* to believe him, so yes, I did. We had a quick chat, I dismissed him under the notion I'd be leaving soon, and before I knew it, he was on me."

Rome inhaled a deep breath, shutting his eyes and all, gathering himself. "Did he actually…"

"Yes," I admitted, "held me down through the entire thing. He even covered my mouth at one point to shield my cries." More tears broke free, leaking down my face in white-hot trails of despair.

And Rome's silence only made them worse, bursting the dam of hell wide open.

"Shhh, just relax," he tried cajoling me, holding me steady with a firm arm around my waist as his hand effortlessly yanked up my fitted pencil skirt. "You know you miss me. I'm sure your cunt misses me, too."

"I said no, Vic. Stop."

The more I resisted, the more he held me down.

The more a smile tore across his face.

I could barely look at him, barely recognized him. The fire in his green eyes was truly alarming. I couldn't believe the direction this was going in, especially when he knew everything about me.

Why was he doing this?

Full-blown panic seized me. My pulse was sky high as every hair on my body stood at attention. "Don't do this, please," I begged him shamelessly, which only seemed to please him more.

He smiled brighter, clamping a hand down on my mouth while the other slipped beneath my panty line and found my sex. I mewled when his middle finger slid between my lips, but it was far from pleasured.

"Goddamn, look how wet you are," he growled, working his finger inside me. "You did miss me."

I shook my head and tried feebly to shove him off, but once again, I was no match for his muscle or his dexterity. In seconds, he had my arms behind my back, my weight keeping them secured beneath me, before he was pinning me down with that palm on my mouth again. I was completely immobilized and at his mercy, laid out on my desk for him to do as he pleased.

And that included ripping my knickers off my body.

"I'm going to fucking kill him!" Rome roared savagely, recapturing me back into the present with a jolt.

It was only then I realized I'd been sobbing, trembling, and judging by the way Rome shook too, I knew I'd probably mumbled some of it aloud along the way.

He'd relived that with me, and now, it was likely Vic was about to find himself six feet under.

Reigning myself in, I wiped the tears off my face and slipped off my desk. "Listen to me—he's not worth it."

"How can you say that?" Offense shined through his demeanor. "He abused you, Lux! Took advantage of you when he knew all about you! Ripping him apart is damn well worth whatever karma throws at me!"

No, it's not.

Call me selfish, but I wasn't willing to risk *him*. *His* life was more important to me than ridding this world of Vic Kane.

"It's okay—I'm okay!" I tried again.

"It's not okay, no, you're obviously not okay either! You just pushed me away because of it!"

"I didn't mean to! The memory flooded me out of no where and I freaked."

"Do they happen often?" he questioned testily.

I shook my head. "No. After it happened, I spiraled for a short period. Started having day terrors again, night terrors too. But they stopped suddenly…"

"What made them stop?"

The silver-lining.

I'd never been more thankful for our obsession with one another until that very moment.

"You," I admitted, closing the distance between us, my arms coming around his middle.

Rome's head nearly snapped off his neck. "Me?"

"Yes, you. Dealing with you, with my confusing, underlying feelings for you, literally kept it all at bay. I guess that's why I spazzed just now. Being here, on the desk, even in a completely different situation, sprung it to the surface with a vengeance."

"Is this why you two weren't on speaking terms?" he pressed on, sliding his hands to the back of my neck.

I nodded.

"So why not just fire him then?"

"I didn't know how. I was afraid he'd snap, run to the cops."

"I get that," Rome sympathized, "but you need to fire him, baby. I don't want him within a foot of you."

Neither did I, but again, it went back to the fact that Vic would flip his shit, whether or not he'd been around much lately. The man was a vengeful bloke, and knowing our history—a history I was *not* about to share with Rome right now—he'd try to destroy me in every way he could.

Imagining the havoc he could wreak in mere hours was truly frightening.

I could lose everything I'd worked so hard for.

End up in prison…

"Rome, I can't. He'll ruin everything, I know he will."

"Make Roscoe do it. He's technically your right hand man now, correct?"

Another nod.

"Then tell him to get it done, stat," he deadpanned.

It wasn't up for discussion.

"I'll text him tonight, okay?" I promised. "Now, let's get out of here. How about we go have a few drinks at Blackbird first, then go home?"

Rome tipped his head and pulled me closer, brushing our lips together. "I could fucking use one."

~

BLACKBIRD WASN'T OVERLY PACKED BY THE TIME WE arrived—thank god. I suspected it was likely due to the fact we were in the middle of the workweek, but in any case, I was grateful for the chill vibe.

Chill is exactly what Rome and I needed right now.

The hostess greeted us and sat us over at the bar where we were tended to right away, our drinks ordered and served within minutes.

It was great, and while we didn't talk much, I was glad we'd stopped in before going home.

I wasn't really in the mood to chat anyway, and I knew for sure Rome wasn't either. What transpired earlier was enough to exhaust us both—mentally, physically. I didn't need forced conversation just for the sake of it, for the sake of pretending everything was alright.

Yes, *we* as couple were fine, but I knew Rome was raging inside; processing, analyzing, debating whether or not he should react on my behalf. Keeping him calm was all I cared about—so if that meant just being there with him, hanging on his arm, and relishing his company as soft jazz played in the background, then so be it.

I'd do it a thousand times over if I had to.

It's not like it was difficult or awkward. It never was. Our ability to be comfortably silent with one another was actually one of the things I loved most about our relationship.

We could sit in silence for hours and it was nothing but serene.

Like now—possessive hand on my thigh, his thumb rubbed back and forth tenderly over my pencil skirt as he stared into the amber liquid within his glass. Every so often, he'd peek over at me and offer a lopsided smirk, leaning in for a chaste kiss that left me humming in bliss.

This right here was all I needed.

And the bathroom, too—two drinks in and I was about to piss myself.

"I'm gonna run to the ladies room really quick. I'll be right back," I said to him, leaning over to peck his cheek.

But he turned his face in entirety, catching my lips with his own instead. A smirked twitched somewhere between us as his hand threaded into my hair, cupping my head. "Hurry—I'm about done here."

"Already?" I grinned, prompting him to nod as he sucked on my bottom lip.

"I need you."

"On the desk again?" I quipped, because although I'd freaked out on my work desk, I wouldn't mind him fulfilling that damned fantasy on my home desk.

"The desk, the couch, in the kitchen, on the bathroom floor. Wherever you want, however you want. I just need you before I lose my shit," he gritted out, flooding me on the spot.

Pussy clenching as those images unfolded in my mind, I hummed lasciviously and pecked his lips one last time. "Three minutes, baby. Get the bill settled."

A tip of his head.

An encouraging swat to my ass.

I squeaked and snatched my purse off the bar top, literally scampering down the dim corridor on the balls of my pumps, both from my bladder on the verge of an explosion and my libido racing into overdrive.

I couldn't get into the stall fast enough.

Couldn't piss fast enough.

Wash my hands fast enough.

All I could think about was the tsunami that was about the go down the second we stormed through the doors of my flat. I whimpered a little as I pulled a paper towel from the dispenser on the wall. The drive home was going to fucking kill me. A quick scan over my reflection and I was off, squeezing the shit out of my clutch in anticipation.

But as I emerged from the hallway into the main room, I tripped over my feet and stopped short at what I walked in on.

Lilac—one of Rome's hurricane sluts.

She was all over him, standing between his legs, her arms around his neck. I couldn't see his face, but I could see hers, and I recognized the fire in her eyes.

It's the same fire that had burned within my own just seconds prior.

I watched fiercely for several moments, my blood boiling, but when he made no move to fend her off, I'd had enough. I couldn't watch anymore. I wasn't even going to bother confronting them. Didn't have the energy for that. Not to mention, I'd likely beat her to a pulp, and I wasn't looking to walk out of here in cuffs.

So, I retreated slowly instead. Walked right out the front doors without a glance back to my G-Class.

Once I was behind the wheel, I pulled out my phone and sent Rome a quick text.

The last text I'd be sending him for the night, too, and possibly tomorrow as well, depending on how I felt after a night's rest.

This was Lux Mercier in all her petty glory, people.

Me: *I'd say I'm surprised, but I should've known better. Hope you and Lilac have a wonderful evening. x*

40. MAN ON A MISSION
Roman

♫ *Mine - Bazzi* ♫

Me: *Answer, please.*

Me: *This is all a misunderstanding.*

Me: *I swear to you, baby, nothing happened.*

Me: *I didn't touch her. She came on to me and I declined.*

Me: *Lux, please listen to me. Answer me. I can explain everything.*

From last night to this morning, I'd sent Lux over fifteen text messages and called her a dozen times, if not more.

Every message went unanswered.

Every call was sent to voicemail.

I was anxious, pissed right the hell off, too. How to the fuck was I supposed to fix this mess when she was giving me the cold shoulder?

Unrightfully so, I should add.

What she saw from her vantage point, what her mind had obviously led her to believe, was *not* what happened.

Not even close.

Azalea had completely caught me off-guard when Lux ran off to the restroom.

I was stewing after the Vic revelation, consumed by thoughts of both murdering him with my bare hands and burying myself in Lux straight through next week. It was all I could see on the glistening surface of the whiskey in my glass.

But then a small hand draped over my arm from the other side of the bar…

"Why so miffed, handsome?"

Snapping my head up, I'm met by regal gray eyes. I recognize them immediately, the long lilac waves of her hair too.

"What are you doing here?" I ask her.

Azalea looks at me like I'm clueless. "I work here, silly. I must have been on my break when you walked in."

"I see," I nod, taking a sip from my glass.

"So how've you been?" she presses, keen on continuing our conversation.

I, on the other hand, would rather not.

"I've been better," I grate dryly, hoping she'll take the hint.

"I figured. You look like—"

"Yo, Zay!" A voice from somewhere behind me interrupts her. "Table five needs refills; two Corona's and a Blue Moon!"

"Coming right up!" she answers, then goes on to squeeze my arm, flashing me a coy wink. "I'll be right back."

I would prefer she didn't, am about to tell her as

much, but she's gone to the other end of the bar before I can utter two words. Perhaps seeing Lux at my side when she returns from the ladies room will warn her off from approaching me again.

Minutes later, there's a tap at my back. I swivel around, expecting to see my Queen, but it's Azalea. She settles herself between my already spread legs and throws her arms around my neck.

"As I was saying, you look like hell. I can make it better, though," she coos.

"I'm going to pass," I deadpan, trying to move her off me, but she holds on tighter still and pushes me back against the ledge of the bar top.

"C'mon, Rome—let's finally finish what we started during the hurricane. And this time, you don't have to worry about Kelsey. Just me."

"Again, I'm going to pass, Azalea."

"I'll put the pep back in your step, babe. Suck your cock so good you won't even remember what you're so angry about."

"Third time's the charm perhaps? I said I'll pass. I have a—"

My phone vibrates in my pocket, pulling my attention away from the woman trying to seduce me.

I fish it out and the message on my lockscreen rises every hair on my body in a panic.

My Queen: *I'd say I'm surprised, but I should've known better. Hope you and Lilac have a wonderful evening. x*

See?

She had it all wrong.

It looked terrible, I know, but fuck—hadn't I proved myself to her? Hadn't I proved that she was it for me?

That she was all I wanted. All I needed.

I tried putting myself in her shoes, tried thinking about how I would've handled seeing some wanker all over her, and while I definitely would've felt the green-eyed monster possess me from the inside out, I never would have jumped to conclusions.

Never would've left her there with nothing but a text.

But Lux was a woman, a damaged woman who'd never experienced a real relationship, so I couldn't bring myself to blame her.

Did her silence play on my nerves?

Absolutely.

But I wasn't going to push her.

I'd done my part. Now, all I could do was wait for her to come around.

She had twenty-four hours.

Otherwise, I was taking it back into my own hands again before this spiraled into something worse.

I didn't hear from Lux until later on that evening, and I was no where near my phone when the calls started. I'd been out in the pool, swimming laps to ease my mind from the stress of the last almost twenty-four hours.

When I got back inside, I was surprised—and a tad

unnerved—by the amount of calls and voicemails clogging my lock screen. She's been calling as frantically as I had, and it appeared that, for every call, there was a voicemail that went along with it.

Most of them were of her singing, *very drunkenly,* to one of Rihanna's more vintage sounds. She wasn't alone either, cajoling Suki into singing along with her at some point as well. Each voicemail was literally a continuation of the last, and by the time I listened to the last one, I was in stitches.

Relieved.

Showering and dressing in record time before I jumped in the Benz and called her back.

"There you are," she said lazily.

"Do you enjoy serenading people in a drunken stupor often?" I joked, gunning it down I-95.

"It's only fun when they"—*hiccup*—"answer the phone." The smile tugging her lips was utterly palpable.

I couldn't help but laugh despite knowing she'd been drinking, very likely, because of what went down last night. "Christ, you're fucked up."

"Am n-not."

"Okay, pissed out of your mind is more like it."

"Rome!" she whined, to which Suki mimicked in the background. "Knock it off! I'm not pissed!"

"You were earlier," I pointed out, and I wasn't referring to alcohol anymore.

I hadn't even meant to say it. It just…came out.

The line fell completely silent, so silent, in fact, I

found myself glancing at the screen to ensure the call hadn't dropped.

"Lux, you there?" I asked.

"I'm here... And I know," she admitted softly, the volume of the music fading dramatically. Then a door clicked shut. "It was stupid and immature, and just... Ugh. I'm sorry."

Flipping on my blinker, I cut off some old geezer—who was driving 30 miles per hour—and dropped a gear, the engine roaring powerfully beneath my foot flooring the gas. Hearing her apologize was a relief. Not that I needed an apology, but it served to confirm this tiff was nothing. "Don't be. If I caught some bloke blatantly trying to get so chummy with you, I'd have done the same, too."

"Worse, maybe." Lux laughed, but I could tell it was only half-genuine. Not a word followed the dismal sound either, drowning the line in another thick bout of silence.

Silence drenched in guilt, more specifically.

Personally, her jealousy spike was nothing short of adorable. I loved the fact that she was possessive in her own way.

But this wasn't a game anymore.

She was mine, and I was hers, and propriety wasn't something either one of us took lightly.

"I know Suki's there," I said after a beat, finally easing onto I-95 with nothing but determination and urgency thrumming through my veins. "But do you need anything?"

"You," she whispered meekly.

One word.

That one little word was all I needed.

All I wanted.

Mine.

"I'm on my way," I warned her, weaving in and out of light traffic in a hurried fashion.

Horns blared above I*magine Dragons* as I cut people off and I could give all of three fucks.

A man on a mission was a force to be messed with.

Honk, wankers.

"Really?" she squeaked.

I nodded regardless of the fact she couldn't see me. "Fuck yes. Don't fall asleep. ."

"I won't."

Damn right you won't.

"And Lux?"

"Yeah?" she drawled.

"Get Suki the hell out of there. I know she's probably blasted, too, but call her an Uber or some shit," I growled, flipping off another twat through the passenger window.

"What? Why?" she queried, clearly befuddled at my request.

A delighted, sinister smirk colored my expression. "Because I highly doubt she'll want to hear your screams carrying through the walls."

Click.

THE DRIVE WAS NOTHING MORE THAN A RESTLESS BLUR OF muttered expletives and my hand slamming down on the wheel in frustration at each red light that held me back from Lux a little longer. I was dying to get to her and these American cunts had not a clue how to drive. Miami wasn't nearly as chaotic as New York, but nonetheless, it was maddening in its own way, and my patience had about reached its end.

Especially after almost thirty minutes just to arrive at her damn flat.

I couldn't get out of the car fast enough, hustling from my seat to the revolving doors in an equally blind trek, fueled by fierce adrenaline and a desperation I didn't know my heartless soul was capable of. I didn't even acknowledge the cheery doorman, brushing past him like a bat out of hell.

My thoughts were on Lux, and Lux only.

But yet again, the extent of my patience of was put to the test. It seemed that, the more I smashed my thumb into the call button, the longer the lift took to arrive.

And when it finally did, it fucking lagged all the way up.

The second the doors peeled open on the penthouse floor, I ambled my ass through the foyer to the front doors as though sweltering flames threatened to incinerate the floor behind me. With no neighbors to alarm, I banged the side of my fist against the door twice, bouncing on the tips of my toes in anticipation.

Time stood still as I waited…and waited…and waited.

My heart banged furiously, pulse racing faster than a speeding bullet. I hadn't been this nervous to see her in what felt like ages. What the hell was taking her so long?

Had she fallen asleep? Was Suki still here? Christ, I hoped not. My dick was screaming in fucking agony.

C'mon, Lux—open the door.

Less than thirty seconds later, the locks were coming undone. My chest instantly deflated with a breath I hadn't even realized I was holding, my palms stinging from the force of my nails embedding into my skin.

Then the door flew open and I couldn't move, gaping at her like a mindless imbecile. Just the mere sight of her in her little black robe was enough to undo me, a lovesick bastard unraveling piece by piece.

This is what she did to me.

How she ruined me.

Even in her blitzed state, with glassy, bloodshot eyes and that wild hair, she was one stunning creature, a creature who, clearly, needed a reminder of who I was and what my intentions were. I was all but on my knees before her, aching to mold her against me, to devour her, *worship her*.

I needed to. Needed her.

Needed her to know *she was mine*, and if that required fucking the concept into her thick skull until her cunt ached, then so be it.

Lux Mercier would learn tonight.

Blue eyes sparkled in the bright lighting, a knowing smile touching her lips. She knew damn well what I was thinking, what I was feeling.

Thoughts and feelings I sensed oozing off her, too.

Mine. So fucking mine, it wasn't even a question.

A savage growl tore free my chest, one that was a

hundred percent irrepressible, and while she hadn't said a single word, I wasn't looking to waste time on pleasantries or anymore unnecessary apologies.

At this point, 'I'm sorry' was as irrelevant as our spat.

Eating up the space between us, I swallowed her frame in my grasp and stormed us inside her home, slamming the door in our wake. Lux immediately wound herself around me like a vine to a trellis, not an ounce of hesitation or uncertainty in the way she crashed her lips to my own. Thighs in my grip, I dug her into the nearest wall, deepening her feverish kiss with impatient laps of my tongue along the seam. Idly, I felt Wednesday wriggling her way around my feet, little mewls of protest echoing below us, but I'd acknowledge her later.

Right now, I was all about my Queen.

"Fuck, I missed you," I mumbled into her mouth.

"It hasn't even been a whole day," she breathed.

"And yet it felt like an eternity. Is Suki gone?"

"Mhmm."—*kiss*—"Stryker came to get her."

"You're in trouble now." That was the one and only warning I was going to offer her.

The only one.

Taking off through the house, I barreled down the corridor to her room in hasty, determined strides.

The second we burst in through the double doors, I tossed her onto her bed, every ounce of frustration and anxiety from the day flooding me in an instant. "That was some dumb shit you pulled last night. This morning, too," I growled, pulling my shirt over my head.

"I know," Lux agreed, fumbling to undo the knot of her robe. "I fucking know. I'm sorry."

My belt was next, the buckle jingling as I pulled it free from the loops of my jeans. "I don't need an apology, Lux. What I need is for you to finally get it through your head that *you are mine*. You're all I want, all I need…"

"I do know!" she protested, prompting me to lay a finger over my lips.

"And yet you don't, but you will by the time I finish with you tonight. Come here—get on your knees."

Without hesitation, she did as I asked, scooting to the edge of the bed. Blue eyes trailed up my bare chest, meeting my stare with such curiosity and adoration, I nearly tossed her backward and impaled her right there.

My cock was already up for the challenge, straining painfully against my jeans. But I held on tightly to my restraint.

All in due time.

Soon enough, I'd be buried so deep in her pussy, she'd never doubt me—*or us*—ever again.

Slipping the belt around her neck, I secured it in one fluid movement and gave a little tug, pulling her body flush against me.

"What are you doing?" she whispered, hands flying up to clutch the belt, her fingers slipping beneath the studded leather.

"Subduing you." I wrapped the end around my hand until the very tips of my knuckles grazed her jaw. "We're doing shit my way this time, baby."

A meek little moan bubbled in her throat, compelling me to yank on the belt.

Harder.

Tighter.

It was abundantly clear she liked it, squeezing her eyes shut as my lips skated roughly up her cheek.

I hummed, appeased by her irrepressible reaction. "You like that, don't you?"

Lux nodded, trembling in my grasp.

I hummed again, brushing the black silk off her shoulders. "Let's see how much you like it once I'm fucking you. Turn around."

"No." She shook her head briskly, unbuttoning my jeans in a flash. "Not yet."

Her objection caught me off guard, so much so that I didn't grasp what was happening until my back had already hit the bed, her face still inches from my own from my hold on the belt.

"Let me service you," she purred, licking at my lips. "Then you can have your wicked way with me."

Fucking hell.

I couldn't deny her even if I wanted to.

No sane man would; control be damned.

Unraveling the belt enough to give her some leeway, she sunk her small frame between my legs, raking her nails down my torso deep enough to leave markings in their wake. Even in the dim lighting of her bedroom, you could see them raised through the ink on my body.

I hissed, and she smiled salaciously, flicking her tongue against the head of my dick.

Then down the rigid, veiny shaft to my balls.

Small hand working the tip, she sucked them into her mouth, steadfast blue eyes watching me beneath her lashes.

The sight of her worshipping my cock was an instant high.

"Motherfuck," I groaned, threading a hand into her silvery locks.

Pleased by my reaction, Lux laid the flat of her tongue at the base, and made her way back up to the tip with a torturous swaying motion that sent my eyes to the back of my head.

She sucked me with such gusto I could barely fucking see straight.

Could barely contain my hold on the belt.

I was lost to her touch, flying high in the fucking sky.

Hand now at base of my cock, her mouth bobbed up and down on the head, hitting that damned spot over and over again. I clenched my eyes tightly as ripples of pleasure diverged through my body, driving me toward the edge.

My hips thrusted reflexively, hitting the back of her throat.

But it didn't faze her in the slightest.

Instead, a satisfied hum vibrated against me, intensifying every last bit of her ministrations.

Then I felt it, my climax. Just within reach, looming closer and closer. Throbbing, the ache for release was almost too much to subdue, especially after stealing a glance at her between my legs.

"I'm gonna come," I warned, but she kept on, sucking harder, faster, her hand working the base with equal fervor.

The thought of coming down her hot little throat nearly set me off right there. I would have, too, and I would one day, but in that moment, I wanted her decadent taste on my tongue when I exploded.

Yanking on the belt, my cock popped free from her mouth as I dragged her toward me, her chest heaving, lips swollen and glistening with her saliva.

She seemed confused, regarding me with wide eyes.

"Turn around, Lux," I demanded, grabbing a greedy handful of her ass. "Put your pussy in my face."

Scandalized—she was downright scandalized, and yet so turned on, not a single objection followed.

With a quick hand, she unhooked the belt from around her neck, tossed it somewhere on the bed, and positioned herself over me, stretching out along the planes of my body to put my dick back in her mouth.

I dove right in, too, death-gripping the backs of her thighs as I dragged my tongue from clit to slit. Over and over again, I repeated the same act, adding swirls over her swollen bud and deep laps inside her tight little hole in between.

Drawing moan after moan from deep in her throat.

Each one reverberated through me as her scent invaded me.

Essence coated my tongue.

Legs quivering, she was flooding for me, and I hadn't even fucked her yet.

"Rome," she moaned suddenly, peeking over her shoulder.

Our eyes met and, immediately, I knew what she was about to ask me. She wouldn't have to ask twice either— my dick was begging to fill her.

"I need you," she grated, mouth falling lax as I licked her one last time for good measure.

"Face down, ass up, kitty kat," I instructed, tapping her off me.

Scrambling desperately into position as I rose onto my feet, she arched her ass in the air for me, offering herself to me.

All of her.

Such a glorious sight, all wet and primed, ready to be owned like she'd never been owned before.

Not even by me.

Settling behind her, I stroked myself a few times and dragged the head along her slicked entrance.

"*Please,*" she moaned softly. "Rome, please…"

"Please what?" I asked, slapping my length on her swollen lips.

Another moan. "Fuck me, please fuck me!"

And then I was inside her.

In one simple thrust I was filling her.

Stretching her.

Impaling her to fucking hilt.

Lux gasped so profoundly, it sounded like all the air just about left her lungs. "*Oh my god…*"

I eased back slightly as her body retreated from the

sudden intrusion, then dug back in, slowly increasing the pace as she accommodated to me.

"Go, go, keep going," she urged me, fisting the sheets for purchase.

But I needed her closer.

Needed to claim her mouth and swallow her cries while I possessed her, *all of her.*

Winding both arms around her shoulders, I pulled her back onto her knees toward me, pressing her back to my front as I powered into her.

"Tell me," I gritted in her ear. "Tell me who you belong to, tell me you know I'm yours."

Throwing her head back against my shoulder, she squeezed her eyes tightly, panting, moaning.

She couldn't answer me.

Could barely breathe from this angle.

"Say it," I demanded again. "Tell me who you belong to."

Still she couldn't respond, shaking her head as if to let me know words were failing her.

But she was going to.

"SAY. IT. LUX, or I'll make you scream it," I gritted out, slamming her down onto my length over and over again almost punishingly.

"You," she panted, "You, I belong to you!"

"Louder, say it louder."

"YOU—I belong to you!" she bellowed, unleashing the beast in entirety.

That was it.

The need to consume her whole—mind, body, and soul obsessed me in a way I'd never experienced before.

Pulling out of her dripping cunt, I spun her around and shoved her back onto the bed, taking her in with manic eyes.

She looked like a goddess, like my Queen, *like my fucking forever*.

On a turbulent growl, I loomed over her, hitching her legs around my waist as the overwhelming thought settled deep within me.

In my core.

In my mind.

In the heart she'd risen from ashes and somehow stitched back together.

And then in a single roll of my hips, I was inside her once more, fucking her with everything I had.

Making love to her with everything I had.

"I love you," I grated out, nearly breathless as the words left my mouth. "Do you hear me? I love you with every"—*thrust*—"fiber"—*thrust*—"of my fucking being."

Lux trapped my neck in arms and nodded frantically, her heart thrashing ferociously against my chest. "I love you, too," she moaned," I love yo—oh god, I'm gonna come!"

Euphoria.

It was fucking euphoria.

That magnificent burst of ecstasy consumed her, consumed us both, our climaxes erupting one after the other. It was so intense my entire body rippled against her, goose pimples littering every inch of my skin as my balls clenched with every spurt inside her.

I'd never come so hard.

Had never loved so hard.

I loved her more than anyone I'd loved in my life.

And should anyone try to take her away from me—may God be with them.

I'd kill for this woman.

Raise hell for this woman.

Mine.

41. LEFT FOR DEAD

Roman

♫ *Circus For A Psycho - Skillet* ♫

Noir Coast was dying.

I'd tried my best to keep that shit afloat, but Vic was still acting dodgy as fuck. So, after several months of minimal contact with the wanker, I stopped giving a fuck.

Washed my hands of it without a word.

Just as he'd done to me.

Like passing ships in the night, I literally hadn't seen him since the Vybe fiasco. Calls and texts were few and far between, but for the most part, I didn't answer anymore.

Didn't feel the need to respond to his repugnant, irredeemable ass, especially after Lux telling me of what he'd done to her.

That was nearly three weeks ago. It'd been one hell of a struggle not to reach out to him and lure him into a trap.

To do away with him, even if it was only putting miles between us.

It's not like anyone would miss him…

What sobered me whenever the thought of revenge hit was knowing that, if I reacted, if I sought out Vic, she'd ask questions.

Questions I'd been harboring the truth about for quite some time now.

Truths I was terrified to share.

After I told her I loved her, I had contemplated when and if would be a good time to finally tell her, but I could never go through with it. I knew I had to, and a part of me knew that for us to ever be fully bared to one another, to be as real and raw as our fierce connection, she needed to know all my truths.

And I needed to know hers.

So when she rang me to let me know Roscoe had finally fired Vic, I knew the time had come. I'd be getting a call from from the bastard soon enough and it was about to go down.

Soon turned out to be a mere hour soon.

The moment his blasted name popped up on my screen, that violent surge of animosity consumed me. I had to breathe through it, deeply, willing myself to calm down.

If I answered then, he'd call me out on it, and this point in time, I wouldn't hold back for shit.

I let it ring through to voicemail instead, stalking my screen for the new voicemail drop down that was about to appear at any moment. Like clock work, the small alert box descended at a the top of my screen about a minute later.

Except it wasn't a voicemail.

It was a text.

Vic: *SHE FIRED ME.*

He was livid, a concept I found comical to say the least. I played it off as though I had not an inkling as to what he was talking about.

Me: *For what?*
Vic: *Technically, the little bitch didn't fire me herself. She had Roscoe do it. He says it was his decision as new head of everything, but I know that's bullshit.*
Me: *Either way—what did he fire you for?*
Vic: *He said primarily because they didn't need me anymore but, evidently, my attendance played a role in the final decision, too. Are you free later?*
Me: *Possibly. Have to check my schedule.*
Vic: *Make time, brother. We need to chat.*

He was right; we *did* need to chat.

This was it.

Vic was finally going to get what he deserved, and I was going to love every bloody second of it—no pun intended.

Me: *I'll meet you at your place. 7pm.*
Vic: *Speak soon.*

As soon as his final text came through, I tapped into my recent calls and rang my Queen, my heart already racing from the burst of adrenaline. We had dinner plans set for the time I'd just promised Vic, and as much as I hated to cancel on her, it simply had to be done.

It was time to cut him loose once and for all, for both our sake. And once he was a thing of the past, I vowed to myself I going to sit her down and finally come clean.

Up on our spot.

High over our kingdom.

Our love demanded honesty, and I had every intention to right by it.

"Hey, baby," she answered, whirring sounds of the printer going off behind her.

"I have semi-bad news for you," I came right out with it, hating the fact I had to disappoint her.

I could hear it already.

"Oh, no—what happened?"

"We have to cancel dinner for tonight."

"Whyyy?" she whined, amping me up all the more for my visit with Vic.

He was going to regret every single decision he ever made, especially fucking with my girl.

"There's something I have to take care of," I answered simply, not wanting to intrigue her too much.

"And what is that?"

"I can't tell you."

"What do you mean you can't tell me?!" she screeched adorably.

I had to stifle the villainous chuckle that nearly broke free. "I promise I've got it under control, baby, okay?"

"Roman King, what is going on?!" she pressed, her tone both demanding and a little anxious.

Grinning, I dropped to the edge of my bed, and slowly pulled open my top nightstand drawer, withdrawing my pistol from within. "I'm ridding our kingdom of vile peasants, my Queen. Worry not—the King will make it up to you later tonight."

~

"So how've you been?" Vic asked awkwardly as we stepped into his study.

The air was thick with tension between us, hence his need for small talk. I fucking loathed small talk and he knew that.

"Just peachy," I answered, peering around the room to avoid pummeling him on his ass right there. Or pulling my weapon out. "Listen, I've got somewhere to be soon, so why don't you go ahead and get on with whatever it is we need to chat about."

"Geez, King—at least let me offer you a drink first," he chuckled, ambling over to the liquor cabinet.

"I'm good, but thanks." I smiled dryly.

Vic held my stare for a moment before hitching a shoulder and pivoting around. "Suit yourself."

A couple of minutes passed us by before he finally stalked to his desk and took a seat at the edge. "Please, sit," he offered, motioning to one of the chairs before him.

Lifting a hand, I shook my head. "I'll pass. Get on with it, Vic. What do you want?"

"I was going to discuss shutting down Noir Coast since we *obviously* don't need it anymore, but now I'm quite bothered by your shit attitude." He took a generous sip of his whiskey and set the glass down on a coaster, crossing his arms. "What the hell is your problem?"

The way he said obviously piqued my fucking interest, but I didn't care enough for him to elaborate. He was probably referring to the fact I'd not done shit lately.

"I'm in a hurry, Vic. Got places to go, people to see."

"Who, like Lux?" He smirked wittingly.

I nearly went rigid, not expecting him to say that, but managed to remain indifferent in my shock. "You're joking, right?"

He couldn't know...

"On the contrary... I haven't spoken to her personally yet, as I explained earlier, but it's clear both of you must seem to think I'm an idiot," he snapped, jerking my head back indignantly.

"You're cracked, mate. Seriously—what are you going on about?"

Vic sighed irritably and leaned forward slightly, looking me dead in the eye. "I know you're fucking her."

Shit.

Him knowing complicated things a hell of a lot more.

"What the fuck?" I barked, trying to play it off still. "I am not—"

"Save it, King. *I have you two on tape.*"

Everything around me went eerily still as the demon of wrath uncoiled inside me. Fuck it that he knew.

He had us on tape?

"You what?"

Nodding, he started around his desk. "After your little performance at Vybe, I made it a point to hang back in the shadows, to observe from afar hence my frequent absence lately. Evidently, you both forgot Black Widow has cameras installed both inside and outside the building." He pulled out three cd's from one of his drawers and held them up for me to see. "Not to mention the ones I installed in both your homes, and the few I scattered on top of the Panorama."

This motherfucker...

"You went in my fucking house?!" I seethed, barely containing myself from strangling him.

"You left me no choice," he sneered, leaning onto the desk. "I trusted you to finish her, to see our plan through, promised you everything you wanted and more, only for you to end up screwing me over. It's fucked up, Rome. *Really* fucked up."

Anddd snap.

There was no controlling it anymore.

I went off like bomb, charging toward him with a savage growl as I cleared his desk, clatters and clangs of all sorts erupting around us from all the items clashing to the ground. My fist collided with his face just once before I gripped the front of his dress shirt and lifted him off his feet.

"You wanna talk about fucked up?" I roared malevolently, throwing him into the wall like tattered doll.

His head hit with a monstrous bang, leaving a mass dent in its wake as his body fell weak.

Seeing him down on the ground awoke every demon I'd tried keeping locking away. I was raging inside, positively vehement.

Even the devil himself couldn't best me right now.

Chest heaving, I stormed over to where he laid, my boots thundering against the tiled floors. In one fluid movement, I fisted the front of his shirt and dug his vile ass back into the wall. "You raped her! You fucking raped her, you sick fuck!"

Vic—now pale as a ghost—shook his head nervously, a trail of blood dripping from his nose. Gallantry gone. "Not true! That's not true! That's what she wants you to believe!"

Growling, I slammed my fist in his face a second time. "Why the fuck would she want me to believe such an atrocity?"

"Because that's what she does, always plays the victim card." He spat more blood to the floor beside us. "Once she's got you invested in her bullshit, she'll ruin you, just like she's done to me and anyone else standing in her way! It's not true, I swear!"

I didn't believe him for a split-second; the terror in Lux's eyes when she'd recounted me with the sordid tale was all the proof I needed.

"What do you mean *like you*? She didn't ruin you! You ruined her!"

He was clearly sick in the head.

"Of course she ruined me, you idiot—why do you think I wanted to take her down?" he countered, maxing out my ire to capacity.

"Well, I wouldn't know because you never told me, remember?" I bellowed, shoving him towards the wall again.

Vic stilled for a fleeting moment, stumbling to regain his footing, but his expression quickly recast from panicked to stout. A poisonous smile turned up the corners of his bloodied mouth as he righted himself, lifting his chin.

"Oh my... I see what's going on here," he rasped, wiping the veil on crimson staining his chin. "Did she tell you about how she met me, Rome?"

"Some, yes..." I nodded, fist coiled at the ready.

"What do you know?" he pressed, amusement coloring his tone.

"How you met her, what you did for her and Suki..."

"And did she tell you how she fucking robbed me of it?" he gritted out. "Just when I was close enough to the top, to my rightful reign as King, she snatched it all from right underneath my fucking feet. Worked her charm to relinquish all of my loyalties, all of my connections, for herself. Went behind my back and weaseled her way into the throne. And then, she led me on—to keep the peace and still use me to her advantage, she slept with me. Made me think eventually she'd be my Queen..."

Silence ensued.

Complete silence.

His Queen.

I couldn't speak—didn't know what to say. The visual stomping through my mind was more than I could bear to entertain. I'm not an idiot...I'd had in inkling he'd slept with her—at least once—based on how she was always a sore topic for him, but I didn't think it went this far.

Far enough that she wouldn't tell me about it.

Then again, the night she laid her soul bare to me, I'd cut her off right as she began explaining how she met Vic.

Had I let her continue, would she have told me?

"What's wrong, Rome?" The bastard's grin widened. "Let me guess, she didn't tell you that? She didn't tell you that she'd slept with me, right?"

"No," I admitted, jaw nearly ground together.

"I'm sure you've not told her about me either. Otherwise, she wouldn't have given you that pretty little pussy. It's so fucking pretty, isn't it? So tight, and warm. Such a pretty shade of pink..."

A deep-seated, possessive growl seethed within me. "If you value your life, you'll shut up right about now."

Vic chuckled darkly. "Look at you so hung up over her, even after I've just told you she's been lying to you. Never thought I'd see the day again after Liza."

"Shut. Up." I warned a second time, but his taunting continued.

"You're like two peas in a pod—two lying, backstabbing, pathetic little peas in a pod. You'll eventually grow tired of her, though, might even resort to taking her by force to teach her a lesson, *just like the rest of us.* Don't say I didn't warn you when you find yourself snapping in a manic episode and—"

The tip of my handgun met his forehead.

Dead-center.

"Go on," he laughed sardonically, holding his hands up in mock-surrender. "Do it."

Growling, I pressed the tip deeper, my lip curled in a snarl.

I could've blown his brains to bits and spared the world from his revolting existence, but my finger twitched on the trigger.

Putting a bullet through his head would be too easy. Like Lux's father, he deserved much worse.

Slow and painful.

So I rushed him instead.

Holstering my weapon back at my side, I finished him off with my bare hands, repeatedly throwing my fist in face, each time harder than the last. The most pathetic part of it all was how he didn't even try to defend himself.

He just took it with a demented smile, until he was nothing but a bloodied, swollen mess.

Once he was down on the ground, I kicked him several times for good measure, relishing the sounds of bones cracking and howls of agony finally renting the air with each one.

He didn't move when finally retreated, his blood staining my hands, spattered on my clothes. My chest heaved from exertion, demons stated from our feat.

And yet, I found myself pulling my pistol out once more, aiming it at him with a firm hand.

"You ever come near her again, a measly two-fucking-feet, and I'll finish you off for good, you lying piece of shit. Stay the bloody hell away from her," I advised, my voice ragged in tempo but deathly low in severity.

Green eyes, now barely visible behind swollen lids, dragged up to where I stood—and that's when I pulled the trigger.

Bang!

42. CUTS OF THE TRUTH
Lux

♫ *Love The Way You Lie - Eminem & Rihanna* ♫

Dripping wet, he carries me through the house and up the stairs, his lips working against mine, tongue lashing viciously in and out of my mouth. It's like he can't get enough of me, desperate for another fix, another high. I can't lie and say it's not the same for me, 'cause it is. God, it is. His mouth can do some deliciously wicked things and I want it all over me. Correction—I want him all over me; on me, in me, everywhere. I want him to consume me, to suffocate me in his darkness and embed me into the fabric of his being.

"That pretty little cunt better be ready for me, Lux," he warns as we burst into his chamber, the doors slamming harshly against the walls. "Because the second I drop you on this bed, I plan on sliding my cock home and stretching you out all night long."

"Sounds like torture," I breathe, all but shivering in anticipation from the overwhelming sense of lust ripping through me.

"Oh, it will be." He laughs darkly. "And you're going to love every bloody second of it."

No sooner do the words leave his mouth before he flings me onto his bed. His hands make quick work of yanking my drenched bikini bottom down my legs and shoving them apart, exposing me to his hungered stare.

The growl that rips free from his chest is so deep and predatory, I feel myself slickening in anticipation.

I want to taunt him, to show him what he does to me, but I don't move, I don't speak.

I can't.

His reaction to my body leaves me completely hypnotized.

How his brow furrows, the way he licks his bottom lip, the way his chest heaves, how with every second he gazes a little longer his dick twitches and rises at attention.

The tiniest moan bubbles in my throat, snapping his attention up to my face. He must like what he sees because that devilish smirk plays on all his features as he sinks to his feet between my legs. With exquisite slowness, he grips my ankles and stamps featherlight kisses up my legs, first the right, then the left. They're so soft, I barely feel them, and yet I'm trembling, pooling at the gentleness of his touch.

His eyes glow demonically in the dim lighting, literally glow, racking another pussy-clenching shiver down my spine. Like a beast stalking his prey, he comes for me, slithering his way up my body until I'm trapped beneath him with nowhere to go.

"I love you," he vows, sliding into me in one fluid stroke. "I fucking love you."

Balls deep in my own fantasy, I was sheer seconds

away from falling over the edge within the confines of my shower, when my bloody phone started ringing.

Blaring.

The vibe harsh on the marble countertop.

Fingers freezing over my clit, I groaned frustratedly and shut off the water, rushing out to check the caller ID.

A quick scan revealed the last name I expected to see; Vic.

My stomach churned violently.

No doubt this had to do with Roscoe firing him.

Wrapping my towel around myself, I swiped the screen and connected the call, throwing it on speaker.

"You're wasting your time if you're trying to get your job back," I answered, deciding my usual bitchy demeanor would probably be best.

Vic laughed weakly, but it was far from one of amusement. "Trust me, Lux—the last thing I want is my fucking job back."

"Then what the bloody hell do you want?" I snapped, sauntering into my bedroom to get dressed.

I was supposed to meet Rome soon.

"To ruin you." That's all he offered, and he sounded deathly serious.

Goose pimples prickled my skin at the vengeful edge of his voice, an uneasy chill rapidly working its way through my being.

Rather than revealing my cards, than revealing the depth of my trepidation, I laughed out loud, pulling a tank top free from my dresser. "Is that so? Go on, Vic. Humor me."

"He's lying to you," he deadpanned, stilling me in place.

"Who?"

"Your boy toy."

His faint snicker widened my eyes.

There's no way he knew about Rome and I. We'd been so careful...

"You must have me confused with someone else." I tried playing it off, pulling the top over my head. "I don't have a—"

"Cut the crap, Lux. I know all about you and Rome. I *have* for a while now," he sneered. "Your little performance at Vybe was quite entertaining. Not exactly a convincing one, but very entertaining."

I nearly swallowed my tongue.

Realization rushed me with such speed, my head almost spun.

He'd been at Vybe...and he matched the stalker description to a T...

"Apparently, the two of you thought I was a fool," he continued as I stood there processing. "Turns out, the only fool here is you."

My head reared back in ire. "How am I a fool?"

"I told you, he's lying to you."

"And what exactly is he lying about?" I pressed, sliding into my knickers and a pair of denim shorts.

"About me."

"What do you mean about you?"

"Roman didn't just magically decide to start a war with you, sweetheart. He came into your life *because of me*. Might be a newsflash for you, but I'd been planning to take you down for quite some time. Knowing how difficult of a task that would be, I enlisted Rome to lend a helping hand—you know, since we worked so well together on the streets of London as young lads."

Forget his mention of taking me down—that didn't concern me. Plenty of imbeciles had tried to overrule me before. All I heard, all my brain could focus on was the last bit.

"Young lads?" I hedged, shuffling over to my bed.

Something told me I needed to sit—stat.

"Indeed. Rome and I have known each other well over a decade."

Well over a decade...

I let that sink in, let what it possibly meant sink in.

If this was true then...

No, it can't be.

"So you mean to tell me, this whole time, you knew who Phantom was?"

"Knew who he was, what his next move would be, where to find him," he chuckled darkly. "Watching you run around like a chicken without a head was quite comical."

"How do I know you're not lying?" I pressed, praying like I'd never prayed before that it was all a lie.

Not for his sake, but for Rome's.

"Why would I lie about knowing the wanker?"

"To fuck with my head."

"Meh. I'm over that," he chortled. "I'm just looking to

even the score after he beat me to fucking a pulp over you."

"I don't believe you," I gritted out, but deep down, knowing what Rome was capable of, a part of me did. "When did this supposedly happen?"

"An hour ago, maybe a little more. Motherfucker left me nearly unconscious with a few broken bones and a bullet graze to my side. I'm sitting in the emergency room as we speak."

I cringed at the visual that unloaded in my mind's eye. "I want proof," I demanded, praying harder still.

The timelines added up perfectly.

Our dinner—the one cancelled last minute—was supposed to be at 7…it was now 8:23 and I'd still not heard a word from him.

A minute later, my phone pinged. "Check your texts," Vic claimed.

Exiting the call screen, I tapped my way into my text messages and clicked on Vic's name now bolded at the very top.

"Oh my god." The image he sent was absolutely horrifying.

He was black and blue, dried smatterings of blood clinging to his skin. His entire face was mostly swollen, too, but the worst of it all was around his eyes. It looked like he'd been stung by a swarm of wasps. And the images of his body—I couldn't even stomach them. They were gnarly.

"Mhmm." Vic piped up again. "He did the same when he caught Leo and I with Liza."

At the mention of their names, any hope I had just about shriveled away.

"You *and* Leo?" I asked, my voice suddenly clogged with emotion.

"Indeed—in the Milani's office. Wasn't the first time we'd fucked her, together or otherwise. That little bitch was a twisted, cock-loving whore. Not that Rome knew, of course. He was too busy playing King of the streets with her."

Vic chuckled at the memory, meanwhile I sat there withholding an ocean of tears in disbelief.

It was true.

As deceitful, backstabbing, and despicable as Vic was, it was all true. There's no way he'd know about Liza *or* Leo, or any of that otherwise.

Which meant Roman had been lying to me since day one.

The knot in my stomach tightened all the more, shooting bile up my throat like a bullet. I wanted to wretch all over the place.

How could he do this to me?

"I need to go, Vic," I croaked.

"Mmm, I'm sure you do." The bastard sounded so damned pleased. "Off to call to your King, I'm sure?"

Just the sound of that name wounded me all the more, the ache in my chest so piercing, I almost couldn't breathe.

"I said I need to go," I gritted out, a lone tear trickling down my face.

I didn't wait for a response, or a fare well.

I simply ended the call and fell back on my bed as my entire world began crumbling into tiny pieces.

Everything suddenly made sense.

Ev-ery-thing.

How he always knew where to find me.

How he knew how to press my buttons.

How he always seemed to be two steps ahead of me.

How any mention of Vic always seemed to put him off.

Silent tears sprung free in raging streams as grief and an abundance of self-loathing dispersed through my being. How could I have been so stupid? So naive?

How had I not have caught onto it?

Really, the question I wanted to know the answer to was why?

Why would he fucking do this to me?

I thought he loved me…

Bringing my phone up to my line of sight, I typed out a simple message. It was all I could manage with shaky hands and a shattering heart.

Me: *Where are you?*

I wasn't so sure how'd I'd fare seeing him right now, but it had to be done. I had to know.

At the very least, I didn't have to wait long for his response. It came through within a minute or so.

My King: *Our spot.*
Me: *How much longer?*

My King: *Until you get your ass up here.*
Me: *Twenty minutes.*
My King: *I'm waiting...*

And he was.

When I made it to the Panorama, I spotted his Mercedes before I even parked myself. The entire walk to the lift and the ride up to the roof was beyond the point of simply nauseating. Every emotion possible seemed to hit me all at once, and with such speed, too, my head felt like it could spin 360 degrees.

How could he do this to me?

A choked sob grated it's way up my throat, a sob so hard I found myself gripping the steel railing for support. My eyes watered as realization sunk it's way a little deeper, clawing into my soul, slowly tearing it to shreds.

It hurt.

It hurt so much I couldn't see straight. Couldn't breathe. Never in my life had I felt anything like this before.

Ding!

My heart just about stopped as the lift came to a full stop.

This was it.

The end.

And yet, as shattered as I was about it, the second I saw him at the other end of the building, his broad back turned to me, red hot rage instantly thawed my despair. It took me over. Consumed me. Fueled me.

Like it used to when we first met.

This I could handle.

Hate was easy, welcomed at this hour.

Straightening my spine, I lifted my head high and stalked toward him with renewed purpose. Tears may have streamed down my face, but pure fire burned through my veins.

How could he do this to me?

How could he fucking do this to me?

Those incessant thoughts only made me angrier.

At the sound of my boots clipping against the concrete, he peeked over his shoulder.

A smile sat painted on his face...until he really saw me. Then his entire demeanor flipped. It ran ice cold. His face fell, dark brows bunching together as he spun around entirely.

"Who fucked with you?" he gritted out, skyrocketing my rage to capacity.

He had some fucking nerve.

"You, you lying bastard!" I roared.

And then my palm made perfect, unparalleled contact with his cheek, resounding around us above the sounds of the city.

43. IMPLOSION
Roman

♫ *End Of Me - Ashes Remain* ♫

"Why?" she barked, tears rolling down her cheeks, steam all but billowing from her ears. "Why the fuck would you lie to me?"

Face burning, I was taken aback at first, shocked by her abrupt strike and the tornado in which she'd touched down.

But it hit me rather quickly, shooting my heart up to my throat.

Vic.

Despite my warning, despite the fact I'd left him in nothing but a mangled heap, he had to have called her after I took my leave and told her everything.

And if everything included what I thought it did, I was fucked.

"What are you talking about?" I asked, needing her to confirm before I opened my mouth and possibly made shit worse for myself.

"Really? You're gonna stand there and play the clue-less card?" she seethed, narrowing her blue eyes.

"What have I lied about?"

Her head jerked back in ire. "Oh my god, are you serious right now, Roman?!"

Roman.

The way she spouted my name so venomously—it stung more than it should have, nearly knocking the wind out of me.

She had to know...

"Just tell me!" I begged, feeling the ground tremble beneath our feet from a looming implosion.

"You knew Vic this whole time!" she yelled back. "You knew him this whole goddamn time, since you were fucking kids! You were helping him take me out, for fucks sake! Knew he was the stalker, too!"

And there it was.

Out in the open.

Freed from the shadows.

She knew it all.

"I can explain..." I stepped toward her, heart thrashing frantically, but she stepped back holding a warning hand up.

"Don't. Touch. Me," she gritted out. "You can *try* explaining from right there, *but I won't hold my breath.*"

If words could kill, I'd have been six feet under right then and there.

Swallowing deeply, I raked an anxious hand through my hair, wondering how the hell I was going to fix this. "It started out that way, yes. But then I fell for you..."

Lux looked at me in pure disgust, lip curled in a snarl and all as she shook her head. "So that's supposed to make it all okay? The fact that you "supposedly" fell for me?"

"Not supposedly, I did! I fucking love you!" I bellowed, wounded by her use of air quotes as if she didn't know I loved her with every last facet of my being.

"You expect me to believe that? You've had plenty an opportunity to come clean, to tell me about Vic, and you've done nothing but lie from start!"

"I did it to protect you!" The desperation in my voice was clear, but Lux didn't seem to be affected.

In the slightest.

Crossing her arms, she cocked her head to one side. "Protect me? From what?"

Silence.

I didn't know how to answer. It sounded so good in my head, all made perfect sense—how I'd so valiantly done it to protect her, but now that I heard it aloud, it sounded more daft than anything I'd ever heard in my life.

What was I really protecting her from?

"That's what I thought," she growled, wiping the moisture building in her eyes anew.

The sight of her so clearly distraught, so hurt... I couldn't bear it, rushing toward her to pull her in my arms. "Baby, please, I swear to you...I never meant to keep it from you this long. It was just so—"

"Save it, Roman." Her palm, firm and steady, hit my chest, holding me back. "I don't wanna hear it. I don't wanna hear none of it. *We're done.*"

Those two little words... They immobilized me, rooting my feet to the ground. "What?"

"It's. Over." she enunciated, with finality nonetheless.

A finality that crippled me, like she'd ripped the soul she'd gifted me from body.

"Baby, don't do this," I pleaded, snatching her wrists in grasp.

"I didn't do shit! This was all you!" She struggled, trying to wriggle herself free.

"You have to believe me, it wasn't malicious! I just didn't know how to tell you!"

"Lying *is* malicious, you bastard!" she hissed. "I hate you!"

And that right there was where I drew the line.

As marred as I was hearing those three words come out of her mouth, three words she'd told me countless times when we first met, I drew the line right there.

I refused to go down like this.

Refused to let *us* go down like this.

She was going to listen to me if it's the last thing I did, even if I had to sit here all night and explain every detail down to the nitty gritty, like I should've done in the first place.

Like we both should've done…

"I'm not the only one who's lied," I said calmly, abruptly ending her struggle.

"What did you just say?" she asked.

"I know about you and Vic, too."

Lux's eyes widened, her face paling just slightly. "I...I…"

"I'm not mad," I explained, pulling her into me. "I

know why you didn't tell me. Should you have at some point? Yes. But I get it, baby, I really do."

Time stilled for a moment as we bore into one another. Me, hoping like hell this revelation would turn the tables around for the better.

And her...well, I couldn't decipher it exactly.

She seemed astounded, and yet, incredulously enraged all in one shot.

It wasn't until she scoffed profoundly and pushed me away once more that I realized this wasn't going to change a thing.

"Just like that, huh?" she huffed. "Even after knowing what you know, you're okay with it just like that?"

I shrugged, trying to remain as level-headed as possible. "You did what you had to do to survive."

Lux threw her head back and laughed, but it wasn't amused. "Unbelievable. Un-be-fucking-lievable! You find out I willing slept with him, and that I kept it from you, and you're standing there acting like you get it. Using this as a ploy to subdue me and sway me right back into your arms. You're fucking disgusting!" she bellowed, shoving me away again.

But I caught her wrists a second time, unwilling to let her go. How could she think that?

"Lux, stop."

"Let me go," she gritted out. "You're disgusting and fucking daft if you think forgiving my indiscretions changes anything for you. I didn't hide my relationship with Vic for the same reason you did! You were playing me for a fucking fool!"

"Listen to me, please—it's not a ploy," I said evenly, tightening my hold on her wrists as I walked us backward.

"Fuck you! Let me go!"

"No, stop. Just listen to me."

"Let me fucking go, Roman," she snarled, gasping when her waist hit the roof's ledge, cars honking and zooming hundreds of feet below us.

"No—knock it off already and listen to me!" I barked.

"Let go!" *Elbow to my side.*

"NO," I growled, holding tighter still.

"LET GO!" *Knee to my thigh.*

"NO!"

"LET FUCKING GO!"

"NO, FUCKING NO! STOP! STOOOP!" I roared at the top of my lungs, the enraged sound carrying through the busy city around us.

My voice fucking echoed. In the city.

That's how loud I was. How I suddenly angry I was.

And she flinched because of it.

Lux Mercier actually flinched.

Then she froze, her chest heaving, pale blues barely holding back fresh tears. Her stare didn't falter, though, and what I saw run through there—what I finally saw such clarity—hit me like a bucket of ice water.

Resentment.

Anguish.

Suffering.

Betrayal.

Every emotion was my doing, my fault. I'd truly, truly hurt her, and while that had been the plan at one point in time, the plan became null and void the second I fell for her.

But I'd done it anyway.

I'd managed to fuck everything up.

Managed to fuck *us* up.

It physically wounded me. Crippled me all over again, worse now than before.

The heart I spent years without, the one she stitched back together, felt like it was breaking.

Shattering.

Imploding.

My grip slipped as indescribable pain lanced right through my being. She tore herself away on a growl and shoved at my chest over and over again until we were in the middle of the roof.

"I hate you, I fucking hate you!" Tears were flowing free once more, slapping me in the face harder with every one that rolled down her cheeks.

My chest heaved wildly like I'd been running a mile.

She hated me and I hate this.

I hated me.

"I'm sorry!" I yelled it, clenching my hands, swallowing down the tsunami of emotions threatening to break free. "I'm fucking sorry!"

"You're sorry?" She yelled back incredulously. "YOU'RE SORRY? That means absolute shit to me, Roman! Look what you've done to me! You've ruined me, completely fucking ruined me, and not just for other men, but for everything! EVERYTHING!"

I was two seconds from uttering something that would

probably only dig me a deeper grave when she started toward me on another growl, shoving me back again repeatedly.

"I opened up to you." *Shove.*

"I trusted you." *Shove.*

"I gave you my fucking heart!" Her voice cracked. "And what did you do with it? Played it like a fucking violin, then smashed it into millions of pieces and sprinkled it around like confetti with your fucking bullshit lies. I fucking hate you!"

"Baby, please. Please listen to me," I croaked, falling to my knees in front of her.

Bowing at her altar.

"Just stay away from me, Roman," she hissed, tsking at my blatant display of weakness. "Just stay the fuck away from me like you should have done in the first place."

But what was a King without his Queen?

44. TORN, TATTERED, AND SHATTERED

Lux

♫ *Elastic Heart - Sia* ♫

I thought I'd been low before, thought I'd experienced pain of great magnitude before.

But I'd never been this low.

This broken.

This torn.

So completely shattered to the point only slivers of me were left.

A part of me died the night Roman's betrayal emerged from the shadows, and although the other half of me was drowning in a deep depression, begging to be saved, I had no intention of rising the stupid bitch from the dead.

After all, she's the reason why I fell for Roman in the first place.

She wanted love, happiness, all the things I knew weren't meant to be a part of my life. But I listened to her anyway. I let her cloud my better judgement, let her convince me destiny couldn't be overruled. Let her convince me that what Roman and I had was real.

I let her kill me.

So now, she could rot in hell for all I cared.

The same went for Rome.

Thinking about him was both excruciating and infuriating, a maddening loop that went on day in and day out, even after the relentless phone calls, voicemails, and text messages stopped. One second, I missed him with every piece of my mangled being, wishing we could rewind time and do it all right from the get-go, and the next I hated him again, wishing him an eternity in satan's fiery playground as punishment for making a completely and utter fool out of me.

We were going on almost a month of this shit and I was losing my goddamn mind. I couldn't take it anymore, had to expel these soul-sucking demons somehow.

Suki and Ramsey didn't know what to do with me either. They'd tried on more than one occasion to pull me free from the darkness, to help me move on with my life, but their attempts were feeble.

Nothing worked.

Nothing helped.

Except the thought of destruction, of raising hell on earth so everyone could suffer along with me.

Selfish, perhaps, but this agony within me, the malevolent blaze that had festered because of it, demanded mayhem.

I craved it.

The ideas presented to me were insane, deranged, and yet, the thought of bringing them to fruition promised me peace.

A semblance of sanity.

Whether that was a result of the devil's work or not, I was willing to try anything at this point. I'd sell what remained of my soul to feel anything but this godforsaken torment.

Which is why I found myself outside of Noir Coast one night with two plastic canisters of gasoline in my trunk. I hadn't told a soul in fear they'd try to talk me off the ledge. Consumed by rage, my vision had tunneled on one thing and one thing only, that fucking building. It may not have been solely his, but he'd put his name on it, had helped Vic build the company from the ground up, and that was enough for me.

He wanted to play me, to fuck me over, right?

Well now, I was really going to fuck him.

Inexorably.

Everything he'd acquired and built upon since arriving in Miami was about to go up in sweltering, ruthless flames.

I smiled victoriously. Heinously. The mere thought of his demise brought me that inept sense of peace I'd been seeking, one that allowed me to take a deep breath and collect myself before I unleashed the gates of hell. And should anyone get in my way while I did so, they'd be thrown in the wreckage, too, left to burn alive while the world around them turned to ash.

I took one last look at the solidarity of the darkened building. In about five minutes, it wouldn't be so dark anymore. Another smile drifted across my face. To be a fly on the wall when he received a call his micro-empire had gone up in smoke…

Stepping out onto the gravel, I shut the driver's door softly and walked around to the rear end of my truck, popping the trunk open. Inside were the two plastic canisters I'd filled to the brim with gasoline on my way over here. One would be carefully poured around the lower level while the other would drown the entirety of his office upstairs. I wanted everything he owned as decimated as he'd left me—his database, his files, his contacts, his fucking art work.

Everything.

He'd have *nothing* left by the time I drove off the lot.

I wasted no time after picking the lock and forcing my way inside, pouring stream after stream of gas all over the different stations that made up the ground level. When that canister spilled its last drop, I tossed it in the middle of the room and started upstairs with the other container in hand, taking care to shed a trail behind myself. All the while, every moment Roman and I had shared played in an unsought repetitive loop that made me impossibly angrier.

With an infuriated growl, I kicked his door wide open and took in the sight of his obscure office. It smelled of him and that vexed me, too, because why the hell could I so vividly remember how he smelled? Then it was like his scent flooded me with those unwanted memories, the ones where at our most savage points I'd felt that hellfire rip through my being as those icy orbs possessed me from the inside out.

I laughed softly at my inner-thoughts, shaking my head in only slight amusement. Who the fuck was I kidding? It wasn't just those eyes that possessed me. It was every-fucking-thing about him.

Those eyes.

That grim smirk.

His unfazed laugh.

His feral growl.

His ability to corner me faster than I could blink.

How from one moment to the next he could subdue me to his liking.

How his hands on my skin stung gloriously like a million taser probes.

The way my body sang the loudest of Hallelujahs while he impaled me without mercy.

How he made me fucking fall in love with him…

"Ahhh!" I growled again, dropping the canister of gasoline to the ground.

Each tick on the list had fueled my rage to capacity. I bound toward his desk and swiped everything off its surface in one big huff. Pens rolled on the floor. Papers flew in the air. His so-called antique lamp split in two while the bulb bursted like a bomb. It wasn't enough to calm me and with my chest heaving, I ripped his keyboard from the monitor and flung it across the room right into a wall. The monitor was next, crashing to the floor with a monstrously loud bang. All his art work on the walls came down, too, the glass of each frame shattering into hundreds of tiny pieces. By the time I'd sent his chair flying through one of the windows, his office was a complete war zone.

And I was about to turn it into ground zero.

I doused everything in gasoline. Every last thing from the curtains to electrical to the contents of the mess I'd made. When the last drop hit the ground, I catalogued this gruesome image to memory and took off down the stairs like a bat out of hell, laughing almost manically. Clearly all the fumes were getting to me, that or the extent of my depravity far exceeded what I thought possible.

In any case, the container held captive in my hand met its pair in the middle of the factory, and without so much as a glance back, I followed the trail I'd spilled upon first walking in to the front doors. Then I pulled a matchbook from the back pocket of my jeans and tore one free from it's family, meeting the match head to the striker. Seconds later, the smallest flame came life, hypnotizing me with all its layers; golds, reds, oranges, and a small sliver of a blue, each one melding together seamlessly to create a singular powerful source. I glanced down at my converse-clad feet, zeroing in on the shiny path I'd so kindly laid out before them.

Do it. Drop it, the antagonizing demon on my shoulder whispered, *In three… Two… One…*

So I did.

I took a simple step back, dropped the match, and walked away as that little flame ignited the track that would set Rome's world ablaze. What was dark just ten minutes ago was suddenly brighter than the sun, the entire first floor of the building engulfed in wicked flames and smoke as I made it back to the G Class, and threw myself into the drivers seat.

It'd only be a matter of time before the fire spread and fire department was dispatched, and by then I'd be gone, waiting for peace to take me over.

Peace that unfortunately wouldn't come any time soon...

45. TIME'S UP
Roman

♫ *Venom - Eminem* ♫

A month.
An entire excruciating month without Lux had gone by, and I was feeling it now more than ever, especially after she left Noir Coast in flames.

I knew it was her.

The fire department and everyone else working the case may have been baffled, left scratching their heads from lack of evidence or a determinable cause, but I knew.

And it hurt worse than any hell.

The building and everything inside its confines meant shit to me. It's what the act itself proved.

She was battered.

Raging inside.

Self-destructing.

And there wasn't anything I could do to help her.

The last thirty-days proved she wouldn't let me.

I spent the first two weeks after our break-up calling her relentlessly, texting her dozens of times throughout the day. I even went as far as reaching out to her friends, who I'm sure you can imagine, had zero inclination to help me.

But nothing.

Radio silence mocked me every single time, from any and every angle.

All I wanted was to explain myself, to have my day in court. I wasn't expecting forgiveness or even to win her back. I just wanted her to know why I'd done what I'd done.

The more time passed without the opportunity to do so, though, the more it began grating on my psyche.

Deranged, convoluted ideas of how I could *force* Lux to hear me out plagued me on the daily—from stalking to breaking and entering, and possibly everything else in between. I was so deep in my desperate state, I actually began considering seeing one through.

But one day, it all just clicked into place for me.

I don't know how or what triggered it, but I stopped calling her, stopped texting.

I gave up and let her be.

Lux had been forced into too much throughout her life for me to go and do the same, for me to be another disgraceful bloke on that list.

The problem with letting her go was that desperation quickly mutated into an enraged insanity, and my demons were all too pleased.

Viciously elated.

They fed off my weaknesses and whispered nefarious solutions, ones to paint the town red.

Ones of bloodshed.

Of death.

They taunted me with Lux's father, with Vic, producing image after damnable image of such violent delights.

I turned to the drink for help, stupidly hoping to numb myself in entirety, but it only made it worse.

So I started hitting the gym instead.

Worked my anger out in a positive outlet.

I went every single day, harder and longer still after the blaze at the factory.

The regimen seemed to be working, but I suspected that was only because I was exhausting myself to the point I'd go home, shower, refuel, and pass the hell out.

Today, though, I made the sudden decision to stop somewhere on the way home. I hadn't been to the Panorama since the night Lux and I broke up, but something was calling to me, urging me to visit the roof top.

To deal with my strife head-on.

It was painful to say the least, leaving me no other choice but to relive what took place up here. I stood near the ledge for quite some time, time traveling through them all; the volatile ones while we were enemies, the tense ones during our transition phase, the tender ones after I claimed her as mine...

All of them.

When it was all said done, when there was nothing left to look back on, I felt more hollow than before, yet sobered from the fog I'd been living in for weeks.

Folding in on myself, I sunk to the ground in poignant

distress, regretting every decision that had led me to this point in my life.

Except Lux.

I missed her—with every fiber of my goddamn being, and for the first time since she left me up here, I wondered if packing my bags would be the best solution for me.

If yet another move would be what helped me heal.

A fresh start—far away from the memories this city now held.

And that's when my phone rang, a call that, unbeknownst to me, was fate catching up to me.

On autopilot, I fished it out of my pocket.

I didn't recognize the number, and yet I answered it anyway. A small part of me—as stupid as it sounds—had me believing it could be Lux. "Hello?"

"Hey, stranger."

I. Fucking. Froze.

Went more rigid than the concrete settled for years beneath me.

That voice.

"Liza…" I growled, balling my fists in my lap.

"Miss me, baby?" she asked, using her most sultry voice.

A voice I once loved.

Cringing, I shot onto my feet and surveyed everything around me. She could've been anywhere. "Quite the opposite, actually," I snapped, repulsed.

"Ouch—such hostility. Why?"

"Ask yourself that question. You're the reason why we're here."

"You led me here," she countered viciously.

"And you led me on," I tossed back. "Guess we're even."

"I don't want to be even. *I just want you.*"

I cringed again. I'd rather be dead than give my ex another chance. "Might as well give it up, Liza, because I can assure you, that's never going to happen."

"Oh, but it is," she stressed.

"It's most definitely not. You wanna chase me down for the rest of our days because I killed your precious Leo, then go right ahead—be my fucking guest. You'll never have me, though."

"I don't give a fuck about Leo!" She laughed cynically, manically almost. "I've been after you for *you.* Sure, it may have started out in Leo's honor, but I had a change of heart recently."

I rolled my eyes, continuing my sweep of the perimeter. "I'm sure you did."

"It's true. Seeing you with Lux made me realize how much I missed you. Seems like you subconsciously missed me, too."

Disgust etched itself all over my face, my head rearing back. "What the hell are you talking about?"

"*Lux*, Roman. She looks an awful lot like me, don't you think?"

The satisfaction coloring her stone knocked me stock-still a second time.

Knocked me sick.

"At first, yes, there was a resemblance—but it faded

over time. She's different, better than you," I sneered with purpose, intending to wound her.

Not that it wasn't true, though. Lux *was* better, and after the initial shock of their similarities, the more I got to know her, the more they became uniquely her own.

But Liza wasn't fazed, a scoffed laughed bursting through the line. "Whatever helps you sleep at night, baby."

I cringed a third time, the abhorrent feeling now settling deep within my gut, churning it in revolt. "Fucks sake, stop calling me that!" I barked.

"Get used it, *baby.* We'll be together real soon. As a matter of fact, your bags are already packed and ready to go. You should probably run home and fetch them. Your flight leaves soon."

I'd heard every bit of that.

Every single part.

But the severity of what it meant didn't sink in for several moments.

"What?!" I snarled in disbelief. "You're bloody-fuck-ing-insane if you think I'm going anywhere with you, much less getting on flight to God knows where."

Liza hummed in earnest. "I'm afraid you don't really have a choice, Rome. You see, either you come willingly, or in about sixty seconds, an expert sniper has been instructed to pull the trigger."

Eyes bulging, my heart-rate skyrocketed.

With my chest heaving, I pivoted around slowly, scanning every roof top at my level. I couldn't see shit, or rather, anyone. Everything was clear, bathed by warm rays of the Miami sun.

"How do I know you're not lying?" I questioned, spinning around faster and faster.

"You don't, and you won't either. Just get on the plane," she ordered.

"Goddamit, Liza!" I roared, feeling a sense of hysteria consuming me.

How could I have been so fucking foolish?

She'd caught up to me. She'd made it clear as day.

And when nothing else happened, when all resumed to normalcy, I dismissed all thoughts of her to the recesses of my mind.

I lived my life without borders, like she hadn't been chasing me for almost two years straight.

"Plane. 2 p.m. Will I be seeing you there?" she pressed, as everything around me spun out rapidly.

"I'm going to kill you!"

"Tick, tock, baby." She chuckled. "Thirty seconds."

"I'm going to make sure you—"

"Fifteen."

She couldn't be serious. There's no way. "I regret every single moment we—"

"*Five, four, three—*"

"Yes, okay, yes!" I interjected, defeated, clamping my eyes shut. "You'll fucking see me there!"

"Stand down," she instructed, her voice further away from the phone.

The line scratched out for a split-second before a man's voice, fuzzy and distant, sounded off.

"Secured?" he asked.

"He'll be there," Liza agreed.

Walkie talkies… She wasn't lying.

Had I not agreed, I'd be…

"You made the right choice, Roman, but I think you already figured that out. Am I right?" Amused, satisfied, her voice was like that of a toxin.

Infecting me.

Debasing me with lunacy.

I loathed her all the more. "I'm done talking, Liza. Just tell me how to get to you."

"Just get to the airport. I'm not having anyone personally escort you there because I trust you value your life. Don't think I won't have eyes on you, though," she explained surely. "When you get to Miami International, you'll find a man entrusted with a sign that says *Ryzhkov*. Go with him."

That name.

I remembered it instantly from that night at the gala with Vic.

"How the hell do you know *Ryzhkov*?" I questioned.

Liza giggled wickedly. "I thought you were done talking?"

"Tell me how you know him!" I demanded furiously.

"Goodbye, Roman. I'll see you soon, my love."

Click.

46. OBLIVIOUS

𝔙𝔦𝔠

♫ *Sarcasm - Get Scared* ♫

I could hardly wait to see Roman's face when his appointed escort threw him in the backseat and he saw me behind the wheel. We hadn't seen or spoken to one another since the night he beat me to a pulp, and I was more than ready to seek my retribution. A little banged up still with healing bones, but ready as I'd ever been none-theless.

Liza promised I could bring him an inch of life as long as she got to finish him off. So I agreed, had a plan all set in my head. Before a single drop of blood was shed, I'd wear down his psyche to the bone.

To nothing.

A shell of the man he once was, he'd be so numb and broken afterward, he'd beg for mercy.

Unfortunately for him, there'd be no mercy to come.

No absolution.

And the glistening cherry on top would be the sight of me toying with his precious Lux, as Liza ended him and sent him straight to the fiery depths of hell once and for all.

Speaking of Lux…

It was time to fill her in and hook her into the plan.

Minutes before Benji emerged from arrivals with Roman in tow, I scrolled through my contacts and selected the little bitch's name. It rang several times, so many I was sure she'd let me ring through to voicemail, but then suddenly, her voice erupted through the speakers of my rental SUV.

"What the hell do you want now, Vic? Don't you think you've caused enough—"

"If you have any hope of keeping your man alive, you'll shut up and listen very carefully to the words that are about to come out of my mouth," I said—calm, cool, collected.

"What do you mean keep my man alive?" Unmistakable panic rang out in her tone.

"I have him. Well, I will. His flight just landed."

Lux gasped, the horrified sound filling the cabin of the SUV. "What have you done?"

"Everything Liza asked me to do," I cooed, grinning, my eyes glued to the doors of the airport.

"You're working with Liza?!" she squeaked.

"Correction—I've *been* working with her for quite some time now."

"You slimy ass backstabbing motherfucker! So help me God, when I get my hands on you, you're going to regret every single choice you've made." It was all an outraged growl, and while I knew what Lux was capable of, I wasn't at all concerned.

In fact, I found her to be quite amusing.

Liza had a million times more crazy on her.

"Somehow, I doubt that. Unlike you, Liza and I are partners."

"And somehow, *I* doubt that, and I don't even know the chick. Where is Rome?" she questioned.

"About to get tossed in my rental."

"Rental? Where are you?"

"Heathrow," I explained, checking the time on the dash.

"You're across the pond?! Are you bloody kidding me right now?!"

Regardless of the fact she couldn't see me, I shook my head. "Cross my heart."

"Let him go." The softest snarl left her.

"Can't do that, Lux."

"Let. Him. Go, Vic," she gritted out.

"I told you, I can't do that. If you make it here in time, you may be able to save him, though."

And there he was, only half-struggling, pushed along the way by Benji towards the SUV. We'd zip tie his wrists together once he was inside to avoid any sudden outbursts.

"'Cause you're gonna tell me how to get to him, right? Do you think I'm—"

"It's not a secret, sweetheart. Liza *wants* me to tell you." It was the complete and honest truth. "Now, here's the deal. Rome's about to get in the car. Either you stay quiet or—"

The rear passenger door flew open.

"Get the fuck off me, mate!" Roman roared, resisting

Benji's attempts to toss him in the back. "I can get in the damned car myself!"

As he slid inside, I slung an arm over the passenger seat and waited for him to notice me. When our stares locked and his expression morphed into that of confusion, I flashed him a subtle grin.

"Top of the mornin' to ya, ol' chap."

"Vic? What the actual fuck is going on?" he asked incredulously, completely oblivious of Benji securing his wrists behind his back until the door slammed shut.

"Rome!" Lux bellowed, igniting a raging fire in his eyes.

I sighed impatiently, squeezing the bridge of my nose. "Jesus-fucking-Christ, Lux, did I not tell you to be quiet?"

"Where is she?" Rome growled.

"Back home where you left her, safe and sound."

"I'm coming for you, Rome, do you hear me? I'm coming for you! Vic, you better text me that information —I've already bought the next flight out. It leaves in two hours."

"Excellent." I nearly rubbed my palms together. Everything was falling into place famously. "In the meantime, here's a little motivation to get you moving faster in the event you thought I was joking…"

With lithe speed, I reached for the pistol tucked between the seat and flung my arm back, whacking the damned thing against Rome's head.

Roaring in pain, he fell back into the seat as deep crimson blood began trickling from his temple.

"Stop! STOP!" Lux screamed in terror. "Don't touch him! Don't fucking touch him!"

"Oh, I won't be, but I'm sure Liza can't wait to get her hands on him one last time," I mused.

Very slowly, Rome turned toward me, squinting through the aftermath of my assault. "Liza?" he rasped.

"The very one."

"They're working together!" Lux yelled, widening Rome's expression in tenfold.

"You're working with fucking Liza? Are you shitting me?!"

"How do you think she found you, *brother*?" I flashed him another grin.

But it didn't last long.

One second I was lucid, and the next, well, I wasn't.

The world around me was fading.

Fading.

Closing in on me.

Black.

47. PLAYTHINGS
Moxie

♫ *The Devil Within - Digital Daggers* ♫

I've been called crazy more times than I can count.

I like to think I'm poetic.

Passionate.

Maybe a little twisted, and a whole lot spoiled.

I have daddy to thank for that. He spoiled me rotten, like he did all his girls.

His women.

My mum included.

He loved me best, though, I know he did. Loved me more than most daddies love their daughters.

Even at my youngest age, I knew it was wrong; we both did, but we couldn't stop.

Until one day, when my first crush came into my life. Daddy didn't like it one bit. He didn't like him, didn't try to get to know him. He wanted to keep me for himself is what he'd said.

I tried to sway him.

Tried to explain he would always be my daddy and I'd always love him.

But he didn't listen, wouldn't hear me out.

So I killed him.

Killed mum, too, when she finally figured out our dirty little secret and tried throwing the blame at my feet.

To the world, it looked like a heart-wrenching homicide, a sordid tale of how a young girl killed her father in self-defense after he killed her mother.

And that's how I left it.

I never told anyone the truth—not even Rome.

Promised myself I'd take that to the grave.

I mean, why would I ever come clean when all it had done was help me get by in life? Help me rise to the top.

Everyone who knew my story saw me as poor little Liza the orphan, the orphan who deserved the world for being so brave, for persevering despite the awful hand life had dealt her.

I had everything handed to me on a silver-fucking-platter, had everyone eating out of the palm of my hand—the boys especially.

Roman.

Vic.

Leo.

Every last one of them.

They were my puppets, and I was their master.

I wanted them all, wanted to love them all, wanted to play with them all, just like my daddy used to do with his girls.

But Roman ruined it in his selfishness.

He killed my Leo, almost killed Vic before that.

For a while, I loathed him. I wanted him dead. Chased

him all over New York, reminding him I was never too far away.

It was under those pretenses I came into contact with Vic again. He was supposed to help me corner Rome, help me kill him. And in return I'd help him end his precious Lux.

But that was then, *and this is now.*

Very soon, I'll have my playthings back together. Maybe not all of them, but two will suffice. I might even keep the little bitch, too.

They'll serve me like the Queen I am…and I'll love them.

Forever.

And ever.

And ever.

48. IN THE NAME OF LOVE
Lux

♫ *In the Name of Love - Martin Garrix and Bebe Rexha* ♫

Landing in Heathrow was surreal.

The last time I'd been here was more than ten years ago, and even the fifteen-year-old version of myself never imagined I'd come back. In fact, that was the plan as Suki and I barreled through the terminals, hoping we'd make it on the flight without incident.

Neither one of us had anything here, and we surely weren't going to miss it either.

But plans change, and now, Rome needed me.

Despite what he'd done to me, despite how it all ended, he needed me.

It was that simple.

Vic was dangerous, so was Liza, apparently. Together they'd likely best me without question.

Yet I couldn't leave the man I loved to die. If I didn't come after him, he'd take his final breath under their rule.

And that was no way for the King to perish.

"So, do you have a plan?" Suki asked as we exited the airport, throwing on our coats. Unlike Miami, the U.K. actually experienced all four seasons.

I slipped my carry-on over my shoulder. "No, but we should probably get to a hotel in the mean time. Vic hasn't text me the information yet and I'm not about to wander the streets waiting for him."

"Well, let's get a taxi then, shall we?"

Nodding, I glanced around in search of one as well. "Did you tell Rams?"

Suki froze for a beat, then turned back toward me with an exaggerated smile on her face. "No."

"Suk, really?!"

"I didn't want her worrying!" she explained, drawing several eyes in the near vicinity our way.

"Because leaving without telling her isn't going to worry her?" I whisper-hissed.

Reaching for my hand, Suki pulled me to her side and laced her fingers with my own, offering a supportive squeeze. "I'll call her, okay? What we need to focus on is a plan."

"And yet, we can't do that without that damned information. I can't map shit out if I don't know where they are."

"Have you text him since landing?" She waved an arm manically as a cab slowed within the airport traffic.

"No."

"Do it then. Let me worry about about the taxi."

As Suki went about whistling and bouncing around to get us some transportation, I fished my phone out of my bag, powered it on, and opened my thread with Vic. He still hadn't responded to my last message before take off, but I assumed it was done with purpose, as was the way our call ended so abruptly after I'd bought my ticket.

Scare tactics and all that shit.

Me: *Just landed.*

I waited and waited, boring into the screen impatiently, but nothing came through until we were actually in the back of the cab several minutes later.

Vic: *Excellent.*
Me: *Where's the info?*
Vic: *What info?*

"Really?" I muttered aloud, indignation striking deep in my gut.

Suki shifted her attention away from her phone and glanced over at mine. "What happened?"

I let her read the message.

When our stares met, she rendered the same dubious look already settled on my face.

Me: *Don't play stupid now.*
Vic: *Call me.*

My eyes almost rolled out their sockets.

Of course he was going to make this more difficult than it already was.

Clicking through a couple of screens, I selected his number and set the phone to my ear. It rang only twice, but I didn't give him the chance to speak even a word.

"I should've known you weren't going to give me those details, you lying bastard," I snapped.

His voice never followed, though. Instead, a woman's sultry chuckle met my ears.

"So angry…"

I knew who it was immediately, my heart-rate spiking to a dangerous degree.

"Liza…" I gritted out, whipping Suki's head toward me as Liza hummed appreciatively.

"The one and only."

"Where's Rome?"

"He's a bit tied up at the moment," she mused, evoking a growl so savage within me, even Suki's eyes widened in alarm.

"If you hurt him I sw—"

"Settle down, little girl. I have no plans to hurt him." Another chuckle. "I just want to love him."

Sure you do.

"How do you plan to make that work when he doesn't love you anymore?" I questioned, noting Suki was holding out her earbuds beside me.

Taking them from her open palm, I plugged them into the jack and passed one side so she could listen in.

"Oh, he does," Liza cooed, sounding so sure of herself. "Deep down, he still does. He always will. I *am* his first love and all."

"You sure about that?"

"Positive. And should he deny it, should he *try* to play

hard to get, I have little ways to remind him of where his heart stands."

Suki twirled a finger beside her head, depicting my exact thoughts.

"You really *are* insane," I stressed.

"Is that what he told you? Did he tell you Liza was crazy?" she queried, cackling maniacally.

"Not verbatim, but he might as well have."

"And you believed him… Bless," she crooned.

My blood boiled.

I'd had enough of her mind games. The chick was clearly unhinged and I was not about to feed into it.

"Where are you, Liza?" I barked.

"Oh, you know, around," she sang childishly.

"You know that's not what I meant… Tell me where the fuck you are!"

Suki shook my arm in haste, typing something out furiously on her phone when I cut my eyes to where she sat. Turning the phone toward me, I read the message on her notepad.

CHECK HIS LOCATION!!!

My best friend was a fucking genius.

I had to refrain from taking her face in my hands and smacking a million kisses all over her.

Of course—tracking his location! Why hadn't I thought of that?

"What do I get in exchange for our location?" Liza asked as I got to work on my phone.

"What do you want?"

"Hmmm? How about fifty-thousand pounds?"

I scoffed. "Is that all he's worth to you? Fifty grand?"

"Oh, no—he's worth much more. That should be enough to get us out of here, though," she clarified, knocking me still.

"Umm, I'm not handing over fifty grand for you to leave *with* him. You want the money? Let him go."

"For a business woman, you really have shit listening skills," she jeered. "The money was in exchange for the location, not for Rome. I'm not releasing him to you or anyone else for that matter. *He's mine.* You can try taking him from me but I promise you, you won't make it out alive."

Suki and I both rolled our eyes. Poor girl clearly thought she was invincible. Too bad she didn't know how crazy my girl and I could be.

"We'll see about that," I countered.

"What's it going to be, Lux? The clock is ticking. Am I to expect fifty thousand at some point today?"

"No—I'll find you my damn self. Be prepared, Liza. You have no idea what you're up against," I warned her, grinning triumphantly as Vic's location popped up on my screen.

"Neither do you, babe. Neither do you. Speak soon, I guess."

Click.

49. THE DEVIL IS FEMALE
Roman

♫ *Secret - The Pierces* ♫

I expected for escort bloke to knock me out after watching him put Vic down, but he never did.

In fact, he didn't speak to me at all. He merely tossed Vic's limp body into the backseat beside me, slid behind the wheel, and pulled out into airport traffic—cool as a fucking cucumber.

We drove for quite some time in complete silence, shrouded by the dark of night.

Every instinct within me told me to fight back, to demand answers and get a better understanding of where he was taking me—since Liza hadn't divulged a thing—but I remained tight-lipped throughout.

Stoic.

Seemingly unaffected by the gravity of the situation.

My mind was in the red, though—flags waving, alarms blaring.

Liza had finally caught up to me, in real time, and without an ounce of actual physical force, she coerced me into her trap.

Into her web of madness and revenge.

Like she'd done to Vic. She'd obviously lied to him as well, had led him to believe they were equal partners in whatever the full extent of their arrangement was.

I wasn't afraid of death, but the thought of dying in her hands was a fucking nightmare.

Worst yet, Lux was coming after me...

What would happen if I was dead by the time she found her way to me? *If* she found her way to me...

Would Liza kill her, too?

Within that depraved loop is where my thoughts remained for the rest of the drive. Leaving the hustle and bustle of the city behind us, we ended up on scenic country roads where the plots of land grew larger and further apart with every twist and turn.

Eventually, we pulled into a long, narrow driveway that led to a massive estate. Securing said estate was a tall, iron gate. Escort wanker punched in the code and the doors opened slowly, granting us access to the semi-lit perimeter.

In any other circumstance, I would have ventured to say it was a gorgeous sight, all old-English style with hints of goth provided by the gargoyles at the top of the castle-like roof.

But my architectural appreciation quickly faded the moment the SUV slowed to a stop at the steps before the front doors.

Two men, who appeared to be hulking butlers based on their classic attire, came barreling down toward us. I was expecting them to yank my door open and pull me into their possession, but both men went around the back end, and opened the door opposite of me instead.

Where Vic laid, still passed the hell out.

One grabbed his arms, the other grabbed his legs... And then they were gone.

Seconds later, escort bloke was opening my door. Once again, he didn't utter a single word, simply tipping his head by way of direction. I hopped out onto the pavement without protest and craned my head back, taking in the clear, late-night sky.

After all, it might've been the last time I'd ever get to see it.

And in some sense, it was—because *that's* the moment when they finally knocked me out.

I didn't even see it coming.

There was a brief whooshing sound.

Then a screeching blow to my head.

And then the world around me gave to darkness.

I woke with a start, gasping for air as I shot up from the...

Bed?

A massive plush bed no less.

My head protested immediately against the sudden movement, pounding violently to the point I thought it might explode. The back of it felt tight and sore, as though something were keeping my aching skull closed.

Stitches, I presumed, based on the images all coming back to me now.

Squeezing my eyes shut, I willed myself through the onslaught with deep breaths, clutching the sheets around my body for support, my jaw ground to avoid making a sound.

When the agony subsided, I cracked my eyes open once more, slowly, finally noting the night had passed me by. Warm streams of daylight now poured in through the bay window not so far away, bathing the room with its incandescent rays.

I peered around, observing my ornate surroundings. Vintage floral wallpaper, gold-trimmed Victorian furniture, what had to be imported, luxury area rugs. Above the bed hung a chandelier, and in the far corner were two parlor chairs set up like a sitting area with a bookcase in between.

And then there were the doors, both a cream color with simple golden knobs.

Where did they lead? Were they locked? Guarded?

Swinging my legs off the end of the bed in an attempt to investigate, it was then I noticed I sat in nothing but my briefs.

No t-shirt. No pants.

Not even my bloody socks.

What the hell?

Panic took its hold on me as my mind began racing millions of miles per hour.

Why the hell were my clothes off?

I'd not even had a proper minute to think it through

when one of the doorknobs jiggled, followed by a lock coming undone.

There went one of my questions answered.

Bracing myself, I rose onto my feet, ready and willing to tackle whoever was on the other side, and run out just like this should I have the opportunity to do so.

But the moment I saw Liza saunter through the threshold, I couldn't fucking move.

"Good morning, sunshine!" she quipped cheerily, a silver tray balanced on her palm.

She was clad in only a silky white robe, pepping goosebumps all over my skin in alarm as my stomach churned about.

No.

Shutting the door with her bare foot, she sashayed toward me with an equally cheery smile.

Or at least she was aiming for such.

In reality, it was nothing short of creepy and deranged.

"How'd you sleep, baby?" she asked, setting the tray down on the pristine nightstand beside the bed, a lush spread of breakfast items set on its polished surface. "I'm sorry we had to sleep apart. I promise tonight you'll get to sleep in my bed like the King you are."

I couldn't do anything but stare at her, blinking, shocked to my damn core.

Her body was Liza—all five-foot-two of her—but the person within her mind… I didn't recognize that person at all.

And that's saying a lot because Liza had always been a little strange—eccentric, if you will.

This, however, was a whole different ballgame. I hadn't picked up on it much over the phone, but now that I was seeing her in person, now that we were face to face...

It was so blatantly obvious.

The girl had snapped.

"What do you want, Liza?" I finally asked, watching her warily.

Dropping down onto the edge of the bed, that creepy smile of hers widened. "I told you already. I want you, *and now I have you.*"

A chill rolled down my spine.

That's what she'd said on the phone... Swore none of this was about Leo. I didn't want to upset her, because who knows what she was capable of at this point in time, but I was interested to see how she would react if I brought him up.

"What about Leo?" I hedged, gauging her closely.

Her blue eyes darkened, narrowing into tiny malignant slits. "He's dead. You killed him, remember?" she snapped.

"Of course, he deserved it," I boasted, lifting my chin high as she shot onto her feet.

"No one deserves to die!"

"And yet, here we are. You've stalked me, finally got your hands on me. Isn't the next part of your plan to kill me?"

Liza groaned in exasperation and thrusted her fingers into her blonde hair. "Why don't you listen to me?! I've already told you—I don't want to kill you! I just. Want. You!" she screeched demonically.

"What does that mean, though? You want me for what?"

"It means I want you for me. I want you to serve me, to love me. I'll love both of you back, I swear it." Her voice was much softer now, tears bubbling in her eyes.

She made no sense whatsoever, and my head was starting to spin from her demented behavior. "Both of you?"

Liza nodded, toying with the belt of her robe. "You and Vic."

Vic. That's right—he was here, too. After the bash to my head, I'd forgotten all about him.

"Where *is* Vic?" I asked.

"In his room. Don't worry, I gave you the better one. You can't tell him, though—he may get a little jealous," she giggled.

Like a child.

Alarm bells blared once more as a heaping dose of nausea twisted my gut like a sodden towel.

What that statement subtly implied…

"How long are you expecting us to stay here?" I questioned, praying to whatever deity might hear me that she was not about to say what I thought she was.

"That's a silly question, baby." She advanced several steps forward. "*Forever,* obviously."

It was.

Fuck, it was!

I had to get out of here.

This wasn't what I'd signed up for, involuntarily or otherwise. I certainly didn't want to die at her hands, but again, I wasn't afraid to meet the grim reaper.

I'd take death over this fresh hell…

On quick feet, I dashed around her and held a hand out in warning, my back now to the door. "You can't be serious! You can't keep us here like prisoners!"

"You're not prisoners—you're my men, my beautiful, devoted men," she cooed, advancing toward me again. "We're going to have such a wonderful life together, Rome. All of us."

She really *had* lost it.

Completely fucking lost it.

Had Leo's death affected her this much? Or was this a result of something else? Her parent's death?

"You're fucking insane!" I barked, chest heaving, my eyes scanning every inch over the room for a weapon.

"No, I'm not!" she bellowed.

"Yes, you are! You've taken two men hostage for some deranged, twisted fantasy you've conjured up in your head! How is that not crazy?!" The veins in my neck bulged from the sheer volume of my voice.

Tears welled in her eyes once more. "Because I love you!" she cried. "I love you both!"

"This isn't love, Liza! I don't know what the hell happened to you after we broke up, but you need help—serious help!"

"I don't need help, goddamit! I just need my boys!"

"Yeah, well, you'll be down to only one soon because

I can assure you I'm walking out that front door right now."

It was only after I said it that I realized I shouldn't have uttered a word…

Wiping the wetness clinging to her cheeks with quick hands, she stared at me, tilting her head slowly to one side. "You can try," she cackled. "But you won't get very far. There's guards at every door and they've been instructed to drag you down to the basement if either one of you try to leave."

Of course there are.

"I don't even want to know what you could possibly have down there."

I really didn't.

"That's right, you don't," she agreed, crossing her arms, a satisfied smirk playing on the corners of her mouth.

"Let me go, Liza," I tried, moving back yet again as she stepped forward. "I'll give you whatever you want."

"I just want you! Jesus Christ, Rome, don't you get that!"

"And I've told you, you can't have me."

Silence ensued, but only long enough to fool me.

In a blur of movements, Liza bound up to where I stood and managed to cuff my arms behind my back.

"And yet I already do," she murmured, running a polished fingernail down my bare chest.

Cringing under her touch, I tried wriggling myself free, but it was useless. These weren't costume cuffs, they were the real deal. "Let me go!" I demanded, despite knowing it wasn't going to do a damn thing.

"Shhh—let's calm you down."

"I'll calm down when your psycho ass gets tossed in the looney bin!"

"So cranky." Another child-like giggle bubbled in her throat. "Don't worry, baby—we'll make that better."

Her hand made contact with my chest.

I stumbled back from the force of her shove, falling right into one of the parlor chairs I'd seen earlier.

It wasn't until she slithered into my lap that I fully understood what she meant.

"Don't you fucking dare. The answer is no," I gritted out.

Unperturbed and quite determined, Liza leaned forward and flashed her tongue out against my neck, licking all the way up to my ear.

"Relax," she cooed, grinding herself against my dick.

Again I cringed, trying and failing to get away from her. "Get off me."

"But I wanna get *you* off, baby. I want you inside me again."

"No."

"Just play nice, Rome. I wouldn't wanna have to hurt you," she growled, her tone low.

Deadly.

"You're fucking crazy!" I yelled, struggling beneath her.

"Not the first time I've heard that." She chuckled, biting her lip as she leaned back, her hand smoothing over my length, palming it. "Ugh, this cock. I missed it. So big, so thick…"

"Don't…" I clamped my eyes, willing my dick not to fucking react. It was already twitching with every roll of her hips.

"Look at this pussy, Rome—your pretty little pussy. So wet, aching for you, ready for you. Imagine it sliding down on your cock…"

My eyes snapped back open to find Liza naked, hovering above me, her fingers spreading her cunt wide open.

I wanted to fucking wretch.

"Don't you fucking dare!" I roared, full—blown panic seizing me.

Crippling me.

Is this what Lux felt when…

Lux.

I swallowed a heap of air as her beautiful face, the one I loved so much flashed into my mind. Tears leaking down her face, sadness and betrayal swimming in her eyes…

As agonizing as that image was, that's what I held onto with all my might as Liza stripped me of my freewill, of my dignity and my sanity, impaling herself on my semi in one fluid move, gasping her praises.

"Fuuuckkk! Oh my god, I fucking missed you, Rome! I missed you so much!"

And I missed my Queen, whom I hoped like hell would find her way on the twisted path that led to me.

50. LONG LIVE THE KING
Lux

♫ *Die For You - The Weeknd* ♫

Vic's location steadily showed as somewhere in the countryside—for hours.

Literally hours.

Suki and I didn't think that was right, but we decided to look into it anyway. A quick Google search revealed a massive estate on a large plot of land, entirely secluded and surrounded by trees.

No neighbors in the near vicinity.

Away from prying eyes and vigilant ears.

My gut told me this was it, but it also screamed danger, especially with Suki and I unarmed.

We drove out there regardless, though. I mean, what other choice did we really have? It was our only lead after declining Liza's offer for an exchange, which I was seriously regretting now.

By the time we made it out there, night had fallen upon us. The sky was clear, littered with dozens of stars from the lack of streetlights on the winding roads. Suki suggested we use the darkness to our advantage, but I shot that down before she could even finish uttering her reasoning.

Stealth was great, but we weren't familiar with the grounds. And again, being unarmed put us at a huge disadvantage.

We needed daylight desperately if there was any hope we'd be able to get to Rome *and* make it out alive.

All of us.

The one thing we did have at our advantage was the thicket of trees across the street from the estate. I was able to reverse the rental car a ways in, enough that the greenery shielded us from plain sight.

From there, we could do nothing but play the waiting game.

We used the time to get a better feel of the land with Google maps and tried to devise some sort of concrete plan. The night seemed to go on forever, though, and eventually, Suki passed out in the passenger seat with the heater hitting her at full blast.

I knew I should get some rest, too, knew I needed to recharge before what laid ahead of us the following day— whatever that may be—but I couldn't sleep. I was too nervous, too anxious, far too fucking worried about Rome to even think about resting.

And that's when the floodgates opened.

As hard as I tried not to cry, as hard as I tried to keep it together and remain strong, I couldn't hold them back any longer. I'd been tamping them down since we got on the plane at Miami International, but no more.

I couldn't anymore.

I wept quietly behind the steering wheel, expelled every white-hot tear that came until there was nothing left to cry.

Until I was bone-dry and hollow.

Until the early sun began streaming through the tops of the trees.

"Suk," I hissed, shaking her awake.

She jolted upright, disoriented, her platinum blonde locks a wild mess. "What happened?"

I laughed weakly at her disheveled appearance, motioning around us with a whirl of my finger. "Daylight, that's what."

"Oh, right." She rubbed the sleep from her eyes and stretched out to the best of her ability with a boisterous yawn. "I need coffee."

"We don't have any," I pointed out.

Suki groaned. "I can't function without coffee, L."

"Gonna have to, baby girl." I shut off the car and peered over her way, reaching for my coat in the backseat. "It's show time."

Our trek out of the thicket and across the street onto the estate's property was made in complete silence. All that could be heard were our footsteps crunching through the grass and an odd bird here or there, chirping it's early morning song. The sky was as clear as it was the night before, only now, it was painted in splashes of pink and gold, the temperatures equally as chilly, if not more so with the sun not yet having reached its peak.

As per our plan, we ducked low and stayed as close to the tall Italian Cypresses surrounding the estate as possible, taking careful steps to the backyard. From the main road it wasn't visible, but evidently, behind the estate was a small lake. Google Maps showed the security gate had a back entrance as well, one that led out to said lake and appeared to be much smaller in scale than the brawny gates up at the front. Should that image be accurate, it might be our one and only ticket inside.

Once we made it to the back, the tall Cypresses came to an abrupt end, waist-high bushes taking their place along the rear gate. They lined the pathway down to the lake as well. Suki and I ducked lower behind them, peeking over their rounded tops to scan the backyard for any signs of life.

But there was no one.

All I could see was a decently-sized pool and a lavish patio area, all well-kept and fully landscaped.

"Should we try the gate?" Suki whispered, holding tight to the crowbar she'd found in the trunk of the rental before we'd left.

It was our only weapon at the moment.

"I doubt it's just going to be open, Suk. Gates are meant to keep people out," I whispered back, dragging my gaze over every window on the estate.

"It's worth a shot, L. You never know."

"Then you check it," I hissed.

"Fine." She rolled her eyes, passing me the crow bar. "Don't lose it."

"Where the fuck am I gonna lose it?" I hissed again, prompting her to flash me the bird behind herself as she inched toward the gate.

Poking her head out around the bushel closest to the pathway, she glanced both ways as if she were crossing a street, and bound right up to the gates. All she did was tug it gently with a single finger and it gave away, falling open slowly.

My mouth popped open in utter shock as she turned to me, satisfied smirk curling her lips. "I told you," she mouthed, motioning for me to follow her.

I couldn't believe it.

It seemed *way* too simple, suspiciously so, but nevertheless, we had a way in.

I scrambled from the safety of the greenery around me and joined her out in the open, gripping the crow bar for dear life.

"That seemed too easy," I whispered, as we treaded carefully through the patio to the large French doors.

"Agreed, but don't overthink it. Could be a total lucky coincidence."

"If that back door is open, this was premeditated."

"L…" Suki whirled around in a flash and took my face in her hands, shaking me softly. "Stop overthinking and focus. Rome—we gotta get to Rome, babe."

The sound of his name paired with the urgency of the moment brought tears to my eyes. "How do we know he's in there?" My lip quivered.

"We don't, but it's all we've got. I have a good feeling though—I can feel the bastard." She grinned, prompting me to grin, too, with a little scoff in tow.

"There's my girl." She shook me again. "Ready?"

Passing back the crow bar, I nodded. "Ready."

We made it to French doors leading into the house without incident. There wasn't a single light on within the estate, but I figured that was likely due to how early it was.

For all we knew, whoever was in there was still asleep.

But not for much longer...

"You remember the plan?" Suki asked as she set her hand on the golden knob.

"Yes—but you're sure you wanna do that?" I countered, my voice wary and uncertain.

It was a good plan, don't get me wrong, but it put us both at risk for different reasons.

I was perfectly fine with risking my own life—I'd fucking die to save Roman if it came to that.

But thinking about risking Suki's life, for something that, technically, had fuck all to do with her, didn't sit right with me.

Made me as sick as thinking what Rome might've had to ensure the last two days.

Suki nodded surely, lifting her chin high. "Positive. Based on what I can see of the inside, it'll work."

Always so gallant, that one.

"You know I love you, right?" I couldn't help getting mushy with her. We'd been through so much together, and in the end, she always had my fucking back. No matter what.

"Stop it." She grabbed my arm thoughtfully. "We're *all* getting out of here today—except that crazy bitch."

"I'm serious, Suk. You always help me out of every

shit hole I get myself into. I love you," I stressed, pulling her into a heartfelt hug."

I love you, too, L," she squeezed me back, "now focus, before I fucking kick your ass into gear. You're making a bitch all teary."

Chuckling into her shoulder, I squeezed her one last time before easing back. "You wanna do the honors?"

Suki shook her head, a wicked smirk coloring her expression. "Absolutely not—that's all you, baby girl. Let's raise some hell."

I nodded and inhaled a steady breath, readying myself as Suki jiggled the knob.

It actually turned, dispersing rivulets of adrenaline through me in seconds flat.

On another nod, she pushed the door open carefully.

It squeaked softly as ever, barely audibly, but I was more worried about tripping an alarm. Nothing happened, though.

That's when we busted in, clearing room to room quickly as we made our way to the front. Once we were in the foyer, two spiral grand staircases on either side of us, we made our presence known.

Or really, I did.

Suki hid herself in the shadows.

"Oh, Lizaaa," I sang, hands cupped around my mouth. "Come out, come out, wherever you are!"

The same stillness that had followed us since leaving the rental remained firmly in place, and still, my heart was galloping.

Why was nothing happening?

I was expecting a calvary to flood around me within milliseconds, but there was literally not a soul in sight.

To be heard.

Until suddenly, a distant thunder erupted from the second floor.

It's on now.

I braced myself for the worst and bounced my eyes between every entry point around me, hoping we had the right place and hadn't just stormed into some innocent family's home.

Less than a minute later, five disheveled men—who'd clearly been asleep—appeared at the landing, each one pointing their rifle at me. I lifted my hands in cooperation, intent on showing them my lack of a weapon, and shook my head slowly. "I just want to have a little chat with her."

They extended them further, to the point I cringed a little at the thought they might pull the trigger, but then someone cleared their throat.

"Move aside, boys," a female voice commented thereafter. "I've been expecting her."

Liza.

This *was* the right place, thank fuck.

A single blink, and she was there, standing between them.

Smirking.

Leaning against the oak banister.

"I must say, I'm pleasantly surprised you actually made it," she said amusedly.

But I barely heard her—I was too busy staring.

She looked so much like me.

Not identical, yet I could see similarities.

It was unnerving, and I wondered if Rome had seen them, too. If they'd contributed to our initial attraction...

I didn't know how to feel about that, but I guess it didn't really matter in that moment now, did it?

"What's wrong, Lux—suddenly mute?" she quipped, throwing my focus back in place.

"Where's Rome?" I gritted out.

A smug, satisfied look settled on her features. "Asleep, in my bed."

This bitch.

"Let him go."

"Really? Did you honestly come in here expecting to hit me with that once and get your way? C'mon, sweetheart—be smart," she sneered.

"I mean, your doors were open, sooo..." I pointed out, my tone condescending.

Liza rolled her eyes. "I *left* them open for you."

"Then obviously you knew I'd be coming in here asking you to let him go, so let's try this again, shall we? Let him go, Liza."

"Yeah...no," she chortled, snapping her fingers in the air. "Take her to the basement, boys. I'll handle her after breakfast."

It was right about here a weapon would have been fucking helpful. I could have easily put the five of them down with Suki's help and stormed up the stairs after Liza, forced her to take me to Rome.

But that wasn't the case, unfortunately.

I could do nothing but let them temporarily restrain me and lead me to what could possibly be my doom, along with hoping that Suki would be able to execute her part unharmed.

The basement was honestly nothing like I was envisioning on the way down there. I'd assumed it'd be dark, damp, a grimy cellar possibly wreaking of death, but it was the exact opposite.

Completely furnished in reds and golds.

Filled with light.

Spacious.

I was flabbergasted, immediately taken aback by its beauty as they threw me inside and locked the door. If she'd killed someone in here before, one would never know.

Literally.

Not a thing was out of place.

Everything was pristine.

It was bizarre.

I didn't know what to do, what to think. I didn't feel threatened or at any danger. If she planned to kill me, certainly she wouldn't have thrown me in here, free to roam regardless of the door being locked.

My head spun.

What was this?

Aside from Rome, what were her motives?

Why did she want me to find her?

After God knows how long of me oscillating from question to question, I finally fell onto one of the couches and simply stared up at the ceiling.

I was starting to get anxious, a little nervous, too.

Why was she taking so long?

What was taking her so long?

Surely, she was done with her breakfast by now…

Sheer moments later, the click of the lock sounded off by the steps as if I'd been voicing my thoughts aloud. I shot onto my feet, steeling myself for what could turn quite ugly rather quickly.

Down came Liza, now dressed for the day, and behind her—

I gasped.

Behind her came Rome—unscathed and in one piece. Or so I thought.

When our eyes met, I saw nothing. His gaze was hollow, lifeless. And yet, there was a tortured agony bleeding out from his soul.

Begging me to help him.

I could feel it.

My vision blurred over as bereaved tears welled at the surface.

"Figured I'd let you see him one last time," Liza explained, shrugging nonchalantly.

Like it was the sweetest gesture in the world despite the fact that, the man standing beside her, was *not* the man I'd left on the Panorama.

"What have you done to him?" I asked, regarding him in anguish.

"Stop asking questions and say your goodbye's while you can, Lux. I can assure you he will *not* be walking out the front door with you when I send you on your way."

Out of all she'd said, *goodbye* stood out for me most, lurching me toward him almost violently as grief rolled down my cheeks.

I'd die in this fucking basement before I said goodbye to him ever again, but she didn't need to know that yet. She'd figured it out soon enough anyway.

Throwing myself at him, he caught me without missing a beat, molding me to the planes of his body as I squeezed him for dear life, sobbing into his neck.

"I'm sorry." It came muffled against his skin. "I'm sorry, I'm sorry, I'm so fucking sorry!"

Rome shushed me quietly, threading a hand into my hair to pull me back, enough for our eyes to meet again.

And again there was nothing.

What the fuck had she done to him?

"Are you okay?" I asked him, taking his face between my palms.

I wanted to kiss him all over, shower him with love until that fire in his gaze rekindled brightly, until the blue of his irises returned to full vibrancy.

Until he was Roman-fucking-King—not this shell of a man.

All he offered me was a shake of his head, though. No words. I didn't know whether he truly couldn't speak, scarred from whatever atrocities he'd obviously endured, or if she'd instructed him to do so.

"Wrap it up," Liza barked. "And if you put your mouth on him, so help me—"

"What?" I turned my head toward her, suddenly enraged. "What are you gonna do about it?"

Rome squeezed me once more, a gesture of silent warning, but there was no way in hell I was heeding it. This woman had clearly hurt him in some way, shape, or form, and now, I was going to fucking hurt her.

Wriggling free from his hold, I landed on my feet and inched closer to her, cocking my head to one side in a coaxing fashion. "Go on, Liza. Tell me what you're gonna do about it."

"You don't want to test me, Lux." She chuckled darkly, standing her ground. "You really don't."

"I'm not afraid of you," I bit out. "I'm disgusted, if anything. What the hell did you do to him?"

"Why do you ask so many questions?" she queried in frustration.

"Why don't you answer any of them?"

"Because it's none of your business what I've done to him. He's mine—I can do whatever I please with him."

I laughed. I laughed cynically, right in her face and burst into her bubble, my gaze piercing hers just inches away. "I hate to break it to you, sweetie—*but he's mine*."

The switch flipped.

I watched it happen.

From amused to manic, her lip curled, posture tensing. Crazy Liza had come out to play. "You're gonna regret saying th—"

Bang! Bang! Bang!

The three of us fell stock-still as shots continued to go off above us, one after the other. My first thought was Suki, jolting my stomach up to my throat, especially when everything ceased and silence replaced the sudden chaos.

But then thundering steps echoed down the stairs, and there she was, in one full piece, blue eyes scanning the room.

And she wasn't alone.

In her grasp was Vic, her newly acquired pistol aimed at the side of his head.

Well, shit.

I deflated like a damned balloon.

"Your men are dead," she sneered at Liza, breaths ragged from exertion.

Then she shoved Vic to the floor.

He looked as empty and lifeless as Rome, green eyes pleading for help.

"I found him in a room upstairs," Suki explained, turning her aim on Liza. "He told me everything. She's been molesting them, treating them like fucking puppets, the sick bitch."

I stopped breathing.

I stopped fucking breathing for so long, my knees buckled. Bile shot up my throat with such ferocity it almost spewed out of my mouth like venom.

She'd been molesting them.

She'd been fucking molesting them.

As horrible as it sounds, I didn't even give a fuck about Vic. He deserved it—you reap what you sow.

But Rome, my Rome—*my King.* She'd done to him what all those men did to me.

What Vic did to me.

His current state made so much sense now.

Liza growled then, exasperated and outraged, spinning

around like a demon picking its next victim. "Why?!" she roared malevolently. "Why the fuck can't everyone just leave me alone? Why can't everyone just let me have my happily ever after with my boys. They're mine—both of them! Mine!"

Woah.

I'd never seen anything like it.

The woman completely unhinged in the span of seconds, faster than when the switch initially flipped.

This was a million times worse—like the exorcist.

If provoked enough, her head might actually spin.

"They're not toys," Suki snapped. "They're human beings with freewill. You can't force them to be with you."

"Yes, I can!" Liza countered. "My daddy did it with his all girls, *with me*. He had us all, got to play with us all, love us all."

Vic turned to her in horrified realization at the same moment Rome's voice boomed. "Your father did this to you, too?" he asked, stupefied.

"Did what? Love me? Spoil me? Give me everything? Then yes, yes he did," Liza barked.

"If your father did what you've done to these men, that's not love, Liza—that's rape," I stated, luring her incensed stare on me.

"It's not rape if I wanted it!" she screeched, the extent of her depravity clear as day in her eyes.

She really *was* crazy.

"And it's clear they didn't want it, so for them it's—"

"Don't let their forlorn faces fool you," she interjected, teeth bared. "They wanted it. They wanted me. They fucking fought over me! So I made them mine—I'll never let them go again!"

"You're insane," I tossed back, reaching back for Rome's hand when his body heat enveloped me from behind.

"No, I'm not! I'm passionate!" she argued.

"Yeah, passionately insane."

That did it in entirety.

On a raging growl, she came rushing for me.

Manic.

Hellbent.

Mad as a hatter.

I'd braced myself for impact, rearing an arm back to smash my fist dead in her face, when a singular boisterous bang filled the room.

Liza stilled a mere three feet away from me, mouth ajar.

The light in her eyes dimmed out right before my very own.

And then she collapsed.

It was then as she laid on the floor that I noticed the bullet hole to the side of her head, a pool of blood quickly spreading beneath her.

Stunned at the rapid turn of events, I glanced at Suki first, wondering how she'd gotten her from that angle, but she shook her head and motioned to Rome.

When I turned my gaze on him, I found him with his arm extended firmly, gun pointed right where Liza once stood.

"Finally," he breathed.

Relieved.

Releasing such a profound sigh, I felt myself doing the very same.

He was going to be okay.

"Thank you," Vic then said weakly on the floor, literally throwing himself at Rome's feet. "Thank you, fucking thank you!"

Rome regarded him for several moments, unspeaking, unmoving.

And then he lifted the pistol, aimed right at the center of Vic's, and pulled the trigger.

The monsters had been slain.

The King had been saved.

And he walked out of that asylum hand in hand with his Queen, as they returned to their rightful places within the kingdom.

EPILOGUE

♫ *Nothing Without You - The Weeknd* ♫

Three months later…

L ux and I stand on top of the Panorama, *her back to
my front as Miami zooms below us.*

*The night is especially humid, but a cool breeze rolls
by every few minutes, offering brief moments of relief.*

*Inhaling deeply, I tighten my arms around her shoul-
ders and bury my face in the crook of her neck, nuzzling
the delicate curve. Her pulse beats steady beneath my lips.*

"You sure you wanna do this?" I ask.

*She nods simply and grips my forearms, offering a
little squeeze of reassurance. "I do."*

*Those two little words do something to me. They
shouldn't, because I shouldn't even be entertaining such
thoughts, but nevertheless, they do.*

Insanely so.

*My heart races at the visual, a visual I'd never imag-
ined myself envisioning. A visual I'd never imagined I'd
want to envision.*

But I shouldn't be surprised.

I want everything with Lux, everything and anything the future has in store. The good times, the bad times.

Everything.

Tamping down the sense of urgency thrumming through my veins, I squeeze her tighter and nod myself. "We need to get going then. Don't want to be—"

"I know," she interjects, her voice wavering slightly. "Just five more minutes, though."

I don't miss the way she sighs or how her body rattles with the tiniest shiver. "What's wrong, baby? Talk to me."

Lux shrugs, burrowing herself deeper in my hold. "I'm just going to miss the girls, that's all."

"They promised to come visit twice a year one we settle down somewhere," I say, hoping the remainder will somewhat soothe the ache of leaving them behind.

"I know, but twice a year is nothing. I'm going to miss out on so much, especially with Suki being—"

"Look at me." I spin her around with a quickness, halting the words on her tongue. Cupping her face, I lay my forehead to hers, my gaze m boring into blue pools. "We don't have to go."

"We don't, no," she agrees, clasping my wrists. "But I want to be with you, and I know this is something you've wanted for a long time."

"What I want is you," I counter, drawing a genuine smile on her plump lips.

"You have me already. You'll always have me, for as long as you want me."

Forever wouldn't be long, but I don't dare say that aloud. Not now.

"*Do you trust me?*" *I ask instead, backing her into the ledge like I've done so many times before.*

"*Yes.*"

"*Do you love me?*"

She nods, wrapping her arms around my neck. "*With every fiber of my being.*"

"*Then let's go. Let's get away from it all. See the world. Live. We can come back to Miami when it's all said and done if that's what you want. I'd live under a bridge as long as you're by my side.*"

My girl laughs, drawing me closer with a leg at my waist. "*And to think you wanted me dead just a few months ago.*"

"*I never wanted you dead, baby,*" *I chuckle,* "*I just wanted what you had, but I learned real quick it meant fuck all if you weren't part of the package.*"

The briefest silence falls between us.

Time stands still as she gazes at me, boring into me with such emotion I feel it in the deepest, darkest parts of me.

"*I love you, Roman,*" *she declares after a beat.*

The words hit me, harder than ever, puffing up my chest. "*Say it again,*" *I demand.*

Lips brushing against my own, she takes ahold of my face and holds my stare. "*I. Love. You,*" *she enunciates.*

Again they hit me. The course through me with such speed, my cock twitches beneath my jeans.

"*Mmm—I'm one fucking lucky bastard.*"

"*You are, now tell me you love me goddammit,*" *she*

growls playfully, her claws raking along my jaw, luring me impossibly closer.

The heat between her legs nearly does me in.

I want to devour her right there, take her on this rooftop as our farewell to Miami, but voicing how much I fucking love her, how much I want her until the end of time, is far more paramount than my insatiable appetite.

Threading my fingers in her hair, I hold her steady, firmly. "Lux—*my vicious little kitty kat*—Mercier, I. Love. You, and one day, whether it be near or far, I hope you'll do me the honor of being a King."

Her eyes widen, but she recovers quickly, clamping her teeth down on her bottom lip as a flush colors her cheeks. "Every Queen takes her King's surname."

Kiss.

"I'm holding you to it."

Kiss.

"You can count on it." *She smiles devilishly.* "Now, let's go—adventures await us, my King."

And they lived happily—and darkly—ever after.
THE END

ACKNOWLEDGMENTS

Every publishing journey has its moments of both trials and triumphs, one more than the other in some cases. Volatile Obsessions had plenty of both. Now, I want to take a moment to thank the people who saw me through this one, because it was one hell of tumultuous a ride.

To Victoria, my fucking amazing PA. Thank you for your undying support and for all that you do. You're my rockstar, lady.

To my best friend, Hazel Grace, I love you more than words can express. Thank you for always sticking by me and always having my back.

To Natasha, my favorite Canadian. Your fierce love for these characters motivated me to keep pushing when I wanted to give. I'm honored knowing they have a place on your literary sleeve, and I'm honored to rock the pieces you drew for me. We need a meet up soon!

To Magical Ri, my unicorn reader. Thank you—just thank you. For everything. I love you something fierce.

To my Devils, all of you...thank you. Our little group has become my safe haven. Getting to know you and building friendships has made this journey incredible despite all my trials. Your love and support mean the world to me.

To Ena from Enticing Journey, thank you for putting up with me. I know all the schedule changes and delays must have driven you up the wall, but you still found it in your heart to help me. I appreciate you more than you know.

And lastly, but certainly not least, to my readers, YOU are the reason I keep pushing so hard for this career. Thank you for reading, thank you for loving my characters, my worlds, my stories. They're all possible because of YOU.

XO,

ABOUT THE AUTHOR

Self-published dark romance author Dee Garcia was born and raised in Miami, Florida. A voracious fan of romance novels and long time lover of the written word, her mission is to craft unique, compelling, and deliciously dark stories that will give her readers a thrilling escape from the monotony of everyday reality. With fierce, headstrong heroines and sinful, possessive Alpha males weaved into her rousing tales, Dee hopes to leave her mark on the Indie world, one decadent plot twist at a time.

Website
https://www.authordeegarcia.com

Reader's Group
https://www.facebook.com/groups/deesdevils

a amazon.com/author/deegarcia

BB bookbub.com/authors/dee-garcia

instagram.com/deegarcia_author

facebook.com/authordeegarcia

pinterest.com/authordeegarcia

youtube.com/authordeegarcia

twitter.com/deegarciabooks

g goodreads.com/authordeegarcia

ALSO BY DEE GARCIA

STAND-ALONES:

• SNARE (ZOMBIE APOCALYPSE/DYSTOPIAN)

• JAGGER (EROTIC ROMANCE)

• THE ASHES OF BLACKLIER MANOR (DARK GOTHIC ROMANCE)

———————

DUETS/SERIES:

• **THE ROSEWOOD REALM SERIES**

(INTERCONNECTED STAND-ALONES)

VENOM (BOOK ONE)

LOST GIRL (BOOK TWO)

• **THE SCARSI FAMILY SERIES (MAFIA)**

X-394 (BOOK ONE)

DEAD OR ALIVE PART 1 (BOOK TWO)

BOOK THREE TO COME

- **THE BLOODSHED DUET (MMA FIGHTER)**

  I AM LIONESS (BOOK ONE)

  HEAR ME ROAR (BOOK TWO)

Made in the USA
Monee, IL
20 October 2021

80492964R00277